Also available from Diana Palmer and HQN Books

DIANA PALMER

DIAMOND SPUR

HQN™

PLEASE RECYCLE

THIS PRODUCT IS RECYCLABLE

ISBN-13: 978-0-373-77994-9

Recycling programs
for this product may
not exist in your area.

Diamond Spur

First published under the name Susan Kyle by Popular Library,
an imprint of Warner Books

This edition published by arrangement with Harle

For questions and comments about the quality
please contact us at CustomerService@Harle

® and TM are trademarks of Harlequin Ente
corporate affiliates. Trademarks indicated
United States Patent and Trademark Offic
Property Office and in other countries.

www.HQNBooks.com

Printed in U.S.A.

For Dean and Donna DeSoto
and Doris and Ben McCord in San Antonio;
for editors Claire Zion and Beth Lieberman in New York;
for Pat in PA and Melinda in Lewisville, Texas;
for my agent Maureen Walters of Curtis Brown Assoc. Ltd.;
and last, but not least, for my husband, James,
my son Blayne, daughter-in-law Christina, grandkids
Selena and Donovan, my family and friends and my own
very special category readers. God bless you all.
—Susan Kyle (aka Diana Palmer)
Habersham County, Georgia 2014

CHAPTER ONE

THERE WERE HUGE live oak trees sheltering the Donavan place from the south Texas heat. The impressive pale yellow Spanish-styled stucco house sat between barbed wire fences, far back off the ranch road at the end of a dusty, winding driveway. Kate Whittman was glad to be poking along on the old quarter horse Jason had given her instead of driving. It had been dry in this part of Frio County, Texas, for some weeks now, and the dust was much less noticeable on a slow-moving horse than in a car.

The Donavan driveway had never been paved. The ranch covered thousands of acres and spare cash always went into buying more cattle, not into modernizing roads. In these days of low cattle prices and overwhelming interest on ranch loans, it took a business mind like Jason Donavan's to keep the wolf away from the door.

Her green eyes scanned the horizon. It was roundup time, Kate knew, and on an operation this size, the spread had to be broken down into sections. Each camp had its own crew and foreman, and Jason would be riding around from one to the other to keep an eye on things. During roundup, somebody always got hurt. While broken bones, burns, contusions, and abrasions were part of the usual demands of ranch work, herding cattle and branding always brought grief. This time the boss himself had run afoul of a maddened mama longhorn, and the ranch foreman had gone sneaking over to Kate's house to fetch her. Any time Jason got hurt, they sent for Kate, because Jason Donavan wouldn't let anybody else near him. He trusted Kate because she wasn't afraid of his temper, and because she alone could manage him when that temper was at flash point.

Kate sighed wistfully, thinking about all the times she'd come down this winding driveway. She and Jason didn't date; in fact he hardly seemed to notice her as a woman. But she'd been friends with his younger brother Gene, and with the housekeeper, Sheila, long before that odd kind of friendship developed between Jason and herself, born out of an equally odd confrontation one night when he'd been drinking. He didn't let anyone very close, even Kate, but she was allowed privileges that no one else was. He was protective of her, in a rough sort of way; a kind of unrelated older brother. Of course, that wasn't at all what Kate wanted from him. But it was as much as she could expect from a man who kept to himself the way he always did.

There was a lot of road between the open range with its spacious improved grazing land, green now that spring had arrived, and the house resting in its solitary nest of trees. In one pasture, cows with new calves were grazing. In another, young castrated bulls made up the steer crop. In still another, huge Santa Gertrudis bulls had been turned out with hearty longhorn-Santa Gertrudis crossbred cows for the third stage in Diamond Spur's three-crossbreed breeding program. In still another pasture, purebred longhorn bulls had been introduced to the crop of two-year-old heifers for their first breeding. The longhorn papas would insure that the new mothers dropped small calves, insuring an easy delivery and less herd losses.

Kate smiled at the efficiency of it all. Jason was a wizard with cattle. His sprawling cow-calf commercial operation had a spotless reputation with its customers, and a large part of it was due to Jason's personal interest in his ranch and the time he spent overseeing every part of its operation. He was always the first to try new techniques, to use better methods of production. That ability to change with the times, to bend to the demands of modern cattle marketing, had kept his Diamond Spur Ranch solvent. When, several years back, other ranchers had turned to investing heavily in new land acquisitions, Jason was experimenting with artificial insemination and embryo transplants and innovative methods of nutritional supplementation.

Kate pushed back her long, dark brown braid and settled lower in the saddle. She grimaced as her jean-clad leg brushed over a nail peeking through the leather. She'd designed and decorated these jeans herself. She hoped they weren't torn because they were part of a collection she hoped to sell to the manufacturing company where she worked. She really couldn't afford any new denim. Things were in bad shape at the small place she shared with her mother, but she didn't want Jason to know just how bad. Anyway, he didn't need any more worry at the moment. The cattle industry was depressed, and even a man with Jason's business sense could go broke. If he lived, she thought with black irritation, remembering how impossible he was about injuries. Jason never would go to a doctor with a cut. He'd try to treat it himself and the only way he'd have it seen about was if it got badly infected, or if Kate stuck her nose in. For Jason's foreman Gabe to run off in the middle of a roundup hunting her, and risking the boss's temper asking her to intervene must be pretty bad this time.

Nobody ever seemed to guess that she wasn't as confident as she pretended to be with Jason. He intimidated her, too. After all, he was thirty—almost ten full years her senior. But she'd learned over the years to hide her uncertainty. Now her dark, slender eyebrows drew together as she wondered if he'd done some irreparable damage to his tough hide. He was male perfection itself, as most of the single women around San Frio would have agreed. It was a pity that he'd become such a dyed in the wool misogynist. She wondered how he'd ever get an heir for Diamond Spur with that attitude. And if anything happened to Jason, his younger brother Gene would never be strong enough to hold the family finances together.

The Diamond Spur had belonged to Jason Donavan since the death of his father, although Gene would inherit a good share of it. Old J.B. Donavan had drowned when the Frio River came down in flood one spring morning eight years ago. But the ranch's name went back a lot longer than eight years. Back in 1873, a Civil War veteran named Blalock Donavan had chanced to sit in on a poker game in San Antonio. In a game that went on all night, and during which one man was killed for cheating, the young Confederate sergeant from Calhoun County, Georgia, won the last hand with a legendary straight diamond flush—and without any wild cards to make that impossible feat any more possible.

In the pot had been a total of one hundred Yankee dollars—and the deed to a broken down cattle ranch in Frio County, Texas. The ranch hadn't had a name at the time. Everyone locally just called it the Bryan place. But Blalock Donavan had won it on a Royal Diamond Flush, with a silver spur in the kitty as his part of the ante. So the Diamond Spur it became. The Diamond Spur it remained. And a Donavan still owned it, 113 years later.

Kate's pale green eyes softened as she saw the heavy-set woman bending over a pan on the front porch. Diamond Spur was one of the richest cattle ranches in Texas, enabling Jason to drive a Mercedes and a new very classy black Bronco. The interior of the house was like an antique museum, with pieces from around the world. And Jason entertained on a lavish scale. In fact, Jason's kitchen had every modern convenience, but his housekeeper, Sheila James, still did her own canning.

Sheila was an institution at the ranch. Rumor had it that she'd been madly in love with old J.B. Donavan, but that gentleman had no use for women after his Nell deserted him and his two sons. The old man took to strong drink and became a holy terror. They said even Sheila had grown afraid of him after that, but that she'd stayed on to look after the boys. She had character and an uncanny tolerance for people. She had a lot of perseverence, too, because old J.B. Donavan had been a hardcase with a mean temper. Jason still was, although Kate could reach him when no one else could. That was something of a joke locally, Kate knew, but nobody laughed about it in front of Jason.

Sheila looked up from the lazy rhythm of the front porch swing, her blue eyes sparkling as Kate came closer. "I sent Gabe after you. I hope you don't mind," she said apologetically. "I figured Jason would bleed to death and become an eyesore out there because his men would be too scared to bury him."

She paused in the act of snapping green beans and stringing them, the shallow pan across the knees of her brilliant green and yellow checked housedress, her salt and pepper hair short and sweaty. She was fifty and looked it. Even Jason gave her a measure of respect, but Sheila was no match for his temper when it was aroused.

"Can't you do anything with him?" Kate replied mischievously.

"Not without a loaded gun," came the dry reply. "Gabe told me that Jason finally stopped the bleeding and bandaged himself, but the blood was still seeping through when he went out again. I'm afraid it needs stitches."

"Well, I'll see what I can do," Kate promised. "Is he where Gabe left him, with the crew out on the Smith bottoms?"

"That's what Gabe said. Thanks, Kate," Sheila replied.

Kate smiled as she turned the horse. "Old-fashioned transportation, isn't it?" She grinned. "But it's a long walk, and Mom has the car at work, since it's grocery store day."

"And you wouldn't ride over with Gabe because he's sweet on you?" Sheila asked knowingly.

Kate, who was twenty and a little nervous about men because of an extremely sheltered background, nodded. Her father and mother had raised her in the same strict fashion they'd been raised. They were old-fashioned, church-going people. And even though her father was dead, her mother was still a stickler for morality and didn't hesitate to ask Jason's opinion of Kate's infrequent dates. That rankled, too, but Kate's mother, Mary, thought the sun rose and set on the man. Kate's late father had been Jason's foreman, and she sometimes thought that was one reason Jason seemed to feel responsible for her and Mary.

She drew her mind back to the present. "Gabe is a very

nice man, but I want to be a fashion designer. I don't want to get married for ages yet."

Sheila nodded, thinking privately that Kate and Jason got along so well because both of them wanted their independence. Jason would probably never marry since that Maryland woman had thrown him over for a movie contract.

"Good luck," she murmured. "He was already wound up and cussing when he went out the door this morning. Had some terrible things to say about what I did to his eggs." She sniffed, snapping beans with renewed vengeance. "Nothing wrong with salsa and refried beans on top of them. Well, is there?" she asked Kate.

Kate knew how Sheila made salsa, and having tasted the extremely hot sauce once, she had every sympathy for Jason. "Why did you put salsa on them?"

"Because the minute his feet hit the floor, he started cussing because he couldn't find where I put his jeans, and then he swore the detergent I used gave him an allergic reaction, he said there wasn't enough cover on his bed…" Sheila's thin lips flattened. "I guess I cause cancer, too, although he stopped short of accusing me of that!"

Kate shook her head, laughing softly. "You ought to short sheet his bed for him."

"Oh, don't you worry, I'll get even," Sheila replied. "He loves cherry pie. Hell will freeze over and shiver before he gets another one."

That wasn't quite true, of course. Jason would get hungry for that cherry pie and start flattering his housekeeper, and he'd have his cherry pie like a shot. He and Sheila had these blowups almost daily, and both forgot them just as frequently.

"Well, I'll go try to patch him up so you can get your own back on him," Kate offered.

"If you can get him back here, I've got some nasty antiseptic...!" the older woman called.

Kate shook her finger at Sheila and rode on. But once she was on the narrow, rutted path through the grass that led to the holding pens, she felt a little nervous. Jason in a temper wasn't the most pleasant person to be around. Part of Kate was still a little afraid of him, although she wouldn't admit it or show it. He was a very masculine man, and he didn't bother to hide his faults; he just let them hang out for everyone to see. He'd never have made it as a diplomat.

Kate smoothed her hands down her jeans and fumbled to tuck the shirttail of her faded blue print blouse back into them. Down the road, a deep, drawling male voice called out orders with more than the usual amount of venom, rapid-fire Spanish reverting quickly to English and back again. Jason spoke both. Since most of the local ranch hands were of Mexican-American descent, being bilingual came as naturally as wearing boots around San Frio. Cattle bawled and dust was everywhere, with men on foot and men on horseback trying to keep some kind of mad order in all the confusion.

This rural part of south Texas hadn't changed a lot since the Civil War. There was less native grassland because of the enormous amount of grazing that had been done back in the cattle era. These days ranchers who wanted good grass had to plant it, so the local Soil Conservation Service people were Johnny-on-the-spot with help for those who wanted it, as Jason had. But, too, there was a lot of scrub and more prickly pear and mesquite than anybody wanted. Despite the drawbacks, the open country was the same;

wide and spread out and endless, with just a few scattered trees here and there to signal houses hidden from the sun. It was pioneer country. Cowboy country. And Kate, who'd been born next door to the Donavans, loved it with all her heart. Sitting astride the quarter horse with the wind blowing the grass down and teasing her shirt, she felt as free and unchained as the land itself.

She left her horse at the big makeshift corral and moved along on booted feet, tugging nervously at her long swath of hair. Her hair was a deep, rich brown, down to her waist when she didn't braid it or put it up. She had a pretty oval face with wide-spaced green eyes under long lashes, and a straight nose and a bow mouth. It wasn't a particularly beautiful face. It was thin and high-cheekboned. But Kate had a sweet personality and a kind of unabashed honesty that overshadowed her lack of beauty.

Just ahead, a large fenced area held a number of bawling calves and unhappy cows who were having their babies taken away for branding, tagging, and a disease check. There was a long chute down which calves were herded singly to a tilt tray that held the bovine head in a kind of vice while the rest of the protesting animal was branded, tagged, and vaccinated. A lot of ranchers had recently gone back to the old-time way of using a corral and doing each animal out in the open with ropes and cutting horses. But Jason liked this new technique and his men had it down to an art—they could usually tag, brand, and vaccinate an animal a minute.

Most of the victims were calves, but new bulls and replacement heifers had to be screened, too. They were given the same treatment, and many of them protested. Jason ran purebred longhorn cattle in this section of the ranch, so the horns on some of them were frankly dan-

gerous if a cowboy let himself get backed into a corner. That was what Gabe had said Jason had done. Jason
didn't like mistakes. He didn't make them himself, and
he expected the same perfection in other people. So naturally he wasn't admitting that he was badly hurt. That
unforgiving attitude was a source of worry to Kate, who
was afraid that someday she might make a slip and be
crossed off his list of friends forever.

Jason was leaning against the chute, tall and powerful and darkly elegant in his unconscious pose, one worn
boot hooked on the lowest board of the chute while he
watched big blond Gabe drive a calf up it to be worked.
But before Kate was halfway to him, his dark eyes had
found her. He always seemed to see her before anyone
else did.

She could see that he was favoring his right arm, resting it on his propped-up leg. He looked good in Western
clothing. Faded jeans and a worn black Stetson, leather
boots curled up and matted with dirt from long use and
a dusty chambray shirt made him look like a handsome
desperado.

He was handsome to Kate, anyway—even if his high-
cheekboned face had overly craggy features and he wasn't
shy about speaking his mind. He was dark-eyed, dark-
skinned, with a deceptively lithe build. Tall and powerfully muscled, Jason had one of those physiques seen so
frequently on the screen and so rarely in real life. With
the misshappen black Stetson pulled low over his eyes,
he had that dangerous look. Kate came closer.

"I wondered why Gabe vanished all of a sudden," he
mused in a deep, south Texas drawl. His dark eyes cut
upward to where his forearm was trying to look invisible.

"My God, are we so hard up for help that we're kidnapping seamstresses?"

"I'm a designer, not a seamstress," Kate pointed out pleasantly, smiling up at the tall man. "And if you don't think I can throw a calf, stand back and watch me. My daddy was foreman of this outfit before Gabe was, and he taught me all I know."

Jason's dark eyes softened as they searched her creamy complexion, lingering on her thick, dark eyelashes. "I guess he did, but most of these calves outweigh you, honey," he murmured dryly.

His casual endearment made her heart dance, but she kept Jason from seeing it. "Your arm's bleeding," she remarked, nodding toward the bloodstained sleeve.

"NO!" he exclaimed in mock surprise.

"You need to see a doctor," she continued, unabashed.

"It would be too embarrassing for both of us if I bothered Dr. Harris over a little scratch like this," he said reasonably.

"If you don't, I'll stand here all day and get heat stroke," she sighed. "But just go ahead and step over me while you work. If you don't bleed to death first," she added darkly.

Gene would have laughed at that, but Jason didn't crack a smile. Jason's younger brother, Gene, was a live wire, ever since his marriage to Cherry Mather. But Jason had always been the quiet one, the deep one. He hardly ever smiled, except when Kate was around.

"I don't have time," he muttered.

"Yes, you do," she said stubbornly. She put her hands on her hips and moved closer, staring doggedly up at him.

At close quarters, the effect he had on her nerves was dynamite. She'd always had a kind of crush on him, but suddenly it was being translated into something new and deliciously physical that attracted her and frightened her, all at once.

She didn't know that her proximity was giving him some problems as well. Little Kate who'd always been like a little sister was beginning to make him nervous and irritable. He'd avoided her lately for that reason. Now here she was, getting on his nerves again, when he needed it least.

"I told you, my arm's all right," he said curtly, his voice more cutting than he meant it to be, because her unconscious posture was bothering him. Her firm young breasts were all too visible under the thin fabric of her shirt, and the tight belt she wore with those tailored jeans brought his dark eyes down over her tiny waist and full hips and long, graceful legs. That made him madder and he forced his eyes back up to hers.

But she wasn't looking. She'd taken possession of his arm while his attention was diverted.

She unfastened the cuff and began to roll the sleeve up. "Go ahead and growl, I don't mind." Touching him even in this casual way made her tingle all over, so she resorted to humor to hide her reaction. Her green eyes danced up to his. "I'll give you a peppermint stick if you let me drive you to the doctor, Jason."

As usual, her light teasing knocked the fire off his temper. He gave in, chuckling in spite of himself as he watched her dark head bend. She was so full of fun, so unlike him. She bubbled through life, always finding the bright spots, while he brooded in the shadows. She'd always been able to make him laugh. Nobody else did, God knew. If he had a surefire weakness, Kate was it.

She drew the fabric carefully up his arm, noting first

the terribly complicated black watch strapped in the dark hairs on his wrist, then his muscles as she uncovered a blood-soaked white handkerchief; linen, too, with the initials JED in one corner, for Jason Everett Donavan.

"If this is a little cut, I'm George Washington," she muttered, grimacing as she moved the bandage aside to view the deep gash above his elbow. She looked up, searching his eyes. They were very Spanish, like part of his ancestry, and he had a way of looking at her that made her knees go weak.

"My, my, how you've changed, George," he mused.

"It needs stitches," she said. "It's too deep to bandage."

"It isn't. But I'll let you patch it up," he sighed irritably.

"We'd have to go back to the house. And Sheila's there," she added, smiling mischievously. "Waiting, with a bottle of nasty antiseptic and just bristling with evil intent. Dr. Harris, on the other hand, is a kind man who wouldn't hurt you. He's the lesser of the two evils."

"Damn it, a little blood won't hurt me," he countered, his dark eyes daring his very interested cowhands to say a word.

"Will gangrene hurt you?" she challenged, losing her patience as she was losing the argument. He could be so bullheaded! "Do you want to lose your arm because you're too pigheaded to see a doctor?"

"You tell him, Miss Kate," Red Barton agreed from his perch atop the fence. He was just out of his teens, a good cowboy with a tendency toward alcohol that would probably have kept him off any other ranch. But he'd saved Jason from a diamondback the same week he'd signed on at Diamond Spur, and he'd be there for life, if Kate knew her taciturn neighbor. Jason never forgot a favor.

"Gangrene's a turrrrrible thing," Barton continued.

"First she gets red stripes running down, then green, then the whole thing starts to rot off..." He shuddered as his pale eyes widened and his hands gestured theatrically.

"Oh, shut up, Barton!" Jason shot at him. "I don't need any advice from a man who almost lost his own damned foot to a mesquite thorn!"

Barton lifted his chin, "Well, at least I finally did go to a doctor, didn't I, boss man?" he challenged.

"Sure," Jason agreed. "Feet first, in an ambulance."

"No need to rub it in," the cowboy replied with a grin.

"All the more reason for you to go willingly, now," Kate told Jason. "Think," she said conspiratorially, "how your men would gloat if you had to be carried away."

Jason looked quietly furious. In fact, he looked hunted. He glared at Barton, who looked like a cheshire cat, and then back at Kate, who stood just looking at him, her arms folded.

"I give up," he said heavily.

"Don't worry, boss, they'll give you a bullet to bite on," Barton called after him.

"Save one for yourself, and a gun to use it in, if that lot of calves isn't done when I get back," Jason snapped back. "Hey, Gabe!" he yelled to his foreman.

The big blond man turned with a hand to his ear.

"I'll remember this!" Jason told him.

Gabe made him a bow guaranteed to incite any half-enraged man to violence. Jason's eyes flashed and he took a step forward.

"He's young, Jason." Kate got between him and his quarry. "They're all young."

He looked down at her with smoldering eyes under his jutting, scowling brow. "So are you, cupcake," he said.

"That's right, old man," she returned. Then she frowned

a little. "Well, not too old," she amended. "You're just thirty. I guess you've got a few good years left."

He cocked an eyebrow. "My God. Look who's talking about age—a child of twenty."

She glared at him. "Almost twenty-one," she amended. "The same age as Gene."

"Yes, Gene." He spared his branding operation another wistful glance. "They'll never get it done alone," he muttered. "If only I could get Gene to hold up his end, I could show a profit. Damn it, why does he want to fool around with painting? He's chasing rainbows, and on my time!"

"Gene isn't a boy anymore, Jason," she reminded him as they walked toward his big black Ford Bronco. "He's a grown man, with a wife."

"Some wife," he said harshly. "Cherry couldn't boil water, and her idea of married life is to watch soap operas and walk around with her hair in curlers."

"She's just eighteen," she said.

"I tried so damned hard to get them to wait." He opened the passenger door and helped her up into the high cab with a steely hand and closed it. Before she could get him to listen to her protests, he was under the wheel, managing very well with his right arm. With the bucket seats so close together, she was almost touching it, too. Kate was fascinated by the inside of this vehicle. It had power windows and cruise control, a stereo radio, tape deck, and two gearshifts—one for automatic drive and one for four-wheel drive. The old Ford that Kate shared with her mother was a straight shift with no frills, and by comparison, the Bronco was sheer luxury, right down to the comfortable fabric-covered seats.

"You aren't fit to drive," she complained.

"Nobody's driving me anywhere, unless it's to the

cemetery one day," he returned. He fumbled for a cigarette, but he couldn't manage the wheel with his injured arm. "Damn."

"I thought you'd quit," she mused. She took the cigarette, lit it, and handed it to him, making a face at the tangy, unpleasant tobacco taste.

"I did," he agreed with a faint grin. "I quit for a week, in fact. And I quit last month, too. I quit religiously about every third week."

"Your ashtray looks like it," she observed, watching him thump ashes over a pile of finished butts the size of a teacup upended. "How can you stand that mess?"

"If I clean it out, it will depress people who ride with me."

She stared at him. "Come again?"

"Most of my men aren't neat. If I start cleaning out ashtrays, they'll think they have to do it, too. They'll feel threatened and they'll all quit, and I'll have to handle roundup all by myself."

He had a dry wit that few people ever experienced. Kate, sitting contentedly beside him, felt constant amazement that of all the people he knew, she was the only one who ever got this close. He seemed never to see her as a threat, which was more irritating to Kate the older she got. She was becoming a woman, and he didn't even seem to notice.

Well, he did hate women, she had to admit. He didn't date, or he hadn't in the past few years. Not since that Eastern tenderfoot had come out to visit a neighbor and Jason had fallen head over heels in love with her. He'd been all set to propose, with the ring bought and everything, when she suddenly announced that she was off to Hollywood where she'd been offered a movie career. Jason had tried to talk her out of it, but she wouldn't be budged. Men were a dime a dozen, she'd laughed at him. Movie contracts were thin on the ground. Sorry, sucker, in other words. And Jason had gone on a three-day drunk that had become legendary in local circles, all the more shocking because he never touched liquor in any form. That prejudice was a holdover from his childhood because J.B. Donavan's drinking had brought violence down on his sons' heads.

Although Kate had grown up next door, and her father had worked for the Donavans, Jason was so much older that she'd had very little contact with him. But Gene and Kate had gone to school together, and she often helped him with his grammar. He'd talked occasionally about their upbringing, and it had softened her toward Jason who one afternoon just after his almost-fiancée's defection, had chanced to come growling out of his study, dead drunk. Jason's unexpected appearance had first disturbed, then shocked Kate. She'd never seen him anything except cold sober and in complete control of himself. Until then.

"Little Miss English tutor," he'd laughed coldly, those dark eyes frankly insulting as Gene had tried unsuccessfully to push him back into the study. "Is English all you're teaching my brother in these cozy afternoon sessions?"

"Come on now, Jay," Gene had coaxed, half a head shorter and not a fraction as strong as the jean-clad, unshaven man he was trying to budge. "Don't pick on Kate."

"I don't want damned women cluttering up my house! Not even your women!" Jason had stormed, black eyes flashing, his lean sharp face as hard as marble. Stone.

But Kate knew the look of pain. She had an uncanny empathy for people who were hurt; she could see it through anger or bad temper or even drunkenness. Jason's heart was broken, couldn't Gene see how much he was hurting? It was like watching a poor, wounded animal trying to escape from a bullet.

Ignoring Gene's frantic signs to go away, she went right up to Jason and took one of his lean, strong hands in hers. "Come on, Jason," she said, her voice as soft as it was when she talked to the kittens at home. "You're tired. You need to lie down."

Gene's pale, broad face winced as he waited for Jason to knock her down. But, amazingly, his brother's sharp features relaxed. Through a haze of alcohol, Jason went with her like a lamb back into his study.

"How about getting Sheila to make a pot of coffee, Gene?" Kate asked him, nodding as her eyes told him to step on it.

"Sure. Right now."

He was gone and Kate closed the door, coaxing Jason to the long leather lounger. She helped him down and sat beside him, her slender fingers gently stroking back his disheveled hair. He was beautiful, in a rough sort of way, she thought, her eyes going over his chiseled sharp features, the stubborn jutting chin, the beautifully carved mouth. He lay quietly, watching her with eyes that only half saw, black and intent.

"It's only been a few months since Daddy died," she said, keeping her voice low and soft. "He was my whole world, the only person who ever cared enough to let me be myself. He didn't want me to marry money or be famous. He loved me just the way I was. At first," she continued, because he was really listening, "I thought the pain would never stop. But day by day, little by little, I got through it. You will, too, Jason. One day, you won't even remember what she looked like."

He caught the soft fingers stroking his damp brow. "How old are you?" he asked unexpectedly.

She smiled. "Eighteen."

"A very wise old eighteen, little girl," he replied. His drawl was a little slurred, but his eyes never wavered from her face. "What the hell do you care if I mourn myself to death?"

"Jason, you've been awfully good to Mama and me since Daddy died," she said gently. "And I guess nobody else looks deep enough to see how bad it's hurting you…."

"I'm not hurting," he interrupted curtly. "No damned woman is ever going to hurt me!"

She closed her fingers around his. "Of course not," she agreed, soothing him back down. "You're just worked to death. But you need time to get your life back in order. Why don't you go away for a week or two? Gene says you never rest. A vacation would put the bloom back in your cheeks," she said with a mischievous smile. "The vinegar back into your black heart…."

"Shut up or I'll throw you out the front door," he replied. But there was a faint glimmer in his eyes, and it didn't sound like any serious threat. "God, you're brave."

"Somebody has to save you from yourself," she sighed. "Alas, I guess I've been chosen. Now how about a nice bowl of razor blade soup and an ugly pill?"

He burst out laughing. Gene and Sheila came in the study door together with stunned amusement suddenly claiming their faces. And that had been the beginning of an odd and beautiful relationship. From that day on, Jason became Kate's responsibility if he got sick, or hurt, or in a fight. He never touched liquor again, but he seemed to have a knack for accidents. Especially the past few months. This was the third time since winter began and ended that Kate had been summoned by someone to look after the big man. And he reciprocated in unexpected, and sometimes unwelcomed, ways.

She became the object of a rough kind of affectionate, almost brotherly overseeing. In fact, Jason had taken on a lot of responsibility that Kate hadn't appreciated. Like helping Kate and her mother to buy their father's property while he managed it for them. Like finding Mary, Kate's mother, a job in the local textile factory. Like checking up on the infrequent dates Kate had and making sure those men didn't take advantage of her. But Kate had managed to keep her temper, and her sense of humor, as she'd survived his first attempts at affection.

But when, a few months ago, she'd begun to notice Jason in a new way, he backed off, as if he sensed the almost imperceptible shift in her attitude toward him.

Not that it was blatant. Kate hadn't realized it herself until a month or so ago. But Jason had suddenly left her to run her own life. Actually, he'd given up running it last year, although he'd protested when she wanted to study fashion design. There was a school in Atlanta that she'd favored, and Jason put his foot down hard. Her mother needed her, he said. Atlanta was just too far away. There were home study courses. He'd find her one. He had, despite her objections. Kate was almost through it now, studying at night.

She worked as a serger on the pants line at the manufacturing company where her mother sewed on the shirt line. It was interesting work, and Kate loved anything to do with the construction of clothes. But serging was becoming sporadic, and today there hadn't been any work for her, so she was sent home by her floor lady.

"Why aren't you at work?" Jason asked after a minute.

"They ran out of pants for me to serge," she said. "They've got Mama doing repairs that were sent up from that Central American plant they opened last year."

He glanced at her sideways. "Do you really like that job?"

"I like it." She smiled at him. "I love the textile business."

"And you're still hell-bent on being some famous designer, I gather," he said tersely.

"Why not? If you're going to dream, dream big." She eyed him. "You did."

"I had more than the usual amount of drive," he replied. He winced as he brought the cigarette to his mouth with his sore arm. "Damn, this thing hurts!"

"You should have let me drive," she said.

"I'm not crippled."

"You're incorrigible, that's what you are."

"So you keep telling me."

He shifted, and she caught the scents of leather and tobacco that clung to him. He hadn't taken off his hat, and she noticed how battered the poor old black thing was.

"Don't you ever buy new hats?" she asked unexpectedly.

"I've just gotten this one broken in," he protested. "It takes years to get a hat just so."

"You've worn that one since I was in grammar school."

"That's what I mean. It's just getting comfortable."

As the big vehicle rumbled over a country bridge, one of the few wooden ones left, Kate glanced down at the trickle of water below. Any day now, the rains would come and the rivers would fill up, and low places like this would become dangerous. Even the smallest dip could become a river with rain, because there was so little vegetation to contain the water.

"Look here, you aren't giving Gabe any encouragement, are you?" he asked so suddenly that she jumped.

Her pale eyes fixed on his dark, somber face. "What?"

His eyes held steady on the road as the burly vehicle shot down the long, level stretch of road that led into San Frio. "I don't like the way he looks at you lately," he added, glancing at her in a strange, possessive kind of way that even her inexperienced eye recognized. "And I sure as hell don't like him coming over to the house when your mother isn't there."

She didn't quite know how to handle what he was saying. She watched his averted face nervously, trying to measure the amount of feeling that had been in his terse statement. Her heart was going crazy. "He didn't even get out of the truck," she began.

"Gabe likes girls, and you're filling out." He didn't look at her as he said it. He didn't want her to see how disturbed he was at the thought of Gabe making a pass at her. "Don't lead him on. He's a good man and I'd hate to lose him. But, so help me, if he ever touched you, I'd kill him."

Kate felt the ground go out from under her. She couldn't even speak for the shock, she just stared at him. There had been a trace of violence in that threat, and the normal drawl had gone into eclipse as he spoke.

"Jason, didn't you notice that I was riding Kip?" she asked after a minute, and the words came out roughly.

He frowned. "So?"

"Gabe came in the pickup," she said. "I wouldn't ride over to Diamond Spur with him. I know he thinks he's interested in me. He'll get over it. Last month it was little Betsy Weeks," she added with a forced smile. "He's a typical love 'em and leave 'em cowboy. He's no threat."

He glanced at her sideways. "Okay."

"Anyway, I can handle my dates, thank you," she said.

"I remember the last time you said that," he replied with a faintly amused smile. "Do you?"

She hated that smile. Of course she remembered the last time, how could she forget? She'd defended to her mother the reputation of a boy she wanted to date, only to have to suffer the embarrassment of calling home from a pay phone in the middle of the night to be rescued. But Jason had come in Mary Whittman's place, and Kate had never heard the end of it. In addition, Kate's erstwhile date had sported a black eye for several days thereafter and subsequently joined the Marine Corps. It had all but ruined her social life. Local boys knew Jason, and since the incident, Kate had spent every weekend at home. There was nothing between her and Jason, but his attitude had created that impression. She wondered if he realized how people looked at his possessive attitude, or if he cared.

She glanced at him, frowning. He was possessive, all right. But was it only because they were friends, or was he feeling the same odd longings that were kindling inside her? She looked away nervously.

"Would you like to listen to some music?" she asked, her voice edgy and quick.

He glanced at her and smiled. "Okay, honey. End of discussion. Turn on whatever you like."

What she liked was country-western, and that seemed to suit him very well. If his arm was hurting, he made sure it didn't show. Kate sat back against the seat with a sigh, while turbulent sensations came and went in her taut body. She couldn't even breathe properly. What if he noticed?

Things were getting totally out of hand. She felt almost uncomfortable this close to Jason, but in an exciting kind of way. She shifted, wondering at the remark he'd made about Gabe. Had it been just a joking statement, or had he meant it?

Well, he'd never so much as made a pass at her, and knowing how he felt about women, there was no future in mooning over him. She'd already realized that. But it was easier to tell herself he was off limits than it was to do anything about it. And what good would it do to drive herself crazy with doomed hope? She leaned back, closed her eyes, and listened to the rhythmic strains of the music as they drove toward town.

CHAPTER TWO

DR. HARRIS WAS a small, stout, bespectacled man in his fifties who knew Jason Donavan all too well. With a resigned smile, he put in fifteen stitches, injected Jason with a tetanus booster, and sent him home. Kate and the doctor exchanged speaking glances behind the tall rancher's back and Dr. Harris grinned.

"See how easy that was?" Kate said as they reached the Bronco. "A few stitches and you're back on the job."

He didn't bother to answer. He opened her door for her with exaggerated patience, closed it, and paused to light a cigarette on his way around the hood to his own side.

San Frio was a lazy little south Texas town with a pioneering history but not much of a present. It boasted a grocery store, a post office, a small clinic, a pharmacy, a weekly newspaper, a small textile company, a video and appliance sales and service store, and an enormous and prosperous feed store. It seemed to Kate to be more an outgrowth of the ranch than a town, however, since Jason had a resident veterinarian, blacksmith, mechanic, accounting firm, computer specialist, and other assorted employees who could do everything from artificial insemination of cows to complicated laboratory cultures on specimens from the cattle.

Huge oak trees lined the cracked, crumbling sidewalks that supported as many deserted buildings as occupied ones. The drugstore had the same overhead fans that had cooled Texas ranchers sixty years before, and there was a hitching post that Texas rangers had used as long ago as the 1890s.

"It never changes," Kate said with a smile, watching two old men sit in cane-bottom chairs outside the grocery store, exchanging whittled pieces of wood. "If it lasts a hundred years, San Frio will still look like this."

Jason closed his door and fastened his seat belt. "Thank God," he said. "I'd hate like hell to see it turn into a city the size of San Antonio."

"And what's wrong with San Antonio?" she demanded.

"Nothing," he replied. "Not one thing. I just like San Frio better. More elbow room. Fasten your seat belt."

"We're only going to the ranch...."

He looped an arm over the back of the seat and stared at her with pursed lips and a do-it-or-I'll-sit-here-all-day look. After a minute of that stubborn, concentrated scrutiny, Kate reached for her seat belt.

"You intimidate people," she muttered. "Look at old Mr. Davis watching you."

He glanced amusedly toward the store where the stooped old man was grinning toward them. Jason raised a hand and so did the old man.

"My grandfather used to pal around with him," Kate said. "He said Mr. Davis was a hell-raiser in his time. And look at him now, whittling."

"At least he's alive to do it," he replied.

"My grandfather couldn't whittle, but he used to braid rope out of horsehair," Kate recalled. "He said it was hard on the hands, but it worked twice as well as that awful Mexican hemp to rope cattle."

"The best ropes are made of nylon," Jason replied. He

started the jeep and reversed it. "After it's properly seasoned, you can't buy a better throwing rope."

"You ought to know," she mused. She studied his dark face, her eyes skimming over the sharp features, the straight nose. He had an elegance about him, although she decided he wasn't handsome at all. In his city clothes, he could compete with the fanciest businessman.

He caught that silent scrutiny and cocked an eyebrow, looking rakish under the brim of his weatherbeaten hat. "Well, are you satisfied, now that I've been stitched and cross-stitched?"

"I guess." She settled back against the seat as Jason roared out of town at his usual breakneck pace, bouncing her from seat to roof and down again. She grimaced. "At least you'll heal properly now."

"I'd have healed properly alone, thank you. God knows why everybody on the place thinks I'll die if they don't drag you over every time I scratch myself," he muttered.

"Because to you everything short of disembowelment is a scratch," she replied. "People do make mistakes from time to time, even you. It's human."

"That's the one thing I'm not, cupcake," he replied dryly. "Ask any one of my men during roundup, and they'll tell you the same thing."

He turned off the city road onto the long, sparsely settled ranch road that led eventually to the Diamond Spur. Clouds were gathering against the horizon, dark blue and threatening as they loomed over the gently rolling landscape.

"Those are rain clouds," Jason remarked. "The weatherman was predicting some flash flooding this afternoon." He scowled. "If the Frio runs out of her banks before we finish the bottoms, we may lose some cattle."

"You and your blessed cattle," she grumbled. "Don't you ever think about anything else?"

"I can't afford to," he mused. "Ranchers are going bust all over. Don't you read the market bulletin anymore?"

"Only when I can't find a fashion magazine," she returned.

"Speaking of which, how are you doing with that designing course?"

"I'm almost through it, thank you," she sighed. "Although I still think I'd have done better at a regular design school." She glared at him. "Thanks to you, I never made it out of Frio County."

"Atlanta is too far away," he replied imperturbably. "Besides, you'd get claustrophobia down in Georgia. Too many trees."

"I like trees. I'd have made friends."

"Your mother would have missed you," he said, glancing at her as they sped down the deserted road. "She isn't half as capable as she makes out. She needs looking after."

"Apparently you think I do, too," she replied, feeling argumentative. "And that can't go on, Jason. I'm a grown woman now, not a teenage girl."

"You were pretty wise, for a teenager." His eyes narrowed as he stared down the road. "I don't guess you knew that time how dangerous it was to come that close to me when I'd been drinking."

"Which was probably a good thing, or I'd never have had the nerve," she recalled with a warm smile, studying him. "But you needed someone. Gene was too frightened of you to do any real good, and so was Sheila."

"They remembered too well what happened when the old man got loaded," he said, memories tautening his jaw.

One corner of his mouth twisted mockingly. "He used to hit. The drunker he was, the harder he hit. I don't drink often, or very much." He shifted against the seat, his eyes narrow. "I guess I've always been afraid I might end up like him. And who knows, if you hadn't come along at the right time, I might have."

"Not you," she said with conviction, her quiet eyes adoring his profile. "You're not a cruel man."

"Neither was he before he started drinking," Jason said. He sighed. "You were lucky, honey. Your father never touched the stuff."

"I was lucky in a lot of ways," she agreed. "I still am." She wondered if Jason knew that she'd heard about how his father had once extended his blind fury to Jason and Gene's mother, that he'd beaten Nell Donavan once and only once, and that she'd vanished the next day, leaving her sons at his mercy. Probably he didn't realize that Sheila had passed that bit of gossip on to Kate. He hardly ever talked about his childhood, even to her. It was a mark of affection he had for her that she knew anything about those dark days. Jason was a very private man. "I've never been really afraid of you," she said absently, "even when you were drinking. That night, I never thought that you might harm me."

He smiled at her. "You saw deep that night," he said quietly. "Right through the anger to the pain. Most people never look past my temper, but you did."

"I liked you, God knows why," she said, smiling back. "And there wasn't anybody else who seemed inclined to look after you after that blond sawmill got through with you."

"She taught me a hard lesson," he replied. "One I'll never forget. In my way, I loved her."

"One bad experience shouldn't sour you for life," she told him. "All women aren't out for what they can get."

"How would you know?" he asked bitterly. "You with your little girl crushes on movie stars and pinup boys? My God, the men you've dated weren't even men in any real sense. They were geldings you could lead around by the nose," he said shortly. "You haven't even been intimate with a man, have you?"

Her face went stiff. Amazing, she thought angrily, that it was the twentieth century and she still couldn't toss off sophisticated chatter with any credence. "How could I have managed that, with you and my mother bulldogging me at every turn and keeping me away from men who knew anything?" She turned in the seat, her green eyes accusing. "My goodness, after Baxter Hewett joined the Marines, all the local men decided you were too much competition and I've spent my evenings at home ever since!"

He lifted his cigarette to his mouth with a faintly surprised glance in her direction as they bumped along the ranch road. "I didn't realize that."

"Think how it looks, when you beat up men who try to seduce me," she sighed.

"I don't want other men seducing you," he said without thinking. "Especially not a ladies' man like Hewett."

"Why not?" she burst out, exasperated.

"There's a question." He turned off onto a dirt road. "God, it's dusty!" he muttered.

She spared the thick yellow dust a glance and turned her attention back to him. "Go ahead, avoid the question. That's what you always do when you don't want to talk about things."

He lifted an eyebrow as he glanced at her. "Well, it

works, doesn't it?" he asked reasonably. "All right, if you want to know the truth, sexual freedom may be in vogue all over the world, but I'm an old-fashioned man. I believe God made women to have children and be the foundation of a family. To my mind, that doesn't mix with easy virtue and high-pressured careers."

She gaped at him. "You reactionary!" she accused. "You mean you think the little woman should stay at home, chained to a stove and slave to a man's hungers?"

"What would you know about a man's hungers, Kate?" he asked suddenly, his dark eyes cutting and intent as they met hers across the seat.

She shifted restlessly. "What do you know about a woman's heart?" she returned. "With an attitude like yours, you'll never find a woman to marry."

"Praise God," he replied easily. "A wife is the last thing on earth I want."

"Well, you'll never get an heir for the Spur without one," she returned.

He frowned thoughtfully through a thin veil of smoke. With a brief glance in the rearview mirror, he pulled off onto the grassy shoulder and cut off the engine. All around them was open land, and Kate noticed the familiar Diamond Spur logo on each gate. What Jason had was a small empire. It stretched practically into San Frio, and encompassed large tracts of bottom land up and down the Frio and small tributaries.

"I want to show you something." He got out, moving around the Bronco to open the door and help her down from the high cab.

She was briefly close to him until he reached past her to shut the door. Then he leaned back against it, his long legs crossed, the cigarette dangling from one hand.

"Blalock Donavan had a cabin out there," he said, nodding toward the flat plain that led to the Frio River. "The homestead burned down a month after he took possession, and he and some of the vaqueros put up a shanty just for him to sleep in. Soon after that, he married a Mexican girl and had seven kids in rapid succession. He built a house very much like the one I live in now, but the legend goes that he and the Mexican girl stood off a Comanche war party in that very cabin."

"Where the mesquite stand is?" she asked, gesturing toward a thick grove of trees with long, feathery green fronds blowing in the wind.

"The very one. There's a legend that she saw her patron saint standing beside the river, and he promised her that she and her husband would be spared. The name San Frio came loosely from it—San for Saint and Frio for the Frio River." He glanced at her and grinned. "Even legends have some truth, but Blalock was a gambler and a realist. He wrote in his diary that it was rain as much as divine intervention that saved them."

She leaned back against the Bronco's door beside him, trying not to notice the powerful lines of his body, or the thick shadow of chest hair that peeked out at the unbuttoned neck of his shirt. "Rain?" she coaxed.

"Comanches lashed the arrowheads on their arrows with rawhide," he explained. "When it rained, the humidity, so the story goes, made the rawhide relax." His dark eyes twinkled down at her. "So the arrowheads had this tendency to fall off in wet weather, before they got to the intended victim."

She laughed gently at the irony of it. Of course, those warriors surely had other weapons just as deadly, and they were fabulous horsemen and fighters. But it was one tiny Achilles' heel in an otherwise terrifying memory, and she liked knowing that even those men had one.

"The things you never learn in history class," she mused.

"They say that one of my ancestors was a Comanche," he remarked. "A lot more were Spanish and Mexican."

"I guess most of mine were Irish," she sighed. She watched the horizon, fascinated with the broad reach of open land. "There can't be a more beautiful place on earth than this," she said suddenly.

"It's that," he agreed, smiling with faint possession and pride as he followed her gaze. He lifted the cigarette to his mouth. "From a few scraggly longhorns to this," he mused. "It was a long road, Kate."

"And a hard one," she murmured. Her eyes lifted to his face, tracing the hard lines. "Your age tells on you sometimes."

"I guess it does. I feel it more these days." He turned his head and looked down at her, and without warning, the world narrowed to black eyes and green ones. Around them, the skies were growing dark, the thunder rumbling. The wind kindled like cool fire, whipping across Kate's face as she met and wondered at the sudden lack of expression in Jason's features, and the curious narrow glitter in his black eyes as his chin lifted slightly and his body stilled.

Lightning striking, Kate thought while she could. Her heart was as wild as the wind around them, her breath stuck like a cactus in her throat. Jason was looking at her in a way he never had, not in all the years she'd known him. Something in that look made her toes curl in her boots, making her body feel as if his hands had stroked it.

He shifted, the movement slow, easy, turning so that

his side was against the Bronco. His right hand, holding the dead cigarette, rested on the open window. The other was suddenly at Kate's neck, brushing stray wisps of long, dark hair, tracing an artery that was pounding crazily.

Jason was so close that she could smell the tobacco and leather scents that mingled with his spicy cologne. She could feel the warmth of his muscular body, the quiet threat of his masculinity. His dark eyes searched hers quietly with a new kind of curiosity. And then, all at once, they dropped to her soft bow of a mouth and lingered there with veiled intent.

The static from the CB radio was overloud drifting out the open window of the deserted cab, and Kate tried to concentrate on it, not on the very disturbing way Jason was looking at her. Any minute, everything she felt was going to start showing, and she couldn't bear to have him know how vulnerable she was.

But he already did. His dark eyes had caught every single giveaway movement of her body—her swollen breasts, her quick breathing, the yielding softness of her eyes. He wasn't all that experienced, and for the past few years he'd lived almost like a monk because of Melody's painful defection. But Kate was even less experienced than he was, and everything she felt was visible.

It gave him an odd sensation to know that she was aroused by him. He wasn't a handsome man. He was rich, and his wealth had given him opportunities with women even if he was still too bitter to accept them. But he couldn't remember a time when a woman had wanted just him, craggy face, mean temper and all. Even the one woman he'd loved had only wanted what he could give her. But Kate was looking at him in a way that made his blood run hot, and he realized suddenly that if he tried to kiss her, she'd more than likely let him.

When he realized that, reason deserted him. It was a new experience, having Kate want him. Breathing just a little unsteadily, he reached behind her tilted head, loosening the ribbon that held her long braid in place. With deft, easy movements, he loosened her hair and his fingers smoothed it down her back, slowly bringing her even closer to him.

"There's a storm…coming," she remarked in a quick, breathless voice.

"A hell of a storm, Kate," he breathed as his free hand slid to her waist and then around her, roughly pulling her closer so that the tips of her breasts came into sudden contact with his chest.

Kate felt electricity rustle through her body at the feel of him so close against her. Her hands went to his shirt instinctively and pressed there, feeling the cushy softness of his chest hair against hard, pulsating muscle. It was wildly arousing, and she couldn't hide her sudden trembling.

The wind whipped through her hair and the dark skies over Jason's head outlined the set of his jaw, the shadowy darkness of his eyes. "Jason?" she whispered in what was half question, half protest.

His gaze fell to her mouth while his lean fingers dug in and pulled her even closer. He was burning now, the cool wind making the fever bearable as he breathed in the scent of roses that clung to Kate's soft body. All the reasons he shouldn't let this happen fell away at the hunger that drew his head down. He wanted her. She wanted him. There was nothing in the world but Kate and her mouth, parted, softly tremulous, welcoming….

He tilted his head as it bent to hers, and he watched, fascinated, the way her mouth lifted for him, the way she caught her breath, the way her nails drew like tiny claws against his chest.

"The storm," she breathed dizzily.

"Damn the storm!" he whispered roughly. "Oh, God, honey, open your mouth…"

She felt the first tentative touch of his hard, warm lips on her mouth. Just then the loud roar of an approaching vehicle shattered the spell as surely as the pitchfork of lightning that shot down on the horizon and shook the earth seconds later.

Kate actually jumped, her gasp mingling with the odd sound that burst from Jason's lips simultaneously.

He stood erect, his breathing only a little rough as he glanced past her with eyes she couldn't read. "It's Gabe."

"Oh." She hoped that her confused frustration didn't show, but it was too late for camouflage because Gabe was already out of the truck and even with them.

"Howdy, boss man," he told Jason, grinning. He looked past him at Kate, and the grin grew wider. "Miss Kate. I hope you got sewed up proper, boss, because we have got trouble."

Jason dropped the forgotten cigarette in his hand and quietly lit another one, giving himself time to recover before he answered Gabe. Damn his own vulnerability! "When haven't we got trouble? And you have got more than most," Jason said with a cold, level smile. "I know how Kate accidentally happened to ride over to the Bottoms…."

"No time for that now," Gabe said quickly. "You know that black Angus bull of Mr. Henry Tanner's that he put in the pasture next to our heifers in spite of all the threats you made?"

Jason's chin lifted. He knew what was coming. "He jumped the fence?"

"He tore it down," Gabe muttered. "He's having the time of his life with our purebred Santa Gertrudis heifers."

Jason murmured something that sounded obscene and murderous all at once. Without waiting for another word, he helped a still shaky Kate into the Bronco, climbed in on the other side, started it and shot off down the road.

Kate was fumbling with her seat belt, and Jason thanked God for the intervention of the bull. Another few seconds and all his good intentions wouldn't have spared her. He could see her mouth like a vivid color photograph, parted, waiting, hungry… He almost groaned out loud. He was going to have to keep his emotions under control from now on. His life suited him as it was.

God knew what would happen if he gave in to his unexpected hunger for her. The least of it would be the loss of the only friend he had, because Kate was most certainly that. And the worst would be an addiction that he couldn't cure, except with commitment. Jason didn't want to risk that twice. His one brush with commitment had left a bitter taste in his mouth. Kate was young and inconsistent and hell-bent on a career. She was a risk he couldn't handle right now. He could fall in headfirst, but she wasn't likely to. Not at her age.

He looked at Kate with a quiet, calculating intensity. "I didn't mean for that to happen," he said, his voice still too deep, too soft.

"Neither did I," she managed unsteadily. She couldn't think of another single thing to say. She felt tongue-tied and nervous and frustrated, still hungry for a kiss she'd wanted with desperate abandon.

Jason blew out a thin cloud of smoke, keeping his eyes on the road as they turned onto the long dirt track leading up to the Donavan house. "If you want the truth, I've been celibate for a long time," he said bluntly, wanting to ward off trouble before it started. He looked at her deliberately and added, "I guess I need a weekend in the city."

Murderous jealousy stabbed into Kate like a knife. She couldn't even speak for it. Somehow she'd never thought of Jason in bed with another woman. Everybody knew there wasn't a less likely playboy in the state, even if Jason was rich. But now she thought about it, and the mental pictures she saw were shocking and embarrassing and they hurt.

He glanced at her set expression as he pulled up in front of the barn, where she'd left her horse.

"What is it?" he asked.

She swallowed. "Nothing. I'd better get home and start supper."

He caught her arm as she started to open the door. "You and I have never lied to each other," he said quietly when she looked at him with visible reluctance. "It's one reason we get along so well. Don't hide your feelings from me."

"This is different...." she blurted out.

"Tell me," he persisted, his voice deep and slow and insistent.

Her lips parted as she met his level gaze. "I...don't want to know."

"About what?"

"About you. With other women."

His breath came hard. He searched her eyes for a long,

static moment. Everything around them vanished in the green mist of her eyes, the sound of her soft breathing. He'd meant to shock her, but now he didn't like the flash of pain in those soft green eyes.

"I'm sorry," she said abruptly, turning her face aside. "I had no right to say such a thing." Her eyes stung. "Let me go, Jason!"

"For God's sake," he burst out, exasperated. He didn't understand his own confused feelings. Her reaction to his blunt statement had thrown him off balance. She'd believed him. She'd actually believed that bald-faced lie, and it had hurt her more than he'd ever expected.

She shook off his hand and jumped out of the Bronco. "Hi, Red, did you put Kip in the barn?" she called to the young cowhand who'd seen them off, because Kip hadn't been at the holding pen when they'd driven past it. Even upset, she'd noticed that.

"Yes, ma'am, Miss Kate, I sure did." He grinned. "I even mended your saddle for you. That nail must have been uncomfortable, even in jeans."

"It was," she confessed, avoiding Jason's interested gaze. "Thanks, Red, I'll remember you in my will."

"In that case, I sure would love a Rolls Royce," the younger man said. "And a house in Florida, on the bay. And a few bonds...."

"Oh, shut up," she laughed. "If I had half those things, I'd do my best to live forever and I sure wouldn't be riding around Texas on saddles with nails sticking through them."

"Well, it was just a thought," he said. "I'll saddle your horse."

She murmured a thank you and started to follow him into the well-lit confines of the mammoth barn, where several horses were quartered in tidy stalls off a wide aisle neat with pine shavings.

"You didn't mention anything about your saddle being worn," Jason said from behind her.

She could feel the warmth from his tall, well-muscled body and it made her legs go weak. She felt tingly from head to toe and deliberately moved away from the close contact. It was all too devastating a reminder of how close she'd been to him in the field, of the flash of passion that had almost but not quite ripped away the fabric of their casual relationship.

"You've got enough on your mind," she said evasively.

"Kate, don't run from me."

The quiet fervor in that statement brought her head around. She looked up at him with soft, searching eyes. He seemed really concerned about her, regretful almost.

She smiled at him. "Okay." She sighed. "I'm a little off balance, that's all."

"You might not believe it, but so am I." His dark eyes narrowed and he glanced toward the horizon, where the storm clouds had passed over without depositing a drop of rain. "Anyway, honey, the storm's gone. And there's no damage."

She looked up quietly, searching his black eyes. "That's right, Jason," she said. "No damage."

He touched her loosened hair, reminding her blatantly of his part in its dishevelment. She made him feel fiercely male, bristling with protective instincts that he didn't even know he had. She trembled at the faint touch, and he wanted to hold her, to comfort her, to keep her safe from any threat, even from himself.

"This time," he added, his voice deep with shades of feeling, his eyes darkening. "That can't happen again."

She searched his face, feeling lost and alone already. "I didn't do anything," she whispered. "I didn't mean to...."

He actually grimaced. "For God's sake, I know that," he ground out. "Leave it, Kate. Nothing happened." He turned away, dismissing it from his mind. "Red!"

Before she could speak, Red Barton came hotfooting in, leading Kip.

"Here you go, Miss Kate," he said, handing her the reins. "Mind that you don't go near the border over toward Tanner's, there's likely to be a turrrrrible explosion in the near future." He grinned, glancing at the boss.

Jason sighed heavily. "Barton, I don't know why in hell I don't fire you," he said absently.

Red frowned. "Neither do I, boss. I've studied on it for months, and I still haven't come up with a decent reason for you to keep me on. But I'll keep trying, don't you worry." He grinned again and tipped his hat to Kate. "I'll just move those heifers out of range of that lovesick bull, boss, while you explain to Mr. Tanner how many cuts of meat you expect to get out of him."

Jason pursed his lips. "Now that," he mused, "is a hell of a good idea. We haven't thrown a barbecue after roundup in a long time, and Tanner's bull looks like good beef to me."

"Mr. Tanner's purebred black Angus who placed at the national Angus show last November?" Kate asked incredulously. "The same one he paid a hundred thousand dollars for? That bull?"

"Where have you been for the past fifteen minutes?" Jason asked with colossal patience. "Didn't you hear Gabe? Yes, that bull. He got in with my purebred Santa Gertrudis two-year-old heifers that I was about to breed to my purebred longhorn bulls, and God knows how many of them he's managed to breed. We haven't checked that section for several days, so God knows when he got in there or how many of them he's bred already!"

"That's sure going to be rough on them heifers," Red mumbled. "That Angus bull had a birth weight of over a hundred and thirty pounds, as I recall."

"Absolutely." Jason's lips made a thin line as he thought about it and got even madder. "And no bull with a birth weight of over a hundred pounds is considered safe to breed to a virgin cow. First-calf cows have it hard enough without the complication of an oversized sire. The least damaging thing is that my breeding program will be shot to hell, and that bull is going to pay for it. Or Tanner is. Or both. Where the hell is my rifle!"

"Oh, no." Red grimaced as Jason whirled and stalked toward the house with his face set in hard lines that the cowboy and Kate both recognized.

"The Tanner place is five minutes away by truck," Kate coaxed. "You could drive past there on your way to move those heifers, and mention that Jason has loaded his rifle."

Red's eyes popped. "I could get the hell beat out of me, too. You know the boss in a temper."

"That's why I think you should warn Mr. Tanner that he's coming."

Red sighed. "The things I do for the Diamond Spur." He turned. "Okay. But I hope you'll take me in to the doc afterwards."

"I'll sling you over Kip here and ride you the whole way all by myself," she promised. "Hurry!"

He walked quickly toward the pickup truck. Kate, taking Kip's reins, made a beeline for the house. Jason was already coming back out the front door with his Winchester under one arm and Sheila raging behind him.

"You'll end up in prison, I tell you!" she bellowed, her hair standing practically on end. "You can't go around solving problems with a loaded gun! Henry Tanner is an Easterner! He's just learning about the beef business! He needs a helping hand, not blazing guns!"

He wasn't even listening. He was walking with the hard, measured stride that meant trouble, his hat at a dangerous angle over his eyes. Kate, leading Kip, intercepted him.

"I won't listen, so save your breath, Kate," he said shortly.

"I didn't say a word, Jason," she replied innocently.

"Well, you needn't," he murmured. He stared at her. "You aren't going to try and talk me out of it?"

"Not at all." She smiled pleasantly. "I've never been to visit anyone in jail before. It sounds exciting."

"I won't go to jail."

"If you shoot Mr. Tanner, you will."

"I'm not going to shoot Mr. Tanner. I'm going to shoot his bull."

"He'll sue you."

"He's welcome, but his bull will still be dead."

"Jason, you'll be arrested."

"His bull is trespassing," he said. "Trespassing is against the law. I'm making a citizen's arrest, which his bull will resist. Resisting arrest is also against the law. I will pass sentence and enforce it with a bullet. And you and the boys can have a nice steak."

She lifted her eyebrows. "It will be the most expensive steak you've ever served."

He grinned. "Nothing's too good for my men." He tipped his hat pleasantly and walked past her.

"You'll rot in prison!" Sheila was yelling from the front porch, her apron waving in the breeze. "Kate, for God's sake, stop him!"

"Sure. Have you got another gun and some bullets?" Kate asked.

Sheila threw up her hands and mumbled her way back into the house, slamming the door furiously.

Kate mounted Kip with a heavy sigh and rode back down the driveway, pushing the incident in the field to the back of her mind until she had enough time to deal with it.

She hoped Mr. Tanner had his bull insured. It was a pity he hadn't listened when Jason asked him not to put that bull next to heifers in heat with only a double strand barbed wire fence between. It was Tanner's fence, and Tanner was a retired department store manager who'd moved here from back East and decided to raise cattle in his retirement years. Jason had even offered to reinforce the fence and Mr. Tanner had refused to let him. Now he was going to pay the price.

Kate began to whistle as she turned Kip down the road toward home. It would be rather interesting to taste a purebred black Angus bull with a hundred thousand dollar price tag. She hoped Sheriff Gomez would let Jason have a plate of it in his jail cell.

CHAPTER THREE

KATE HAD JUST taken a taco casserole out of the oven and was putting the unmatched plates and cups and utensils on the supper table when her mother came in the door.

"Something smells good," Mary Whittman sighed, as she kicked off her comfortable thick-soled shoes at the door. "Heavens, I'm tired. I can't remember doing so many bundles in one day."

"If you made production, you shouldn't complain," Kate grinned.

"I made over a hundred percent, in fact," her mother replied, "so I expect I'll get a better check this week than last. By the way, Mr. Rogers stopped me on the way out and said for you to come in tomorrow."

"Have they got some serging for me?" she asked.

"They probably will have. We got some new cuts in today for the pants line. But what Mr. Rogers wants to see you about is those designs you left with him," Mary said, her green eyes twinkling. "He's been calling people all week to stop by and look at them. I think he's made a decision."

Kate stopped breathing. "You think they might be interested in using one?"

"Definitely. There's been a rumor about a new line of sportswear, and he loves your Indian designs, especially those bold turquoise colors you've used," Mary added.

"It seems that one of the buyers found a market forecast that predicted blue was going to be big next year. And your styles went over in a big way. I'm just guessing, honey, and I don't want to get your hopes up too high. But, I have a good feeling about this."

"I hope you're right. Oh, I hope you are," Kate laughed. "Mama, I'd be over the moon if they used anything of mine!"

"Well, don't mention that I said anything to you. I overheard Mr. Rogers asking Gwen about some accessories." She flopped down on the couch, her slender body slumping. Her thin, graying, dark hair was limp, and there were bits of cloth sticking to her brown stretch pants and her brown and green over blouse. The pants had come from a garage sale—Mary had brought them home, practically new, for two dollars. The blouse was one that the ladies at the plant had given her for her birthday last month. The shoes had come from a sale at a local department store; they were a little loose, but Mary's feet stayed swollen after walking around on the plant's concrete floors all day, so that was kind of a fringe benefit. She was no fashion plate, but she was decently covered and for a bargain price.

Mary had handed down that instinct for financial conservation to her daughter. Kate had learned to shop for the best fabrics at the lowest prices, and most of her apparel she made herself, even her jeans. She hand-embroidered each pair on the pockets and hems, and had more sewing than she could do for other people producing them after-hours. That was one reason she'd gone to Mr. Rogers with her designs in the first place. She was getting more orders than she could fill, and not only for jeans. And thank God for the sewing machine Jason had given her last Christmas because the old one she'd been using would never have stood the strain.

Kate's original skirt and blouse designs produced even more income. But not enough to pay the bills, keep up a car, and buy food. Her salary and her mother's combined barely did that, even with the spare money Kate made sewing.

"I'll get rich," Kate promised. "Then we can both give up working in the plant and you can parade around in mink and diamonds."

"I'm allergic to fur and I don't like diamonds." Mary grinned. "Give me a new rod and reel and some bass flies instead."

"I'll give you a lake stocked with bass, too."

Mary closed her eyes with a weary smile. "You're a good daughter."

"Yes, I know. Uh, did you come home by way of the Tanner place?"

"Every day."

"Hear any shots?" Kate asked innocently as she took a pan of green beans off the stove and set them on a cold burner.

Mary sat up. "Shots? Why would I?"

"Mr. Tanner's bull got in with Jason's cows. He went over that way with his Winchester."

The older woman leaned forward to light a cigarette, ignoring Kate's disapproving gaze. "I'll die of something one day," she said before her daughter could protest. "Turn on the fan and it won't bother you. Jason took a gun after Henry Tanner?"

"After the bull. It was on his land." Kate pursed her lips. "We've been invited to a steak dinner. Guess who's providing the steak."

"Mr. Tanner, no doubt. Well, Jason's attorneys have had a slack month, they need the business."

"Mother!"

Mary studied her daughter curiously. "How do you know about all this?"

"Jason got hurt and they sent for me. I got him to the doctor and patched up, and the bull was discovered about the time I was getting ready to leave." She shook her head as she poured iced tea into thick glasses, taking time to sip one so that it didn't overflow. "Sheila was screaming her head off. It didn't even slow him down."

"That's nothing new. Poor Sheila. Poor Mr. Tanner." She stood up and stretched. "I wonder what Jason's going to do when you go off to be a famous designer?" she wondered aloud. "I expect he'll die from lack of medical care because everybody else around San Frio is scared to death of him."

"You could take over for me," Kate teased.

Mary's eyes bulged. "Not me. I like living. I hope you didn't put too much cumin in that taco casserole."

"Only half a cup, isn't that what you put?" Kate asked with a blank smile.

"If you poison me, I'll tell Mr. Rogers to throw your designs out the window."

"Okay, I'll behave. Sit down and eat something. You're going to blow away."

"I'm a good size. I can walk through a harp sideways."

Kate turned away to flip the switch on the old rusted table fan that her father had bought when she was just a baby. There was no money for a new one, not even a cheap new one. But money, Kate reasoned, had never made anybody happy by itself. She'd rather have her mother and friends like Jason any day than a bankroll.

"You're very quiet tonight," Mary remarked as they finished off the small casserole and homemade Mexican corn-bread Kate had cooked with it.

Kate linked her hands around her coffee cup. "Well, I've been thinking."

"About what?"

About Jason, she could have said, and that he almost kissed her today. But that was a memory too precious to share, even with her mother.

Smiling, she tilted the cup and watched the ripples move with the overhead light that hung from the ceiling. The kitchen was worn, like the rest of the house. The walls needed painting. They were a dirty unpleasant yellow, and the gold and green linoleum on the sloping floor was torn in places and cracked in others. The stove was almost as old as Kate, and the sink had stains that nothing would get out. Faded yellow curtains hung over the windows, their miserable condition reflecting the stains on the ceiling where a leaking roof had left its mark before its haphazard repair. The house was falling apart, and there was no money for maintenance. Kate wondered sometimes what she and Mary would do if the roof fell in or the floor gave way. She'd seen some winged ants just yesterday. If they were termites, even now the house could be under a death sentence. The only new thing in the place was the new zigzag sewing machine that Jason had given her last Christmas, and it was the first thing she'd have saved if the house had caught fire.

"I said, what are you thinking about?" Mary prodded as she flicked an ash into the cracked glass ashtray with Phoenix, Arizona in faded letters in its gray-caked center.

Kate looked up. "About if the house is going to fall around our ears."

Mary's thin shoulders lifted and fell. "It's lasted fifty years already. I guess it's got a few more in it. And we can always cry on Jason's shoulder if things get desperate. God bless him, he'll do something."

"We shouldn't depend on him too much, Mama," Kate said, her tone hesitant.

"Why not? He doesn't mind, honey."

"I mind."

Mary grimaced. "Katy, pride won't satisfy hunger or fix leaking roofs."

"I know that." She sipped coffee. "But it's not right, to always be asking him for things."

"Did something happen today? Did the two of you argue?" Mary probed.

Kate laughed nervously. "When have Jason and I ever argued?"

That seemed to be a relief to the older woman. She smiled. "Silly thought, wasn't it? It amazes me, the things he'll let you get away with."

"Like taking him to the doctor?" Kate smiled back. "He likes me."

"You like him, too, don't you?"

"Stop digging, Sherlock Holmes," the younger woman said firmly and got up to wash the supper dishes. "You won't find romance. I'm not Jason's type. He'll want a society girl who can organize business dinners and act sophisticated for his rich friends. I'm just his late foreman's daughter and he feels sorry for me."

"Rich men have married poor girls before," Mary said doggedly. A match between Kate and Jason was the dream of her life, and the source of the only arguments she and Kate ever had. Mary had been poor since childhood. She wanted a way out of the rut, at least for Kate.

"I don't want to marry Jason," Kate replied. She ran water in the sink. It wasn't the whole truth, but she didn't dare confess to Mary that she was madly in love with their rich neighbor and would give her left arm to live with him. There was some truth in what she'd said about Jason's future bride, anyway—that he'd want a society girl. She'd never thought about Jason getting married, but inevitably, he would. He'd want an heir for the Diamond Spur. And, although it hurt to admit it, a poor girl like Kate would never fit into his world.

"If only we could afford some fancy clothes for you," Mary moaned. "I'm sure he'd noticed you if you had pretty things to wear. Not that these things you sew yourself aren't pretty," she was quick to add. She was proud of her daughter's accomplishments, but some nice store-bought things would catch a rich man's eye even better.

Mary couldn't know that Jason had noticed Kate. Her eyes went dreamy as she relived that unexpected and exciting interlude in the field, felt his arm around her, felt the warm and vibrant urging of his hard mouth, his body. She was aware of a new, nagging hunger that made her restless, and hoped that she could hide it from her mother. The last thing in the world she needed was to have her ambitious mother pushing her at Jason. He might be her best friend, but he'd already said that he didn't want commitment. Her mother could easily cost her his company forever by making it look as if Kate were trying to trap him into marriage.

"How about some dessert?" Kate hedged. "I made an apple pie."

"Well, aren't you the smart one? I'd love a slice. Make that two slices, I feel like living dangerously."

Kate grinned and got down two saucers to put the pie

in. Thank goodness for her mother's appetite. It saved her from a modern Spanish inquisition.

THE NEXT MORNING, Kate rode into San Frio with her mother. She was wearing one of the outfits she'd designed herself—a simple, loose, sky blue blouse with set-in cap sleeves with lots of embroidery in Indian patterns on the square yoke and bodice and sleeves, and an ankle-length full circle skirt of chambray that echoed the blouse's embroidery around the hem. She finished the outfit with simple suede fringed boots in a powder blue and a matching bag. Jason had given her those for Christmas. They weren't new, but they looked it because Kate kept them for special occasions. She'd put her hair in braids and added big blue bows to each one, and her own natural grace and carriage gave the outfit a charm all its own.

"You look delightful," Mary sighed as she parked the battered old blue Ford Galaxy outside the neat offices of Clayborn Manufacturing Company. Clayborn was the south Texas division of a national manufacturing company with headquarters in New York City.

Kate sighed as they got out of the car. She slammed the door twice to get the lock to catch. "Stupid car," she muttered. "I hate it."

"It gets us around," Mary replied. "And it's a long walk from the house to here."

"Walking is healthy," came the short reply. Kate gnawed her lower lip as Mary opened the door marked "employees only," and was met immediately by the sound of sewing machines running and steam surging through pipes into the pressing department. The colors of the current cut were echoed down the rows of seamstresses in the pants department. Kate waved to two of the girls she sat near and followed Mary down the aisle toward the front office.

The plant was large. It had a shirts line and a pants line, a training room, a huge cutting room and warehouse, a pressing department and quality control department and mechanics who were kept busy making the old machines produce. It smelled of fabric and machine oil and thread, pleasant smells that Kate had grown accustomed to since graduation from high school. She'd worked in the plant that long.

The canteen was empty as they passed it, the long tables spotless, the machines standing waiting for break time. The lady who worked seconds was busy packing them up in brown cartons, and the floor lady over the pressing department threw up a hand as Mary and Kate went by.

The main offices had a payroll department, personnel office, a receptionist and the plant manager's office. The assistant plant manager shared space next door. The cutting room had its own office, far down the hall, where the cuts were processed and records were kept of the coming and going of cloth. There was a quality control supervisor, who shared space with the pressing room supervisor, a storeroom where sewing supplies were kept, and a huge warehouse from which finished goods were shipped. The plant engineer had his own office, too, where he did time and motion studies and helped oversee the seamstresses on the shirt line.

Bundle boys and girls wandered around the floor, carrying stacks of cut garment pieces called bundles to the various seamstresses as each section of garment was quickly and efficiently finished and passed along to the next person and the next step to its completion.

Keith Rogers, the plant manager, was the person Kate wanted to see this morning.

"Hello, Kate," he greeted her in the doorway, adding a cheerful hello to Mary, who paused just long enough to kiss Kate's cheek before vanishing into the pants line where she worked.

"Good morning, Mr. Rogers," Kate said, sounding and feeling breathless. She twisted her bag nervously in her slender hands. "Mama said you had some news for me."

"Indeed I do. Jessie, bring that letter in, will you?" he called to the slender blonde who handled the telephones. She smiled back and went to the filing cabinet beside her desk.

Kate stood in front of the desk. Jessie brought the letter, winked at Kate with twinkling green eyes, and went back out, closing the door behind her.

Mr. Rogers was tall and balding and wore glasses. He had a wife and three small children, and pictures of them adorned his desk. A diploma in textile engineering held pride of place on one wall, and an award for superior production caught the attention on another.

Mr. Rogers leaned back in his chair behind the desk with the letter in his hand. "I showed your designs to our regional vice president," he explained to Kate, looking smug. "He felt just as I do about their potential. He went to the big boss, who also agreed. We want to contract with you to do a new line of women's sportswear for our spring season."

Kate was barely breathing. "Me?" she squeaked.

"You. These Indian designs are new and exciting, and our forecasters and buyers seem to share your feeling for blue and cream colors in the next year's fashions. They also like this silhouette," he added, picking up one of

Kate's sketches from the portfolio she'd left with him. It showed an outfit much like the one Kate had on, with a long full skirt and blouson top. "And denim looks strong for next year, too."

He smiled at her fascination. She tried to speak, caught her breath, and tried again.

"Mr. Rogers, I'm just speechless," she said finally.

"I'm glad you're pleased. You've designed these with an eye to cost control, which pleases the money men, too. They'll be easy to mass produce, they'll be moderately priced, and we'll show a good profit margin if they go well. Which," he added, "we expect them to. Now. Sit down, Kate, and we'll go over the details."

She did sit. She needed to. He outlined the designs that Clayborn wanted to purchase, mentioning a price that to Kate sounded like a small fortune. And her first thought was that she and her mother would be able to afford a better car—maybe even one that was only eight years old or so, and that would seem new after driving the twenty-year-old Ford around for so long.

"Does that amount sound reasonable to you, Kate?" Mr. Rogers prodded.

"Yes, sir," she agreed promptly. "Very reasonable."

His smile broadened. "Okay. I'll have the contracts drawn up. Can you finalize this new line by September, so that we can get it to our sales staff before fall market week in New York?"

"I'm sure I can," she agreed, visualizing nights of sketching and sacrificed weekends. But this was building toward something. This time would be invested in her own future.

Kate gave him a list of the fabrics, accessories, and trim she wanted. He sent her down to the design room and settled her with the head designer. Sandy Mays, fortyish, seemed to be a capable and confident woman, generous with her praise of Kate's new drawings. There was an assistant named Betsy Gaines and another named Pamela Barker, both of whom Kate knew from school. The head seamstress was Dessie Cagle, a middle-aged lady with silver hair and deft hands who could make anything she saw in the finer shops without a pattern. She could copy couture with incredible ease, and had been responsible, along with Sandy, for many of the company's newer casual clothes. It was Betsy's job to coordinate the trims— the buttons and laces, ribbons and belts and buckles that complemented the designed outfits. These were as important in their way as the actual silhouettes, and Kate paid deliberate attention to their use when she put together a new outfit.

The first day was spent getting used to the new location. Kate had a lot to learn about the routine of the sample room and the way things were done. This, Dessie and Sandy were happy to show her. They discussed the fashion business, contacts, buyers, fashion merchandising, and learned a lot about each other. By the time Kate went home, she felt as if she'd become another person. She had a new and vibrant attitude toward designing, replacing the vague anticipation of the years before.

"I'm going to be famous," she told Mary over the supper table. "I can feel it. I'm going to design new lines for each season, and people are going to know my name by my label, you wait and see. I'll make the company rich. I'll make them proud of me."

"I already am," Mary said, her eyes sparkling. "Kate, you have to go and tell Jason."

There was a thought. She turned away, so that her

mother wouldn't see the radiance of her face. "Can I borrow the car?"

"Sure. There's enough gas to get you there and back, and then some," her mother said dryly.

"Our very first luxury," Kate called from the front hall, "is going to be our very own telephone!"

"I hear you!"

She rushed out the door, grabbing up her purse on the way, and was all the way to the old battered blue Ford before she realized that she didn't have the keys. She went back to ask for them with a sheepish grin, then tore out the door again.

It started on the third try, made a loud roaring sound, and clanked when it was coaxed into low gear. She pulled out of the dirt driveway, careful not to scatter dirt in her haste, and bounced off toward the Diamond Spur with barely contained impatience and delight. If Jason wasn't in jail, she knew he'd be pleased about her good fortune. She wondered if Mr. Tanner still had a bull and if not, whether he had pressed charges. Jason usually got his way, but there was always a first time.

CHAPTER FOUR

As she drove up in front of the Donavan house Kate realized something. She had no girlfriends, unless she counted her mother. Her best friend, the only real friend she had, was Jason. It was ironic that she had no one else to share this milestone in her life with.

She smiled about that as she darted up the steps and knocked furiously at the big hand-carved oak door, ignoring the modern doorbell altogether.

Sheila opened it, her eyebrows arching. "What a nice surprise."

"I'll bet," Kate laughed. "Well, is he in jail or not?"

The older woman grimaced. "He belongs there, all right. But Mr. Tanner decided that it would be easier to reinforce his fence and move that bull to another pasture after Jason explained the situation to him."

"I wish I'd been a bug on the fence," Kate said with a mischievous grin.

"Me, too," Sheila whispered. She nodded her grizzled head toward the hall. "He's in there with Gene and Cherry having supper. Go sit down and I'll get you a dish."

"Oh, I've already eaten…."

"The dish," Sheila explained patiently, dragging her inside, "is for peach cobbler. I made one tonight."

"My favorite!" Kate enthused.

"Fancy that," came the tongue-in-cheek reply. "I didn't know, of course, having only made it for you about a hundred times over the past few years."

Kate laughed delightedly. "What would I do without you?"

"Starve, most likely, if you weren't such a good little cook yourself. And I'll pat myself on the back for teaching you how, too, because your sweet mama is the best seamstress and the worst cook I ever knew."

Kate started to argue, and then closed her mouth. "I thought hamburgers were supposed to be black and crunchy," she said under her breath.

Gene and Cherry were whispering when Kate walked into the elaborate dining room. Jason was sitting quietly at the head of the table, impressive in pale slacks and a tailored gray shirt open at the throat. He was tapping his silver fork against the tablecloth, lost in thought, brooding if that scowl was anything to go by.

He looked up suddenly, as if he sensed Kate, and the scowl was still there. But something new kindled in his eyes, something born of their tempestuous interlude the day before. He was aware of her now, and she was just beginning to realize it. Her heart raced as his dark, very Spanish-looking eyes went over her like hands tracing every curve and line of her slender body.

"Did somebody die?" he asked politely. "I haven't seen you dressed like that since the last time you went to church with us."

Kate curtsied to cover her nervousness. "Do you like it? I made it myself."

"It's beautiful," Cherry sighed, propping her head on her hands to stare dreamily at the long full skirt and blouson top with its sky blue colors and detailed embroidery. "Gosh, Kate, you ought to open a boutique."

Kate could have hugged her. Cherry was petite and blonde and blue-eyed, always smiling, always enthusiastic. She encouraged Gene to be himself, to do what pleased him instead of what pleased big brother. But she did it in such an open, sweet way that Jason had become less antagonistic toward her. She was just eighteen now, and to Kate she seemed very young, despite the fact that there was less than three years between them.

"I'll second that," Gene chuckled. He was thinner than Jason, a little shorter. He had lighter hair and dark eyes, but his features were more even and attractive than his older brother's. Jason had the business sense and the steel will, but Gene was the male beauty of the family and had always seemed to have girls hanging all over him.

Kate wondered sometimes if that wasn't why she preferred Jason—he wasn't a ladies' man by anybody's measure, although she was sure that he wasn't naive. He'd had her trembling with need in no time at all. Not that he needed vast experience to accomplish that, when Kate thought the sun rose and set on him.

"Jason would loan you the money to go into business for yourself, wouldn't you, Jay?" Gene asked him with the careless certainty of youth.

"Careers are the ruin of good women everywhere," he commented dryly, leaning back in his chair with his hands behind his head. The posture outlined the powerful muscles of his chest and stomach, and it made Kate tingle to touch him. That must have showed, because his slow smile was knowing and faintly predatory. "A woman's place is three steps behind her man."

Kate stared at him, and even though it sounded like

teasing, it took some of the joy out of her surprise. His mother's betrayal had warped his attitude toward marriage, and his one-time fiancée's defection to Hollywood had compounded the prejudice.

"Not this woman," Kate told him as she sat down beside him at the table. "I think a woman's place is at a man's side."

"Here we go again," Gene muttered to Cherry, who giggled.

"Women shouldn't have careers," Jason repeated, his dark eyes level and somber. "Not unless they never plan to settle down."

"I plan to settle down one day," she said unexpectedly. "And have a home of my own, and children. And a career. I'm going to be a designer."

"Without any help from me," he returned blandly. "I'll be damned if I'll start you on the road to women's liberation."

Her eyes flashed. It wasn't the first time she and Jason had argued about the traditional place of a man and a woman in society, but it was the first time it had mattered.

"I'm on the way already," she shot back, "and without any need to go to you for help, thank God. I've just agreed to sign a contract with Clayborn to design a new line of leisure wear."

"Congratulations! Kate, that's grand!" Cherry gushed.

"I knew you could do it," Gene chuckled.

"What's this? A career designing clothes?" Sheila asked from the doorway, all eyes. "Great! Design something for heavyset women, the moderately priced stuff I can afford makes me look like a tub of lard."

"Don't say it," Cherry gritted as Gene started to say

something. "Not until after we get our peach cobbler, for heaven's sake!"

Gene looked as if he might burst. Sheila glared at him out of gimlet eyes, the bowl of cobbler held protectively against her waist, her head cocked threateningly.

"I'll throw it out," she promised the young man.

Gene sighed. "I love peach cobbler." He grinned. "Sheila, you ravishing beauty, you, how about a taste of that exquisite dessert you concoct with such style and sensuality?" He wiggled his eyebrows.

Sheila curtsied, almost falling over. "Why, thank you, kind sir, would you like to eat it or wear it?"

"I'll eat it, thanks, and I swear," he stood, hand over his heart, "I'll never make another sarcastic remark about your size."

Sheila nodded curtly. "See that you don't. Here."

She set the deliciously browned dessert on the table and laid a serving spoon beside it. "Kate goes first, since we're celebrating."

"Well, I won't argue with that." Gene grinned. "She's earned it. When did you find out?"

"This morning," she replied, digging with the serving spoon through the sugar-sprinkled crust to the sweet smell of sugary peach and dumpling beneath. She filled her dish, aware of Jason's dark glare on her averted features. It was difficult to keep her hands from trembling as she began to sample the dish.

"It's wonderful," she told Sheila, who beamed and went back into the kitchen.

Gene got up and did an impression of the ample-hipped housekeeper waddling away, only to turn and find the object of his demonstration scowling at him from the doorway.

He cleared his throat and sat down quickly. "I lost a button, I was looking for it."

Sheila glared at him. "Ha, ha. You just hold your breath until I cook you that vanilla pound cake you keep begging for."

"I'll repent!" He ran into the kitchen after her and the door closed behind them.

"Disgusting, watching him grovel." Cherry grinned. She grabbed the cobbler. "Maybe if I hurry, I can finish his part and mine before he gets back."

"Evil girl," Kate accused. She glanced at Jason, who hadn't said a single word through all the wordplay. He didn't seem to hear what was going on around him. In fact, he didn't. He was still hearing Kate rave about her career. He'd never realized how ambitious she was. It bothered him because he didn't like to think of losing her to the big city and high fashion. And that was vaguely surprising. He'd been fighting the memory of her soft mouth for a whole day without success, and that hadn't helped his temper.

"Don't you want any cobbler?" Kate asked him.

"I've lost my appetite." He lit a cigarette, daring anyone to object, and leaned forward to stare at Kate while she tried to eat her cobbler. "What will it mean, this job?"

"More money to start with. And I'll get to do a lot of traveling once the designs are finished and we have samples made up," she told him. "I'll go to New York for market week this October and talk to the buyers and salesmen, and if my designs sell well, I'll get to do another collection. All with my own name on it. I may even get to go to Europe to look at styles before I start on my next designs."

Jason stared at her quietly. That wouldn't suit Kate.

She was meant for a kitchen and a house of her own, for children. Not this house, of course, not his children. He didn't want any kind of permanent relationship even with Kate. He frowned. She'd meet all kinds of men in a job like that, predatory men. He didn't like to think about some suave stranger seducing her.

"You're too damned green for a sophisticated job like that," he said aloud, shocking her.

She gaped at him, her fork poised in mid-air. So did Cherry. "What?!" Kate asked, torn between exasperation and laughter.

He crossed his long legs and took a heavy draw from his cigarette. In the overhead light, his dark straight hair seemed to have black highlights. "You'll get in trouble back East, with no one to look out for you."

"Well, you'll probably bleed to death while I'm gone," she shot back, "since nobody else can convince you that blood poisoning is dangerous."

"I've been looking out for myself just fine."

"Oh, of course," she agreed. "Ripping your arm open, trying to shoot people…how's the bull, by the way?"

His jaw tautened. "The bull is alive, through no fault of mine. I had to sell six cows to Tanner because his bull bred them. Luckily, I had plenty of replacement heifers this time."

"How do you know his bull bred them?" Cherry asked innocently.

Jason looked suddenly hunted, his whole expression set and uncomfortable.

"Go ahead," Kate dared him. "Tell her." She knew about the new system of dyes that were used to show a stockman when a cow had been bred, but Cherry had never taken much interest in the cattle. Like Gene, she was more fascinated by art.

Jason took a sharp breath and stood up. "You tell her," he said to Kate, his tone deep and cutting. "I've got better things to do."

"You might congratulate me on my new job," Kate said quietly.

He searched her green eyes curiously, his eyes narrowing on her oval face in its frame of dark, softly loosened hair. "I can't do that. I think you're making one hell of a big mistake."

"You didn't think so when I wanted to take the course in fashion design!" she argued.

"That was just something to help you sew better at the plant, or so I thought. I didn't realize that San Frio was going to get too small to hold you."

She stuck her chin up in the air and stared at him, refusing to be told how to live her life. "You're just jealous because you can't sew a dress, Jason," she replied, resorting to teasing to keep from blowing up at him again.

"Oh, hell." He turned on his heel and walked away without another word or a backward glance.

Kate smothered a grin, sharing a wink with Cherry, who was about to burst with mischief. Jason would come to his senses and then they'd talk about it. For now, he had to get used to the idea, and Kate knew very well how to skirt his moods. She'd had almost three years of practice.

"I never used to believe Gene when he talked about how well you managed to get along with Jason," Cherry grinned. "But I'm beginning to see the light. My gosh, he takes a lot from you, doesn't he?"

"From time to time," Kate agreed with a sigh. "I wish

he could understand that women aren't property anymore. He doesn't like them very much, you know."

"It's hard to miss," Cherry murmured dryly. "All the same, I guess he'll marry a woman someday, as long as she's socially acceptable and doesn't mind giving him an heir."

Cherry couldn't have known how much that supposition hurt Kate, even though she'd already faced it.

"I guess he will," Kate replied, going quiet. She finished her cobbler and poured herself a cup of coffee from the carafe. She took it black, hardly tasting it as she lifted it to her mouth.

Cherry smiled. "I thought he was going to pass out when you dared him to tell me about those bred cattle." The younger girl frowned. "How *do* you tell that a cow's been bred?"

Kate told her absently, and Cherry just shook her head. "I can't imagine a man being a rancher who's too old-fashioned to talk about breeding in mixed company," Cherry remarked.

Kate bit back a defensive comment. She couldn't help it that she felt defensive about Jason. Despite her proud defense, she liked a few of his old-fashioned attitudes. In the modern world, where rough language and frank discussions were a matter of course, it was sometimes refreshing to be treated like a lady. Not that Jason cared much who was around when he lost his temper, she mused, but he'd never let Kate near his cows and heifers at breeding time or expose her to cattle that were being put down because of illness. Apparently he thought women were too delicate for that kind of thing.

She'd asked him once why he didn't want her around the breeding stock, just in passing. He'd said something that had puzzled her at the time—that he didn't want her to get the wrong idea about it because the cows would sound as if they were in pain and he didn't want her to be frightened of a natural process. Now that she was older, and had been exposed to at least one racy motion picture, she began to understand what he'd meant. Passion was violent, if what she'd seen was any indication, and on the screen at least, women looked and sounded as if they were being killed. Kate had wondered a time or two if she'd ever sound like that, but she'd never felt passion with the few hometown boys who'd taken her out. She'd only felt that kind of fiery heat with Jason, the day before, and it was still new and a little unnerving.

"Jay just rattled the windows in the front room slamming out the door," Gene remarked as he rejoined them with another saucer of cobbler. He grinned knowingly at Cherry as she guiltily gulped down the last bite of his after having finished her own.

"It was my fault, I guess," Kate confessed. "I got a little overheated about his opinion of a woman's place. Honest to goodness, I think sometimes that he doesn't know what century this is."

"You know why, though," Gene said gently. "You of all people know why."

Kate sighed. "Yes. But I was so excited about my break," she smiled. "I wanted to share it."

"He'll storm around the barn for a while and then he'll be all right," Gene assured her. "Just drink your coffee, Kate, and remember that even the nastiest storm rains out eventually."

"After it gets through rumbling," she agreed, and sipped her coffee.

She stayed a few minutes longer, telling them about

the new chores she had at the plant and what she was going to work around in her designs. Then, depressed by Jason's sustained absence, she told them good-bye, waved to Sheila, and went out the front door to go home.

It was a glorious spring night. The sky was clear and the breeze was warm, and the stars looked close enough to touch. There was a whisper of jasmine in the air from the thick bushes at the front steps and at the corner of the house, lilac was just blooming. Kate sighed, smelling it, her eyes on the long horizon. Somewhere cattle were lowing softly, and she thought about the trail drives of the last century, when cowboys would sing to the cattle to calm them.

"Leaving already?"

She stiffened at the unexpected sound of Jason's voice from the porch. She turned to find him sitting in the porch swing, barely silhouetted in the light from the nearby window. The orange tip of a smoking cigarette waved in his hand as he pushed the swing into motion. Its soft creaking sound was oddly comforting, but Jason's presence made Kate feel nervous.

She lifted her chin. "Are we still speaking?"

"If you're through reading me sermons on the modern woman, we are," he said shortly.

"I might as well be, for all the good it's done me," she sighed, and smiled at him, because it was hard to fight with Jason. She understood him all too well, most of the time.

He got out of the swing lazily and strode toward her. Seconds later, he towered over her. The soft light coming out of the window lay on the floor in abstract patterns at her feet.

"I hate fighting with you," she remarked to break the silence.

"Then don't do it," he said lazily, and managed to smile.

But as he smiled, he stared. He hadn't really come face to face with her career until tonight, and now that he had, he was concerned. He knew that she couldn't stay a girl forever. But he'd opened up with Kate in ways he couldn't with even his own brother. He could talk to her. Somehow in the past few years he'd come to think of her as his own, and now she wanted to go away and leave him.

His eyes narrowed as they searched her face and then down her slender, exquisite body. Just lately his affection for her had become physical. He'd told himself that he hadn't noticed her blossoming figure, but he had. Ever since that sweet interlude by the Bronco when he'd come within a hair of kissing the breath out of her, he couldn't stop thinking about her. And that wouldn't do. He couldn't give her a physical hold on him. He didn't want commitment with anybody just yet, much less with a girl like Kate who was years younger than he was, and a world apart from him in experience and maturity. She wouldn't fit into his world. Even if she could, he didn't want to let her.

But letting go was hard. "Do you even realize what a change it will be, if you get what you think you want?" he said after a minute. "You'll be thrown into a world you've never experienced," he said.

"It isn't so different from mine," she defended.

He lifted his chin, staring down his straight nose at her. "You're a poor little girl from rural Texas, Kathryn," he said shortly. "You don't even know how to speak the language."

"And I guess you do?" she challenged.

He looked at her half angrily. "Of course I do," he said shortly. "I'm worth a small fortune. I've been moving in monied circles for years."

Her face went blood red. She'd never considered the differences between herself and Jason as much in her life as she had in the past two days. She knew he was a rich man and she was a poor woman, but she'd never really noticed it before.

"You like to go barefooted and groom horses," he said on a slow breath. "The people you'll be associating with in New York will be city sophisticates. You won't understand the discussions they have, or know the people they talk about, or be knowledgeable about the customs they'll take for granted. You've got a Texas drawl that will stand out, and an innocence that some city man will do his best to relieve you of. If you aren't careful, you'll end up a broken flower, used up."

She glared up at him. "What a glowing character reference," she said, almost choking on her own pride. "I'm poor white trash, is that how you think of me after all these years?"

Her voice broke and she turned away furiously. But he was one step behind her. Without bothering to worry about consequences, he reached for her hungrily, locking her in his arms. He held fast, her tearstained cheek against his broad chest.

"I don't want you hurt," he said curtly. His mouth brushed her forehead, his lean hand smoothed her hair away from her face. "You'd be on your own in the city, with nobody to protect you, and you're so damned innocent, honey."

"And who's to blame for that?" she demanded, hitting at his broad chest.

He took a slow breath. "All right, if you want to put it that way, I guess some of the blame is mine," he admitted. He nuzzled her dark hair with his cheek. "I've tried to help Mary keep you out of trouble, and maybe I've gone overboard. It's just that it's hard to let go," he admitted finally, breathing in the scent of her.

She'd hoped for something more. And that was foolish because she knew better than most people how much Jason avoided involvement. He had almost a fear of it, and knowing his past, she couldn't really blame him. He couldn't trust anybody that far, not even Kate.

"You'll have to let go one day," she reminded him.

"I guess so." He spoke absently into her soft hair. "But you're the closest thing to a friend I've got," he added, the words slow and gentle. "I'll miss having you around."

"I won't be going away forever," she laughed, because he sounded so fatalistic. "Just for an occasional week."

"That's what you think now," he said quietly. "That isn't how it will be. Business tends to overshadow everything else, after a while. I've given everything in me to the Diamond Spur in recent years. It's become my life. Be careful that designing doesn't obsess you the same way."

"It won't," she said. She drew back enough that she could smile up into his concerned face. "And if you'd relax a little now and again, maybe you wouldn't have those gray hairs."

"I can't relax," he returned. "The cattle industry has been in a slump for the past few years. Until market prices edge up, the Spur is hanging by a thread."

"You could delegate once in a while."

"Maybe I could, if Gene would hold up his end of the work," he returned. He studied her quietly. "You never seemed so ambitious, Kate. You used to talk endlessly about getting married."

"Well, I've changed my mind now," she said, holding back the fact that she'd changed her mind because she knew she'd never change his about marriage.

He sighed, watching her. With her hair loose around her shoulders and that silky blouse she was wearing, she looked seductive. When she moved her breasts danced with erotic subtlety, and he was sure that she wasn't wearing anything to support them. That made it even worse, thinking about what her full young breasts looked like under their sensuous covering. He even felt vaguely guilty to be considering Kate in that light, when she'd been off limits for years.

"It's strange to argue like this with you," she said finally, smiling faintly. "We've been friends for a long time now. We get along better than any two people I know. And yet in the past two days, all we've done is disagree. It's…it's uncomfortable."

"This is the first time you've really gone against me," he replied.

"I've never wanted anything this badly before," she replied. And it was true, she'd never fought him. How odd to suddenly wake up and find that she'd allowed herself to be dominated by him for years. Her eyes searched his dark face. "You won't change my mind, Jason. I'm going to do what pleases me, even if it doesn't please you."

His eyes narrowed, but he didn't speak. It was frankly arousing to argue with her. His body made a sudden and emphatic statement about what it wanted, and he moved restlessly, trying to convince it that she wasn't fair game.

"I'll drive you home," he said abruptly.

"I have the car," she reminded him reluctantly. His

nearness was already working on her, and she wanted the delight of being alone with him, even if it was just for a few minutes on the way home. Remembering the way he'd looked at her and touched her the day before still made her burn with untried longings.

"That's just as well," he said after a minute. He lifted the cigarette again to his chiseled lips. "I'm in a strange mood tonight."

"I don't understand."

His chin lifted and he scowled at her. "Don't you? Are you going to pretend that nothing happened yesterday?" he challenged, driven by mingled desire and frustration to lash out at her.

She remembered, but she didn't want to. Jason aroused her, excited her, and she was uncertain of his motives. He'd always been possessive of her, but lately he was taking it to new heights. She felt that if she let him, he'd smother her.

"Nothing did happen, really," she faltered.

He moved closer, his whole posture threatening. She could smell his cologne and the scent of leather that clung to his soft Western shirt. Her breath stifled in her throat.

"And nothing's different between us?" he persisted.

She could hardly breathe at all. His fingers were on her hair, lightly touching it. "No," she whispered.

"Then it shouldn't bother you if I have women."

She bit her lower lip until her teeth almost broke the skin. The image of that was unbearable. "No," she agreed. "It shouldn't."

He flicked the cigarette off the porch while the silence closed in around them. He tilted her chin up and searched her eyes in the dim light from the windows.

Her mouth, faintly pink and just a little tremulous,

looked delicious. He wondered idly if anyone had even kissed her properly. God, he wanted to do that!

Kate watched, shocked, as his dark head suddenly bent toward her. She could feel his warm, smoky breath on her parted lips and her own breath came jerkily.

"Don't pull away from me," he whispered deeply as his head tilted, his fingers touching her cheek. His nose nuzzled against hers and his mouth brushed the corner of hers, then drew lightly over the full softness of her parted lips. "I won't hurt you," he breathed against her mouth just as his covered it.

The sensation was explosive. His mouth was hard and warm and faintly hungry. He teased her lips until she went weak in the knees and her heart began to slam at her rib cage. Her eyes, half open, a little frightened, searched his curiously when he drew back to look at her.

"You taste of coffee," he said deeply. She'd never heard that pitch in his voice before, that sensual note. It was exciting and new.

"You…you taste of cigarette smoke," she whispered back, trying to smile. But she didn't know how to play so-phisticated games, and she was out of her depth with him.

He seemed to know that. His lean hands came up to frame her face and he bent again. "Open your mouth this time," he breathed as his lips nudged hers apart. "Deep kisses are an acquired taste, but I think I can make you want mine."

She moaned at the way he said it, at the velvet of his deep voice, at the aching hunger his caressing lips aroused in her body. She let him push her lips apart with his, admitting the slow, tender penetration of his tongue. She felt his tongue touching hers, fencing with it, and her body began to tremble.

One of Jason's hands went behind her head, to support it. The other traced her cheek, her soft throat while he deepened the kiss. His mouth was expert. Warm and hard and knowing, and she could hear his rough breathing mingled with hers in the silence of the porch. Instinctively she tried to move closer to him, wanting his strength to support her sudden weakness.

His mouth lifted a second later, pressing roughly against the side of her neck. He slid his arms around her and enveloped her against him, but when she pressed even closer and felt the sudden changed contours of his body, he gently eased his hips back to prevent the contact.

She wanted to ask him if it embarrassed him to have her know he was aroused, but she was too shy to put it into words. She'd heard girls at school talk about men getting this way. She knew what caused it, and her head swam to think that, at her age, she could have that effect on Jason.

He was having his own effect on her as well. She couldn't seem to stop trembling, and his arms tightened, shifting her soft breasts against his hard chest. She could feel the muscle right through the soft material of her blouse. He had to know that she wasn't wearing a bra by now, and that made her nervous. She tugged gently against his hard arms, but he wouldn't let go.

"Don't fight me," he murmured at her ear as his head lifted. "I won't take advantage of it."

"Of…what?" she faltered, trying to save her pride.

"Of the fact that you're bare under that blouse, Kate," he said. He lifted his head and looked down at her with an odd kind of patient indulgence, but there was a glitter in his dark eyes that made her heart skip beats. "That I can feel how soft you are, lying on my chest."

Her face went blood red. She dropped her eyes to the steady rise and fall of his chest. She felt inadequate. Years too young.

"There's nothing to be afraid of," he murmured. He scowled, gently tracing her mouth with a lean forefinger, feeling its instant shy response. "I told you I was in a strange mood. I should have sent you on home before this happened."

"Are you sorry that it did?" she asked shyly, and her eyes were wide and soft and still hungry when they met his.

"Are you hell-bent on becoming famous?" he countered.

"I just want to see how far I can go," she told him. "No, I don't want to be famous. I just want to use my talent."

"New York is a long way from Texas."

"So you keep telling me. Jason, I won't change."

"You will," he said quietly. He studied her young face quietly. "But I'm not going to have you seduced by some Ivy Leaguer with a line a mile long. I don't want you treated like an appetizer."

"You're very possessive lately," she said, but it flattered her that he cared, that he didn't want anything to happen to her.

"Of course I'm possessive. I owe you my life a time or two." He sighed roughly. "I don't want a man to…hurt you," he said finally, and his dark eyes were troubled. "Inevitably, if you move in those circles, you're going to meet some experienced men, and you won't know how to handle them. You could get drunk one time too many in the wrong company, or you could be flattered too much by a man's attentions. And the first time, if a man isn't damned gentle…." He stopped, frowning as he searched for the right words. "I don't want you used."

She smiled, because she knew what he was trying to say. It delighted her that he had trouble saying it when most men were permissive and worldly and blunt. He wasn't a virgin, she was sure, but he wasn't all that experienced, either. She dropped her eyes to his chest. "I promise I won't jump into bed with the first man who asks me, Jason." She stared at his chest. "Anyway, I don't like it when men touch me. Except that I've always wondered what it would be like…if you did."

He felt the ground go out from under him. Until the past two days he'd never thought of Kate as a woman, and now he couldn't think of her any other way. Her mouth was sweet and responsive and he wanted it again. He wanted to put his hands under that silky blouse and touch her bare breasts, to see if they were really as soft as they felt lying against his chest. He wanted to drag her hips back against his and make her feel the strength of the arousal he hadn't wanted her to know about.

"Don't make jokes," he said tersely.

Her face felt warm, but it wasn't the time for subterfuge. "I'm not," she said honestly. "If I ever…well, if I wanted anyone, I mean…" She was as bad as he was about this, she thought, almost laughing at her own inefficiency. "I can't imagine being that intimate with someone I've only just met," she murmured. "It would have to be someone I knew very well."

"Like me?" he prompted quietly.

Her body tingled. She couldn't quite meet his eyes. "Yes."

"If I'd let you," he said after a minute, trying to lessen some of the tension that was building between them and playing hell with his good intentions, not to mention his agonized body.

She glanced up to find a faint, rather forced amusement in those dark eyes. "Oh, so it's that way, is it?" she took him up, delighted at the new familiarity they were sharing so unexpectedly. "I'd have to seduce you, I gather?"

"Damned straight," he returned. "I'm not one of those fast city boys. You won't get me into bed without a fight."

She laughed, her eyes sparkling, her face radiant. "Well, I never."

"I know," he mused.

She hit his chest with a small, playful fist. "Tease."

"Flirt."

She stared up at him with pleasure and adoration written all over her. "If you're going to play hard to get, I'll just go home."

"That might be wise," he sighed. He dragged a cigarette from his pocket with fingers he had to force to be steady, and lit it. "You're getting me all stirred up."

Her eyebrows lifted. "Well, you started it."

"I guess I did." He touched her cheek gently. "Are you sorry?"

She shook her head. "If we're making confessions, I've wondered for a long time what it would feel like if you kissed me."

His chest swelled. "I've wondered the same thing about you, just lately."

She smiled with aching pleasure. "I thought you were mad at me when you came out here."

"I think I was." He drew from his cigarette, and said, "I just don't want to lose you."

"And I've already told you, I'm just going to a few fashion shows, that's all. I'm not going to have my head turned by fancy living."

"It's easy to say, isn't it?" he asked with faint cynicism.

"I grew up poor, honey. I remember what it was like when we started making money here. But that's something you're going to have to find out for yourself, I guess."

"That doesn't make sense," she said softly.

"It will. Kiss me good night and go home. Want me to follow you in the Bronco to make sure you get there all right?"

She was still staggering from his request. Her wide eyes welded to his, she couldn't be bothered to worry about getting home.

"Kiss you good night?" she whispered.

"Don't you want to?" he whispered back, bending. "This kind of thing can get addictive, especially when it feels this sweet. Come on. Open that soft little mouth and fit it to mine, Katy," he murmured as his face came closer.

She obeyed him, trembling as she felt the moist warmth of his lips so close against her own. She parted her lips and nudged them up against his, and moaned when he returned the caress with biting hunger. The sound worked on his blood like fire. He looped an arm around her shoulders and brought her roughly against his chest while the pressure of his mouth pushed her head back onto his muscular arm. Time hung like the stars while they fed on each other, and it was a long time before Jason could manage to drag himself away.

Jason's eyes were almost frightening with their hot glitter as they searched Kate's. "You and your damned soft breasts are giving me hell," he breathed shakily. "Next time, wear a bra, unless you want to watch me strip you to the waist out of sheer frustration."

Her mouth opened on a gasp and he bent long enough to crush his own over it for an instant. Then he let her go and moved back a step. She tried to stop shaking.

"Jason!" she exclaimed.

"I'm not made of solid rock," he reminded her. His eyes went to her blouson, where the sharp tips of her breasts were straining against the thin fabric. "God, that excites me," he said roughly.

She blinked, because in some ways, her education was a little faulty. "What?"

He sighed wearily. "Kate...this." He brushed the back of his hand softly over her breast, and she jerked back on an inverted breath. "Didn't you know that a woman's body shows arousal that way?" he asked her gently.

"I do now, thanks," she fumbled, wrapping her arms around herself in a flurry of embarrassment.

"Stop that," he scolded gently. "Remember who I am, Kate."

"I'm trying," she replied lightly, her eyes fascinated with him and this new and sudden intimacy. But she moved her arms. Odd, how her body tingled when he looked at her breasts. For one wild instant, she thought about what he'd threatened, about stripping her to the waist and looking at her there....

"Why the wild blush?" he asked, his voice deep and velvety. He kissed her closed eyelids. "If you want to experiment, I'll let you do it with me. At least you'll be safe that way."

"Oh, Jason," she moaned, "I feel so strange...!"

"And so threatened. And there's no need." He pressed his mouth to her forehead. "I'm going to take exquisite care of you. Now go home before things get out of hand. Lovemaking is one thing, but sex is something else again." He lifted his head and searched her eyes. "I won't let you sleep with me, Kate. Virginity is something you should save for marriage."

"Nobody else does," she replied.

"Bull," he shot back. "That's another myth. It's the fashion to be sexually liberated these days, but it's damned dangerous, too. And I don't mean just because girls can get pregnant. It's because there are so many things you can catch that can kill you, or at the very least make you untouchable. You understand me?"

"Is that why you don't run around?" she asked, her eyes curious.

"It's one of many reasons I don't," he admitted. His eyes drew slowly over her face. "Even a man has to be careful these days. I'd cut off my arm before I'd expose you to any kind of disease."

"And that's the only reason you don't want me to sleep with other men?" she coaxed.

His face hardened. "I feel the same way about that as you seem to feel about thinking of me in bed with other women."

Her eyes fell. "Oh."

"Kate, I'm getting in over my head here, and I need a cold shower like hell. So will you please go home?"

She smiled at the way he said it, delighted at the way he was reacting to her, and at the new relationship they were heading for. "Okay."

"Drive carefully."

"I will."

She peeked at him, but he seemed remote now, unapproachable. With a faint grin, she turned and started toward the steps.

"I'll be in Montana looking at Beefmaster bulls for a few days next week," he said unexpectedly. "And at the end of the month, I'll be headed for Australia. I'll bring you back something pretty from there."

"You're doing a lot of traveling," she said quietly. "Will you be in Australia long?" she asked, sounding miserable because she was.

He wished he wasn't going all of a sudden. He studied her face. "I know a man up in the Northern Territory who's experimenting with some new Indian cattle, crossbreeding them with shorthorns. I've been invited to spend a month over there getting familiar with the operation. It's something I'm interested in trying here, so I've accepted, and Gene's going to run things while I'm away, despite the fact that I had to browbeat him into it. I can't spare the time, but I need to see about expanding the operation."

"A whole month away?" she murmured, trying not to let him see how disappointed she felt.

"Yes. But not for a few weeks yet." He smiled. "Don't borrow things to brood about. Live one day at a time."

"That's easy to say," she sighed.

"You'll get the hang of it." He put a fresh cigarette in his mouth and lit it. "Watch your speed."

She nodded. One last glance at his face was all she got before Jason turned and went back to the swing to sit down. When she pulled out of the driveway, he was still sitting there. By the time she got home, she wondered if she might have dreamed the whole interlude. But her mouth was swollen from his kisses and her breasts ached from the gentle crush of his chest. Kate walked in feeling on air, and only barely managed to camouflage her budding emotions from her mother's eagle eye. She didn't want to share her secret just yet. She didn't want Mary to know what had happened. But life had suddenly taken on new meaning, and she felt alive as she never had before.

CHAPTER FIVE

THE FIRST TWO outfits that Kate designed had been cut, and sewn, and Dessie Cagle had them sitting on a mannequin the next day in the sample room when Kate got to work.

Dessie beamed at her, and the designer, Sandy, laughed at the expression on her face.

"There you go," Sandy mused, one hand on her ample hip. Her salt-and-pepper hair was elegantly coiffed, and she wore a simple blue pantsuit. "What do you think? The first samples with the Kathryn of Texas label."

"Almost," Dessie added. "The labels were supposed to come by UPS, but they're late."

Kate sighed over the sky blue and cream combinations, a heavy silver-toned concho belt linking the bottom to its blouson top. "Imagine," she shook her head, astonished. "That's all mine."

"Well, not quite," Sandy said slowly. "Kate, there are a couple of changes in the darts, because of production time. I hope you don't mind," she added, and she showed Kate the minor alterations.

"Oh, that's no problem," Kate said, and meant it. "Mr. Rogers had said already that there might have to be a change here and there. We learned compromise in design school," she grinned. "I don't do these in concrete."

"Thank God, she's not going to be a prima donna," Sandy gushed, dancing Dessie around the room. She glanced at Kate with a rueful smile. "Our last new designer lasted one week. She'd designed us a skirt with eight set-in pockets and sixteen belt loops. We had to alter the design, and we even tried to compromise because it would have cost more to make it than we could have sold it for. Our little designer raised the roof, threatened to sue us individually and collectively, and in her fury overturned a buggy of scraps on one of the quality control ladies." She shook her head. "I don't guess you heard about it out on the floor?"

Kate pursed her lips. "Actually, we all knew about it, and I decided then and there that if I ever sold a design I'd bite off my tongue before I'd argue about production changes. Am I still loved?"

Sandy hugged her warmly. "Of course you are! Now. How are you coming with that new slant bodice on your blouson…?"

Kate pulled out her sketchbook and laid it on the desk to show her boss. But while she was talking, her eyes kept darting to the outfit on the mannequin. Kathryn of Texas. Now she had a label. And she was going to make it one to be proud of.

Mary had lunch with her in the canteen, and spent most of the half hour groaning over the repairs they had to get through. Some of the cuts were farmed out to a division of the company in the Caribbean, where labor was less expensive. But when they came back in, some of them didn't make it through quality control and had to be taken through the sewing line again.

"Those repairs are never going to stop," Mary sighed as she finished her ham sandwich and washed it down with a swallow of canteen coffee in a Styrofoam cup. She rested her tired arms on the polished yellow finish of the long table they were sharing with a few other scattered sewing hands. "I think my body is growing to my machine."

"God forbid," Kate laughed. "There, there, I'll get rich and support you."

"Promises, promises." Mary stretched, looking older than ever in the orange slacks and patterned matching top she'd made. Orange really wasn't her mother's color, but Kate hadn't been able to talk her out of the fabric she'd made them from.

"You'd look good in white," Kate told her mother.

"Sure. Covered with lint in camouflage and khaki shades and smeared with machine oil," her mother agreed dryly. "Any other helpful comments you care to make?"

"Why don't you make eyes at that new mechanic," came the quick comment. "He's about your age and dashing...."

"And the only thing he's ever said to me was, 'Hand me my screwdriver.' No, thanks. He's got a wart on his nose."

"Maybe he was a frog and somebody kissed him," Kate suggested.

Mary gave her a hard glare. "I have to work over today," she said. "Do you want to wait for me or get a ride home?"

"I want to wait until the truck comes in from Dallas and see if it's got my buttons and lace," Kate told her. "They're a day late already. I need to check them against the fabric and make sure they look the way I want them to."

"You picky designers," Mary chided as she got up. "You'll be standing in a retail store, complaining about the way they stick on the price tags."

"Oh, to design clothes so fancy that they wouldn't have price tags," Kate sighed.

Mary just grimaced and left her there. Kate sipped her coffee, her eyes going blankly out the window at the blue skies. She wondered if Jason was still out with the men, and decided that probably he was. Roundup seemed to go on forever. Tempers got worse as it went along and she didn't imagine that she was going to see him for several days. That was vaguely worrying, because he'd be going to Montana next week, and it was already Thursday. Her mind went back to the way he'd kissed her. She smiled, going off into a daydream where she was a famous designer and Jason was her husband, and he was accompanying her to a grand show in New York during one of the market weeks. She'd glitter, and he'd be so proud of her. She'd be hailed on the street in her famous finery, and Jason would accompany her to parties....

She blinked. Jason wouldn't be at any of those parties for the simple reason that he didn't approve of her designing aspirations. He still thought a woman belonged in the bedroom or the kitchen, and he wasn't likely to change overnight.

A part of her mind kept asking why she was mooning over a man who wouldn't want her the way she wanted to be, and who would expect his wife to stay home, have babies, and help entertain his business guests. She couldn't face those limits, so she ignored them. At the moment, all she could think about was the sweet savagery of his mouth and the unexpected pleasure of loving him. If the lovely dream only lasted for a few days, until she came to her senses, she was going to enjoy it while it did. He was right. It was better to live for the moment rather than worry about the future. Because for her and Jason there was no future.

She and Mary were getting ready to leave the house the next morning when Jason unexpectedly showed up at the back door with a basket of beans.

"Sheila sent them," he told Mary, putting them on the counter in their wicker container. "She thought the two of you might like some fresh ones, and she tucked in a bag of frozen ham hocks to cook them with."

"The darling," Mary enthused. "Thank her for us. Would you like a biscuit and some coffee?"

"I'd like that, thanks." He grinned as he glanced toward the doorway where Kate suddenly appeared, breathlessly plaiting her hair with a blue ribbon that complemented her denim skirt and blue dotted Swiss short-sleeved blouse.

"Oh!" Kate exclaimed, stopping short. Her hands froze in midair for a second and her face colored. He was in working gear, jeans and a chambray shirt carelessly unbuttoned at the throat, with a blue bandanna tied at his neck and that battered black Stetson on his head. His spurs jingled on boots too worn to be decent. But he looked very masculine and unbearably handsome to Kate's adoring eyes. She smiled at him unexpectedly, and he held her eyes until she had to drag them away.

"I'll get the coffee," Mary murmured, turning away to get another cup with a knowing smile.

Kate finished tying her braid and sat down at the table where biscuits sat on one platter and bacon and sausage on another. They hadn't bothered with eggs because neither of them cared for them.

"If you want an egg, I'll cook you one," Kate offered as Jason sat down beside her.

"No, thanks, honey, I've had breakfast once already,

about five this morning." His leg brushed hers and he smiled at her nervous reaction. "I like the ribbon."

"Thank you." She glanced into his dark eyes and shivers of sensation ran through her body. It was exciting to look at him, all of a sudden. She felt the magic like electricity as he searched her soft eyes.

"How's roundup going?" Mary asked when she came back with the coffee and broke the spell.

"Oh, not so bad," Jason told her. He took a biscuit and filled it with bacon that was crisp and browned just right. "We had one busted leg, two broken ribs, a crushed foot, and fifteen stitches in a leg. Other than that, I guess it's going fine."

Kate grimaced. "Well, at least it wasn't your fifteen stiches," she said. She creamed her coffee and offered him the faded little cream pitcher that once had boasted a patch of strawberries on one side. Now there was little more than a faded leaf and a few unrecognizable dots of red where it had been.

Jason's lean, dark hand took it from hers and didn't let go for several seconds. Kate could hardly breathe. His touch ignited her like fire. She looked at his somber face, feeling the hunger in him like a living thing because it was echoed in her own body.

She remembered how hungrily they'd kissed two nights ago, and her eyes fell to his hard mouth with frank delight. He saw it, and his lips parted. She looked up again, catching the same need in his dark, narrowing eyes.

Neither of them moved. Life seemed to be locked in slow motion for a space of seconds while their eyes said things their mouths couldn't. Jason abruptly poured cream in his coffee and asked Mary about selling off a few head of the cattle he oversaw for her on the boundary of his own property.

"Go ahead and do what you think best, Jason," Mary said without argument. "You know I've no head for business. If we sell now, will we get enough to make the next mortgage payment?"

"With some to spare," he told her. "The market's up just temporarily. This is a good time to get rid of the culls."

"Are you selling some of yours?" Kate asked, just to show him that she wasn't too tongue-tied to talk.

"I've got a few dry cows and some open ones I'm going to sell off," he agreed.

"Pitiful," Kate murmured over her biscuit. "Getting rid of a poor little cow because she isn't expecting."

"I can't afford to keep poor little cows who aren't expecting," he returned with a faint smile. "In a cow-calf operation, calves pay the bills. If mama doesn't earn her keep, off she goes into somebody's frying pan."

"He's a cannibal," Kate told Mary with a straight face.

"He's a businessman," Mary argued.

"Same difference," Kate returned, grinning impishly at Jason.

He laughed, the sound deep and pleasant in the silence of the cheerful little kitchen. "It takes a cannibal to make money these days," he admitted. He ate his biscuit and sipped his black coffee. "Well, Gene's trying to convince me to back him in an art show. He needs up-front money for supplies. Damn, those paints are expensive!"

"I know," Kate said gently. "But he's good, Jason. He's really good."

He drained the thick white mug, one of the new ones Kate had bought, and put it down on the red-checkered oilcloth that adorned the table. "Kate, there are a lot of good artists in the world. But it takes a great one to make any money. And most of them," he added somberly, "die poor. He's got Cherry to support, and someday there'll be children. He needs to think about them, not about his own pipe dreams. Dreams won't put bread on the table, or clothe children. And I'll be damned if I'm going to support him into old age. He's going to have to start pulling his weight around the Spur."

Kate wanted to argue, but Jason looked dug-in, and she didn't want to start something else. It was Gene's problem, after all, not hers. If he wanted to live his own life, he was going to have to fight Jason himself. Kate didn't envy him that challenge, either. Jason was a formidable enemy.

"How's your arm?" Kate asked.

He flexed it, rippling the muscle under the nice fit of the fabric. "Fine," he said. "I haven't had a problem with it." He glared at her. "And I would have healed just fine without being dragged to the doctor."

"I do realize that, Jason," Kate said sincerely. "And I promise the next time Gabe begs me to look at your torn and bleeding body, I'll put a sack over my head and hold my ears shut."

He pursed his lips, and his dark eyes twinkled. "Would you, really?" he asked. His voice had a new softness when he spoke, his face was more relaxed than Kate had ever seen it.

She sighed, studying him. "I guess not, since you're the only friend I've got."

"I'll put the dishes in the sink," Mary murmured, glancing delightedly from one to the other of them. As she puttered around the kitchen, Kate got to her feet.

Kate hadn't expected Jason to stand up at the same time. She overbalanced and he caught her waist to steady her.

Standing so close to him, her nerves were unsettled, and it showed. She had to force her breath in and out, but she couldn't stop the rustle of it through her lips.

He stared at her mouth until she thought she'd go crazy if he didn't bend those few inches and take it. She swallowed, her tongue going unsteadily to her dry lips, and he made a sound under his breath and almost pushed her away.

"I've got to get back to work," he said curtly. "I left calves scattered all over hell and gone."

"Thanks again for the beans," Mary said. She glanced at him thoughtfully. "Would you like to come over for supper and sample them?"

He lifted his eyebrows. "Who's cooking, you or Kate?"

Mary glared at him. "Why, you horrible man, and I was going to bake you a cake, too."

He tweaked Mary's chin and bent to kiss her cheek. "You're a great cook. I apologize."

"Kate's cooking, anyway," Mary muttered. She shook her head, laughing. "You horrible man," she said again and started toward the hall. "I'll get our purses, Kate, you can lock the back door after Jason."

"Yes, Mama," Kate agreed.

The silence in the room when she left it was deafening. Jason stared at her with all the barriers down. There was no teasing banter now to disguise the desire in his hard face.

He moved toward her, tucking a hand under her soft chin to lift it. "Do you want my mouth as much as I want yours?" he asked under his breath.

Her lips parted. "Oh, yes…!" she moaned.

He bent and roughly opened her lips with his, teasing them in a silence that vibrated with tension. He lifted his mouth and brushed it lazily back and forth across hers, feeling the trembling start.

He bit her lower lip softly. "Do that to me."

She did, and both his lean hands came up to frame her face, to hold it steady while his dark eyes blazed into hers for an instant.

"Now let's stop playing and do it for real," he whispered gruffly, and bent with fierce purpose in his mouth.

Her heart was going crazy when she felt that tentative searching, but before she had time to react to it, her mother's footsteps echoed toward the kitchen door.

"Oh, damn," Kate whimpered under her breath. Jason stood erect on legs that felt weak and looked down at her with black frustration in a face like stone.

"I wanted it, too," he said quietly. "Tonight, I'll give you that kiss, Kate. I'll give it to you with interest…!"

Mary walked in with Kate's purse. "About six suit you, Jason?" she asked the taciturn man who was already at the back door, with his lean hand on the doorknob.

"Six suits me fine," he said, and grinned at them.

"See you then," Kate said lightly.

Neither of them fooled Mary, who saw beneath the teasing tones to the intense tension she'd interrupted. "Don't fall off your horse," she told Jason.

"Hold your breath," he returned. "My God, a man can't walk in the door around here without getting insulted."

"We only insult people we like," Kate assured him. Her eyes traced his face lovingly. She was still shaking with hunger for the kiss she'd wanted so much.

"Good thing I'm not on the bad side of you, then," he

chuckled. He winked at them and went out, leaving Kate to lock it behind him.

"Jason's a character," Mary laughed, shaking her head.

"He's a nice man," Kate agreed without looking at her mother, and she smiled. "Shall we go?"

Nice, Mary thought as they left the house, was a word no sane woman would use when referring to Jason Donavan. She knew suddenly, and with almost tangible delight, that something was going on between Jason and Kate. Now if she could just help things along, she might not have to worry about Kate's future after all.

Kate, blissfully unaware of her mother's plotting, was thinking dreamily of the evening ahead, already tasting Jason's mouth on her own. She'd put the future out of her mind altogether. All she wanted now was as much of Jason's company as she could get, and whatever feeling there was in him for her. She was in love with him, and because of that, she decided, she'd give him whatever he asked of her. Even if that meant eventually getting out of his life altogether.

CHAPTER SIX

ALL DAY AT work Kate felt like she was on top of the world. Early in the morning one of the regional salesmen came by and made some very flattering remarks about the first of her samples, and when that praise was echoed by Mr. Rogers, she could have walked on a cloud.

But even more delicious than that was the memory of Jason's hard face above hers, his eyes glittering with the need to kiss her. The anticipation made it worse, intensified the hunger. She thought about him and her heart skyrocketed, her knees going shaky. It was so new, and things were happening so quickly that it was all a little frightening. She knew that Jason would never hurt her. Or that even if he lost his head and seduced her, he'd make everything right. He'd take such excellent care of Kate that…she frowned…that she'd never be sure that he'd married her because he wanted to or because he'd had to.

Her bubble began to burst. Jason didn't want marriage. He'd said so often enough, and his lack of involvement with women proved it. Kate could get close to him, but until the past few days, that had been a friendly closeness, not an emotional or physical one. Perhaps she was knocking him off balance, just as his fierce kisses had done to her. Perhaps he was as helpless to resist what was happening between them as she was. That disturbed her. Kate loved Jason. But she didn't want to trap him. And unless she was very careful, this physical chemistry was going to get out of hand and push them both into an unwanted situation. If that happened, she'd lose the only friend she had.

But knowing how to handle this delicate balance was just as worrying. There was no one else she could go to for advice. She could talk to her mother, but not about sex. It was the one area that Mary was too reticent to discuss, and Kate was too shy to blurt it out and ask questions. The only other person she might have talked to would have been Jason. While he might not talk about breeding at the supper table, Kate knew instinctively that he'd tell her anything she wanted to know. Nothing was taboo for them to discuss.

Kate had to leave Mary at the plant and go home first to start supper because everyone on the pants and shirt line had to stay to get out a cut that was already late for shipment.

She made spaghetti because there wasn't time to get the beans cooked. And while she worked, she thought about Jason and wondered how they were going to dodge Mary that night. Thinking about his kisses and the way they made her body throb was such delicious pleasure that she put too much coffee in the basket and had to start all over again.

She made a green salad and defrosted sesame seed rolls to go with it all. There would still be time to change after she drove back to the plant to pick up her mother....

A hard knock on the front door stopped Kate in midthought. She went to answer it with her hair tied loosely in back with a ribbon, her makeup worn off, her forehead beaded with sweat. And there stood Jason.

He was immaculate in dark slacks that he wore with

a white silk shirt, open necked, and a navy blue blazer. His creamy Stetson, the one that matched his horribly expensive dress boots, was sitting at a jaunty angle on his head. The look he was giving Kate could have scrambled eggs because it was so warm.

"You even look sexy when you're worn to a frazzle, cupcake," he said quietly, but he looked more solemn than teasing when he said it. There were lines of strain in his dark face.

"I thought you were coming at six," she faltered, because Mama wasn't home, supper wasn't cooked, the house was empty, and she looked like a refugee from a cookoff.

"Yes, but one of the men saw you drive home alone," he returned, letting his dark eyes slide slowly down her body. "So I sent Red Barton to pick up Mary at five-thirty, and I came on over."

It was hard to breathe when he looked at her like that. "Did you?" she whispered shakily.

He took off his hat and moved through the doorway, tossing the Stetson onto the sofa as Kate closed the door.

He turned, his lean hands catching her gently by the arms to hold her just in front of him. "We've got to talk," he said, his jaw going taut. "Things are getting out of hand too fast."

She understood at once. His eyes were already glittering with hunger, and his face was as hard as stone with it. Her lips parted on a caught breath as she looked into his eyes and felt the world stop around them.

"Too fast?" she faltered, because there had been little more than kissing between them.

He searched her face in a silence that throbbed with sensuality. "Don't you think I can see how you react when I come near you?" His hands tightened on her arms. "What happened this morning has haunted me all day. All I've thought about since is your mouth and how badly I want it. And that," he said tersely, "is the whole problem."

"And you don't want commitment," she said, almost reading the thoughts in his mind. "You're afraid of what could happen."

"That's the bottom line, honey," he said, his voice quiet and somber.

She wondered if he knew that his hard words were shattering her dreams. Kate searched his face with wide, sad eyes. "You can't trust even me, can you, Jason?"

"No," he said quietly. He drew in a slow breath. His eyes brooded as he brought her completely against his chest and pressed her cheek to him, bending his own cheek against her dark hair. He could feel the hard tips of her breasts against his chest even now. She was already aroused, and he hadn't touched her. He kept her a little away, because the touch of her was equally arousing to him, and he couldn't hide it if her legs touched his.

"I've had some hard experiences in the past," he said, his voice deep and slow in the stillness of the living room. The eyes she couldn't see were haunted. "First my mother, leaving me and Gene at the mercy of that wild-eyed alcoholic of a father. Then Melody, chasing after rainbows that meant more than I did." His hand touched her long hair, pulling at it idly. "Kate, I wanted marriage then," he said slowly, deeply. "I wanted a woman to love me and make a home for me. I wanted a baby growing in her body, and the hope of a warm, close family like I'd never had. All my life, I've felt like an outsider looking in. I tried to explain it to Melody." His chest expanded roughly. "And then she told me about the movie contract they'd offered her. And how she felt about children. She didn't want them. Not ever."

"Oh, Jason," she whispered sympathetically, because she knew how hard it was for him to share private feelings with anybody.

"She laughed at me, damn her," he said curtly. "She said that only a naive country boy would be dumb enough to expect a woman to throw away her career just to have children. Children, she said, weren't even necessary these days. And then she told me that she'd been pregnant with mine—and she'd gotten rid of it."

Kate felt tears sting her eyes. He'd never talked about the way Melody had left him. He'd never said anything about a baby. She felt the pain in him like a living thing, and remembered how it hurt him even to see a calf put down. So now she knew. Why he'd been drinking that night they first became friends. Why he'd never let another woman into his life. He'd been badly betrayed.

She went into Jason's arms without a second's hesitation, pressing close, holding him, to give him all the comfort she could. "I'm sorry," she whispered. "I'm so sorry!"

His lean hands gripped her shoulders hard enough to hurt before he got himself under control again. "I wanted you to know why. What I am, she helped make me," he whispered roughly. "God, Kate, I can't risk that again. I want you. But I don't want commitment. I'm still too raw from what Melody did to my pride, my manhood."

"Have I ever asked you for commitment?" she whispered, drawing back to look up at him, with soft, adoring compassion in her eyes.

"You never would. You're as proud as I am," he replied. He touched her mouth gently with his fingers, fascinated by its softness. "But if I seduced you, I'd marry you, because you're a virgin. I'd feel a moral obligation to make it right. But I wouldn't want it. And you'd suffer for it."

She pressed her hands flat against the front of his silk shirt. Through it she could feel the hard muscle and warmth, see the dark wedge of thick chest hair that arrowed down into his belt. She touched one of the small shirt buttons idly. "What are we going to do, Jason?"

"I think it would be a good idea if we don't see each other for a while."

She forced a smile. "I was afraid that was what you were leading up to," she said softly.

He tilted her face up to his, and his eyes were very dark and steady. "I never should have touched you like that to begin with. It's becoming an addiction. First the attraction, then deep, hungry kisses. From there, it gets worse and hotter until, inevitably, we'll go at each other like animals."

She breathed deliberately. "Are you sure?"

He nodded. "Yes, honey. I'm sure." He pulled her hips gently against his and watched the reaction in her eyes. "Now consider that this has happened before I've even kissed you. For a man, this kind of arousal can be anguish. And I can lose control. Any man can, with the right incentive. I want you badly. I can't remember ever feeling anything so explosively sweet with a woman." He brushed back the wisps of hair that had escaped from her braid into her face. "Kate, I have a very special feeling for you," he said hesitantly. "I don't want to cheapen it by making you into a convenience. Can you understand that?"

She nodded. She smiled, so that he wouldn't realize

how much the words were hurting her. "I guess I got carried away, too," she said.

His dark eyes went down to the soft hands pressing against his chest. He touched her short nails, caressed their pinkness with his thumb while he tried to convince his body that it should cooperate with his brain.

"That's understandable," he said after a minute. "It was all new to you, and we know each other in more than just a physical way."

"Yes," she agreed quietly, because her voice would wobble if she said much more than that. She'd daydreamed all day about what it would be like when he came to supper. And here he was, telling her that they were going to be friends. There would be no more warm, slow kissing in the darkness. No more consuming passion. He didn't want Kate to get any closer to him than she already had. This was going to be the end of her dreams of Jason. She should have known better than to hope. She should have realized what was going to happen when he realized where they were headed. Jason trusted no woman with his heart, not even Kate.

"So under the circumstances," he continued, "I think I'd better pass on supper."

She managed a careless shrug, and she was smiling bravely when she looked up again. "Sure."

His dark eyes narrowed. "I know it hurts," he said suddenly, with the same perception that she had for his deepest feelings. "But it's for your own good. You want your career and I want my freedom. That's the only reason we've been as close as we have, because neither of us wanted ties."

That simple statement made the whole puzzle crystal clear. She looked up into his impassive face and understood everything. "That's why you let me get so close," she said absently. "I wasn't a threat."

"You were a pretty kid with eyes that saw all too deep at a time when I needed someone desperately. But not physically." He felt her withdrawal even before she drew away from him. His face hardened because it wasn't easy to say these things to her.

"I see," she said. She wrapped her arms around her breasts. She couldn't look at him.

"No, you weren't a threat, Kate," he said, his voice very quiet. He paused to light a cigarette because he needed something to steady him. "You were off limits, and I could talk to you. But that changed, suddenly and without warning. And now if I come too close to you, I go half out of my mind with desire. I can't let that go on. I like my life as it is, now. I want no more complications."

"You just got through saying that you wanted a family, and children…." she began, glancing up.

He forced himself to be blunt. "I wanted that with Melody," he replied. He took a draw from the cigarette and blew out a thin cloud of smoke. "I don't want it anymore. With anyone," he emphasized.

He was afraid, Kate thought, staring at him like someone who'd been unexpectedly shot. She didn't even blink. He was afraid to trust a woman with his heart, so he was smothering the delicate feeling that had been growing between them. He wasn't even going to give it a chance.

She felt as if she were growing up all at once, instead of in easy stages. She reached up and pushed her hair back, trying to look calm. "Well, you never had any problems with me on that score," she told him softly. "I want a career, too, and no complications. So you were safe all along, Jason."

Her tone irritated him. He lifted his chin, scowling. "Safe?"

"From being deliberately led down the path to the altar," she said with theatrical effect. "From being seduced for your money and your name. I don't want to settle down, either. I never did. Marriage is for the birds, Jason, and so are children. All I want is to make my own way in the world and have a respected designer label to show for it. I'd rather die than have to stay in rural Texas all my life, eating dust and smelling cattle all day."

Something darkened his eyes, stiffened his posture. He didn't let it show, but the words stung. He managed a careless smile, though, and took another draw from the cigarette.

"I'm glad you see things my way," he said. "No harm done."

"Of course not." She went to the door and opened it, still smiling woodenly. "I'm going to pay you back for that design course," she said. "I'll finish it next week. When I get my next check, I'll start sending you payments."

He started to protest, but she looked unmovable. He nodded. "If that's how you want it."

"I don't need charity," she replied. "I even told you so when you offered to stake me. It was only with the agreement that you'd let me pay you back. Thanks for giving me my start."

His eyes drew over her wan face, her drawn features. She looked older. All the sparkle was gone, temporarily at least. She'd get over this, though. She'd have her career, and eventually she'd look at another man as she'd looked at him...

"Good-bye, Kate," he said abruptly. He turned on his heel without another word, without a backward glance.

He climbed into the Mercedes, started it viciously, and took off in a cloud of dust.

Kate had no idea of the thoughts that had set him off, and assumed that he was irritated by her offer to reimburse him. She went back inside, closing the door, and fighting tears. Well, at least there'd be something good for supper, for her and Mary.

Her mother knew the instant she set foot in the house that something was badly wrong. She'd been curious when Red Barton showed up to fetch her at the plant, and he'd said that the boss was already on his way to the Whittman place. But there was no car out front, and Kate looked as if she'd been crying.

"Where's Jason?" Mary asked gently.

"He's gone home," she replied. She put the food on the table with a minimum of fuss. She was wearing jeans and a sweatshirt now, her hair loose and no makeup on. She looked depressed and tired.

"Talk to me," Mary said gently.

Kate ran to her, burst into tears, and for an instant they went back in time to Kate's childhood. She was hurt, and Mary was going to kiss it and make it better.

"Come on, tell me what happened," Mary coaxed.

"Jason thinks we're getting too close," came the sobbing reply. "He said…that we could get into a situation, and he doesn't want to be trapped into marrying me."

"Oh. So it's that way."

"He only kissed me," she whispered miserably. "But he says that could lead to something much more serious, and he doesn't want to run the risk of seducing me."

"An honorable man, Jason," Mary said, stroking the dark hair. "You may not realize it, but he's paid you a high compliment with that protective attitude."

"He doesn't want to see me again," her daughter wailed. "We won't even be friends. Oh, Mama, how am I going to live?!"

The thin old arms tightened, and Mary smiled. She knew how it felt. A long time ago, before she married Kate's father, she'd been hurt in the same way by a man who cared too much to seduce her, but not enough to marry her. She rocked her little girl in her arms, murmuring soft nothings. Kate would survive. And Jason might yet come around to marriage. He hadn't been seen with any other women in a long time, and Kate was young and sweet and pretty, and she was close to him. Yes. It might come to marriage, if Kate was patient and didn't run off half-cocked and do something stupid. Mary smiled to herself. She'd see to that, she thought. She'd keep Kate levelheaded, no matter what she had to do.

"There, there," she cooed. "Everything will be all right."

Kate was crying more softly now, her broken sobs growing faint. No, it wouldn't be all right, she thought. But she'd get through somehow. If it was true that work could be a person's salvation, she'd find out. She was going to work herself to death to keep Jason out of her mind. And maybe when she could think about him without crying, she'd have more men than she could manage in her life. And she'd flaunt them all in front of Jason, and she'd be rich and famous. She'd show him. Her tears stopped and she dried them, smiling reassuringly at her mother. Oh, yes, she would. She'd show him!

CHAPTER SEVEN

AT FIRST, KATE thought the pain would never stop. But slowly, one day at a time, she forced herself to go to work and smile, pretending nothing was wrong. She finished her designing course and sent in the last lesson, amazed at how much she'd learned since she started, not only about designing contemporary clothing, but also about the history of costume, the economics of designing, basic marketing, color theory, textiles, and even business law. She felt so much wiser about the industry, and much more confident in herself as a budding businesswoman. But she was going to pay Jason back for that course, all the same, whether he wanted it or not. If he wanted her out of his life, she'd help him. If only it didn't hurt so much.

She missed even the simple things, like the occasional visit when he was just passing, or running into him in town. Now she didn't see him at all, and her heart was hungry for him. She wished at times that she had an excuse, any excuse, just to go to the Donavan house and talk to him on any pretext.

But she was too proud. So she went along from day to day, half alive. And it might have gone on that way indefinitely, except for a chance meeting with Cherry.

Kate had just come from the beauty parlor in San Frio, where she'd had her hair restyled into a short perky cut, when she ran into Jason's sister-in-law coming down the sidewalk at her usual bouncing dash. Cherry, like Kate, was almost always on the run.

"Kate?" Cherry exclaimed. She stopped short to gape at Kate's haircut and sophisticated look.

Kate curtsied, some of her old humor reappearing. It had been three weeks since her confrontation with Jason and she was slowly coming alive again. "The very same. And how *do* you like my dress?" she added with a flourish.

It was a sample of her newest casual jumper, done in denim with lavish embroidery and an ankle-length skirt, and worn with a white round-necked blouse.

"I'd kill for it, that's how I like it," Cherry enthused. "Kate, you're going to be richer than you ever dreamed once those clothes get on the market."

"I do hope so," she replied with a sigh. "Market week is just down the road, in October. I'll go with one of our reps to the markets in Dallas, Atlanta, Houston, and New York. I even got to talk to our house model, who'll be showing most of the collection to the press. That was the high point of my day today. It's so exciting!"

"I don't doubt it. Come and have coffee with me and tell me all about it. Have you got time?"

"It's Saturday," she reminded Cherry. "Mama's sleeping late for a change, and I thought I'd shock her by changing my image."

"You look older," her friend replied. "And very sophisticated. Very...designerish."

"Flattery will get you a fresh blueberry muffin," Kate told her, and dragged her into Jo's Café.

Jo was Jo Rodriquez, a middle-aged Mexican-American woman with a dynamite personality. Her small café in San Frio was known all over south Texas, especially by truckers. Rumor had it that after she'd been deserted by her husband with three small daughters to raise alone, Jo had talked one of the stingiest bankers in the territory into lending her the money for a café with only a used car and a small heirloom diamond stickpin for collateral. Jo had put all three of her daughters through college. Two were doctors, and one was a well-known author. Lately Jo had talked about retiring, but she did that periodically. Nobody took her seriously.

"Blueberry muffins are not enough protein for breakfast," she told Kate and Cherry as she put them on the table, along with two cups of the best coffee in south Texas and a jug of fresh cream. "You should be eating bacon and eggs."

"Steak and eggs!" Kate said in a stage whisper, grinning at a rancher she knew who was sitting nearby. He grinned back, lifting a hand.

"Thanks for your support of the limping beef industry, Kate!" he called across the café.

"You're more than welcome, Bob," she called back. "We only have a few steers, but they do help pay the bills."

"As if you'll need help paying the bills when you can sew like that," Jo sighed, her ample figure neat in a blue denim skirt and silky blue print top. As she shook her head, a few silver hairs gleamed in the overhead lights.

"You're bad for my hat size," Kate scolded as she creamed her coffee. "You'll give me the big head, talking that way."

"Well, I want a skirt like that," Jo replied. "Make it an expensive skirt like that, too. And make me a blouse…."

"I will not make you an expensive anything," Kate returned, her green eyes twinkling. "Not after all the treats you gave me as a kid, and the free sodas...."

Jo bent over, resting her hands on the table. Her deep brown eyes stared into Kate's. "You listen here, *niña,* without your mama, my little ones would have gone to school dressed in rags. She let me pay her as I could to make their clothes, and I don't forget favors. So you shut up. If I want an expensive skirt, you just better let me have it. Or I'll scream discrimination so loud, they'll hear me clean down to the Gulf!"

Kate burst out laughing. "Discrimination, indeed," she scoffed. She laid her hand over the callused one on the table. "Joellen Rodriguez, there isn't a more loved and less discriminated against person in this whole town. Especially by me."

"I know that, *niña.*" Jo bent to hug her warmly, smelling of flour and coffee and the starch from her skirt. "Now you make my skirt. You know what size. And this time I'm a paying customer. I haven't forgotten that wedding dress you sewed for my Jennie last spring, even if you have."

"All right, all right, I know when I'm beaten," Kate sighed. "What color embroidery do you want?"

"Blue and pink."

"It's yours, but right now I'm finishing the last unit in my design course, and pushing to the limit to get my collection out of the way in time for fall market week," she said. "It won't be anytime soon."

"No rush," Jo said. She grinned, showing perfect white teeth in her youthful face. "Although I hear they're having tryouts for the ballet in October, and I'd like to have my skirt to wear. When I audition, you see." She did a pirouette, and the rancher at the next table clapped enthusiastically. "Bob, you come with me," she called to him as she went back behind the counter to work on her pies. "You can be my dance partner. We'll work on those high tosses later."

"You bet, Jo," Bob replied, doffing his hat to her. "Just let me rush out and buy a couple of mattresses first. So you'll have something soft to land on," he added with a grin.

"She's one of a kind," Kate murmured, smiling at Cherry.

"To you, everybody is one of a kind," Cherry mused, smiling back. "I guess I've still got some of my daddy's prejudices, but you like people no matter who or what they are."

"Daddy was foreman on Jason's place," she reminded the younger girl. "And Jason has cowboys that come in all colors and nationalities; there's even a West Indian working cattle over there! Old J.B. might have been a hell-raiser, but he wasn't a bigot. He said a man was a man, regardless of his circumstances of birth. Jason feels that way, too."

"It's nice to know that he has at least one good point," Cherry said darkly.

Kate's heart lurched as she nibbled at her muffin. "Is he back at Gene about ranch work again?" she asked, trying to sound casual.

Probably Cherry didn't know about the friction between them, and it wasn't something she wanted to discuss. Kate was still raw about Jason's determined avoidance, even while she understood his reasoning.

"He's been terrible lately," Cherry sighed over her own muffin. "I mean really terrible," she emphasized, lifting wide blue eyes to Kate's. "I saw Red Barton hiding from him Wednesday before he left for Montana, can you imagine! Red's the only one of the hands who won't back down from him, as a rule, so you can see how rowdy he's gotten. He mutters and glares at everybody. He won't come to the supper table at all, and he and Sheila are having a cold war with Gene and me in the middle. We all gave thanks when he announced he was spending a few days in Montana, but he got back this morning and his mood hasn't improved one bit." She swallowed a sip of coffee. "I think he's in love."

Kate felt sick. She hadn't considered that there might be a woman in his life besides herself, that it might have been the reason he wanted Kate out of his life. "Do you?" she asked, and there was a peculiar wobble in her voice.

"I don't know what you're thinking," Cherry said ruefully. "He doesn't date anybody, and there isn't even a woman he sees regularly as far as we know. But he acts positively lovesick." Her full lips pursed. "And this morning, when Gene asked if he was going over to see you, he went black-eyed and stomped off into his study, and slammed the door so hard that he knocked a picture off the wall."

Kate felt her heart turning cartwheels. If he was missing her, there couldn't be another woman. That made her feel better, even if he was still fighting his mental battle with involvement.

"Fancy that," Kate said innocently. She finished her muffin. "But, then, he's never been an easy man to get along with."

"I've found that out in recent months." Cherry sat back, dusting her hands with her napkin. "Kate, Gene and I need your help."

"You know I'll do anything I can."

"Great! I knew you'd say that." Cherry grinned. "Well, it's this exhibit Gene's been invited to display his work in. You know that Jason's going to Australia for a month?"

Kate nodded.

"Well, the exhibit is during that first week he'll be away, and Jason doesn't want him to leave the ranch. You know and so do I that Gabe can handle things by himself." She leaned forward. "Especially for just a few days. But Jason put his foot down and dared Gene to do it. Now Gene won't go against him, and you know why. Jason's sacrificed for him all these years, he feels he owes it to Jason to do whatever he's asked. But I figured that if you spoke up for Gene when we explained about the giant step it would mean for Gene's career—well, Jason listens to you."

Kate was searching for the right words to tell Cherry about the agreement she had with Jason to stay away from him. They wouldn't come. She was so hungry for the sight of him that it was almost unbearable.

"We thought we'd have a small dinner party tonight," Cherry said, interrupting her thoughts, "just to welcome him back, and Sheila thinks you'd be good medicine for his temper. You know he won't mind."

"Did he say so?" Kate asked quietly.

"It's a surprise," Cherry said. "We can't ask him, but why wouldn't he want you there?"

"Well…" It was impossible to explain it to Cherry without telling her some very private things about the sudden shift in their relationship. Kate flushed a little. "I don't want to impose…."

"It's not imposing. You're family. Oh, Kate, please? Jason will listen if you ask him to. You're the only one he ever listens to. Please? For Gene? For me?"

Kate sighed wearily. She knew she should refuse. But if Jason had missed her as much as it sounded like he had, maybe he'd be happy to see her.

"Okay," she agreed.

"Great! We'll have supper about six-thirty, and wear something dressy," Cherry instructed. "It's going to be one of those parties like Jason throws for visiting dignitaries."

Kate hesitated. "Cherry, I don't know to act at those things…."

"Neither did I, until Gene taught me. Don't you worry, I'll cue you," she was assured. "Do you want me to ask one of the boys to come for you?"

"No, thanks. I've got a car!"

"A what?"

"A new used black Ford Tempo," Kate grinned, her eyes twinkling. "I talked Mama into cosigning with me, and we can make the payments without any problem at all. They even took our old heap in trade. So I have my own transportation. Compared to old faithful, it's a Rolls."

"I guess so. Well, congratulations, you famous designer, you. Speaking of which," Cherry continued slyly, "I want a skirt, too. And with black and green and pink embroidery, in a size eight."

"You and Jo will clash."

"No, we won't. And I'm in no hurry for it."

"Are you sure?"

"I'm sure." Cherry shook her head as Kate stood up. She looked again at Kate's outfit. "What a winner. I can see you now, making national headlines."

"I can see me now, begging for a sale on the sidewalk, where I may be hawking these things if the buyers don't like them," Kate said. "Oh, Cherry, nobody else is doing Indian designs this year, everything's prints and florals like back in the thirties and forties. I feel like the odd man out, and if I'm wrong, and my designs don't go...."

"They'll go," she was assured. "I promise they will. Jo, tell her they'll sell."

"You bet they will," Jo said as she took the five-dollar bill Cherry handed her and made change. "Now, go walk off those muffins so you don't get fat like me."

"If that's fat," Kate remarked, studying the older woman's ample but perfect figure, "I can hardly wait to get that way."

Jo chuckled. "Get out of here."

"I'll go home and think about your skirt," Kate assured her. "Bye!"

She took time to show her car to Cherry, who enthused over it even though she had a Fiat that Gene had given her for her last birthday. I'll be like that, Kate swore silently, as she waved good-bye to Cherry and got in under the wheel. If I ever have a lot of money, I'll always be pleased for other people when they get something new, even if I can afford a Rolls. It was one of the things she admired in Cherry—the girl might be young, but she had a sweet personality.

"I HOPE I survive this," Kate told her mother as she came out of her room that night, dressed for dinner at the Donavans'. The dress she was wearing was one she'd designed and made herself, although she'd never expected that she'd have anywhere to wear it. It had been an experiment in sewing evening clothes. Kate knew that the style was simple and elegant, but she still had her rural ideas about what constituted high fashion, and they were a little overboard. This dress was just slightly too brassy, and since Kate had never been to a local society party of any kind, she had no idea what people wore to them. Her only contact with that kind of evening wear came from watching the fashion shows on television, and society around San Frio was a little too conservative for clothes like those.

The dress she'd designed was black crepe. It fell from spaghetti straps that crisscrossed down the back and laced in front over a high-necked split bodice. It had a straight full-length skirt, with a side slit, adorned only with a thin line of silver sequins on each side of the split bodice where the laces went through. It was the kind of dress that made a man ache to unlace it, and even with its brassy design, it was a witchy dress.

"That is gorgeous," Mary said, as naive about high fashion as her daughter. "I'd forgotten that you made it."

"So had I. Cherry said to dress up. I hope this is what she had in mind. Goodness, I hope it's not some of those city businessmen friends of Jason's. I met a few of them, and I felt like a country hick around the wives. One of them actually asked if I kept pigs and yodeled."

"Don't you worry, Jason won't let them bother you," Mary assured her. "You look lovely. Your lipstick is smeared just here." She touched her own mouth, and Kate went to the dresser in her room and fixed it. She was wearing only a little more makeup than usual, but she felt strange with her hair cut and swept forward.

"Have I got on too much makeup?" she asked worriedly.

Mary grimaced. "Don't ask me, honey, I never use any," she said with an apologetic smile. "It looks pretty heavy to me, but I guess that's the way everybody does it these days. You'll do. And I like the haircut, although I bet Jason won't."

"I wonder if Jason will go through the roof when I side

with Gene," she replied with a faint smile. "This dinner is supposed to be a surprise, but I don't know if he'll even let me in the house. Mama, I don't know if I should go at all, after what he said about keeping his distance."

"Surely he doesn't want to stop being friends, does he?" Mary asked gently. "And how will you find out if you don't ask him? This is a good opportunity to see if he's missing you as much as you're missing him."

Kate grimaced. "I hear he's raising hell every chance he gets. But that's normal for Jason."

Mary touched the short, perky haircut. "You and Jason have had a very special relationship. I can't believe he wants to throw that away completely."

"We'll know after tonight, won't we?" Kate looked worriedly at the clock. "I'd better go, or I'll be late. Wish me luck."

"Honey, nobody who looks as good as you do will need any. Have a good time."

"I'll do my best." She picked up the filmy shawl she'd made painstakingly to go with the dress—black with sequins all over it and fringe down the back.

"You look delightful," Mary sighed. "And so sophisticated."

Kate grinned. "It's still just me inside. I hope Jason doesn't mind having me going over there," she added worriedly.

"He won't. Go on, now!"

Kate did, but as she drove the car along the sparsely traveled road, her sense of foreboding grew. And the closer she got to the Donavan place, the worse she felt. Cherry didn't know Jason like she did. When he said no, he meant it. She was deliberately going against his wishes, and if her presence upset him, all her good intentions wouldn't stop him from speaking his mind in front of everybody.

There were two other cars at the house. One was a Lincoln and the other was a bright red foreign car of some kind with the top down. Kate parked her little Tempo behind the Lincoln and got out slowly. She felt overdressed and under-confident and unbearably nervous. She shouldn't have come.

She went up the steps, noticing as she did that her shoes were terribly worn and not at all the kind she should be wearing with a dress this sophisticated. They were just little black vinyl slings, scuffed badly on one toe and the opposite heel, and the sole was faintly loose. Well, maybe the skirt was long enough that no one would notice, and thank God it wasn't winter, because the only coat she owned was moth-eaten and a hideous color. Clothes were going to be her next major purchase.

She rang the bell. Sheila came to answer it, and when she saw Kate, she darted a glance over her shoulder worriedly and came out on the porch.

"Darlin', you look lovely," she said quietly. "But nobody's dressed up, and Cherry hasn't had the nerve to tell Jason you're coming."

"I guess I'd better go back home…." Kate faltered. She was coloring, and she felt sick with embarrassment.

"Kate!" Cherry came running up in a blue silk pantsuit. "Come on in, what are you standing out here for? Sheila, something's boiling over on the stove," she added to divert the worried housekeeper. "Kate, that's beautiful," she said, looking over Kate's dress.

"You said to dress up…."

"Oh, and I meant to, but everybody came in casual clothes, so I rushed upstairs and changed. But you look fine, honest you do. Is that makeup new?" she added, her eyes darting nervously around as she led Kate into the dining room.

Jason was sitting at the head of the elegant cherry wood table, bending toward a ravishing blonde in a low, white knit blouse. He was wearing a white silk shirt with a tan jacket and matching tie, looking as elegant as the room itself. Gene was on Jason's other side, and opposite each other were two elderly men in leisure suits and one older woman in a red and black pantsuit. They all looked up as Kate froze in the doorway, suddenly feeling like a painted Saturday night special.

Gene, God bless him, stood up. "You look lovely, Kathryn," he said, inviting her into the chair next to his. "Let me introduce you to our guests," he added, ignoring Jason's furious eyes. Kate moved forward on wobbly legs and prayed that she wouldn't pass out.

The blood was beating in her ears so hard that she didn't even hear the names. The older woman gave her a polite smile and instantly dismissed her. The younger woman simply stared at her blankly, as if she didn't exist. The men nodded, equally polite, and Cherry slid into the seat next to hers and gripped her hand, hard, under the table to smile at her apologetically.

Cherry's fingers were freezing cold and trembling. Kate knew that this wasn't anything like what Cherry had planned, but her support didn't help a lot. Jason was angry.

"Good evening, Miss Whittman," he said in his most cutting tone, and he smiled, but it wasn't a smile she'd ever seen directed at her until now. "Excuse me, but I don't remember inviting you over here tonight."

Kate could have choked to death on her pride. She

managed not to burst into tears, but it took every ounce of willpower she had.

"I invited her," Cherry spoke up. Kate saw that she was afraid of Jason, but regret at the pain she was causing her guest overcame it. "I didn't realize you'd arranged to have a business meeting tonight. By the time I did, it was too late to tell Kate not to come. It's my fault, not hers."

"Kate is always welcome," Gene said, glaring at his brother. "She's been like family for years."

"And she's going to be a very famous designer," Cherry seconded, gaining strength from her husband's support.

"You designed that, I suppose?" the ravishing blonde mused, studying Kate's outfit in a way that spoke volumes. "Well, honey, it's not bad, but I'd never want to wear something that brassy in public. I mean, it's the kind of thing a hooker would wear."

Just as Kate was about to respond with an unwise rebuttal, the gray-haired woman across from her turned in her seat and asked, a vacant smile at her lips, "Is that comment from the horse's mouth, Daphne?"

The blonde's eyes popped. "I beg your pardon?!"

"Geraldine!" one of the older men harumphed.

The gray-haired woman lifted her chin pugnaciously. "Shut up, Harold," she drawled. "If Daphne can be rude, so can I." She looked at Kate. "I think your dress is lovely."

Kate could have hugged her. But it was taking too much effort just to keep from crying. She managed a smile, with tears brimming in her eyes before she lowered them.

Jason looked at Kate with an expression that caused Cherry to avert her own eyes. This was all her fault. She hadn't meant to hurt Kate.

"Here it is," Sheila said, entering the room with a huge

roast on a platter. "This came from one of the biggest steers we ever raised on the Diamond Spur. And one of the meanest." She grinned. "I had the pleasure of helping cut him up after he chased me up a tree."

She glanced at Kate as she spoke, and the smile faded. She may have wanted to say something, but the glitter she saw in Jason's eyes made her back off. Sheila put the platter down and went back for the vegetables.

Conversation began again over the delicately roasted meat. But Kate didn't taste anything. She couldn't look at Jason at all, and she was aching to get up and run out the door. But that wouldn't do. Kate couldn't behave in such a cowardly fashion, not in front of Jason.

She thought that if she lived to be a hundred, she'd hate him every single year for the rest of her life. He had deliberately insulted her, embarrassed her in front of his guests. He wanted her to see the difference between her lifestyle and his, and he'd shown her graphically. Kate wanted no part of people like this, and no part of a man who could be that cruel to her.

Cherry and Gene tried to draw Kate into the conversation going on around her, but she sat quietly and stiff-backed, finishing the food on her plate. She wouldn't speak, and every time Jason looked at her, she felt sick.

Kate couldn't know the self-contempt that was making him act this way. She couldn't feel his pain at the sight of her after weeks of loneliness and aching desire. And he couldn't let her know. He couldn't admit to the weakness of caring about her. He searched her sad, wan little face with eyes that were terrible to look into, glittering with pain at the hurt he'd caused her. Damn Cherry! Damn her for putting Kate in a position like this, for not telling her that that black dress was like a clown suit in such sophisticated company, that she was wearing the wrong makeup and too much of it. That she was overdressed and oversequined, and that she looked just like the little unworldly country girl she was.

"Kate, I'm sorry," Cherry said under her breath.

"So am I," Gene said, and loud enough for Jason to hear him. He glared at his brother. "Cherry thought if Kate backed us up, you wouldn't raise hell about me leaving for that art exhibit while you're in Australia. We didn't know you were going to cut Kate up this way, of course. We thought you were friends." He put down his napkin. "I'm going to the exhibit, Jason, and to hell with your opinion."

"Good for you," Kate said on a choked smile. She moved her chair away from the table and stood up on shaky legs. "It's about time you showed him that he isn't the only man in the house. And it's okay, Cherry. Your heart was in the right place."

Kate touched the younger girl's shoulder lightly. As she lifted her eyes and looked straight across at Geraldine she managed a smile. "I don't know who you are," she said gently, "but you've got breeding. Much more than your companion," she added, glaring at the woman named Daphne. "Money doesn't buy manners, even if it does buy expensive sports cars and the best clothes."

"You're insolent for a working girl," Daphne said, tossing back her blonde hair.

"And you're cruel," Kate replied with quiet sincerity. "I'm sorry for you because people have to be very unhappy to want to hurt other people."

Daphne actually blushed, and she didn't say another word.

Jason was glaring at her from the head of the table,

but he didn't speak. Kate turned away with the remainder of her dignity and left the room. Her heart was beating so loudly that she expected everyone to hear it, but she managed to get out of the room before the tears started running helplessly down her cheeks.

She almost tripped over her own feet in her haste to get out of the house. It was just past sunset. The reddish glow on the horizon was rapidly giving way to night, and crickets were singing and cattle lowing in the distance.

But Kate heard nothing over the beating of her own heart. If only she'd listened to her instincts, this might never have happened. She might have been spared the ordeal.

She'd barely made it to the car when she heard quick, heavy footsteps behind her. Seconds later, her wrist was caught and she was swung around to a sudden stop by a coldly furious Jason.

"Let me go," she wept, struggling with the steely hand that had her firmly, but not painfully, by the wrist. "Damn you, Jason Donavan, I hope I die before I ever have to look at you again!"

He caught her other wrist, too, and pushed her back against the door of the Tempo, pinning her with the threat of his body. "Stand still," he said curtly, using the tone that made his cowboys jump even though he never raised his voice. "You're not getting in that car until you calm down."

She could hardly breathe, and her eyes were wet. Mascara was running down her cheeks with tears, and her throat felt as if she'd swallowed a pincushion. "It was Cherry's idea," she said harshly. "I had no idea that I was walking into the Spanish Inquisition, or that I was going to have you bite my head off and humiliate me in front of your latest conquest!"

He scowled down at her. "What conquest?"

"That silky-eyed blonde," she wept. "And I wish you joy of her, Jason, she's just your style; a selfish little money-hungry man-eater who's good in bed and doesn't give a hang about anything except herself! She's even blonde, like that Melody woman…!"

He put a tight rein on his temper, infuriated by the accusation. He'd meant to tell Kate that the blonde, whom he disliked anyway, was married to one of those very rich elderly gentlemen at the table. And that the discussion they'd been having was strictly business. But he'd be damned if he'd tell her now. It would serve no purpose, anyway. It was cutting him to pieces not to give in and pull her into his arms. The past three weeks had proved to him that she could become his Achilles' heel; but that was something he couldn't allow to develop.

Jason let her go abruptly and moved away to light a cigarette with steady hands. "I like blondes, honey," he said with deliberate cruelty, smiling through a cloud of smoke. "And you'd better get used to the idea that women are a permissible part of my life. I don't have to explain myself to you."

She swallowed convulsively. Tears blurred her vision, but that was just as well. She didn't want him to see the pain in her face. She took deep breaths. "No. You don't," she said with the last shreds of her pride. "I'm sorry I spoiled your business dinner and made an utter fool of myself. Cherry asked me to come—I thought it had been long enough that you…you wouldn't mind having me around just for a meal." Her voice broke and she turned away.

Jason felt himself weakening, and that was the one thing he didn't dare let happen. He steeled himself not to give in.

"Now you know that I do mind," he said, forcing carelessness into his voice. "I told you how it was going to be."

She reached for the door handle without looking back at him. "So you did." She opened it, watching the light come on in the headliner. "I should have paid attention."

"Don't come back here again, Kate," he said quietly. "It gives me no pleasure to hurt you."

"We were friends," she whispered. "I hate being a stranger to you."

He drew in a slow, steadying breath. "Don't make this any harder than it already is," he ground out. She was cutting the ground out from under him with her unexpected vulnerability. He'd never heard her cry until tonight. It had taken his last ounce of willpower to keep from going across the table after her inside, when he saw the tears gleaming in those soft, trusting green eyes. Hurting Kate was unbearable. But he had to. He couldn't give in to her...!

"I told you I didn't want you here," he said through his teeth. "Damn it, why didn't you listen? Can't you get it through your head that I don't want you hanging on my neck like a lovesick teenage girl?" he demanded, certain that she'd leave now.

But instead, Kate cried; huge racking sobs. And as she fumbled with the door, Jason's motives went up in smoke. He threw the cigarette away with a furious curse and reached for her.

He caught her, turned her, wrapped her up in his arms and bent, groaning, to her mouth.

Time stopped. He was rough, and she didn't mind.

His mouth hurt, and even the hurt was sweet. She felt him bend her, lift her into the hard contours of his body, and she reached up to slide her arms around his neck. She clung, loving the violence of it—loving the undisguised hunger in his mouth as it burrowed deeper into hers, and the crush of his hard arms, the faint tremor in his powerful body.

"Oh, God," he breathed into her open mouth. "I can't stand it…!"

He backed her against the car, oblivious to where they were, grateful for the concealing blanket of darkness as his hips ground into hers.

She felt him, knew that he was savagely aroused. That aroused her. Jason was suddenly out of control, and his hips began to shift sensually over hers in a frank statement of his desire.

All the while, his mouth moved obsessively on her lips, his tongue probing rhythmically into her mouth.

"Kate," he groaned. His hands contracted on her hips, his lean fingers pegging into her flesh as he tried to get closer to her.

She held him tighter, and her body began to move helplessly. The tears came hotter now, faster, and she was moaning, whimpering into his devouring mouth. His hands slid up to her breasts, cupping them blatantly through the fabric. His fingers held their aroused tips, testing the hardness while she gasped at the sensations he was causing her to feel.

"You damned little fool, I could take you right here, standing up, in front of God and the whole world. And you won't understand why I don't want you around," he whispered hoarsely, his voice dark with quiet fury. "You've got me so aroused that I don't even know if I can stand up straight. Feel me, Kate," he ground out, pushing against her. "Damn you, feel what you've done to me! You're a virgin. Do you think I can just push you down and take what I want without any conscience?"

"I don't care," she whimpered against his hard mouth.

"Well, I care. And you would, sooner or later." He let his mouth slide down to her throat, pressing hotly into the soft flesh. He shuddered. "Three weeks," he whispered hoarsely. "My God, it feels like three years. I could hate you for what you do to me, Kate!"

"Well, I'm just as helpless!" she cried tearfully. "Jason, everyone is vulnerable sometimes."

"Not me. Not with you." He took a deep breath and forced himself to be still. He was shaking, and she had to feel it, to know how out of control he'd been. That made it worse, to have her know how vulnerable he was, but he couldn't help it. Jason took deep breaths and finally levered himself painfully away from her. Kate couldn't see his eyes, but she could feel the anger in him. "Get away from me. And don't come back. I don't want you here."

"What are you afraid of?" she asked, trembling still from his feverish embrace. "I'm not any threat to you."

"I'm not afraid," he said curtly. He breathed deliberately, and then he took out a cigarette and lit it with fingers that trembled. "I told you, I don't want involvement."

"You're so straitlaced," she breathed unsteadily. "So honorable. You don't make mistakes, you don't lose control. You won't let yourself be anything less than perfect and you won't accept imperfection in anybody else. Oh, Jason, do you want to spend your whole life alone?"

"I don't want to be owned, Kate," he bit off. "I won't be owned, least of all by a virginal child who can't even dress properly or behave like an adult in polite company!"

That was the final blow. She'd taken all she could take from him. He was using every weapon he had against her, and he'd finally found one that worked. Kate drew back her hand and slapped him full across the cheek as hard as she could.

"Go home," he said coldly, after a brief silence.

"With pleasure," she managed unsteadily. "I couldn't live up to a man like you in a million years. Thank you for spelling it out for me. Good-bye, Jason."

She got into the car with as much dignity as she could muster and drove off sedately, leaving him standing in the yard, in the dark, alone.

CHAPTER EIGHT

KATE WALKED AROUND in a daze all day Sunday and Monday at work. The blonde's caustic remarks, and Jason's turbulent behavior had shaken her out of her shoes. She felt raw inside. Hurt. Bruised. And the worst of it was that she was certain Jason had been well on the way to feeling something deep and lasting for her. But he was afraid of emotion, and he'd fought it to a standstill. He'd pushed her away last night with finality, despite his loss of control. In fact, he'd very likely pushed her away because of that loss of control. He was used to having vulnerability met with pain, so it wasn't even surprising that he was fighting his new feelings for Kate. She understood. But that didn't make it any easier for her to live with.

At least her line was off to a marvelous start. Kate became more excited with each step as she saw her designs on paper become ensembles on a rack. The hope of making something of herself took a little of the sting out of Saturday night. She was more determined than ever now to do something spectacular. It was almost a fever in her now, to pull herself up out of poverty. To be somebody. To show Jason that she didn't need his pity or his patronage, that she could belong to the world at large.

Kate had long since selected her fabric. It was sitting on flats by the back door of the plant, huge bales of cloth stacked up out in the cutting room, the enormous rolls of it lending color to the drab khaki and camouflage cloth that the workers were sewing for a government contract.

"Pretty stuff," one of the cutters said with a grin as he walked past. "It'll make a nice change."

"You're a brick," she told him. He was one of the men she knew well, the father of a girl she'd gone to school with. "Is that all of it?" she asked, studying the stack of rolls.

"We got shorted two bales," he replied. "But Gloria in the cutting room office has already checked on it, and the warehouse will send it the end of the week. Don't worry," he chuckled. "By the time you get the markers ready for us to cut by, we'll have it all in hand."

"Of course we will," she agreed. And she laughed with sheer delight at the idea of having specially ordered cloth just for her very own designs. It was more fun than she'd ever imagined.

As Kate walked back toward the cutting room, one of the spreaders—the men who spread thirty to sixty ply of fabric on the long tables for the cutters—came by with two samples of cloth in his hand.

"Want to help me shade cloth?" He grinned wickedly because he knew Kate had one slight visual flaw—telling the difference between dark blue and black.

"You go away," she told him. "Both those pieces are black or I'm a truck driver."

He glowered. "Somebody told you!"

She shook her finger at him, and when he left, she called a thank you to the stockroom clerk, who'd been mouthing "black, black!" around a corner.

She walked back down the long corridor, her mind clouded with an old fantasy of having a major designer get excited over her work and offer her a fabulous contract to produce haute couture garments. Then she abruptly came back down to earth, remembering the humiliation of Saturday night. Kate lifted her chin proudly. Well, maybe she didn't know high fashion yet, but she would. Meanwhile, she'd design what she did best, and take it one step at a time.

Her workload grew as the pressure did, and it was hard to be creative with deadlines staring her in the face. October wasn't that far away, and unfortunately, she had dozens of designs to finish for inclusion in the collection. Kate had a difficult time ahead of her. If she hadn't loved what she was doing so much, or wanted it so badly, she might have thrown up her hands and gone back out to sew on the line.

Jason hadn't come near her for two days. But she hadn't really expected him to. He'd made himself crystal clear, and apparently he was going to cut her completely out of his life. They wouldn't even speak anymore. That was painful, because after having sampled his ardor, she dreamed about him all the time now. It was more than just caring, more than loving him. She wanted him, as a woman wants a man. And that was going to make the months ahead unbearable.

Kate started spending her evenings at her work, spreading paper and bits and pieces of lace and trim all over the kitchen table as she laid out new designs. Mary gave up trying to talk to her, and took to reading mystery novels instead. She assumed it was the pressure getting to Kate, and not their absent neighbor. Which was a relief to Kate, because Mary was starting to show some concern about this new career that might take her daughter away from home for good.

One night toward the end of the week, while Kate was

still struggling with one particular gored skirt on paper, Mary came into the kitchen after work to make another pot of coffee.

"You're going to kill yourself if you keep up this pace," she remarked.

Kate only smiled without looking up. "I've got to meet the deadline. We've got a car payment coming up," she added. The car and the phone were great. There were other little luxuries that they were able to afford, too, like a used washer and dryer combination and some paint for the outside of the house, and even some new clothes. It was so wonderful, just to go to the grocery store and not have to budget every penny. Kate bought cheese and lettuce every week, which she considered a godsend. And that was wonderful.

"It's just wonderful, having a few things." Mary touched her hair gently. "I wish I could have given them to you. It doesn't seem right, you having to do for me."

Kate put down the pencil, stood up and put her arms around her thin mother. "Now just hush," she scolded. "I love you. If I want to do a few things for you, that's my right."

"I love you, too." She smiled at her daughter. "Okay. I won't fuss." She moved away to start the coffee. "Want a cup?"

Kate stretched, lifting the hem of her embroidered tank top away from the waistline of her jeans. "I guess so. I'm tired."

"No wonder, the way you've been working the past few days. Oh, I forgot to tell you, Cherry's stopping by this evening to pick up that skirt she had you sew for her. Is it ready?"

"It sure is." Kate went and fetched it, a full circle

denim skirt with embroidery all over the hem and waistband. "I hope she likes it. It was flattering, having her ask me to sew for her."

"She said she was afraid you wouldn't want to come to the house," Mary said quietly.

Kate's face grew hard. "She's absolutely right. I can't remember ever feeling so stupid. Jason's made it very clear that he doesn't want me around anymore."

"You know why," Mary said gently. She sighed. "Honey, he's had a hard life. You can't blame him for being afraid of involvement. Every single person he's ever cared about has hurt him."

"I wouldn't, though," Kate returned, her eyes hurting. "I'd never hurt him!"

"He has to find that out for himself," her mother said. "And, Kate, he's trying to protect you. He's older than you are. He can see things more clearly. He does care, in a way—he cares too much to use you."

"I wish I were rich and beautiful," Kate said fiercely. "I wish I were famous, and sophisticated…!"

"The reason he cares so much about you is because you're not sophisticated," Mary reminded her. "Give it time, honey. Don't worry so. You've got enough to do now with this designing. Don't make things harder on yourself by worrying about things you can't change. If it's meant to be, it will be. But if it isn't, nothing you can do will make it happen."

Kate sighed wearily. "You fatalist, you." She smiled. "But I guess you're right. It's hard, having your dreams go up in smoke…that must be Cherry," she broke off as she heard a car coming up outside. Kate fought to get her emotions under control. All those dreams, and Jason had been so hungry for her. As hungry as she was for him.

And then he just turned it off and walked away. She hated even the memories now, because they taunted her with things she could never have.

"It's Cherry," Mary said. She opened the door, smiling. "Hello! Come in and have coffee with us, I've just put it on."

"I'd love to have a cup, and move in with you, too, if it's okay," Cherry said bitterly. She was a dish in her little yellow frock, every strand of blond hair in place. She smiled at Kate. "Hi! Are we still speaking? I hope you'll be able to forgive me someday…"

"I've already done that," Kate said honestly. "You couldn't have known what was going to happen. I'm just sorry that I ruined the evening for everybody."

"Pity you couldn't have been a fly on the wall after you left." Cherry grinned. "Mrs. Davis gave Daphne hell on the half shell about what she'd said to you, and she told her husband right in front of everybody that in the future she wanted no part of any dinner or gathering that included the very snobby Mrs. Haversham. That's Daphne's last name; you were sitting next to her husband."

Kate felt her heart stop. "She's married? The way she was flirting with Jason, I thought she might be his latest conquest."

"She and her husband have a feedlot, Jason had thought about doing some business with them, but he didn't say another word about it after you left. He sat sipping brandy and looking unapproachable. The visitors left, and he gave me hell, too." She flushed. "I didn't even fuss, because I deserved it, and I told him so. The upshot is that Gene gets to go to his exhibit, but if I'd known how much hurt I was going to cause with my plotting, I swear I'd never have asked you into that hornet's nest."

"No harm done," Kate lied. "And I've got your skirt ready." Kate produced it, and Cherry's eyes lit up with genuine pleasure. "Oh, Kate, it's the prettiest thing I've ever seen," she sighed, holding it against her. "Whatever you've charged me won't be nearly enough. I'd pay well over a hundred dollars for it in any boutique, so that's what you're getting, and don't argue," she added, watching Kate's mouth open to protest. "You know very well that Gene can afford it."

"That isn't the point, you're like family…" Kate argued.

"Sorry, but the ink's dry, I can't change it." Cherry grinned, producing a check from her dress pocket.

"You doll," Kate sighed, and hugged her. "How can I thank you?"

"You've got that backwards," she was assured. "And how you can thank me is by making me a tank top like yours to match it. Okay?"

Kate shook her head, laughing. "This old thing? You're kidding!"

"I am not. I want one."

"Well, all right."

"Now," Cherry said. "How about that coffee?"

"Make mine black," Mary called to Kate as she went to fetch it from the kitchen.

"How's Gene doing with his painting?" Mary asked as they sat on the worn floral cover of the living room sofa.

Cherry sat back with a long sigh. "He'd do fine if he could convince his older brother that he had talent. Jay still thinks he should become a cattleman, but Gene isn't a rancher at heart. Jay is determined to beat him into shape."

"And Gene can't say no to his brother because he owes him so much," Mary said.

"That's about it," Cherry agreed. She looked up as Kate came in with coffee on an old tin tray. "You know how hard it was on the boys, Kate," she added. "With the old man drinking like a fish and beating them bloody if they didn't jump fast enough to suit him. I swear if it hadn't been for Jay, he'd have killed Gene once. Sheila told me about it when Gene and I first got married. Jay was in his last year or so of high school and Gene had just barely started. Well, she said old man Donavan had taken a quirt to Gene for missing the school bus, of all things, and he was blind staggering drunk. He was beating the boy bloody when Jay came running back from the bus and fought the whip out of his daddy's hands. He turned on Jay, too, but by that time the bus driver had backed up and put in his two cents worth. They said that every kid on the bus got an eyeful of the Donavan boys' home life that day, and that even the teachers were easy on them from then on when they were disobedient."

"Yes, I knew about that. It was one of the teachers who tried to have the boys taken away from him," Mary agreed. She sipped her coffee slowly. "But J.B. was cold sober that one day in court, and convinced the judge that he loved his kids. After he told about how Nell had run off and left them, and how they'd suffered, and how Sheila took such good care of them...well, the judge felt sorry for the old man. Most people did, and were shocked at the way he acted when he drank. He was a good man when he was sober. But after that, J.B. must have looked hard at himself, or Jason must have threatened him. Things got better. Frank helped," she added, recalling times when her late husband, Kate's father, had intervened.

"Jason's had a hard life, but it isn't right for Gene to let his older brother plan his life for him. It's my life, too, now. I don't want to spend it on a cattle ranch any more than Gene does."

"Can't you talk to Jason about it?" Kate asked. "He's not an ogre."

"Only you could ever say that with a straight face," Cherry chuckled. "You're the only person he gets along with, as a rule, except that lately he seems to explode if your name is mentioned. But he hates most people, and he just tolerates me because he has to."

"He seems to like Gabe most of the time," Kate murmured, her eyes faraway as she remembered the good days. "And he even tolerates Red Barton, whom most cattlemen would shoot on sight for gross insubordination. That cowboy stays in trouble all the time."

"He does that. By the way," Cherry said with a mischievous grin, "Gabe waylaid me in the driveway on my way out and asked if I thought you might be receptive to going to a square dance with him. I told him I couldn't speak for you."

Kate thought about Jason and his horrible temper and the way he'd treated her. "Tell him I will."

"It's about time. He's been mooning around for weeks; it will be good therapy. I'll tell him." Cherry grinned. She left, with her precious skirt in hand, waving good-bye.

"Jason won't like it, honey," Mary said quietly.

"It's none of Jason's business," Kate said shortly. "If he can ignore me, I can ignore him."

"I thought it bothered you that he hadn't been around

to see you," Mary replied. She hugged Kate gently. "I'm sorry."

Kate had to fight tears. It hurt terribly that, after what had happened, Jason still hadn't come to see her.

"I like Gabe a lot," she said out loud as she tried to sound and feel convinced. "He's good fun and I won't have to fight him off." I hope, she added silently. "There's no reason in the world why I can't date him."

IN FACT, THERE was one big reason why not. And he hit the ceiling when he overheard Cherry and Gabe talking about the upcoming square dance.

"Hold it right there," Jason called to his foreman after Cherry had gone inside.

Gabe had started back toward the corral, but he froze in place and turned, grinning sheepishly.

"I, uh, guess you heard what Cherry said," he ventured.

"Go near Kate," Jason said, his voice deep and slow and measured, his dark eyes glittering, "and you'll leave the Spur in a basket."

So that was how things stood. Gabe liked Kate, but he liked his job even more, and he knew how dangerous it was to cross Jason Donavan.

"I think a lot of Kate," Gabe said gently. "I just meant to take her out on the town. I wouldn't hurt her, in any way."

"I know that," Jason replied tersely. "It doesn't change things. Stay away from her."

"If that's how you want it."

"I'll give her your condolences," Jason replied. He turned and headed for the Bronco, sick of life in general and cattle and philandering, trespassing cowboys in particular. Damn Kate for agreeing to go out with that soft-hearted lunatic, and damn Cherry for sticking her nose in.

He didn't want to seduce Kate, but he sure as hell didn't want Gabe doing it. And then he realized that as long as Kate was free, she was fair game. She was as young and fresh and pretty as a country rose, and men would want her. His face hardened. He started the car with a vicious turn of the key and gunned the engine fiercely as he shot out into the highway, narrowly missing a fence.

Kate had done that to get even, he knew it. He'd hurt her, and then he'd let her think that Daphne meant something to him. But he couldn't let her get involved with Gabe, any more than he could let her get involved with him. His hands gripped the steering wheel hard. If only he could get her out of his system without hurting her any more. But he wanted her even more now, and found himself dreaming of her. He felt her mouth under his every time he closed his eyes. But that wasn't love, it was lust, and Kate deserved something more.

Jason thought as he drove, furious at circumstances. He'd been trying to fight memories of Kate and gain some time to turn things around. He sighed angrily. Life was sure as hell getting complicated.

Kate was back at work on her designs when she heard a car drive up outside. Surely it wasn't Cherry again. Mary was in the bathroom, soaking in a tub of hot water, so Kate got up and went to see who it was.

She opened the door and her heart did cartwheels. It seemed like years since she'd seen Jason. He was wearing dress slacks with a patterned gray shirt and tie, a silky sport coat and his dress Stetson. He looked furious. She didn't need a telegram to inform her that he'd just found out about her acceptance of Gabe's invitation.

Her green eyes glittered as he came up on the porch. She didn't take one step toward him. He was doing some looking of his own, his dark eyes feeding on the sight of her after so many days of trying to remember every detail of her face and body. He didn't like that damned short haircut, and he almost said so. But he had no right to dictate to her. She looked as if she hated him, and that bruised him in ways he hadn't expected.

"My goodness, are you lost?" Kate asked, throwing down the gauntlet with unexpected ease. She even smiled as she folded her arms tightly across her chest. "I can't imagine you'd come here for any other reason."

"You aren't going anywhere with Gabe." Damn. He'd meant to lead up to it slowly, not slam it at her that way. His jaw tautened as he saw rebellion sparkle in her eyes. "And it's no good arguing about it," he added before she could speak. "I've told him if he comes near you, he's through at the Spur."

That was faintly shocking. "Gabe's your friend," she reminded him. "And you'd never get another foreman who'd work half as hard as he does."

"I won't deny that. But all the same, if you go out with him and I find out about it, he's fired. And I will find out about it," he added quietly. "I swear to God I will."

"What does it matter to you who I go out with, Jason?!" she demanded. "You couldn't shoot me off the place fast enough Saturday."

"You know why I've kept my distance," he said after a minute. He paused to light a cigarette, scowling at her. "But this was low, Kate. You're not going to use Gabe to get to me."

It was the wrong thing for him to say to her. He'd dashed her dreams to shreds and made it out to be her fault. "And I suppose I threw myself at you?" she challenged, biting her lower lip to still its telltale trembling.

"Didn't you?" he asked with a cold smile, impatient with her accusations and his own doubts and misgivings.

Her hand went up, but this time he caught her wrist in a steely grasp that had his full strength behind it. She shivered a little in anticipation because his eyes flashed wildly.

"Kate, is that Jason?" Mary called from the bedroom.

Jason dropped Kate's wrist just as Mary came out in her new blue crepe dress, looking very elegant despite her thinness. "Well, hello." She grinned. "Kate, I just called Betty Gallaway and we're going to see that new movie about that wild Australian man together. You don't mind, do you?"

Kate was trying desperately to hold her temper. "No. Of course not."

Mary didn't smile smugly, but she felt like it. She'd obviously just interrupted something violent, and if she left these two alone, there was every chance that they'd finally start talking again. She'd leaped out of the tub when she heard him drive up, dressed, and called Betty in a space of five minutes. Thank God Betty was free.

"Well, I'm off. Don't you two kill each other," she said, kissing Kate good-bye. "See you, Jason."

"Sure," he replied, but he was breathing roughly and still glaring at Kate when he said it.

Mary eased out past them, got into the Tempo, started it, blew the horn and drove away. Kate pushed back her hair, glaring back at Jason.

He took deep, slow breaths, and then he looked down at Kate, whose mutinous fury had passed into lackluster depression. He reached out and held her wrist, smoothing his fingers over the soft flesh that he'd just crushed.

She looked up at that moment, her soft eyes searching

his, and every sane thought went out of Jason's head. He flipped the cigarette out into the sandy yard and eased Kate into the house, closing the door gently behind him.

"I hate you," he said through his teeth. "My God, I could…!" His mouth crushed down over hers in a kiss that was part revenge, part torment.

She barely heard him. Her lips parted softly and she reached around his hard waist, pressing into the powerful length of his body while his searching mouth made rough love to hers in the silence.

The feel of Kate's soft, warm body was the final straw, breaking Jason's will, making him helpless to stop himself.

His lean hands slid under her top, up to her uncovered breasts, and before she could recover enough to protest, his tongue went into her mouth. He backed her into the door. His hard, hungry body pushing down against hers took the last sane thought right out of her mind. He worked at buttons and fastenings and in feverish minutes, she felt his broad hair-covered chest softly crushing her own bare one in an abrasive contact that was as wildly arousing as the feel of his powerful legs against her.

"I tried," he breathed roughly, his voice shaking as he kissed her. "God help me, I did." His lean hands smoothed down her body, brushing her hips against his, holding her to him in an intimacy that she should have protested, but didn't. "I want you. I want you so badly, Kate…"

She touched his dark hair gently as his insistent mouth covered hers. She knew that no one had ever really loved Jason. But she did. She wanted to show him how much. She wanted to teach him that trust and love and emotional ties weren't painful. She wanted to teach him how to love. Perhaps, in this way, Kate might build a future with him. She might give him a taste of the kind of life he'd once wanted, and might stop him from finishing the wall he was building to keep out the world.

There were risks, of course. But this was Jason, and Kate felt that he also needed her. And if there hadn't been a woman for him in the past few years, just the possession of her might be enough to bind him to her forever. Yes. Yes. She closed her eyes and let him settle his aching body over hers, with the door hard and cool at her back and the blazing warmth of his muscular torso brushing hungrily against her as he bent suddenly to lift her.

"Forgive me," he whispered hoarsely, breathing the words into her trembling lips.

Her arms closed around his neck as she fought down the faint fear of his possession. "I love you," she whispered back. "There won't be anything to forgive."

Jason couldn't even speak for the blood hurtling through his mind. He carried Kate to the sofa and laid her down, blind and deaf and dumb with the helplessness of desire.

CHAPTER NINE

JASON EASED HER down on the long, faded sofa, his mouth
still over hers. God, she was soft. Her body trembled
faintly when he began to stroke it, and her legs tangled
with his. She was innocent, but he could feel the buried
passions in her and hadn't he heard her whisper that she
loved him? He wanted her so much. The years of absti-
nence and the sweet feast in sight made him irrational, so
perhaps he'd imagined what Kate had whispered. Right or
wrong, it was too late to draw back. His body was on fire,
his mind drowning in her scent, her softness.

He bit at her lips, lifting his head to search over the
soft pink thrust of her breasts, the smooth line of her
flat stomach as his hand eased her loosened jeans down.

Kate's breath caught and she stiffened. She hadn't
thought about how intimate it was going to get, and this
was just the beginning.

He read accurately that brief hesitation. It was a big
step, and she was frightened. He bent to her mouth, barely
able to speak at all for the shuddering passion that had
overtaken him. "This is part of loving," he breathed
against her trembling mouth. "I know how shocking it
must seem to you, but I swear I won't do anything to
hurt you."

She knew how naive she must seem to an experienced
man. She tried to relax. "I'm sorry..."

He touched his mouth to hers. "Trust me, Katy," he whispered with aching tenderness.

He slid his hand into the thick, short hair behind her head and lifted her mouth up to join with his. He wished to God he knew more about women than he did because he'd never been with a woman who was virginal and he wasn't sure he knew how to arouse her enough to spare her the discomfort of her first time.

Even now, in the back of his mind, he could hear his father raging about sex, about how women used it to break a man's spirit. No real man would let a woman make him weak by tempting him with her body, his father had sermonized. That constant lecturing had scarred Jason, in fact it had kept him away from women most of his adult life, so he didn't have the expertise Kate seemed to credit him with. But he'd certainly learned enough to see him through. He touched Kate hesitantly where he was sure no one else ever had. She jerked, but his mouth hardened on hers, stilling her sudden frantic movement. And then he found her, where she was virginal, and she moaned.

The sensations that shot heat through her body made her shudder. She made a sound, a cry, under his devouring mouth, but she lay very still. He touched her again, more intimately this time, and again the pleasure burned. Her arms reached up to him. She answered the pressure of his mouth, going under in dazed submission as he brushed and stroked and probed.

He lifted his mouth just a fraction and watched her face. Her eyes were half-closed, misty with arousal. Her cheeks were flushed, her mouth swollen and parted, waiting for him to claim. He probed and she gasped, but without protest. It was beyond belief, the pleasure it gave him to watch her. Jason was trembling with his own desire, but even stronger was the tenderness he felt for her, the need to protect, to comfort, to cherish. Later, perhaps, the guilt and shame would come, as it always had before. But now he was in the throes of magic, and nothing mattered except fulfillment. His. And hers.

"There's a barrier," he whispered, holding her eyes as his hand moved. "A very thin one. Let's get rid of it now, little one."

She trembled, feeling him push gently against her, the fear dark in her eyes at the faint stab of discomfort. Kate gasped, but Jason brushed his mouth over hers and caught the tiny sound. It embarrassed her, the way he was touching her, the helplessness of her body in his sight. She was losing control and he was going to see…!

"Don't close your eyes," he said softly. "There's nothing so very terrible about letting me see your pleasure, Kate."

Tears burned her eyes while sensation climbed and climbed. She couldn't answer him. She gasped, arching, her body no longer hers, her face taut, her jaw clenching.

He pushed against her then, gauging the exact moment when he could without hurting her more than necessary, and she moaned like a wounded thing, pain mingled with pleasure in her cry. Blazing torment turned sweet, lifting her. He hesitated then, to see how complete her abandon was, and she began to writhe uncontrollably.

"No," she whimpered as he sat up. "Oh, don't stop!" Her head turned toward him, her legs shifting sensuously, her body racked with a new and involuntary fever.

He got to his feet, and she saw him undressing through a red mist of uncontrollable desire, still moving, like a small animal in a trap, weak and vulnerable. It only took a minute, his tall, powerful body shuddering openly when he reached down to strip her out of the rest of her covering.

He looked down at her taut nudity, his body powerful and tense with its damp, bronzed muscle and the thick hair that curled down his chest, his flat belly to his blatant masculinity.

"Jason," she moaned, trembling.

"You're exquisite," he said roughly, his voice as aroused as her body. "God, you're exquisite."

He eased down over her, every movement slow enough to make her moan with impatience. The fear was gone. Only her body was alive, wanting the power and domination of his with a primitive kind of desire. She'd never realized the strength of desire until now. Trembling with the need for his body, the anguish of emptiness waiting to be filled, she arched up, weeping, as he moved her legs gently to admit the weight of his body.

"I hope I know enough," he whispered enigmatically, sliding his hands under her head to cradle it while he played with her mouth. He eased down, and the words sounded almost reverent, like the tenderness of his hands as he positioned her.

"Jason," she wept. "Jason, please…please!" She moved against his body, urgently, but he held back.

"You have to be hungrier than this," he whispered, his mouth gentling hers. "I can't bear to hurt you now."

"You won't…!"

"Not yet." He touched her as he had before, and she cried against his mouth at the exquisite things he did to her. And all the while, his mouth moved first against hers, and then down to the peaks of her breasts. He kissed her there, his tongue and his teeth teasing, tenderly arousing, insistent. And all the while, she moaned, her teeth clenching in pleasured agony, her body writhing as if in unbearable pain.

"I can't...bear...any more!" she sobbed.

"Neither can I," he breathed into her open mouth. He shifted slowly, despite his trembling need, and she felt the gentle, shocking touch of him and her eyes flew open. His were above her, watching, almost black with desire. "Lie very still for me, honey," he whispered as he moved down slowly, and his hand slid under her hips. "Just for... another second. Just...for a second...yes!" he groaned, and he pushed down.

She looked at him with eyes like saucers, shaking at the slow, bold intrusion that shattered all her previous conceptions of lovemaking. This was the mystery... blatant, intimate, earthy. She gasped as he moved again and her hands caught at his hard arms as she felt a faint spasm of discomfort.

"Kate," he whispered shakenly, holding her eyes as he eased down. "Oh, God, I don't want to hurt you, honey. Sweetheart, is it very bad?"

The tender concern in that deep, slow voice brought tears misting into her eyes. Men weren't supposed to care about a woman's pleasure, were they? But he cared. His face was taut with the strain of trying to hold back for her sake, and that forced the tension out of her. She didn't want to hurt him, either.

She took a deep breath and let her body sink into the sofa cushions, feeling his weight as she began to absorb him. The discomfort slowly lessened, and all at once, there was no more resistance.

She'd never felt anything like it, and not just the physical closeness. Her eyes stared into his, and it was like souls touching. She trembled with the awe of it, and her hands reached up to touch his chest, tangling in the thick hair, feeling the sweat and the throb of his heartbeat and the shudder of his breathing.

"You look as shocked as I feel," he whispered unsteadily. "It isn't…totally physical, is it?" he breathed, bending. "Oh, God, Kate, Kate, I never dreamed I could feel so much sweet pleasure…!"

Her eyes closed as he touched her mouth with his. She slid her hands up over his shoulders as he began to move, and her breath caught with each delicious contact. She was woman and he was man, and it must have been like this when the world began.

Like waves, she thought when the first of them washed over her. Waves of pleasure, sliding against her bare skin. Her eyes opened, to look into his, to share it with him.

He felt her gaze. His own eyes opened, and somewhere in the back of his reeling mind, he realized that he'd never looked before. He'd never wanted to, until now.

He searched her wide, darkening eyes, barely breathing in the utter stillness of the room as their rhythm deepened and slowed and became torturously sweet.

Kate's eyes dilated until they were almost black. She looked into his hard face with wonder, feeling his body intimately joining itself to hers.

He seemed as stunned as she was. "My God," he breathed.

It should have been routine to him, she thought wildly as she watched the expression on his face. But perhaps because of the closeness they'd shared, it was special. Or because she was virginal. Her loving eyes traced his face above her, her breath jerking in sweet surges of pleasure as his movements deepened and quickened, and his breathing began to change.

"I can't hold back any longer," he managed through red waves of building passion.

"It's all right," she whispered. She touched his mouth with trembling fingers, gasping under the hard buffeting of his body. The pleasure was building suddenly. She made a sound she didn't recognize. "Ja...son?" she cried, and felt a surge of fear.

"Don't be afraid of it," he ground out. He caught her wrists and pinned them beside her head, his hips crushing down on hers. His face tautened, his teeth clenching, his eyes glittering into hers. "Don't close your...eyes," he bit off, shuddering. "Oh, God...Kate...let me watch!"

Her mouth opened and she felt the first aching spasm of pleasure as his body became feverish and rough over hers. She looked straight into his eyes as the pleasure slammed into his body. He groaned harshly, and then his face blurred and all she knew was the rhythm and the tide, rushing, rushing, rushing....

It was like a sneeze backing up. A cough that died. She lay under him still trembling, crying. She was sure that he'd felt what men were supposed to feel, but she was incomplete and she wanted to cry.

He seemed to know. Seconds after he stopped shuddering, his mouth moved tenderly on hers and his hand went under her hips where they were still imprisoned by his.

"Oh!" she cried out as the sudden pleasure of his slow movements shocked her.

"Hush, sweetheart," he whispered tenderly. "I know. I'm not going to leave you like this. Just lie still. Now... there?"

She gasped, clutched at his sweaty arms, her nails bending on the hard muscle. She couldn't even speak, but he felt her building pleasure.

She was on a cloud, through it, falling, falling...! She wept, whimpering wildly against his crushing mouth as her body lifted and clung to his and she was thrown against a wall of unbearable pleasure.

Kate felt Jason go very still and she heard him groan. Then he was suddenly heavier, trembling differently now. She stroked his dark, damp hair tenderly, awed by what had happened. It had been like a bonding of souls. A union so complete that it went beyond anything physical.

"My God, that's never happened to me in my whole life," he whispered a minute later.

"So beautiful," she whispered. "That, with you."

He touched her face with wonder. He'd gone to heaven in her arms, he'd sailed on warm winds and touched the sky.

She touched his chest, loving the thick nest of hair that felt deliciously abrasive under her searching hand. "It was...profound." She looked up into his dark eyes.

"Yes." He framed her soft face in his lean hands and bent to kiss her open mouth. There was a tenderness in him that he'd never known. He wanted to cherish her. To give her everything. His mouth opened. He wanted to make her pregnant....

She felt him move, felt the slow exquisite joining in a lazy welcome that made it as natural as breathing. He was hers now, and she could take him. She could touch him any way she liked, she could enjoy his body, she could possess him with her body.

She returned his soft, tender kiss, almost crying from the beauty of it. She loved him so. And he was feeling more than simple desire, she could tell by the way he touched her, by the cherishing of his mouth.

"No. Not here," he whispered when he tried to move and was stopped by the back of the sofa. Breathing unsteadily, he drew her down onto the thick brown rug she'd bought earlier in the week to cover places where the linoleum was worn. She felt its soft pile against her back with delicious sensuality, her eyes searching Jason's as he bent over her.

"Like this," he said, positioning her so that they were curled together in a way that seemed incredibly intimate, his thighs cradling hers, his arms beside her breasts. "I want to cherish you," he whispered over her soft lips. "I want…to…"

She didn't hear the words. He was rocking with her, part of her, and like waves smoothing over the beach, his body was smoothing over hers. The rhythm was slow, sweet, buffeting. The rug slid and his mouth grew insistent, and then there was only the rough jerk of his breath mingling with hers, the hungry rhythm, the…joining.

It was more intense than before. She lay in his arms trembling for a long time after they came shuddering back to earth together. She couldn't breathe, and her heart was beating so heavily that she thought she might die of it.

He rolled onto his side, still locked with her, holding her against him. "Are you all right?" he asked, kissing her face wherever he could reach it, his lips tender and loving. "I didn't hurt you?"

"No," she whispered. She kissed his closed eyelids, his shoulders. "Jason, I thought…I was going to die."

"So did I." He pressed her mouth against his chest.

"Kiss me there. Open your mouth and do it. God, that... burns me up! Do it again."

She did, glorying in the pleasure it seemed to give him. She laughed, wrestling him over and she put her mouth in the center of his chest and bit him.

He laughed, too, his face younger and more alive than she'd ever seen it. His eyes were soft. Almost tender. He let them slide over her with frank delight.

"I adore you," she whispered, and it was in her eyes, her smile, her whole look.

"No regrets?" he asked quietly, as if it mattered.

A few, she thought ruefully, but she'd determined that she wouldn't spoil it. He might give in to his conscience and go away if she said anything.

"No," she lied. She bent and kissed him softly. "Do you do this often?" she murmured.

"Do what...often?" he asked against her nibbling lips.

"Seduce virgins on the floor."

"We started out on a sofa," he reminded her.

"Do you go around seducing virgins on sofas, then?"

He sighed lazily. His fingers touched her soft body, savoring its delicate contours. "I've never made love to a virgin before, Kathryn," he said quietly. "And I've never made love to any woman the way we just did, here on this rug."

That pleased her. At least she was special to him, somehow, even if just as his only innocent.

"It wasn't anything like I'd thought it would be," she confessed. "Even the first time. I thought it would hurt."

"Some men like that," he said, his voice deep and steady. "They like the pain of initiation. But I don't have a sadistic bone in my body," he replied, his voice deep and slow, his eyes possessive. "I'd have done anything to spare you. I don't have to hurt a woman to feel like a man."

"I don't think you could hurt me if you tried," she replied. "Not physically, at any rate."

"Emotionally, I've done some damage, haven't I, Kate?" he asked. "Now it seems unnecessary. I thought you wanted to save your virginity for marriage, and I couldn't offer you marriage." He touched her hair, about to tell her that his attitude toward it had changed during that sweet interlude. He'd decided that marriage wasn't the end of the world. Judging by what he and Kate had shared, it might be the beginning of everything for them. He'd never imagined anything as tender, as profound as what they'd just shared. And because of it, he was going to take a chance. He was going to marry Kate, and to hell with consequences.

But before he could open his mouth, Kate anticipated a totally different attitude. And because she loved him so much, and didn't want him to feel trapped by his old-fashioned conscience, she forced herself to laugh at the idea of marrying him. She couldn't know what the sound of a woman's laughter did to Jason, or the memories it brought back.

"Marriage is for women without any ambitions at all," she told him, reaching for her clothes because she felt uncomfortable sitting with him this way when they were no longer intimate. "I don't have any inclination to be an obedient wife with a string of preschoolers behind me." She added that for effect, feeling her heart break at the very thought of Jason's black-haired babies that she could never have. He didn't want to get married, after all, that was why he'd tried so hard not to be intimate with her. Now he had, and she had her exquisite memory of him to put away for her old age. And she was giving him his freedom, in return for that sweet keepsake. Because she loved him enough to let him go, to spare him the guilt and torment that she was sure he was already feeling.

"I thought you'd always wanted children," he said after a minute. He got to his feet and started getting into his own clothing, keeping his eyes averted so that Kate wouldn't see the sudden darkening in them.

Kate didn't watch. She finished dressing and sat down on the chair across from the sofa and flushed as he moved the sofa throw he'd drawn under them when he'd first started making love to her.

"You'd better put that in the washer," he told her quietly, averting his eyes from the faint red stain.

She took it without looking at it and put it in the washer, starting a load of clothes before she came back.

"Kate, when was your last period?" he asked unexpectedly. He was standing by the window, drawing on a cigarette he'd just lit.

She stared at his back warily. "What?"

He turned, his face hard. "I hate asking, it embarrasses me, too, damn it," he said shortly. "When was your last period?"

She swallowed. That was something she wouldn't tell him. Couldn't tell him. This was her fertile period. She hadn't thought about it in time, and they were both too far gone to think of precautions by the time she had. But she didn't want him to worry.

"It was about four days ago," she lied, averting her eyes.

He thought the quick jerk of her head was because she was embarrassed to tell him. His eyes narrowed suspiciously, but only for an instant. Well, he told himself curtly, it was just as well that she probably wouldn't get pregnant. He'd lost his head and tried to make her that way in a positive fever of need. Probably it was just the excitement of knowing she was a virgin and having been emotionally close to her all these years. God forbid that he should be falling in love with a career woman.

"Thank God," he said deliberately. He drew on the cigarette. "I'd hate to have the threat of an unwanted pregnancy hanging over us."

She felt her heart sink. Unwanted. Well, he'd made no secret of how he felt about ties. She forced a smile to her swollen lips. "There's little chance of that," she lied. And prayed that there wasn't any threat because she'd never be able to have an abortion. She loved him too much not to bear his child, and she'd love it with the same fierceness with which she loved him. But everyone would know. Her mother would be horrified, and everyone in the community would stare at them because in small towns like San Frio, everybody knew everything about their neighbors.

He moved closer, pulling her gently into his arms. He stood holding her, with the cigarette smoke wafting to the ceiling from his forgotten cigarette. He brushed her hair tenderly with his mouth.

She savored the warm embrace, without passion. Her eyes closed, and she sighed, drinking in the familiar, delicious scent of him. "I'll live on today all my life," she whispered.

His hand smoothed her hair. That didn't sound like ambition to him. He lifted his head and looked into her eyes. "You said you wanted a career."

"I do. But I wanted a memory, to carry me through the loneliness and the long nights," she said honestly. She searched his eyes. "Oh, Jason, I'll be a spinster. I'll die before I'll ever let another man touch me."

His face went rock hard. He could barely breathe. His head felt ten sizes too big, and he wanted to cry out with sheer joy. But then he realized that it was reaction. She'd just had her first sexual experience, and she'd had a kind of crush on him in the past few months. He'd just made her dreams come true. She couldn't know how many of his she'd fulfilled. But whatever she felt physically, it must not have gone further, because she'd said that her career came first.

He touched her cheek, thinking about his babies that she'd never have, about the nights he'd spend alone remembering her in passion. He took a deep, harsh breath.

"There will, someday," he said with deliberate carelessness. He managed to smile. "When you're the toast of the fashion world, you'll be fighting them off with sticks."

"Will you miss me?" she asked, peering up at him with a coquettishness she didn't feel.

He brushed back her hair. "I'll miss you."

"That sounds like good-bye," she said, hiding the anguish her suspicions were already causing.

He took her hand and brought it to his lips. He brushed it gently. "Isn't that what you want, Kate?"

It might be for the best, she realized that, but it broke her heart. "For good?"

He shifted. "For a while. I leave for Australia the end of next week."

"I'll miss having you to talk to," she said without looking at him.

"I'll miss it, too," he said quietly. "You're…very special to me," he said tautly, and Kate, who knew him to his very bones, was aware of the difficulty he had in just that simple admission.

She went close to him and held him. "I meant it," she whispered. "There won't be another man."

"Don't," he bit off. His hands contracted on her shoulders and he felt a horrible emptiness. "You'll forget this in time. As I will. It should never have happened."

"You didn't force me, Jason," she reminded him, because she could see the guilt behind those terse words. She was feeling some guilt of her own already, now that the flush of desire was turning cold.

It was a good thing, she thought, that he couldn't see the tears forming in her eyes. She stood very still until she had them under control. He was frozen over again. The fleeting vulnerability she'd glimpsed just as he lay exhausted from fulfillment was gone. He was himself again, invulnerable, unapproachable. Completely in himself.

She drew back after a minute and drew herself erect. "Will we see each other when you come back from Australia?" she asked.

"We'll see. Five weeks is a long time."

"I know," she murmured quietly, glancing up. "That's almost how long it had been the last time I saw you."

He let go of her slowly, watching her move away. He stared at his cigarette, which had burned down to the filter. "Good-bye, Kate," he said quietly. His eyes were eating her, but the minute she turned, he averted them to the door. "It's getting late. I'd better go."

She walked him to the door in a static silence. As he opened it, she slid her hand into his big, lean one, loving its strength. Loving him. She didn't dare look up then, because he couldn't have missed it. "Take care of my best friend," she said in a hushed tone.

"Take care of mine," he said after a minute. He bent, brushing his mouth with infinite tenderness over her closed, wet eyes. "Oh, God, don't cry," he ground out, his hand contracting around hers. "I can't bear it!"

"All right." She drew in a steadying breath and flicked away the tears with her free hand. "It's just that I'll be alone," she said simply.

He stared down at her bent head with eyes almost black with pain. He had to clench his teeth to keep the words from pouring out. That soft hand, so trusting in his, her eyes tender with the aftermath of shared passion; he wondered if they were going to haunt him for the rest of his life.

My God, he thought fiercely, I think I could love her...!

She looked up in time to see the pain, and forced a smile to her lips so that he wouldn't torment himself with the guilt she thought she saw in his eyes.

"I'm all right," she assured him. "You mustn't worry about me."

"Are you damned sure about that career?" he asked abruptly.

She felt the tears threatening again. Why couldn't he just go and stop tormenting her? "Yes, I'm sure," she said doggedly. "I want it more than anything in the world."

He wanted to throw something. She couldn't know that she was putting a knife into his heart. She'd made him vulnerable. He'd thought he could compete with her aspirations, that she cared for him. But apparently she cared for the pleasure she could get from his body, and now that he'd given her what she wanted, she was through with him. Just like that. Melody, all over again.

He felt used. Damn women everywhere, he thought bitterly as he looked down at Kate's bent head. Damn them! And damn her most of all.

He turned on his heel without a single word and climbed in the Bronco. He gunned it out into the road, and he never looked back. Not once.

Kate, watching him go, was grateful that she'd managed to set him off and make him leave so quickly. Tears were pouring down her cheeks. Another few seconds, and she'd have blurted out the truth. That he was all she wanted, ever. That a career would always be second to what she really wanted—making a home for him, and giving him the children Melody didn't want to give him.

She turned back into the house, broken sobs racking her. She didn't hear the Bronco stop just down the road, or see the hard-faced man sitting in it look back with tormented eyes in a face like broken stone. She didn't hear his soft, agonized "Kate!" or hear the faint break in his voice that not one other human being had ever heard, or ever would. She'd never know how close he came in that instant to turning the Bronco around and going back to force her to marry him. Because after a minute, he regained his pride and pulled away, smoking a cigarette as he drove back toward the Diamond Spur. In all his life, he'd never felt so empty, or so determined that Kate would never get past his defenses a second time. She didn't want him. All right. Let her have her career. He didn't want her. He whipped the Bronco out onto the main highway, and left skid marks behind him.

Inside the house, Kate was doing some hard thinking, now that her mind was firmly back in control again.

Well, she'd done it now. She was no longer a virgin. She'd given him her body, without asking for anything, and he'd taken it. He'd taken her all the way to heaven. But despite the tenderness and the pleasure, it was still just sex. Just a mutual physical sharing.

She went back into the house and closed the door. She wondered if she'd ever be able to look at that sofa and rug again without seeing herself nude on them. She felt guilty and shamed and vaguely sick at what she'd done. All her noble motives went up in smoke the minute her clothes and principles were back in place. So much for free sex, she thought with a faintly hysterical laugh. It wasn't free. It came with a price tag of guilt and shame and self-contempt, unless it was done with love on both sides. What a pity, she thought miserably, that she'd had to learn that lesson in such a hard manner.

It got harder, too. Jason went to Australia, and he was gone six weeks, not five. And Kate's period didn't start. But morning sickness did.

CHAPTER TEN

AUGUST SLID INTO September, and with barely six weeks before market week in New York, Kate pushed herself to the limit to finish her collection. As each piece was painstakingly draped in muslin, and then sewn and tried on and adjusted and revised if necessary before it went into the next stage of development, she watched her ideas turn into moderately priced women's casual clothes. A buyer from one of the companies that did business with Clayborn came by to look over those designs, and was so impressed with them that he put in an advance order for a record number of them.

Kate was over the moon. Especially when Mr. Rogers told her that the move was unprecedented by that particular buyer. He beamed, and so did Kate and the design staff. Then came the most exciting news of all. One of their publicists from New York was coming out to interview Kate and get some preliminary shots of the collection for a press kit to be handed out during market week, and in the various merchandise marts. It might even make the pages of *Women's Wear Daily* and *Apparel South!*

So much was going on that Kate was able to ward off thoughts of Jason. During the daytime, anyway. She worked herself to exhaustion. But at night, the memories haunted her, sweet and sensuous. She could feel Jason's hard mouth on her body, taste him on her lips. And at those times, her heart would ache and tears would sting her eyes.

It was for the best, she kept telling herself. Of course it was. He didn't want commitment, and neither did she. She had a career to think about, she was going to be famous and rich. Unfortunately, a lot of hard work went with those things, and she began to realize that a career was going to rob her of any kind of normal lifestyle. She got up early and went to bed late, always thinking of new ideas, always designing. She did cost estimates on the backs of envelopes, because production costs were the bottom line of any collection in a manufacturing company's budget. She thought about threads and closures and trim while she ate. And always in the background was the memory of sewing on the line, which was an eternal threat if her collection didn't market well. She might have talent, but so did thousands of other designers. It took a unique eye toward trends and color and style to make a great designer. It took an understanding of world politics and world economy, because those things influenced fashion. Bad economy made popular a simple black dress because it could be worn more than one season. A focus on military affairs could produce a camouflage phase, or a focus on a certain country could influence bits and pieces of fashion from it. It was difficult to forecast trends, and there were people who got paid to do nothing else. But a good designer, with the proper training, would have a flair for it. Kate only hoped hers would suffice.

The fashion reporter, who was on the staff of Clayborn's New York office, found Kate's accent fascinating and kept her talking over three cups of coffee.

"And you've been sewing on the pants line all this

time, imagine," Roberta Kowalsky sighed. She was petite and dark and elegant, and Kate liked her immediately. "Well, tell me about your background."

Kate told her as much as possible without a single mention of Jason or the Diamond Spur, except to say that her father had worked for it.

"Yes, I know Jason," Roberta said surprisingly. "I met him at a cocktail party in Manhattan. He used to date one of the models I knew. A dish, a real dish. She got a film offer, and now she's making movies in Great Britain. She married a lord or a baronet, or some such royalty, and they have a little girl. What was her name," she mused, while Kate held her breath. "Oh, yes. Melody. Melody Jones."

"I've heard of her," Kate said, her voice unnaturally husky.

"We all thought she'd marry Jason," Roberta sighed. "But I guess no mere rich man could hold a candle to her film aspirations. And she's really very good. I hear her latest film may get an Academy Award nomination next year."

"Good for her," Kate said.

"Yes. I like a success story. Like yours," she added with a smile. "Say, how would you like to fly up to New York with me and see the preparations for market week? You can meet our house model and some of the design staff and get acquainted. And I can photograph you all over Manhattan. It will make a great layout."

"I don't know," Kate hesitated. She tired easily these days, and she still had a lot of work to do.

"Just for the weekend," Roberta promised. "Come on. I'll get the tickets, make reservations for the hotel room, and shepherd you all over town. You'll love it."

Kate sighed. "Okay." She grinned.

"Good girl!"

It was all arranged in no time. Kate wore one of her own embroidered denim outfits, a full circle skirt with a slinky cowl blouse and an open vest, and carried only some casual things. She had no dressy dress except for the black crepe disaster, and she wasn't wearing that to New York to be laughed at. Besides, Roberta had promised her the loan of an original design from one of their own staff.

"Take care of yourself up there," Mary sighed as she told Kate good-bye in the San Antonio airport. Mr. Rogers had driven them there, and Roberta was waiting to accompany her.

"I'll be fine," Kate told her mother. She bent and kissed Mary's cheek. "Lock the doors at night. I'll phone you when I get checked into my hotel, okay?"

"Okay, darling." She hugged Kate once more and reluctantly said good-bye, watching her daughter disappear through the funny box beside the conveyer belt. Mary had never flown, and distrusted airplanes. But Mr. Rogers had promised that Kate would be well looked after.

Kate hadn't ever flown before, either, and her stomach felt distinctly queasy as she eased into the first-class seat beside Roberta when their flight was called.

"Want anything to drink?" Roberta asked her as the plane taxied out to the runway minutes later.

Kate felt sick. "No. Thank you."

"It might calm your stomach." Roberta grinned. "But if you'd rather not, they might have some milk or an antacid."

"It's all right," Kate groaned. "I'll be fine."

But she didn't feel fine. They taxied onto the runway and the plane shot up into the sky, leaving Kate's stomach behind. It felt like one of those space movies, where spaceships were launched and the pilots looked sick. That was how Kate felt. Her head was swimming and she wished she could find a wet cloth.

"Are you okay?" Roberta asked.

"Fine. Just a little nauseated," Kate whispered, leaning back with her eyes closed.

"How about a cold cloth?" the stewardess asked gently. "I'll bring you one, and some cracked ice."

"Thank you," Kate said, and had never meant the words more.

"Don't worry. Lots of people get sick the first time they fly," Roberta said comfortingly. She patted Kate's hand.

But Kate wasn't prone to motion sickness. It had been over a month since Jason had made love to her, and her period hadn't started. She'd assumed that it was emotional upset, because of all the pressure, that had made her late. But this sickness that came so suddenly so often, her paleness, and the ease with which she tired were adding up to lullabies.

"We'll be there before you know it," Roberta assured her. She ordered a gin and tonic with her lunch. Kate drank one cup of black coffee and prayed for the plane to land.

It did, hours later, and then came the long walk from the terminal to the main building, the longer wait at the baggage claim, and then the wait for a taxi into the city.

By the time they weaved over bridges, through tunnels and city traffic, past graffiti-sprayed walls and down wide, crowded streets to the hotel, Kate was ready to throw up her hands and jump in the river. She couldn't remember a time in her life when she'd felt worse.

But oddly enough, it wasn't her possible pregnancy that disturbed her the most. It was how she was going to conceal it from her mother and Jason, if it really was pregnancy. She knew she wasn't going to have anything done about it. She'd wanted babies as long as she could remember. And Jason's, despite their parting, would be a dream come true. She loved him so much. If she never saw him again, that would never end. A baby would be a part of him that she could keep and love and take care of. A little boy with dark hair and dark eyes....

"Here we are," Roberta said brightly as the cab stopped in front of a huge Madison Avenue hotel.

"Wow," Kate sighed.

"It's the best. But so are you, kid." Roberta grinned. She paid the driver, who set their luggage out on the sidewalk for the hotel bellboy to pick up.

"I've never been in a hotel before," Kate whispered.

"Don't worry. Think of it as a restaurant with rooms. This one has a reputation for its Cajun cooking. You'll love it!"

Kate followed Roberta through carpeted space under crystal chandeliers to a desk where no one seemed to be a native American. Everyone had an accent, and Kate couldn't understand a word they said. On the other hand, she was just as unintelligible to them with her Texas drawl. The bell captain came for the bags and motioned the women to follow them, adding something that went right over Kate's head.

"I'll translate for you," Roberta chuckled as she put Kate into the elevator and pushed the tenth floor button.

"Nobody's from here," she wailed. "And you'll be gone. They'll never understand me."

"I'll take good care of you, Kate, my friend. You just leave it all to me. Here." She motioned Kate out of the elevator behind the bell captain, who stopped in front of one of the doors and held out his hand with a smile.

Roberta put the key into it. As he opened the door into the room, Kate caught her breath at the splendor of it. It was as nice as Jason's house on the inside.

"Like it?" Roberta asked, smiling at Kate's fascination. "Thanks," she told the bell captain, tipping him after he'd opened the curtains and turned the lights on.

After he left, Kate kicked off her shoes and looked out at the city with its endless traffic, horns, and sirens. Far away she spotted the river, and down below people scurried past like colorful ants.

"Everybody in the country must live here," Kate mused.

"Half of it, anyway. If you'll be all right for a while, I'll dash home and put up my stuff and check my messages. Then I'll come back for you and take you over to my office. Since it's Friday, there will still be some staff there. You can meet people."

"I'd like that," Kate sighed.

"Okay. Just relax."

"I'll do that, all right." Kate let her out, locked the door, and collapsed on the bed. She was asleep almost instantly.

A loud knocking at the door awakened her. She got up, stopping suddenly at the taste of nausea, then put her feet on the floor.

"I'm coming," she called.

She opened the door and there was Roberta, glaring at her. "Never open the door until you look through the peephole," she was cautioned. "This is the city, not rural Texas."

"I'll remember. Lord, I feel green," she murmured, and weaved toward the bathroom.

"You must have eaten something that didn't agree. Here, I've got an antacid. Try this." She handed Kate a pill. Kate took it, certain that an antacid wouldn't harm her even if she was pregnant. It did seem to help.

She bathed her face and went back into the room, where Roberta was talking to someone on the phone.

"I called your mother," she explained, handing out the receiver with a grin. "Want to tell her you're okay?"

"I think I'd better," Kate said sheepishly. "I went to sleep." She took the receiver. "Hi, Mom."

"What's this about being nauseated?" she was asked immediately. "You haven't picked up any of those viral things, have you?"

"I don't know," Kate replied. "I've been feeling pretty off-color lately. I think it's the pressure."

"I'm not surprised, the way you've pushed yourself. Was the trip all right?"

"It was fine. I'll be back Sunday afternoon. Are you sure you don't mind that drive to pick me up?"

"Not one bit," she assured Kate. "You have fun."

"I'll try. I'll bring you back a present," she promised.

"No, you don't. You spend your money on yourself. I don't need anything."

Kate smiled. "Okay." But she knew she would. She always brought Mary something, even if she just went into San Frio shopping.

"Okay. Be good. I love you."

"I love you, too, Mama," she said gently. "Good night."

She put the receiver down with a sigh. "What do we do now?"

"We travel," Roberta laughed. She was wearing a neat blue business suit with epaulets, which had been designed by one of the staff.

The office was on Seventh Avenue, the heart of the textile district. Kate saw men moving racks of clothing along the sidewalk, trucks loading and unloading, the logos of manufacturing companies everywhere. They came to a building that boasted Clayborn's logo, and Kate felt a surge of pride.

"That's us!" she enthused.

"You bet, that's us." Roberta led her into another elevator—there seemed to be nothing else in this city—and they went up to the offices.

It was a lot like the company back home, except that everyone dressed to the hilt. One woman particularly caught Kate's eye—a black woman with elegant carriage, and the look of royalty.

"Who is she?" Kate asked Roberta. "She's beautiful."

The black woman heard her and turned, her chin at an arrogant angle.

"I'm sorry," Kate flushed. "But you carry yourself so well…most people slouch."

"I never slouch," the woman said with a faint Southern accent. She looked Kate up and down, and she didn't smile. "That's very nice," she said. "You designed it?"

"Yes."

"You must be the Texas girl."

"Not girl. Designer," Roberta said shortly. She glared at the woman, who averted her eyes and went back to work. "Don't mind Clarisse," she told Kate. "She thinks she's God's sister."

Kate wasn't listening. She was watching the woman's back stiffen, even though she didn't reply or even turn her head. There was pain in that exquisite carriage, and more than a little fear. Odd, when the woman was so lovely.

"This is Bates. She's our head designer." Roberta indicated a heavyset woman of fifty or so with black hair, snapping eyes, and a ready smile. "And these are the other girls." She introduced at least six more women, whose names went right past Kate. "And Clarisse LeBon, you met," Roberta added, indicating the black woman who was standing apart from the others, putting trim on a dress that graced a fitting form.

Kate went through the motions. She talked to the women and made modest noises when they spoke favorably about her own designs. She toured the office and looked at their own sketches and sample garments for the coming shows. It was no surprise at all to discover that Clarisse was the house model.

"She doubles as receptionist and secretary during slow seasons," Roberta told her, glaring toward the black woman. "If she'd unbend a little, she might go further. I hear she has design ambitions of her own, but she'll never get a chance with her nose in the air. She's been here three months and none of us like her."

"She's the only black woman in this office," Kate said gently. "Didn't it ever occur to you that she might feel uncomfortable?"

Roberta eyed her curiously. "You're from Texas, aren't you?"

"Of course. But that doesn't make me a bigot," Kate returned.

Robert shook her head. "Well, well. Miss enigma."

"I don't know what that means," Kate replied. "But I like people."

"What a story I'm going to get about you," the shorter woman mused. "Okay. Let's go see about that dress I promised to loan you. There's a cocktail party tonight that I want to take you to."

"I don't drink." Kate winced.

Roberta's eyes grew a size larger for a second. "Well, don't worry," she said. "You can imbibe club soda if you'd like."

The dress they found for Kate was a rainbow of colors, muted and soft, on sheerest chiffon with an underlay of satin. It had a fitted bodice and spaghetti straps, a cinched waist and a skirt that had to have at least six yards of fabric in it. It was the most beautiful thing Kate had ever seen, and it was almost a perfect fit, except for the waist.

"I thought you were a perfect ten." Roberta frowned when the zipper wouldn't close.

"I am." Kate sighed. "Well," she hedged, "I've put on a little weight lately. Too many sundaes and milkshakes," she added, neglecting to mention her possible pregnancy that was more than likely the real reason.

"We can let it out."

"Who made this beautiful thing?" Kate asked gently. "I did."

Clarisse stared at Kate without smiling, but there was something in that high-cheekboned face. Pride. Satisfaction.

"It's like a butterfly," Kate told her, smiling despite the lack of response. "I feel frumpy just wearing it. It needs a face like yours to set it off, not a plain one like mine."

Clarisse's face changed. It was almost imperceptible,

but Kate caught it. "You aren't plain," the other woman said. "Your face has character. You have good bones, and you carry yourself well. No. You carry the dress off much better than I would have."

Roberta went off to get Bates to do the hem, which was a fraction of an inch too long. Kate stared at Clarisse.

"You were supposed to have worn this, weren't you?" Kate asked. "I won't go…!"

"You will," Clarisse shot back. "I don't mind loaning it to you. I have another for myself. A different style with a similar fabric."

"I hate cocktail parties anyway," Kate muttered softly. "I don't drink and I think I'm pregnant…." She'd blurted it out. Now she started, her breath catching in her throat as she wondered if it had been wise to trust that secret to a woman who didn't like her.

But Clarisse only smiled. And it was a real smile. "I won't tell them," she said quietly. "You aren't married."

Kate shook her head. She looked down at the floor, remembering the sight of Jason's back as he walked out of her life. "He didn't want commitment, you see."

"But you love him."

Kate looked up, her eyes blazing with it. "Oh, God, yes," she whispered huskily. "And I want this baby. I've never wanted anything so much, not even a career."

"Why not have both?" Clarisse asked. She bent to the hem, ignoring the shocked looks on Roberta's and Bates's faces. "Here, I can do it," she volunteered. "May I have the pins, please?"

It wasn't until later, when they were on the way to the cocktail party in a cab, that Roberta mentioned that incident.

"I could have fainted when I saw Clarisse pinning up

that hem. She'd raised hell about your wearing the dress in the first place. And now she seems to like you, when she hates the rest of us. What did you do to her?"

"I told her a secret," Kate said, and glanced out the window at the beautiful city lights. "And it's still a secret," she added with a wicked grin.

Kate got through the party by the skin of her teeth because the nausea and fatigue were almost unbearable in combination. She met Roberta's brother, Curt—the Curt whose designs were internationally known—and had time for another longer and interesting chat with Clarisse, with whom she formed an unexpected friendship. And it hadn't been at all bad. Kate found that people accepted her just as she was. And they were kind enough to explain the things they discussed that were foreign to Kate's lifestyle. It wasn't at all as Jason had led her to believe. She learned, in fact, that people were people, regardless of the geography.

By the time she and Roberta got back to her hotel room, she felt as if she'd had a taste of another world, and not at all an unpleasant world. And with that, Kate fell into a deep sleep.

CHAPTER ELEVEN

MANHATTAN WAS FASCINATING. Kate spent the next day after the interview with Roberta, learning the shops and visiting with some of the marketing people. The hectic pace was a little rough, but it had kept her mind from brooding over Jason and her possible pregnancy at least.

Despite the fact that it was Saturday, Roberta seemed to know where to find everybody. They gave Kate the grand tour, and she learned rapidly that New Yorkers weren't the cold people that they were labeled. They were warm and friendly up close, and Kate couldn't remember a place that had made her feel more welcome.

But the day was a long one, and her head was swimming with facts and figures when they got back to the hotel. Roberta invited her to supper with her and her famous brother, but Kate only wanted sleep.

"Your brother is a character," Kate remarked with a smile as they parted company in the lobby.

"He likes you, too." Roberta grinned. "He was fascinated with the way you made friends with our Clarisse. So was I," she added. "She's not a friendly person."

"She's a scared, bitter, disillusioned person, though," Kate said gently. "And she's had a hard time of it. If people meet her halfway, she's very nice. You'll all find that out eventually."

"Maybe we'd better give her a second look." Roberta

grinned. "Well, I've got all my photos and enough for ten interviews. I hope we'll see each other again after I put you on that plane to San Antonio tomorrow. It's been an experience."

"I hope we do, too. I've enjoyed it," Kate said, and meant it. "Roberta, those merchandise mart shows, will I go to them, too?"

"We've scheduled you for Dallas and Atlanta, for certain," she was told. "Think you'll feel up to it, after the flurry of getting ready for the markets?"

"I hope so," Kate replied.

"It would really be to your advantage to go, Kate," Roberta said gently. "Even if you have to push yourself. I can introduce you to the media in both places, and you'll have southern and southwestern coverage. That will do us a lot of good in our regional sales, and I think your biggest market will be in those areas."

"If it makes that much difference, then certainly I'll go," Kate said.

"Good. I'll make the arrangements. Mr. Rogers can put you on the right planes, and we'll have marketing people meet you." She smiled. "Now get some rest, and don't worry about tomorrow. I won't send you to Hawaii or Italy, I promise. How are you feeling, by the way? Tummy better?"

"Some," Kate said. "But I think I'm just tired."

"As much time as you've put in, no wonder," Roberta said. "You get some sleep. I'll leave a wake-up call for you at the desk, and I'll be here to pick you up at eight sharp. Okay?"

Kate smiled. "Okay."

She waved Roberta off and went upstairs, dragging a little. She didn't like to think about going home because she was surely going to have to see a doctor. She wondered if Jason had said when he was coming home. Not that it mattered. She didn't know how she was going to cope, but she had to make a decision soon as to whether or not to tell him about the baby. If there was a baby, she corrected. But her symptoms were pretty concrete. And a baby was a hard thing to hide in a small community. If she decided not to tell him, she'd have to go somewhere else. That would be easier for her anyway, if her designs sold. Everything hinged on that. Kate had to support the baby. If the designs didn't market well, she was back to sewing on the line and textiles were a depressed industry. There might not be a job at some other plant.

She put on her gown and went to bed, not even calling Mary. She was too tired. Besides, she'd be going home to Texas in the morning.

The flight back was only a little easier than the flight to New York. Kate felt queasy the whole way, and this time the stewardess had her eye on a rich businessman a couple of seats behind Kate and spent the entire flight catering to his needs. Kate managed to get down a cup of coffee, but she couldn't eat anything.

Once on the ground in San Antonio, her mother's face in the waiting area was the most beautiful sight she'd ever seen. She rushed toward her, feeling the ceiling move toward her. Before she could reach her mother's arms, she fainted dead away on the terminal floor under a painting of a Texas windmill.

She came to lying on a couch in an office. Mary was hovering worriedly and there was a damp paper towel over Kate's fevered forehead.

"Goodness," she exclaimed, sitting up. "I can't imagine how that happened."

Mary tried to smile, but she looked pale herself, and worried. "Poor baby," she said, sighing. "Poor, poor baby."

"I'm all right," Kate said soothingly. "I just fainted, that's all. Where am I?"

"In the security office," she was told. "Can you walk, darling?"

"Of course." She stood up, feeling oddly fit. She even smiled. "Okay. Let's go wait for my luggage and then we can go home. I've got so much to tell you."

The security man came in the door as they were going out, and Mary thanked him and helped Kate out into the hall. The baggage was just shooting out onto the round claim ring, and Kate found her case immediately.

"No," Mary said, when Kate would have picked it up. "Don't you dare, in your condition."

Kate gaped at her mother.

Mary touched her daughter's hair. "Oh, baby, I'd never have let you go if I'd even suspected...."

"How do you know, when I don't even know for sure?" Kate asked in a hoarse whisper.

"Darling, you never faint," Mary said gently. "Or go white as a sheet. Your skirt is unbuttoned because your waistline is thicker, and you haven't had your period. I was pregnant with you. I remember the symptoms."

"I guess I thought I was going to get away with pretending it hadn't happened," Kate said on a sigh. "Most girls don't get pregnant the first time."

"Most girls are prepared," Mary replied. "Does he know?"

Kate assumed an innocent stare. "Does who know?"

"Don't insult my intelligence," Mary said, holding

Kate's arm to guide her along toward the exit. "Who else?"

"Another hopeless subterfuge," Kate laughed. "You're the limit, Mother."

"I'm smart, that's what I am. I should never have gone to that movie," she said shortly.

Kate flushed wildly. "It was my fault."

"It was not," Mary returned. "It takes two. He could have stopped, or you could have. I'm ashamed of both of you. Sex isn't a toy, or an amusement. It's for making babies and keeping a marriage happy."

"Now you tell me," Kate mused.

"I kept telling you. You just didn't listen. And he's still in Australia. Nobody's even heard from him." She glared at Kate. "If he doesn't come back, you'll write to him. It's his baby. It's his responsibility."

"We'll talk about that when we get home," Kate said firmly.

"There's nothing to talk about." Mary tried not to sound smug. At last, Kate was going to be looked after, even if she never became a designer. Jason would marry her, of course. And money would never be a problem for her baby again. Or her grandbaby. She felt glowingly happy. All that, and a son-in-law like Jason to boot. What a stroke of luck.

Kate didn't feel the same exultation, though. She was wondering how she was going to keep her secret until she knew Jason's heart. Her mother was going to be a major obstacle.

"Don't you dare tell anybody," she warned Mary as they climbed into the black Tempo. "Not one person. I swear I'll vanish if you do."

Mary stared at her. Kate was usually a sweet, obedient

little soul who never made trouble. But this determined woman didn't sound like Kate. She was at once more mature, more sensible. Mary sighed. "All right, baby," she agreed, when she saw that Kate meant it. "It's your right to tell Jason. I won't interfere."

"Thank you." She touched her mother's hand gently, and smiled. "I know what I'm doing. At least, now I do. And babies are sweet, whether or not they have the right name. I want this one, so much."

"Well, I never doubted that," Mary said, and she smiled back. "I know how you feel about Jason. I knew before you did."

The problem was, how did Jason feel about her?

Kate took the next day off because she was still tired out from her trip. Mr. Rogers agreed that it wouldn't hurt their schedule. And Mary went to work, reluctantly. Two hours later, Kate was in Dr. Harris's office, and hearing something that she was already expecting to hear.

"I'll phone you tomorrow after we have the results from the pregnancy test," he said. "But there's nothing they're going to tell me that I don't already know."

Kate sat quietly in his office, absorbing it. While it had only been a threat, she hadn't been afraid. Now she was. The thought of being responsible for a little human being was terrifying.

"Scared to death?" he asked gently, and smiled at her startled expression. "That's normal, believe it or not. We're all scared to death at first. But considering that the human body doesn't come with an instruction manual, people have done pretty well over the centuries."

"I'm not married," she said.

"When Jason finds out, you will be," he said imperturbably.

Kate went beet red. "Don't you dare…!"

"I'm a doctor," he reminded her. "You know, oath of silence, privileged information, not even if he tortures me, that kind of thing."

"And how do you know it's his?" Kate asked curtly.

He only smiled. "Who else could it belong to?"

"Maybe somebody I met in the night…."

"Cut it out," he interrupted. "I'm too busy to sit and listen to fairy tales. I delivered you, for God's sake. Don't you think I know that you'd never be intimate with a man you didn't love? Mary raised you that way. And Jason, despite this obvious setback, helped her instill those repressions."

"Some setback," she sighed. "Now what do I do? You know how Jason feels about marriage."

"Most men feel that way, until they become husbands and fathers. He likes children, Kate."

"There's just one thing," she said hesitantly.

"Well?"

She shifted in the chair. "I had a little spotting last night. And some cramps, just for a few minutes." He looked concerned, and she decided not to mention the other times she'd had it. She didn't want to have to face the possibility that she could lose this baby.

He folded his arms across his chest and perched against his examination table. "Let me explain something about first pregnancies to you," he began. "Sometimes, for reasons no one really understands, things go wrong. There can be an abnormality in the fetus, or even in the mother's reproductive system. Whatever the reason, the womb expels the fetus. That's called spontaneous abortion. Now symptoms like yours very often herald that." He held up a hand when she stared to interrupt. "Let me finish. I'm not saying that you'll lose the baby. I'm telling you that it can happen."

"What can I do?"

"We can do an ultrasound and an amniocentesis in a couple of weeks. That may tell us if there's an abnormality, but in all honesty, Kate, it doesn't about ninety-five percent of the time, and it can't guarantee a baby without defects." He shrugged. "There are simply no tests at present to reveal all the abnormalities. And if we found one," he continued, his eyes narrowing as he watched her expression, "would you want an abortion?"

She shuddered. "I know it would be sensible. But..."

"But, you couldn't," he said, smiling gently. "So, the only other alternative is that you can go to bed for the duration. You can avoid exertion, or emotional surges, and you can live like a nun. And after all that care, you can still lose the baby."

"You're not very encouraging," she sighed.

"On the other hand, you can go on living a normal life," he continued. "And if you're meant to have that baby, nothing will stop it from being born."

"That sounds metaphysical," she said with a faint smile.

He smiled back. "I'm a doctor. I've delivered a lot of babies. Sometimes a child with everything against it will grow up to be a football player. Sometimes a very healthy child dies, for no apparent reason. Miscarriage is a risk every pregnant woman takes. And, Kate, you're young and very healthy. One episode of cramps and spotting isn't necessarily the start of a miscarriage. So stop worrying." He jerked away from the table. "I'll write you a prescription for some prenatal vitamins that will help you lift Mack trucks, and something for the morning sickness. Then I'll refer you to a good obstetrician in San Antonio."

"That's a long way."

"It's a good hospital. And the obstetrician and I went through medical school together."

She watched him scribble on his prescription pad. "If I don't tell Jason, you won't?"

He finished writing and handed her two prescriptions. The look he gave her through his spectacles was a speaking one.

"All right. I'll tell him," she muttered.

"I'll have Becky get you an appointment with Ben Johnson and call you with the day and time. More than likely, it will be a month or so before he has an opening because he's good. Anyway, you're just in the early stages, and I'll look after you. If you have any more spotting or cramps, I want to know. All right?"

She almost told him. She tried. But she was so afraid of what he might say. She only nodded.

"And stop worrying."

She opened her mouth.

"I know, that's easy for me to say," he stole her thunder, and grinned as he let her out of the office. "I'll phone you the test results," he said. "But don't expect any surprises."

"I wasn't," she confessed, and smiled as she went out to pay Joan, his receptionist.

She felt odd, as if everyone was looking at her, smirking at her. It made her feel cheap, and she flushed as she paid the bill.

Before she could leave, Becky came out in her white uniform and pulled her out the door, away from the eyes and ears of six other patients.

"Nobody's staring at you," Becky told her gently, and smiled. She'd been a nurse for a long time, and she had a heart as big as her buxom body. "And nobody's going to look down on you. For heaven's sake, everybody will know that it's Jason's, and that he'll make it right," she chuckled. "Now go tell him."

"I think you're terrific," Kate said impulsively, and hugged the older woman. Then, before she could burst into tears, she ran for the safety of the Tempo.

Amazing, she thought as she drove home, how everyone was certain that the baby was Jason's. But Kate wondered if Jason would be equally certain. Perhaps because of the friction between them, he'd automatically suspect it was some other man's. He might even think that Kate had used him as a stepping stone to other men. That thought was sickening.

She stopped by the pharmacy and had her prescriptions filled before she remembered that the petite brunette who was the druggist's clerk was a friend of Cherry Donavan's. But chances were slim that she'd mention them to Cherry. The girl might not even know that Cherry was acquainted with the Kate Whittman on the prescriptions.

After she finished at the pharmacy, she stopped by the town's only drive-in and got herself a strawberry milkshake. It probably wouldn't be the best source of protein, but it was delicious and it stayed down.

It was a beautiful summer day. The fields, underneath beautiful blue skies, were still dotted with wildflowers. As Kate sipped her milkshake, she found herself oddly at peace with the world. Well, creation made her one with the earth, after all. The trees put out new leaves in spring. The grass sprang from seed. So did flowers and vegetables and fruit. The earth was constantly in the business of renewal, and now Kate was part of it. Her fertile body had absorbed a seed and would produce a small, human fruit. It seemed profound.

She turned into the dirt driveway that led up to the white clapboard house she shared with Mary and almost went into the ditch when she saw the big Ford Bronco parked at the steps. Jason was standing beside it, smoking a cigarette.

With trembling hands, she managed to stop the car and park it without undue commotion. He looked as if he'd been working. He was in denim jeans, very dusty, with his old boots and black hat and a thin blue-checked Western shirt. He lifted his chin as she got out of the Tempo, and Kate's heart ran away at just the sight of that lean, powerful body. Time hadn't helped her hunger for him.

"Hello, Jason," she said gently.

His dark eyes went over the denim skirt and sleeveless blue blouson top she was wearing with a singular lack of visible emotion. And when Kate saw his face up close, she was sure that the weeks away had closed up the last cracks in his shell. He was free of her. He looked at her as if she were a stranger.

"Kate," he acknowledged. "You look well."

She forced a smile to her numb lips and lifted the milkshake to them. "I should. I can afford junk food now."

He took another draw from the cigarette. She looked paler than he remembered, but there was a new maturity about her. "Yes. I suppose you can." He wanted to tell her he'd missed her, but he was too used to holding things inside. Even now, he couldn't express emotion.

"How was your trip?"

"It was productive," he replied. Productive, hell, he thought bitterly as his eyes ate her. He'd spent five of those long weeks trying to put the memory of her out of his mind, and the last one resigning himself to the fact that he never could. He'd actually thought he could walk away from her. Until he'd tried.

"Thanks for all the postcards," she said with a short, bitter laugh.

"I had better things to do than send postcards." He tilted his hat back. "I was doing my best to forget that you even existed, if you want the truth," he added curtly. "My conscience hurt for a while, but I got over it. I guess you did, too," he said pointedly, in an attempt to smoke her out. He didn't want to expose himself to any new wounds until he found out how she felt. Oh, God, she had to care about him. She had to!

But Kate was as cautious as he was, and she couldn't see through his mask. She took his words at face value. So his conscience didn't bother him anymore. Only his conscience, not his heart. All right, she thought, if that's how you want it, if you want me to absolve you from the guilt, I can do that.

"Yes, I got over it," she told him easily. "Like you, I didn't take it to heart." She thought that something touched his face, but she couldn't be sure. "You don't have to worry about my throwing myself at you." She managed a smile. "If you hadn't come over, I wouldn't have gone looking for you. It was all just a mistake. An accident. But no harm done."

Jason stared at her quietly. "I'm glad you're taking it so well," he said, his voice cold because he'd had dreams. A lot of dreams, about finding her sick with missing him, hungry to live with him, to share his life and give him children. And here she stood, putting her damned career first. Again.

"Oh, I'm doing fine," she replied airily. "I'm getting sophisticated. I've been to New York, and mingled with the social set. I'm even going back up there in November for market week."

He took a soothing draw from his cigarette and averted his eyes because sometimes she could read them. Yes, she'd have her career. She'd be independent. There might be other men, now, and she'd learn how to cope with a social lifestyle—the difficulties he'd taunted her with wouldn't matter. He'd known they wouldn't from the beginning, but he wanted to keep her at home.

"You might try to look pleased for me," she said after a minute. The milkshake was freezing her fingers, and she changed hands with it. "Although I guess you really aren't. You never wanted me to have a career in the first place."

"That's right, I didn't. But now I don't give a damn." His eyes challenged, mocked. "I just wanted to make sure you weren't hoping for a proposal of marriage. Sorry, but I don't feel that guilty."

She'd never had anything hurt so much. If she'd seen his face, she'd have known that he was lying through his teeth, but she didn't.

She had to grit her teeth. "Neither do I," she replied.

"Of course not. You're going to be a career girl. Maybe. Personally, I don't think you'll fit into that kind of lifestyle any more than you would have fit into mine," he said deliberately. "You'd never have managed that, judging from the way you handled yourself at the dinner Cherry invited you to."

Her face flamed. She glared at him. "I'll learn," she returned. "I can learn. And most people aren't snobs, like that Daphne person."

"Go ahead and try, honey," he chided, broken up inside from her whole attitude. "Get famous. Get rich. But no matter how high up you get, you'll still be just plain little Kate Whittman from San Frio. You'll still be as country as a plow and as out of place in my world as a weed."

"I'm not a weed," she said huskily, fighting tears. She was carrying his child, and he wouldn't even give her a chance to tell him. He was making it impossible.

"Well, you're no orchid, either," he bit off. "Weeds are hearty. They have character and style and they serve a useful purpose in the order of things. An orchid looks pretty, but it doesn't survive well under hardship." He tilted his hat over one eye. "I'll tell you something, Kate. Given a choice, I'll take the weed every day. At least it's honest enough to be what it is, warts and all. It doesn't try to be something it was never meant to be."

"If that's a slam at me, trying to make something of myself, then I'll prove you wrong, Jason. I'll show you that I can pull myself up out of poverty by my own talent."

"To be a career woman," he taunted. "But it will never suit you. You're too homey, Kate. You like flower gardens and going barefoot in the summer. You'd be right at home surrounded by those squalling preschoolers you don't think you want. But you won't admit it."

She pulled herself erect, her face pale. How could he know that she wanted nothing more than what he'd just described, but she was going to have to settle for the career. Jason didn't want her for keeps. Only for an afternoon, just long enough to satisfy the hated desire she raised in him. But that loss of control would have been a weakness to him, and he'd fought to overcome it. He had, judging by his impassive expression. "That's right, Jason," she replied. "I don't want children."

He looked down at her stomach with black eyes. "Least of all mine," he breathed, his eyes shooting back up as she was about to speak. "And that's good, Kate, because I'd rather be impotent than risk giving a child to a woman who's already said that her career comes first. I've already seen how a career woman deals with an unwanted baby."

Kate felt as if he'd slapped her. She stared at him with the pain going all the way to her toes, swallowing her up. She'd made him believe that, she'd told him her career came first. It didn't, she'd only said it to spare his pride. But to do that, she'd had to sacrifice her own. Tears stung her eyes.

"A career woman can't afford to be tied down by a child," she agreed huskily.

His pride felt lacerated. He glared at her. "Then you'd better take a crash course in precautions before you spend another lazy afternoon with a man, honey," he said. Contempt glittered in his black eyes. "If you're going to be liberated like all the other free women, then you'd better be prepared for anything. Of course," he added icily, "there's always abortion."

Her hand clenched around the milkshake so hard that it almost ran out the top. "Yes," she said. "There's always…that."

Pain flashed over his face for an instant before he erased it. "So it's a good thing I didn't make you pregnant, isn't it?" he asked harshly.

She swallowed hard. "It's a good thing you didn't."

The sky started spinning around her. She couldn't know that he was striking out at her in his disappointment and loss, that he didn't mean a word of what he was saying. She almost threw his own lack of precautions at him, but that was too risky, he might guess about the baby.

"Well, you've sure got the makings of a party girl, honey," he added coldly. "You gave in to me fast enough."

She closed her eyes. She was getting sicker by the second. She had to make him leave before she fainted and aroused his suspicions.

Her eyes opened and she stared at him furiously. "You lost control, yourself, as I recall," she threw at him. "And you seemed to enjoy it enough at the time."

She hit the target. That remark got him in the heart, that attack in his weak spot, his pride. He couldn't even speak. His black eyes seared into hers for one long, hateful second. Then, without a word, without a single sound, he turned on his heel and got into the Bronco, driving away without looking at her.

Nothing had gone as he'd planned it. He'd meant to feel her out, to see if she cared anything about him, if she'd missed him. Now he had his answer. No, she hadn't missed him. She was only glad she wasn't pregnant because she didn't want him or his child.

He lit a cigarette with eyes that didn't see and drove blindly toward home, dreams lying dead in his black eyes.

Back at the Whittman house, Kate made it into the bathroom just in time to be agonizingly sick. Remembering Jason's taunt about preferring impotence to fathering her child made the nausea even worse. Then she remembered what she'd said to him. Tears rolled down her white cheeks. Amazing, that it could be so painful to hurt him, even when he deserved it. The nausea came again, and cramps with it, but she prayed even now that she wouldn't lose the baby.

CHAPTER TWELVE

IT WAS LATE afternoon before Kate got over the shock of what Jason had said to her. The harsh speech was totally unexpected. Part of her had believed that everything would be all right when he knew about the baby. But he hadn't given her the chance to tell him.

She went through the motions of housework, but she was worried about the future. She couldn't stay in San Frio now. She was going to have to go somewhere else to live, and that might mean the loss of her job. Clayborn had other divisions, though, and perhaps she could work for the one in San Antonio. There would be an apartment to get, and she'd have to be without her mother at a time when she was going to need her desperately. Not that people would gang up and tar and feather her. No, it would be a much more subtle kind of torment than that. Pitying looks. Whispers. The kind of small cuts that killed pride. And not only she and her mother would have to bear it. So would the Donavans, because everyone would know that Jason was the father.

She wondered how she was going to break the news about the argument to her mother. She decided that it would be best to wait until the next day. Mary had borne enough lately. She could have one more good night's sleep before she knew. She went into the kitchen and started supper, her mind riveted to the future and how she and the baby would cope. If they would. Dr. Harris's ominous words about the possibility of a miscarriage were still ringing in her ears, complicating her problems. She hadn't meant what she'd said to Jason, about getting rid of her baby, but if she lost it, those words might come back to haunt her.

SEVERAL HOURS LATER, Cherry Donavan sat down absently in the dining room where Gene was waiting impatiently for Sheila to serve dinner. He looked up from a book on art, glaring.

"Where have you been?" he grumbled. "First Jason goes off into his study with a bottle of whiskey for supper, and then you vanish."

"I had to go into San Frio to get my allergy medicine refilled," Cherry murmured.

"Hey. What's wrong?" he asked, aware that her expression was deeply troubled, not like her at all.

She sighed. "Oh, Gene," she whispered, biting her lip as she cast a watchful eye toward the doorway.

"Well?" he asked, impatient now.

"Kate Whittman's taking prenatal vitamins," she whispered.

He stared at her without total comprehension. "So?"

"And medication for morning sickness," she added.

He sat very still, hardly moving at all. "She's pregnant?"

"Debbie thinks so. She works for Dr. Cadez at the pharmacy. Not that she'd tell just anybody," she said firmly, "but she knows that Kate and I are friends." She shrugged. "I never thought Kate would get in trouble. I mean, she hasn't been near a man in months except…" Her eyes widened like saucers. "Except Jason."

Gene said something curt under his breath. "I wonder

if he knows. He left earlier and when he came back, he took that bottle in there. You know, he hasn't touched a drop in three years. If Kate had told him, he sure as hell wouldn't be drinking. He'd be over at her place browbeating her into marriage." He got up. "You stay here," he said. "I don't want you around Jay when he's sauced up. And keep Sheila out. I may get my nose broken for what I'm about to ask him."

"Oh, Gene, be careful!"

"Don't worry, I know how to handle him," he said, and mentally crossed his fingers.

He went to the study door and knocked gently. He waited, but there wasn't a sound. He knocked again, louder.

"Hell!" came a rough reply. "Come in."

He opened the door. Jason was sitting behind the desk with a brandy snifter in his hand, but it didn't contain brandy. It was filled to the top with whiskey.

"Come right in, little brother," he said with a cold smile. It was like old times, before Kate had come along to make the hard man laugh. This was the Jason that Gene remembered from childhood, the one who'd shouldered a man's burden barely out of his teens. The world beater.

Gene closed the door behind him and leaned back against it. Damn it, Jason made him feel like a kid. "You haven't done that in a while," he remarked, nodding toward the snifter.

"I haven't needed to for a while. I need it right now." He toasted Gene and downed several swallows. "Not bad. It takes the edge off, anyway."

"Jay, have you seen Kate today?" he asked.

Jason glared at him. His head tilted at an arrogant angle. "Yes, I've seen her," he said curtly.

Gene pushed a little harder. "And…?"

Jason shifted uncomfortably. "She looked straight through me and gave me the rundown on how her career's taking off, on how rich and famous she's going to be." He took another swallow of whiskey. "What the hell do I care. I don't want some damned career girl. I told her so," he added with a hard glance in Gene's direction. "I told her what she could do with her career, and how far."

Gene's eyes closed. It was worse than he'd dreamed. They'd argued again, and this time Jay had dug his own grave. Why, Gene didn't understand. There was a part of Jason Donavan that nobody ever saw; a hidden part that kept secrets of any emotion he might feel. Even Gene didn't know how he really felt about Kate. He wasn't that privileged. Only God was.

"Why did you ask me that?" Jason demanded.

Gene moved closer. He didn't want Sheila to hear. "Jay, Kate picked up a prescription in San Frio today," he began quietly. "For prenatal vitamins and morning sickness pills."

Jason didn't move. He didn't breathe. But suddenly, without warning, his work-strong hands, lean and dark-skinned, contracted around the brandy snifter and shattered it, sending glass and whiskey everywhere. The face that never showed emotion contorted with it, went white.

"Oh, God, no," he breathed.

Gene heard stark horror in his brother's husky exclamation. Jason got to his feet, knocking over the chair, and moved past Gene toward the door.

"Jay, wait a minute, I'll drive you."

"Oh, God!" was all the reply he got. Jason was out the door and gone before Gene could make it to the steps.

Jason had never felt such cold terror in all his life. He remembered vividly now the things he'd said to Kate, her white face and deathly stillness as he flung those insults at her. She wouldn't fit into his world, he'd said. He didn't feel guilty enough to marry her, and that she had the makings of a party girl....

He felt sick all over as he gunned the Bronco down the road and broke speed limits getting to the Whittman place. He didn't know how in hell he was going to convince Kate that she had to marry him now, after what he'd said to her. He cared about her, but she wasn't going to believe it anymore.

The lights were on, so she had to be home. He jerked out of the Bronco and onto the front porch, knocking hard and urgently.

Mary answered it, frowning slightly at his face. "Jason?" she asked, because she hardly recognized this bareheaded, haggard looking man who smelled like a brewery.

"Kate," he whispered hoarsely. "Where is she?"

So he knew. Mary relaxed a little. "She's in the kitchen, working on some new sketches...."

He went past her without breaking stride.

Kate was just adding a new embroidery pattern to a sketch when she heard voices, then heavy, quick footsteps. She looked up, and there was Jason.

She made herself sit very still. She looked at him with all the contempt she could manage, almost hating him for the torment she'd been through since his visit.

"You know," she guessed, reading it in the undisguised horror in his face. "Do you feel guilty enough to marry me now, Jason?"

She sounded tormented, and he felt sick. He reached down and caught her arms, pulling her up very gently to stand before him while he tried to find the right words to mend the wound he'd caused.

"Why didn't you tell me?" he ground out.

"I'm glad I didn't," she said with her pride intact. "I'm glad I found out first how you really felt. I was just another body in place, wasn't I?" she laughed bitterly. "Just another conquest, and you don't want me to have your baby…!"

"Don't!" He pulled her against him, enveloping her, his face in her throat as he rocked her. His tall, powerful body trembled, and his breathing was unsteady. "Kate, I didn't mean it. I swear to God I didn't mean it. I didn't know you were pregnant."

Tears stung her eyes. If he hadn't been drinking, and he had because she could smell whiskey all over him, she might have been less rigid. But it was the liquor talking. He'd found out about the baby, God knew how, and now he'd come running, full of fortified remorse, to make everything right. Except that nothing was right. Least of all, a proposal spurred by an illegitimate child.

"If you're here to ask me to marry you, it will be a waste of breath," she said, her eyes staring past his dark head at the ceiling. "I don't want to marry you."

He lifted his head after a minute, scowling. "And what about the baby?" he asked.

"The baby won't be a problem," she returned curtly, and meant it. It would be hers, and she'd be everything it would ever need.

"You'll get rid of it, is that what you mean?" he asked. His eyes were terrible with the memory of what she'd said outside, in the yard, just before he left earlier in the day. "You'll have it removed, like an unsightly birthmark…?!"

"No!" She put her soft hand over his mouth, guilt-ridden about that impulsive lie. "No! Oh, Jason, I didn't mean that," she whispered tearfully. "I'd never do anything to hurt the baby."

He actually shuddered. The memory of Melody doing exactly that haunted him for years. Did Kate mean it, or was she just trying to make amends? Carving a career was going to be rough with her pregnancy.

He drew in a deep breath. He had to reason it out. He had to make her see sense. But it was damned hard, when he was all but shaking inside at the sight of her. Everything had gone wrong so suddenly. Kate had been all the color in his dark world, and he'd driven her away because she'd wanted her career more than him. She'd accused him of losing control, and she was right. He'd done this to her. He'd lost his head and hadn't protected her, and she was pregnant.

"Who told you?" she asked quietly. "Was it Dr. Harris?"

"No, and never mind who told me," he returned. He searched her wan face. "Are you all right?"

"No, I'm not all right," she replied. She sounded and felt cold. Ice cold. "I'm sick and alone and I've never been so frightened in all my life...!"

"It's my baby, too," he whispered. He touched her dark hair, savoring its silky feel. "There's nothing to be afraid of. I'll take care of you."

"I don't want you to take care of me," she said shortly. "I don't want you."

"Yes, I know." He drew her cheek against his chest and held her there. His eyes closed when she quieted and he felt the wet shock of tears even through the thin fabric. She needed him, and he liked that. It gave him a small hold on her, even if she blamed him for her condition.

"Listen," he said at her head, while he stroked it, trying a different tack, "whatever our own feelings, we can't turn our backs on family, Kate. Your mother and my brother and Cherry shouldn't have to live down what we've done."

"You said you'd hate me for trapping you..." she began.

He drew her chin up and looked at her. "Damn my soul, I said a lot. I told you I didn't mean half of it."

"You meant it," she replied coldly. "And I won't trap you into marriage. I can go to San Antonio to live and have the baby there."

"That's no solution at all." He set his jaw. "Listen, honey, I'm not having you away from me while you're carrying my child. You can have separate bedrooms, if that's what you want. But you'll marry me if I have to carry you kicking and screaming to the altar. For the baby's sake, if not ours." She still hesitated, and he asked bluntly, "Kate, do you want people to call him a bas..."

"No, I don't want that." She stared at his chest miserably, her eyes still wet with tears of bitter regret. Not like this, she thought. Not like this. Marriage should be because two people loved each other, not as a punishment. She sighed wearily. She was so tired. "All right, Jason. I'll marry you."

He couldn't remember ever feeling so helpless. But at least he'd managed to convince her to marry him. That was encouraging.

"Let's go and tell Mary." He took her hand in his and led her back into the living room, pulling her gently down beside him on the sofa. "Kate's pregnant," he told Mary without any softening or preamble, and he looked her straight in the eye. "It's mine. She isn't overjoyed about the prospect of marrying me, but I've browbeaten her into agreeing. Now how do you feel about having the wedding a week from Friday at the house? I could do it in three days under Texas law, but she's not going to want a rushed ceremony. I do," he added. He threw a sharp glance at Kate, who was numb with mental pain. "I'm convinced that she'll cut and run if she has time to think. But in a week we can get out invitations and we can buy her a dress at Neiman-Marcus."

"Cherry and I can arrange everything," Kate said quietly. "And I'll sew my own dress."

"Hell, no, you won't," he returned coldly. "Your damned career almost cost me that child you're carrying. I don't want you in the fashion business at all. Once you finish out this collection, you'll resign."

Kate stood up. "I won't."

"We can discuss it later."

"We won't discuss it at all, Jason," she snapped, determined to fight for her rights. It was now or never. "If I bow down to you now, I'll be doing it for the rest of my life. You aren't going to make a slave of me. I have a right to choose what I do with my life!"

"Sure you do. But not while you've got my baby under your heart," he said with dark intent. "I haven't forgotten what you said about careers and babies not mixing, and I don't damned well trust you!"

"Jason, damn you…oh!" She bent over suddenly, racked with pain.

Jason forgot the argument. He picked her up and sat down with her, cradling her. "Do you need the doctor?" he asked quickly.

"Just…let me sit…and breathe."

"Oh, baby," Mary moaned. She sighed heavily, touching the dark head lying on Jason's broad shoulder. She met his repentant eyes. "You can't upset her. Not now, of all times," she whispered.

"I should have known that," he said. He held her closer. "Honey, is it any better?"

"It's easing off." Only a little, but she didn't want him to know that. She'd had twinges like this before, and a good deal of spotting. She remembered with horror what Dr. Harris had said. She wondered if it was honest to withhold that information from Jason. Things were so strained between them that it seemed impossible to communicate with him at all, and she'd already made him doubt her intentions.

"We won't talk about the future," he said firmly. "There won't be any more arguments. The baby has to be our first concern."

She sighed, looking up. She wanted to tell him that she had no intention of risking the baby, career or no career. But the words wouldn't come. She relaxed against him, weary. "All right."

Mary smiled at the picture they made. She'd never felt so smug in all her life. "I'll make some coffee."

"Should she have coffee?" Jason asked, his tone deep and concerned.

Mary winked at Kate. "A little won't hurt. I drank two pots a day while I was carrying her, and nothing happened. I didn't get cancer, either."

"Don't get her started," Kate moaned. "She's good for two hours on what she thinks of research studies."

"I'll remember that," he mused.

Mary vanished into the kitchen, and Jason looked down into Kate's wan little face hungrily, although he hid it immediately.

"I'm sorry," she said, searching his dark face. "I'm really sorry. I wasn't going to tell you at all...."

His face hardened. "I realize that," he said curtly. "No

doubt you'd have gone away and put the child up for adoption if I hadn't found you out by accident. Your career would have suffered otherwise, wouldn't it?"

Let him think what he liked. "At least you want the child," she said coldly.

"Yes," he agreed. "I want this child." She didn't know how desperately he wanted the child's mother as well. "Do you have an obstetrician?"

"Yes. Dr. Harris is getting me an appointment." She took a slow breath. "I'm a little scared," she confessed. "If anything went wrong…" She was going to add that Jason would probably blame her.

He interrupted. "Nothing's going to," he said shortly. He laughed bitterly. "My God, I'd go out of my mind if anything did, now."

That stopped her from telling him about her symptoms. She couldn't. She'd put the knife in her own back, with her taunt outside.

Her soft eyes searched his. "You do want this baby?" she whispered.

His gaze dropped to her waist and one lean, tender hand moved down past it to her flat abdomen. "I want it." He put more feeling into those three words than she'd ever heard in his deep voice.

Her fingers touched his hesitantly, and his hand turned to catch them, hold them.

"I won't fit into your world, Jason," she said suddenly. "You were right, I'll never manage…!"

He bent and kissed her forehead. "You'll learn. You said earlier that you could, now I'll let you prove it."

That was what bothered her. He'd tutor her and take her over, and the baby would be the wedge he used. He'd decide every move she made, every step she took and she'd have to fight for any inch of leeway she got from now on.

"I can't let you own me," she remarked. "You're a reactionary, Jason. You're the kind of man who won't let a woman breathe unless you tell her when and how. I can't bear being nothing but an extension of you."

He studied the warm hand in his. "I realize that," he replied. "You want fame and fortune, don't you? But that will have to wait, until this child is born. Afterwards," he added, searching her face coolly, "we'll discuss terms."

She drew in a slow breath. Now she knew that it was going to be a fight all the way. But marriage was an unexpected bonus, even if he hated her for trapping him. She and the baby might turn his life around. She might make him like captivity. So she gave in. "Okay."

He searched her eyes for a long moment. "There's one good thing, Kate," he said. "We know each other as well as two people ever do without actually living together. We've managed to get along for three years. Maybe we can regain the friendship we had."

Was that all he had left to offer, she wondered miserably. She sighed. "Yes, but don't you see, that wasn't on an intimate basis." She looked, and felt, worried. "You said I'd never fit in."

He stiffened. "You may need a little educating in social graces, not that Mary hasn't done well by you. But you'll handle yourself well enough. And once you join a few social groups...."

It was getting worse by the minute. She felt trapped already. "Social groups?"

"There are always coffees and teas and benefits," he said carelessly. "Things to welcome new people to the community or honor brides-elect, or help the poor. You'll learn all about that. Then there are the inevitable business conferences and business dinners. We do a lot of entertaining at the Spur, but Sheila will be a godsend when you start organizing them."

"I don't know if I can cope," she confessed nervously.

"You'll get the hang of it in no time. Now sit up. We've got some plans to finalize before I leave here. Stop worrying. Everything will work out," he promised.

But it wasn't going to be that easy, Kate knew it even if he was trying to pretend differently. She came from a totally different background than he did, from a different world. All the things he'd warned her about long ago, when he found out that she was ambitious, suddenly applied to their marriage. She wasn't the kind of woman he'd have chosen to marry, she was almost sure of it. But she was pregnant, and he wanted the baby, so he'd do whatever was necessary to get it.

She wondered as she heard him outlining the wedding ceremony what he really felt about having to marry her. He'd never tell her, she knew that. He wanted the baby, but she knew he didn't really want her.

TIME PASSED ALL too quickly. Kate went into work the next day despite Jason's objections and her mother's pleas. She couldn't stay home and think about things or she'd go crazy.

Dessie and the others were tickled about the forthcoming marriage, and their first question was about where was she going to get her gown.

"I wanted to design it myself," Kate sighed, sitting down heavily in her chair. "But he wants to have it from Neiman-Marcus."

"A waste of good talent," Dessie scoffed. "Honey, you

sketch that thing out and we'll donate the materials and the talent," she buffed her nails on her dress front with a haughty smile, "and we'll have you decked out in the prettiest outfit since Lady Di married the prince."

"But you don't have time…." Kate protested.

"We'll make it. Get busy," Dessie said.

The others seconded the offer. Kate gave in. Well, this was an act of rebellion, and it would irritate Jason. On the other hand, she had every right to design her own dress. At least this way, it would fit on the first try and there wouldn't be the inevitable alterations for her waistline from buying a perfect size at an exclusive store. She turned to her desk with a smile and opened a clean sheet on her pad.

Jason was there when she got off from work. She'd planned to wait until Mary finished her overtime, but now she could leave the car with her mother.

"Here," he said, "I'll take her the keys to the Tempo."

"But you can't go in, you're not an employee…."

Useless to tell him that. He just kept walking, towering over everyone as he went through the door that said "employees only." He was back scant minutes later, looking smug.

"Your mother thinks I'm the berries," he informed Kate as he slid into the front seat of the Mercedes beside her.

"You knew that already," she sighed. She leaned her head back against the leather seat and turned it sideways to study Jason's sharp features.

"Looking for male beauty?" he taunted. "Sorry, honey, ugly goes all the way to the bone, as the song says, so we'd both better hope that our boy takes after you."

"Our boy or our girl," she corrected. "And you're handsome enough."

He laughed softly, reaching into his shirt pocket for a cigarette as he drove. He was wearing suit slacks with a white silk shirt and tie. The jacket was helter-skelter in the backseat. He looked like a tired businessman, and Kate realized suddenly that she'd see him every day now.

"Why did you come after me?" she asked, curious.

"It seemed like a good idea. We're barely engaged. People might think it odd if I didn't."

"Oh. I see."

"No, you don't," he shot back. His dark eyes glittered across the seat at her. "You don't know me at all, Kate."

"You won't let me," she replied softly, and even laughed a little. "Nobody's that privileged in your life, Jason, not even me."

"People can hurt if they get close enough," he said. "I learned that the hard way, when I was just a kid." He laughed coldly as he drove, his face hard with the memories. "My dad used to put on a big show when I'd made him mad. He'd hold out his arms and smile at me, and talk really sweet. And then, when I was close enough to catch, he'd beat the hell out of me. I never knew when it was coming. I could never tell. It was safer to stay out of his reach—physically and emotionally."

"And now you stay out of everybody's reach because of it," she said. Hers, included.

"That might have been different if my mother hadn't saved herself and left Gene and me at his mercy," he replied. His voice got even colder as he went on. "My mother, damn her soul, put her own needs first. He was a hellion when he drank, but it was because of her that he gave in to alcohol. He went over the line when she left. He missed her every day he lived."

"Is she still alive?"

He glanced at Kate with a curious expression. After a minute he smiled bitterly. "Oh, she's alive. She's very much alive. Every year, on my birthday, she sends me a card and another tearstained note begging me to come and talk to her. She never elaborates, and she never gives up. And I never go."

Kate stared at him without speaking. Jason sounded bitter and cruel, and the face she saw then frightened her. He never forgave people. Kate wondered if someday, somehow, she'd fail him. And he'd look at her with that cold smile and push her to one side without mercy. She shivered a little.

"Your birthday is in April," she recalled.

"When is yours? I keep forgetting."

"In January. I'll be twenty-one the next one."

"An old lady," he said, his dark eyes twinkling. They softened on her. "By then, you'll look very, very pregnant."

"You sound smug." He didn't elaborate, but he felt proud, too, that he'd managed to get her pregnant the first time he'd tried. He could talk about wanting his freedom, but he'd wanted Kate until she was his major obsession. While she was pregnant, she was his completely. No other man would look at her with desire or want her, and her career would have to take a backseat to motherhood. And she'd have to lean on him, just a little. That made him feel fiercely male, and he liked the feeling.

"Have you told Sheila and the others?" she asked.

"It was too late when I got home last night," he said, "and I was up and gone early to Dallas for a meeting. I thought we'd go tell them together."

"It will be embarrassing," she said nervously.

"Hell! They're family."

She thought about that, and relaxed a little. Yes. They were family, and none of them would ostracize her.

If Jason had expected to surprise Sheila, he was doomed to disappointment. She was waiting at the front door with two skeins of pink and blue wool and her knitting needles under one arm.

"Thought I'd get a head start," she told Kate, grinning wickedly. "Are we having a boy or a girl, or hasn't his lordship here decided yet?" she jerked her head toward Jason.

Kate burst out laughing and hugged Sheila warmly. "Oh, Sheila, you angel."

"Be careful that she doesn't stab you with her angelic pitchfork," Jason muttered. "She overstarches my shirts and changes detergent every second week so that I break out all over...."

"Keep it up," Sheila glowered at him. "Just keep it up and I'll teach you the true meaning of the term 'burnt offering,' because that's all you'll get from now on."

"And what do you mean, 'from now on'?"

"Where's my broom?" Sheila muttered, looking around.

"I think Barton borrowed it to fly to town on," Jason offered, and sidestepped as the bulky woman swung, grinning at her.

"Your brother and sister-in-law are watching a movie in the living room," Sheila called after him as he caught Kate's hand and guided her down the hall. "At least, she is. I think he's painting her."

"When isn't he painting something?" Jason asked curtly. "Everything except those new fences we put up, and the wagon...."

"I heard that!" Gene called through the open door.

He was working at an easel while Cherry, in a beige pantsuit, was curled on the couch watching a soap opera.

"Why, Gene, that's very good," Kate exclaimed, peering at the half-finished canvas that depicted Cherry in a lazy, sultry mood. It captured her elfin quality completely. "Cherry, you'll love it, you're gorgeous."

"So are you, honey," Cherry laughed. She got up to hug Kate. "I'm so happy for you."

"Same here." Gene grinned, glancing past her at Jason. "And stop smirking, will you, big brother? Lots of men get to be fathers."

"Most of them don't manage it on the first attempt," Kate mused, watching Jason look uncomfortable.

"Well, well," Cherry said with a speculative look at Jason, who pretended not to see it.

"How about a toast?"

"Only with caffeine-free tea or something harmless," Jason said. "No alcohol. It isn't good for the baby."

"Yes, sir, Dr. Donavan," Kate agreed, and smiled.

He lifted an eyebrow. "Go ahead. Argue."

"Not me. I agree wholeheartedly."

After they all toasted her health and the baby's, Kate took Cherry off to one side and enlisted her help with the wedding. The younger girl was delighted to assist in planning. Sheila would be pressed into service as well, to deal with the caterers. Kate and Cherry planned to go together to choose the invitations the next day. Thank God Jason was rich; he could pay for the rushed printing job.

Afterward, while Kate went upstairs with Jason to look at the master bedroom, Gene and Cherry went back to their painting.

"He never does a damned thing around here," Jason said shortly as they went down the wide hall. "Except paint and have exhibits. But he never sells anything. God, Kate, he's my brother and I love him, but I can't break my back supporting him for the rest of his life."

"Yes, I know." She slid her hand into his big one, shocked at the way he actually flinched. She started to draw it back, but his fingers contracted suddenly.

He looked down at her. "I'm not used to being touched," he said softly, pausing before an open door. "It had been over two years since I'd had a woman, that afternoon with you."

She was shocked. Actually shocked. Her eyes stared into his without total comprehension.

"Did you think I was a playboy?" he asked, his eyes intent on her face.

"I guess I did," she confessed.

He searched her eyes for a moment, wondering how shocked she'd be if she knew just how inexperienced he really was. He led her into the big bedroom. It had exquisitely large furniture, very dark and obviously hand-carved. The bed was king-size, and had four tall posters with a chest at the foot. The dresser and chest of drawers were on opposite walls, across a thick beige carpet. The coverlet on the bed was quilted and depicted a Western landscape. The earth colors in it were reflected in the woven drapes as well as in the two leather armchairs beside the rock fireplace. There was even a daybed, a holdover from the post-Civil War days.

"It's very masculine," Kate said.

"No woman has even set foot in here since I've been the head of the household," he replied. He lifted his cigarette to his lips and looked down at her. "You'll be the only woman I've ever made love to in this room."

She trembled at the husky warmth in his voice as he

said that, and she almost took a step toward him. But the spotting and the cramps had frightened her, and she knew now that intimacy had a kind of violence all its own. A violence that could harm the baby.

"What is it?" he asked. "Something's upset you. What?"

"The baby," she whispered, searching his eyes worriedly. "It's dangerous, the first three months...."

"I see." He lifted his chin and studied her eyes. "Did Harris tell you to avoid intimacy?"

"No," she said honestly. "But, it might be as well if you talked to him," she added hesitantly, because she didn't really want that.

"Only at gunpoint," he said mockingly. "I don't need a lecture on my evil ways. And I can wait. I know what you're thinking. We're a pretty violent combination when we make love. I don't want to hurt the baby any more than you do."

She managed to smile. It would make things harder, of course, if they didn't have that physical bond to ease them over the rough spots. But there was a very real risk that she might lose his baby, and she didn't want him to blame himself if something went wrong.

"I'll understand if you want me to sleep somewhere else," she faltered. "I mean, I know it's difficult for men..."

Jason drew her closer, his lean hands gentle on her arms. "Kate, I don't want you anywhere at night except beside me," he said bluntly.

She sighed. "I was hoping you'd say that," she whispered, her eyes on his chest. "But I was afraid to ask."

His hands contracted. "Why?"

"Because I know you're marrying me because of the baby, Jason," she said quietly. "You don't have to pretend it's out of undying love. You aren't any more in love with me than I am with you. And because of that," she said, carrying off the lie beautifully, "I didn't feel right about asking for any special favors. But I'm scared and I don't want to be alone."

He didn't move. After a minute, he released her and moved away, looking quietly out the window. "It isn't a special favor," he said finally. "There's a daybed. I'll sleep on that, and you can have the big bed. If you need anything in the night, I'll be handy."

"I'm sorry about everything," she said hesitantly.

He laughed coldly, and he didn't look at her. He couldn't. What she'd said about not loving him hurt. "So am I," he said.

She turned away toward the door. "I guess I'd better get you to take me home, if you don't mind. I have to get supper for Mama and me."

"You can stay to dinner with us," he said, turning.

"Mama and I will only have a few more evenings together," she replied. "I'd like to enjoy them."

He shrugged. "Suit yourself," he said carelessly. "Come on, then. I'll drive you back."

She followed him down the hall, but this time she didn't try to hold his hand. She felt as if he'd just slammed a door between them and locked it, and she wondered if it was because she'd asked him not to sleep with her. That only reinforced her earlier idea, that what he'd felt for her was nothing more than desire. And that had already burned out when he came back from Australia. It was going to be a rough marriage. She only hoped she could stick it out long enough to show him how much she loved him. And maybe when the baby came, he might feel a little more for her than he did now.

CHAPTER THIRTEEN

KATE WONDERED AT the power of easy cash, when she saw how quickly their wedding invitations had been printed and mailed out. Jason had reluctantly agreed to wait two weeks so that Kate, Cherry, and Sheila would have time to get caterers, organize a reception, and have the invitations engraved and mailed.

Kate was a bit relieved about the delay, because she and the design staff were tearing their collective hair out trying to manage the last samples before the salesmen carried them out the door. The showings were barely three weeks away, and Kate's stamina was wearing thin. It was the worst possible time to get married, but Jason was adamant. He didn't want Kate showing when they spoke their vows.

"I'll never get it all done in time," Kate moaned as she and her mother ate supper two nights before the wedding. "I'm worn to a frazzle already, and I still have another week's work ahead of me with twelve-hour days. Even with Cherry and Sheila helping, organizing the wedding is killing me."

"Can't some of the other girls help with the design deadlines?" Mary asked.

"Not with the actual designs, no," Kate sighed. "And I'm helping do a couple of the patterns, too, to save the pattern makers some time. They're already behind. It's such a mess. Why does Jason want to get married this fast? Most people know I'm pregnant; does it really matter if they can see that I am?"

Mary smiled gently. "It matters to your future husband."

"My future husband is going to be one big handful," Kate told her mother. "I can see what a peaceful relationship we're going to have because he's already making angry noises about the time I'm spending at the plant. He hates the whole idea of my having a career."

"You'll change his mind."

"I'll have to, won't I?" Kate asked with a bittersweet smile.

"Kate, you do love him?" Mary said unexpectedly, the green eyes so much like her daughter's narrow with concern.

Kate hugged her. "More than my own life," she confessed, "although he doesn't feel that kind of loving for me. But I wonder if he's really capable of giving himself, Mama. He's been locked up in his shell for a long time."

"If he has, then you're the only one he ever gave a key to," Mary reminded her. "Think about it. He never would let anyone else get close."

"I'll try to remember that," she agreed. She didn't add that Jason's attitude had grown more and more distant since her visit to the house the night they became engaged. He was pleasant and attentive and overwhelmingly concerned about her. But it was a surface kind of thing, and the man beneath the mask was as enigmatic as ever.

The sight of her dress on Dessie's rack the next morning caused Kate to catch her breath. The other women gathered around, all smiles, to watch as she held it against her.

"It's glorious," Kate sighed. "It's just glorious."

"You designed it, darling," Dessie reminded her. "I just

put the pieces together. And it will knock their eyes out, you mark my words. Try it on. Let's see how you look."

Kate didn't need encouraging. She ducked behind the screen that the models used and fumbled her way into the yards and yards of satin and alençon lace.

It had an exaggerated keyhole neckline and an empire waist, with a long train because she'd always wanted one. The leg of mutton sleeve variation tapered to a point over the back of her hand, with pearl buttons to close them at the wrist. Kate had used the satin mostly without a lace overlay, except for the skirt and lace appliqués at the cap of the sleeves and on the long point of the cuff. The skirt was elegantly full, and there was a delicate feathering of alençon lace appliqués on the hem. The gown was accented by a Juliet cap from which the veil was draped, and when Kate looked in the mirror, she felt exquisitely beautiful.

"Wow," was all Dessie had to say.

"I can't believe I designed that." Kate shook her head, delighted with the fit. It was as comfortable as it was lovely, and she wondered at the talent she wasn't even aware of having. Sometimes she felt as if she was looking at someone else's designs, because the ideas came out of thin air and seemed to settle on paper before her startled eyes.

"Well, you did. And it is gorgeous!" Dessie assured her. "You'll be on the cover of *Vogue* in that!"

"I'll settle for not passing out at the altar," Kate whispered conspiratorially.

"Well, we, uh, did rather wonder at the waist measurement," Sandy confessed with a smile.

"A bit large for a perfect size ten, which you were," Dessie agreed.

"Not large for a pregnant lady," Kate reminded them.

She sighed. "I know it's jumping the gun and all that, but I'm just shockingly thrilled about the whole thing," she added with a flush. "I've wanted a baby since I was eighteen. Not that this is exactly the most orthodox way to get one...."

"If you want it, and you're going to love it," Dessie began, "and your future husband wants it as much, I'd say that's going to be a very happy baby."

Kate smiled. "He does want it. Very much."

"Congratulations, then," Dessie said, hugging her. "And thank you for sharing the news with us, before it's official."

"I hope your invitations came?" Kate asked hesitantly, because Jason's list had some very prominent people on it and Kate's friends were largely plant people. Considering her feelings about her career, it wouldn't be unlike him to simply cross them off the list if he disapproved the invitations.

"Got mine this morning," Dessie said, and Kate could have dropped with relief when that news was echoed by the other staff. "I hear Mr. Rogers got one, and that Roberta even had one. She's flying down for the wedding."

"Oh, how lovely," Kate laughed. "She was so nice...." She hesitated. "And Clarisse?"

"If that's the black designer, she said she can't come," Sandy said. "She's been given a huge break. Roberta's brother has hired her for his couture house! She's working as an assistant designer!"

"But she insulted him," Kate gasped. "She told him off royally, at his own party, too."

"He likes spunk, I'm told. Anyway, Clarisse said to say thanks for the invitation, and only getting ready for her own show at the Waldorf would stop her from coming to your wedding. She says she'll see you in New York when they show your collection with the other Clayborn lines."

"I'll look forward to that," Kate said, and meant it. "Being on Seventh Avenue during market week is going to be an experience. And thank you so much for my wedding gown. I can't tell you how grateful I am…."

"Sure you can," Dessie assured her. "Go ahead. And you just remember me when you get your own house and you need a sample hand."

"And a cooperative and highly talented designer," Sandy seconded.

"And two marvelous assistants with great taste in trim purchasing," Pamela and Becky added.

Kate hugged them all. "You bet I will!"

But when she finished, late, and went home with her beautiful dress carefully bagged, she was worrying about that trip to New York. Jason had been adamant about making her give up her career. And since she was pregnant, she had a feeling it was going to mean one royal battle to even get to go. He'd be busy with roundup again during those two weeks, and that might be her out. If Kate had to, she could sneak away without his knowing. It felt dishonest, and if anything went wrong with her pregnancy, she was going to hate herself. But as Dr. Harris himself had said, all the precautions in the world weren't going to help if she wasn't meant to have the baby. And in the past few days, there had been no spotting and no cramping. So perhaps her worries were over.

The day of the wedding dawned with rain in the forecast. Kate was at the Donavan house, getting into her beautiful dress helped by her mother, who was in a beautiful lavender floor-length dress that Jason had taken her to buy. Kate moaned when she heard the report.

"Why does it have to rain?" Kate asked the mirror as she fixed her face. "Why today, of all days? I'm only ever going to get married once in my whole life, so why can't the sun come out?"

"Rain is a good omen," Sheila assured her blithely.

"The best," Mary agreed.

"Sure," Cherry added, "anybody can have a sunny wedding. Yours will be special."

"Has anybody seen Jason at all?" Kate asked quickly as they fastened the hooks of her wedding gown. "I haven't seen him since I got here with Mother."

"He was in his room getting dressed when I came upstairs," Cherry assured her. "Now, don't worry. He isn't going to do anything terrible like leaving you at the altar. Have you got your something blue?"

She did. A blue lace handkerchief. Her something old was a small garnet ring that her grandmother had left her. Her something new was the gown itself.

"I don't have anything borrowed," she exclaimed.

"Here," Sheila put a small coin in her hand. "That's an English sixpence coin. A boyfriend of mine gave it to me, long ago, and its been my good luck piece ever since. It will bring you luck, too."

"Put it in your shoe," Cherry suggested, and Kate slid it into the toe of her white pump.

"I'll pass out at the altar, I just know I will," Kate groaned. "I feel nauseated already."

"Did you take that morning sickness tablet?" Mary asked.

Kate hesitated. "I don't like to take medicine of any kind," she confessed. "I'm so afraid of hurting the baby."

"That's understandable," Mary agreed, "but Dr. Harris is as stubborn about drugs as you are, and I guarantee he wouldn't have prescribed anything he thought might hurt the baby."

That made sense. Kate reluctantly took the pill with a swallow of juice and finished dressing.

The huge living room was clear of furniture, and chairs had been placed there for the ceremony. There was an altar with candles on either side, and huge pots of ferns and flowers everywhere. An aisle ran between rows and rows of strange faces in elegant dress. A pianist played a medley of wedding songs in one corner, and the minister of the local Presbyterian church, Reverend Samuels, was talking to Gene at one side of the altar. The Donavans had been Presbyterian for two generations, while Kate's family had been Baptist for an equal length of time. Since Jason had been so easygoing about the invitations, she hadn't made a fuss about having his minister perform the ceremony.

Kate, standing quietly on the staircase, felt more nervous by the minute. There was no one to give her away, since her father was long since dead. She'd have that long walk alone. Cherry was her matron of honor, as Gene was Jason's best man. It would be a very simple but elegant ceremony, although Kate was sure that she noticed at least two reporters. They had huge cameras and tape recorders.

Kate felt her mother's gentle touch, and turned to see her smile. She smiled back, nervously, her hands clutching the bouquet of white orchids Jason had sent her.

The prelude suddenly began. Jason was already at the altar. Cherry went next. And then the wedding march announced Kate. She almost tripped getting down the steps, but she recovered quickly. She had to appear calm. She had to look regal. That was her gown she'd designed, she couldn't disgrace it by fumbling down the aisle.

Her chin went up. She smiled cooly. Her eyes found
Jason at the altar, his dark head with its back to her, and
she walked toward it. He had a sexy nape, she thought
irrelevantly. Kate felt dozens of eyes watching her. She
wondered how many of those elegant guests knew that
this was a sort of shotgun wedding.

At last she reached the altar. In a daze, she heard the
minister performing the ceremony while Jason faced
straight ahead and only looked at her when they exchanged rings. Jason had purchased simple gold bands
for both of them, nothing frivolous. Later, he'd told Kate,
she could have a different design if she wanted it, but
these would suffice for now because they didn't have the
time to shop for permanent rings.

As Kate looked down at the thin band of gold on her
finger, she heard the minister, somewhere in the back of
her head, pronouncing them man and wife. She looked
up into Jason's steady, quiet eyes as he slowly lifted her
thick veil out of the way and looked at her. After a brief
hesitation, during which his eyes darkened, he bent and
kissed her. His lips were cool and brief. He lifted his head
a fraction and searched her soft eyes.

"No," he whispered, "no, not like that. Like this…."

And he kissed her again. This time, it was everything
it should have been. Kate grasped his muscular arms
through the fabric and held on while his hard mouth
warmed hers. A long, exquisite moment later he drew
away, and the smile he gave her, although she knew it was
only for the benefit of the guests, like the kiss, was the
tenderest she ever remembered seeing on his hard face.

After they left the room, Kate ran upstairs to change.
They were flying to Jamaica for three days, a short honeymoon because of work pressures on his part and Kate's.

They were to leave following the reception. It was all very rushed, but Jason had insisted that it was the only way to do things.

The reception was very brief. Kate spoke to Roberta and introduced her to Jason. She wasn't quite prepared for Roberta's very warm attitude toward her new husband or the frank desire in the woman's eyes. Kate was having second thoughts about her newest friend. She hadn't realized that to Roberta, a wedding ring had never been a barrier. Not that Jason responded. It was fascinating to see his black eyes turn Roberta away without a single hard word to mar the day. He couldn't have made his disinterest more obvious if he'd worn a hands-off sign. Kate had seen him back down fighting cowboys with nothing more than that level, cold, unblinking stare. It had a sobering effect on most sane people.

But Jason's friends were the hardest to deal with. They talked mostly to Jason after realizing that Kate wasn't knowledgeable about big business or the latest business trends. They weren't snobby about it. They were simply like Jason, feeling that women had no place in the business world.

Their wives were distantly pleasant, congratulating Kate on her "catch" and also on the lovely gown she had worn.

"Neiman-Marcus," Jason informed them, toasting his lovely wife.

"Kathryn Whittman Donavan," Kate corrected gently. "I designed it myself, and the sample room staff made it up for me."

That produced an unexpected flutter of exclamations, and renewed interest in her gown. And not only from the guests, but from the reporters as well. This was a nice little tidbit to add to an otherwise routine society wedding story. The bride was a budding designer and had done her own gown.

Jason didn't like it. Not one bit. He and Kate had discussed this before, and he'd made his opinion known. He didn't say anything, but Kate knew he would. No way was she going to get out of this without a fight, but she was ready for him. They might as well settle the career question now, at the beginning of their life together.

After she helped him cut the cake, they mingled until everyone was full of cake and conversation. She'd been sticking close to her mother and Sheila and Cherry, and with one eye she'd watched Roberta mingling with the rich men present. Roberta was like a butterfly, beautiful and vaguely surface with her emotions. Kate liked her, but she was secretly glad that the woman wouldn't be around Jason very much. Even a man of principle could be tempted by a woman that lovely.

Kate wore a pale mauve suit for the getaway. Her bag was already packed, although she imagined Jason wasn't going to like having the shabby thing next to his in the airport. Hers was old and tattered and the handle was half off. But it was all she had.

She barely had the chance to kiss everyone good-bye before Jason escorted her out the door and into the Mercedes. Minutes later, they were speeding away from the house. Married.

"I thought I told you to buy the gown at Neiman-Marcus," he remarked quietly as he pulled out into the main highway. He didn't look at her even then.

She took a deep breath. Just as well to get it over with now, she supposed. "You did," she replied.

"Then why did you deliberately go against me?"

He didn't look that angry, but with Jason, it was hard to tell. She couldn't see his eyes, and they would have told her what she needed to know.

She studied him silently for a moment, absently registering how handsome he looked in a light gray suit and a matching Stetson and boots. He was her whole heart, although she wouldn't be able to tell him that. It was the first time they'd been alone since the day he'd come for her at the plant, and despite the wedding ring on her finger, she felt nervous with him.

"It wasn't a matter of going against you," she said finally. "Jason, I design clothes. It's what I do for a living. I just wanted to create something special for my own wedding, that's all."

"You aren't going to do anything for a living," he said, and now the anger was creeping into his deep voice. "Not while you're my wife." He glanced at her. "And that includes being a designer."

She lifted her chin, glaring at him. "I gather that we're going to spend our honeymoon having this out?" she asked coldly.

"What did you expect, honey, that I'd back down?" he countered. "Kate, you know me better than that by now."

"I know very little about you," she said, her voice as quiet as his own. "I can't get near you, Jason, especially since the wedding invitations went out. I feel as if you're doing your best to push me right out of your life."

"I told you I wanted the baby," he said tersely, which was no answer at all. He lit a cigarette as he drove and blew out a thin cloud of smoke. "I meant it."

Of course he wanted the baby. He just didn't want Kate. She leaned her head against the seat and stared out at the passing landscape with eyes that hardly saw it.

"You haven't had any more problems, have you?" he asked unexpectedly.

"No," she said flatly. She glanced at him as they sped down the deserted highway. "I guess if I said I had, you'd turn the car right around and go home."

"I'm not risking the baby for a holiday," he told her.

"Listen, Jason, if I'm meant to have this baby, I will, and nothing in the world will stop it from coming," she said heatedly. "On the other hand, if it isn't meant to be, all the protective instincts in the world won't save it."

"I suppose that means you don't plan any falls down a flight of stairs?" he asked mockingly.

She felt the first tears sting her eyes. She'd worked herself half to death trying to organize her wedding and finish her collection, now she was on the threshold of a career she'd worked toward for years, and she'd been made pregnant and forced into a marriage Jason didn't want. Now he was making snide remarks about the baby. She hated him. She hated the whole idea of marriage. She wished she could take off the ring and throw it at him.

Her silence caught his attention. He looked toward her with narrow eyes that saw the glimmer of unshed tears. "Hell, I didn't mean that," he bit off.

"I didn't get you pregnant," she said through trembling lips. "I didn't force you to marry me. All I ever wanted was to make something of my life. I'm sorry if you feel trapped, but you might consider that I'm just as trapped as you are." She choked back a sob. "You should have stayed away, Jason. It would have hurt for a little while, but we wouldn't be in this mess."

That took some of the anger out of him. "Did you miss me, Kate?" he asked, and now there was gentleness in his deep voice.

She stared through tears at her folded hands. "Yes, damn you," she sobbed. "You were the only friend I had…."

"You were the only friend I had, too," he replied quietly. "The only woman in my life that I ever liked." His jacket strained against powerful muscles as he turned at a crossroads onto the road that led to San Antonio. "I'm sorry it turned out like this."

"We should have taken precautions," she said defensively. "I didn't even know how. I thought you were going to…you know."

He had, he thought bitterly. But he'd lost control completely, and that loss of control was half his problem now. His father had drilled it into him, that desire was the weapon a woman used to control a man. Sex was something a man who was a man could do without, his father had raged. It was only meant for the act of creation, anyway, and there were better things to do with a man's time. Jason had been little more than a child, he hadn't understood how deeply his father had been grieving for his wife or how hurt he'd been at her desertion. Jason had taken the words for gospel. And because he had, they'd warped his attitude toward women and sex. Sex brought guilt, and loss of control was devastating to him.

Even now, remembering his weakness was causing him some problems. He couldn't let that happen again, he couldn't let Kate know how vulnerable he was to her.

"In the heat of passion, men forget, too," he said cooly. "Going over it won't do any good, Kate. You're pregnant and we're married. Now we have to live with it."

"I suppose we do." She drew in a slow breath and dashed away the tears. "Can you spare the time to go to Jamaica, really?"

"Every couple needs a honeymoon of some sort. Three

days is better than nothing, and I thought a little time away from that damned textile plant might convince you that the world doesn't begin and end there."

"Can't we…not argue, just for the next three days?" she asked, and looked across at him with faintly pleading eyes. She smiled shyly. "I'll be your best friend."

Jason felt his heart soar. That was the Kate he remembered. The laughing, happy Kate who'd taken his mind and then his body, and ultimately possessed him. He reached across the seat with his free hand and linked it with hers gently.

"You'll like Jamaica," he said lazily, neatly dismissing the subject of her job. "We're going up to Montego Bay, where it's a little less hectic than Kingston. We'll laze on the beach and drink piña coladas and go disco dancing."

"Your baby and I will not have a piña colada, and neither of us is up to disco."

His eyebrows went up. "Excuse me, little mama. Make that a pineapple punch and a two-step."

"That's better." She wrapped her slender fingers around his and pressed them warmly. He returned the pressure.

It was going to take time, a lot of time, for him to adjust to the loss of his freedom. Well, she had that, didn't she? She was content with her lot for now. She was going to make him the best wife he'd ever believed possible, if she could just make him give her enough freedom to be herself and not try to remake her in his own image. He and the baby were the most important things in her life, but if she lost this chance to show what she could do with her talent for design, she was never going to be truly satisfied. But for now, she was going to enjoy being with Jason and try not to think about the future.

That resolution carried her aboard the big Air Jamaica

jet, where they had first-class seat reservations. It was nice and roomy and she had Jason's hand to hold during the two hour-plus flight to Montego Bay.

Aboard the plane she'd gotten accustomed to the musical West Indies accent, but she heard a lot more of it when they got into the airport in Montego Bay.

When they got off the plane, the tropical breeze hit Kate in the face like a warm wet towel. She actually caught her breath, not only at the moist heat of it, but also at the floral scent. What she could see of the landscape was unencouraging, but then airports wouldn't be likely to locate downtown.

Jason got their carry-on luggage on a small cart with wheels that he'd packed, and now she understood its purpose. The little luggage rack was perfect to save them the discomfort of lugging their bags the distance from the plane inside the terminal, and through immigration and customs.

Kate, who'd never been out of the country at all except once to Mexico, was fascinated with the procedure. Jason had obtained a voter's registration certificate for her, since she didn't have a passport. He had one, which he gave to the official at one of the multilaned counters. They were welcomed to Jamaica, asked if they had tobacco or alcohol, drugs or firearms, and then sent to a window to cash in their traveler's checks for Jamaican currency.

"It's been illegal to spend American currency here," Jason explained to her, "because the Jamaican economy has been in bad shape. It's improving, but it's still against the law to take their money out of the country."

"I like their money," Kate mused, examining her bankroll as they climbed into a cab and were driven off toward the big Holiday Inn where Jason had reserved rooms for them. "It's so colorful."

"First time on the island?" the cabdriver asked with a big, welcoming smile in the rearview mirror.

"Not for me. But my wife hasn't been here before," Jason replied, with an indulgent smile for Kate. "We're on our honeymoon."

"Best place for that," the cabdriver laughed. "No place like Jamaica, to live or to vacation. You must see the banana and coffee plantations, and there are some houses you might enjoy seeing. Also many historic places here. Much to see."

"How about taking us around, then?" Jason asked. "I'm not much on boxed tours, and I'll bet you know Mo Bay better than any of the tour guides."

"You bet I do, man," came the laughing reply. "I'll have you hooked on reggae before you leave, too."

"Reggae?" Kate asked hesitantly.

The cabdriver turned on his radio, flicked a switch, and a strange, new kind of music filled the car.

"That is reggae, ma'am," he told Kate. "You'll hear a lot of it on the island. I'm Barton Cox, by the way."

Jason introduced himself and Kate, and set a time with the driver early the next morning for a day-long tour. They agreed to meet in the lobby of the hotel at nine, which would give them time to sleep in.

"Don't forget the time difference," they were reminded as Barton pulled up in front of a modern modular hotel complex surrounded by palm trees of half a dozen different species and a glorious flame tree in full bloom.

"We're two hours behind Jamaican time," Jason told Kate.

"I'll reset my watch," she said.

But Jason had already set his before he paid Barton and helped Kate out of the cab.

Barton set their bags on the sidewalk, where a uniformed bellboy came to pick them up. "Hello, cousin," Barton called to the bellboy, who grinned and called the greeting back. "See you in the morning now," he told Jason and Kate, and was gone, his rickety yellow cab leeing a little as he sped out the round drive.

"You folks just get in?" the bellboy asked politely as he led them inside the luxurious hotel.

"Barely off the plane," Jason returned. He took Kate's arm. "Is there a big crowd this week?"

"Hardly anybody. There was a riot in Kingston," the bellboy said with a resigned sigh. "Everybody thinks we'll kill all the tourists if they come down."

"Too bad," Jason replied. "I suppose you think the United Stated is the gangster capital of the world every time you read about a gang murder?"

The bellboy grinned. "Now you're talking sense."

Jason laughed. He looked younger, Kate thought as they went to registration to check in and get their room key. He looked like a different man. This was going to be a marvelous honeymoon, if only she felt like enjoying it. She hadn't told Jason how queasy she'd felt on the plane, or how shaky she felt now. She didn't want him to worry. But she was getting greener by the minute, and the thought of being bounced all over the island in a cab made her worse. She had to get better. She just had to.

The bellboy carried their luggage to the first module of the spacious hotel complex, where they had a room with an outdoor patio overlooking the bay. Kate opened the sliding glass doors first thing and drank in the breeze. It swept the graceful casuarina pines outside the door and stirred the flowering hedge bush near the sea wall. This was like paradise, and Kate sighed, closing her eyes as she felt her nausea slowly disappear.

"Want anything to eat?" Jason asked.

"I'm a little nauseated, but it could be lack of food that's causing it," she laughed, and looked up at him helplessly.

"Uncomfortable?" he mused.

"Green! I'm sorry."

"Good Lord, why?" he asked. He bent and lifted her effortlessly and carried her to one of the huge double beds, their green and white patterned coverlets corresponding beautifully to the green of the carpet and the white of the curtains.

"I didn't want you to know," she sighed, leaning her weary head against his shoulder with her arms linked around his neck. "I'm not much of a companion for a holiday, I'm afraid."

"All that damned overtime didn't help," he said shortly. He laid her down, looming over her. "Tell me what suits your fancy and I'll go get it."

She searched his dark eyes. "You'll laugh."

"Not likely," he said, smiling.

"I want oysters and strawberry shortcake, a piña colada with no rum, and a cup of that Blue Mountain coffee I can't afford back home."

"Whatever turns you on," he said with a glimmer of amusement in his eyes. "Okay. Just take it easy. I'll be back as soon as I get it organized."

Considering that the hotel didn't offer room service, Jason still managed to have the meal catered, white-coated waiters and all. God alone knew where he'd found the exquisite meal, but Kate had everything she wanted and then some. And since she'd reluctantly taken one of her nausea tablets before she ate, it even stayed down. She was just tired now, and content to be alone with Jason and feast her eyes on him.

"That was just delicious," Kate sighed when the remains of the meal had been taken away and they were alone again. She stretched out on the bed with a weary sigh, relaxing with a smile. "Thank you."

"My pleasure, Mrs. Donavan," he returned. "Now just lie there and rest for a little bit. And when you feel better, I'll help you change clothes."

She looked up at him with dawning traces of her old sense of humor. "How exciting," she mused mischievously.

"That's what I think, too," he said with reluctant interest. She was getting to him again. He laughed softly and walked out onto the patio to smoke a cigarette, standing tall and quiet in the semidarkness. After a minute he was back, rummaging in his suitcase for casual clothes. He hesitated, glancing at Kate. Then he turned and started toward the bathroom.

"I thought that the woman was supposed to rush into the bathroom to dress, not the man," she pointed out.

He glared at her. "I've never undressed in front of a woman except you, unless it was in the dark." His eyes glittered. "Go ahead. Laugh."

"I can't. I'm just delighted." She smiled, and meant it.

He started to laugh at his own self-consciousness. "Hell."

He threw his clothes down on the bed and took off his suit, aware of Kate's frank, curious stare as he stripped down to his underwear and pulled on his tan Bermuda shorts.

"It was good for me. Was it good for you?" she asked with a wicked smile and a leering eyebrow.

He laughed softly, with pure delight. "Just when I think I'm getting used to you, you knock me off balance again," he remarked gently.

"You never used to smile at all," she replied. "When I first met you, and Dad took the job as your foreman, I was scared to death of you."

"Are you still?" he asked with a speculative glance.

"Sometimes you intimidate me," she confessed. "But I haven't been afraid of you for a long, long time. And I like seeing you smile."

He felt as if he had bubbles in his bloodstream when she looked at him like that. She aroused him more every day. As his dark eyes slid down her body in that becoming garment, he thought about her the way she'd been that day in her own living room, beautifully nude and soft under him. His body reacted immediately to the mental pictures and he felt it going taut. There it was again, that threatening desire, the consuming arousal that stole his mind, his ability to reason. When he was with Kate, he seemed to be a totally different man.

She watched the expressions cross his face, fascinated by their complexity. She was learning new things about Jason all the time, exciting things. Her eyes noted the changed contours of his powerful body, and knowing that he was aroused in turn aroused her. She stretched slowly, her eyes on his bare, broad chest with its feathering of hair, wanting to touch him there, to kiss him there.

"Could you help me on with my tent dress, Jason?" she asked in a voice that sounded husky and odd, but what she wanted was much more than that. And it showed in her eyes.

CHAPTER FOURTEEN

THE SOUND OF the surf outside on the beach was suddenly dim compared to the beat of Jason's own heart. Kate's voice made him tingle. He remembered that husky note in it from the first time he'd made love to her, and the memory was already causing him some problems.

He lifted his chin and his dark eyes went over her soft curves like hands, masculine appreciation in his smile.

"Will you?" she repeated.

"Will I what?" he murmured.

She cleared her throat. "Help me change."

"Is that all you want?" he asked bluntly, his eyes alive with sensuality.

She shifted again on the bed. "No."

He sat down beside her, pushing back her unruly hair. "We can't," he reminded her. "Now stop tempting me."

"I never used to think I could," she confessed as his lean, deft fingers worked the buttons of her jacket to unfasten it. They were exciting even through three layers of fabric, their touch warm and knowing.

"You don't know the half of it," he murmured. He helped her out of her jacket, and then the white blouse under it. He hesitated at her bra, his eyes narrowing on its obvious inadequacy to hold the blossoming curves under it. "Isn't this thing too small?" he asked curiously.

He hadn't seen that many women in bras, but this lacy thing didn't look big enough to give any support.

"I'm pregnant, Jason," she said gently.

His bewildered gaze lifted to her face. "What does that have to do with it?"

"My breasts are swollen," she explained softly, amazed that it didn't bother her at all to discuss intimate things with him. Well, they were lovers, after all, and they were married.

He scowled. It still didn't register.

She reached behind her hesitantly and unfastened the lacy garment and slowly peeled it away. His eyes stared down as if he were mesmerized, darkening with that intent, fascinated stare as he studied her full, soft breasts with their pretty pink and mauve contrasts.

"See how many veins there are?" she whispered. "These little changes make it possible for me to nurse him...."

"My God." He made it sound reverent. His lean fingers went to the dark aureole of one swollen breast. He touched it, very lightly, watching it stiffen. "You're darker here than you were."

"Yes." She tried not to tremble at his intimate caress, but she couldn't help it.

He looked up into her eyes. "Do you want to nurse him?" he asked unexpectedly.

Her face colored. "I want to," she whispered.

His lips parted on breath that was coming hard and quick as his hand grew bolder and openly caressed her. "You're trembling," he whispered back. "Does it excite you when I do this?"

"More...than you realize," she managed huskily.

He sat up, his hands going to the elastic waistband of her skirt, which allowed for her thickened waist. "I want to look at you," he said quietly, searching her eyes as he hesitated. "I've never seen a pregnant woman."

"Not even...her?" she asked, muted anger in her tone because she was jealous even of that shadowy figure in her past.

He scowled. The memory came down between them like a wall, and he started to draw back, but she suddenly sat up.

She forgot immediately what her original intention had been because the tips of her breasts brushed his hard, hair-matted chest, and knocked the thought right out of her head.

She caught her breath at the feel of him. Her hands went to his muscular arms. They were cool and his skin was a little rough, but he felt so good to touch. She drew her fingers down to his elbows and back up again, and she swayed helplessly against him, her breasts touching and then not touching, brushing, the tips growing harder. She wanted to be closer than this. She wanted all of him.

He felt himself shudder. She was seducing him. He didn't want this, he didn't want to risk the child. But her breasts were warm and hard-tipped, and every time they brushed his chest, his body reacted more.

He caught Kate's upper arms with the vague thought of pushing her away before things got out of hand. And then her head fell back and she looked at him. Her green eyes were half-closed, misty and soft with desire, her full lips parted, waiting, her body moving with helpless sensuality. His eyes went to her taut, swollen breasts, and his reason deserted him. God, her breasts were exquisite!

She reached up to his cheeks and pulled his face down as she arched. "Please," she whispered, her voice odd, soft, shaking. "Please. Jason, kiss me there...!"

Yes, he thought, his lips already parted even as he bent

to her body. His hands held her as he nuzzled against one perfect breast and took it, hard tip and all, right inside his hungry mouth.

She moaned at the wave of pleasure that his mouth was giving her, and the sound made him even more reckless. He took her deeper into the warm moist darkness of his mouth and felt the softness of her like silk against his tongue.

His hands were moving. He only vaguely realized that they were against her skin now, having gotten everything else out of the way. His mouth went down her, onto her soft belly, where his child lay. He pressed his lips warmly there, and onto her hips, and her long, elegant legs. She was still moaning, her body fluid in his grasp. He was going out of his mind and she was pushing him over a sensual cliff. He couldn't stop. His body was already thrusting against her hip, so fevered that he was in agony.

He found the snap and the zip of his Bermuda shorts and stripped them off while his mouth slowly teased the inside of her silky thigh. She made a new sound, a different sound.

"Jason," she whimpered, blind and deaf and dumb to everything except her sudden, overwhelming need to join with him, to lock her body with his and know him in every way there was. "It's so sweet, it's so sweet, Jason…!"

His mouth traveled, open and warm, back up to her breasts while his hands touched her, probed and explored and excited her. Then his lips found her mouth, and locked with it, and she felt his hard body moving over her soft one.

She arched, on fire, burning up. She had to have him. Her feverish eyes didn't even see him. She clutched at his broad shoulders, her voice shattering, her body eager and taut, trying to fit itself to his.

"Oh, God, honey, you'll make me hurt you…!" he ground out. Her urgency was throwing him more out of control by the second. He'd never dreamed how sensual she could be, how passionate.

"Now," Kate cried. Tears ran down her cheeks at the intensity of desire he'd aroused in her. "I can't bear it, now, please now, Jason, don't stop…!"

He went over the edge. His mouth ground down into hers as his body intruded powerfully in one smooth, hard thrust.

She moaned, but not in pain. Her nails bit into his back, and her hands went trembling to the base of his spine to dig in, pulling him, holding him. Her hips arched and arched, and she made noises he'd never heard come out of a woman's throat. It shouldn't have happened so quickly, but her mind barely registered that. She was part of him. He was filling her…!

He gave himself to her. Completely, in a feverish, passionate giving that robbed him of anything except the raging, thrusting need to possess. He pushed down against her in an unconscious rough buffeting, the sound of the surf overshadowed by the rasp of their breathing and the sound of skin sliding against damp skin.

He whispered things to her as the tide became red and hot. He whispered things he'd never said to a woman, intimate things, secret things that she only vaguely heard. His mouth slid over hers and his tongue matched the quick, hard rhythm of his body as passion turned to insane urgency, and all at once everything exploded in a sweet, blind rush of heat and color and light that went on, and on, and on….

Jason felt her softness a long time later, when consciousness came filtering back. She was gasping for breath, as he was. Kate's warm body was wet with sweat, her heartbeat matching the frantic throb of his. "Kate?" he whispered at her ear. His voice sounded unsteady. "Kate, did I hurt you?"

"No," she whispered back. Her lips brushed at his throat, his chin, his shoulder. Her eyes rubbed there, and there were tears in them. She wept softly. "Darling," she whispered brokenly.

Jason felt the heat stab through him. She'd never used endearments, not even the first time he'd made love to her. Such a surge of tenderness welled up in him that it became terrifying. He kissed her soft face with lips that cherished, possessed. It had been like dying. He'd never dreamed of such a surrender. It had been that. He'd given himself to her, he'd given up control. And as he realized that, and that she knew it, his lips grew cool and he began to feel a stirring of stark fear.

"What is it?" she whispered.

She'd felt the mood swing. That bothered him, too. She saw too deep, knew too much. He wanted her obsessively, and now she knew it. Would she use that against him?

He lifted his head to search her soft eyes. His own were very dark and quiet.

She touched his mouth, her whole look one of wonder. "We're like…one person, aren't we?" she whispered, letting her eyes run boldly down the length of their intimate contact.

Heat surged through his body at the question. Yes, they were. In ways he didn't like to consider, ways that had nothing to do with the physical intimacy they were sharing.

And then he thought about the baby. And he froze.

"Kate…the baby," he whispered roughly.

She stopped breathing. In that mad, wild joining, her

only thought had been to get as close to Jason as possible. Tears stung her eyes as she realized what they might have done.

"I didn't think," she whispered tearfully.

"Neither did I," he said half angrily.

He lifted himself slowly away from her, his body throbbing at the way she intently watched him unlocking his hips from hers. She grimaced and he drew in a harsh breath before he jerked off the bed and went into the bathroom. She heard water running, and he was back with a warm wet cloth before she had time to miss him.

Kate laid still while he bathed her gently, his dark eyes almost black with concern. There were streaks of blood on the cloth.

She wept, but after a minute he laid the cloth aside and pulled her against his wet, hair-matted chest, holding her gently.

"It's just a little," he whispered. "Do you hurt at all? Is there any pain?"

"No," she said. She dabbed at her eyes with the back of her hand. "I just wanted you so much…."

He pressed her cheek against his chest and kissed her dark hair. "I wanted you, too, honey," he confessed quietly. "But we can't do that again. We're too violent with each other. I can't seem to be tender with you when I'm that aroused. I'm sorry. We'll have to wait until it's safe, Kate. Even if that means separate beds."

Safe. He meant that the baby came first, and perhaps he was right. But Kate felt him slipping away from her by the minute, even after that exquisite closeness. She wondered how she was going to hold him without the lure of desire. She knew Jason wanted the baby, and part of him wanted her with the same desperate passion she felt for him. But hers was tempered with love, and his wasn't. And if she lost the child because of her hunger for him, she'd have nothing at all. Only an empty marriage with a man who felt trapped.

She closed her eyes with a weary sigh. At least, she thought, she'd have her memories.

He felt that sigh and wondered how he was going to survive nine months of keeping his distance. His loss of control shocked and frightened him. Did he have no pride with her, no restraint at all? If he let her, she could take him over, and he wasn't risking that. She'd already told him that she wanted her career more than marriage. If it hadn't been for the baby, she'd never have married him in the first place.

He stroked her dark hair quietly, worried. He couldn't put the child at risk again. He'd just have to get himself together. If that meant keeping Kate at arm's length, so much the better. She was his first and only weakness. He couldn't let her discover how vulnerable he was, or she might turn it against him. The one lesson life had taught him so far was that trusting women was dangerous. It was a hard lesson to forget, even with a woman he…cared about. He didn't love her, of course. That kind of weakness was something for men with no pride, no manhood. He wouldn't love her. But he'd protect her and take care of her, and when the baby came, she'd forget all this career nonsense and stay home with him, where she belonged. He laid his cheek against her head. Yes. She'd be his, once the baby came.

After a minute, she stirred, moving away from him. It was still new, and strange, to have her clothes off with a man. Not that he was any better dressed.

"Are you sure I haven't hurt the baby?" he asked as she got up and reached for her briefs and bra.

"I'm not hurting or anything," she said gently. "I think it will be all right, Jason. Really, I do. Don't worry."

"How can I help it?" he asked, his voice deep and quiet and moody. "I shouldn't have touched you."

While she was digesting the sting of that bitter pill, he moved away to pull on his undershorts and Bermuda shorts with brief, quick movements. She took advantage of that diversion to get dressed herself.

He turned away to light a cigarette, and she pulled out the red and white polyester dress she'd brought with her. It was sleeveless, ankle length, and one of those one-size-fits-all things that was very comfortable to walk around in.

She pulled it over her head, and Jason glared at her when he turned and saw it.

"Where in hell did you get that?" he asked with unexpected irritation.

Her eyebrows arched. "Why, at a thrift sale," she faltered. "It had only been worn once or twice...."

He stiffened with outraged pride. "Don't ever let me hear of you going to another thrift sale. You go to one of the department stores in San Antonio to shop. Neiman-Marcus or Joske's. I've got charge accounts in both stores."

"A thrift sale is something even high-class women go to," she began.

"They most certainly do not," he shot back. "They go to bazaars to benefit charity."

"Thrift sales benefit poor people," she reminded him. "That is charity."

He glared at her.

She glared back.

After a minute, he made a rough sound, glared at the dress, and went out the sliding doors.

It was dark now, but the brilliant white of the beach and the reflection of the half moon in the crashing waves was idyllic. The dark silhouettes of the feathery casuarinas waved back and forth in the eternal breeze that blew off the Caribbean.

"It's so beautiful," Kate remarked, joining Jason on the patio.

"This was a pirate stronghold back in the eighteenth century," he remarked as he smoked. "So were the Bahamas, and most of the Caribbean islands. Henry Morgan and his privateers held sway around Kingston for many a long year until Morgan became governor and threw his buddies off the island."

"Shame on him," she said.

"A man has to think about his own throat," he said quietly. He gestured toward the front of the complex. "There's a plantation house not too far away called Rose Hall. The woman who lived there reputedly murdered her husbands and used voodoo on her workers. They called her the White Witch of Rose Hall. We can go up and look around tomorrow, if you like. There's an old bar in the basement where you can get a soft drink, and a small gift shop."

She shuddered. "You'll think I'm strange, Jason, but I don't like things like that," she confessed. "I'd have nightmares."

His eyebrows arched. "Chicken," he accused.

She made a noise like a clucking hen.

He laughed and puffed on his cigarette. It was the first pleasant sound she'd heard from him since they'd dressed. "Okay. Then how about a ride around the island and a look at the country and the people?"

"That," she assured him, "is much more my style."

"Then that's what we'll do," he replied gently.

She wanted a look inside the small boutique she'd noticed just past the lobby, too, but she didn't want to start another argument, so she didn't mention that. She leaned back and smelled the fresh, florid scent of the breeze. Kate thought of long days and gentle nights in the distant past, when other married people sat and enjoyed it as she did now. She glanced at Jason, but he was staring moodily out at the bay, and she quickly averted her eyes.

She wondered if his lack of control had disturbed him. She'd knocked him off balance and he didn't like it. But it had been so urgent, so sweet. She knew she'd remember it all her life. Except...

Her hand went to her abdomen. There were some faint cramps now, and there had been a little bleeding. What if that violent lovemaking had hurt the baby? And it would be her fault, because she'd incited him. She'd invited it.

With a wistful sigh, she closed her eyes and listened to the calming sound of the surf and the wind in the casuarinas. The baby would be all right. She just had to keep telling herself that; she had to think positively.

They strolled along the poolside, watching the swimmers in the beautifully lit blue water, and they sat down in white wooden chairs to sip fruit drinks under the avocado trees. Just before bedtime, they walked along the beach, Kate with her sandals held loosely in her hand, Jason smoking his eternal cigarette.

He'd put on a shirt when they went to sit beside the pool, but he'd unbuttoned it when they got to the beach. He towered over her now, lithe and powerful and graceful silhouetted against the sky. Kate stopped walking and just looked at him.

He caught that scrutiny and stopped, turning back toward her. "What's wrong?" he asked.

"Not a thing," she replied, smiling. "I like looking at you. Do you mind?"

He frowned slightly. That honesty of hers took some getting used to, and he wondered if she realized how it affected him when she said things like that. He couldn't afford another lapse like the one he'd had that afternoon in their room. He couldn't put their child at risk just because Kate aroused him to madness.

"No," he said absently. "I don't mind."

"It was just a comment, Jason," she murmured as she fell into step beside him. "I mean, I'm not planning to wrestle you down on the sand and tear your clothes off or anything."

He chuckled helplessly, glaring at her even through it. "Damn you, stop that."

She smiled up at him. "At least you've stopped looking like one of the Roman senators in those intimidating statues," she commented. "You never used to laugh at all."

"I've never had much to laugh about," he said. His dark eyes smoothed lazily over her face as they paused to watch the surf curl onto the white beach. "Then you came along and started getting under my skin."

"You didn't used to mind."

He took a long draw from the cigarette and lifted his head, letting the ocean breeze rip warmly through his thick, straight black hair. "You made everything bearable," he said stiffly. "I got to where I even looked forward to getting hurt, because it meant somebody would stick his nose in long enough to get you. And you always came. Patch-ing cuts. Bandaging wounds." He smiled slowly. "Nobody ever gave a damn about me, Kate, until you did."

Her breath caught in her throat. "Sheila loves you. So does Gene."

"In their way," he agreed. "I didn't mean family." He turned toward her, looking very masculine, and very much older than she was. "I meant women."

Amazing, she thought, how he could still make her flush with a look like that, even in the semidarkness. "I won't believe that none of your lovers ever cared about you," she replied coolly.

He studied her without speaking for a long moment. "You might be shocked to know how many women I'd had."

She moved restlessly, averting her angry eyes. "I don't want to know."

"Are you sure?" He crushed out the cigarette under his sandal and took her gently by the shoulders, resting his chin on her dark hair. It was a letting down of barriers that he might regret later, but she was his wife now, and he needed to make her understand. "Kate," he said quietly, "you could count the number of women I've had on the fingers of one hand."

She wouldn't look at him. His closeness was having its own effect on her, making it hard to speak. "Pull the other one, Jason," she said, disbelieving.

His eyebrows shot up. "What?"

She turned, glaring up at him. "You don't have to make up fairy tales for me. I may be grass green, but what we did...what you did..." She shifted restlessly. "You didn't learn that by reading books."

His face changed. Softened magically. His dark eyes searched her mutinous features with a kind of subdued amusement behind the tenderness. "Not all of it, no," he confessed. "But instinct goes a long way."

"You're serious," she said after a minute, her eyes darkening as she realized that he was telling her the truth.

"Dead serious. I'm not much more experienced than you are." He lifted his chin in that arrogant way he had, daring her to laugh, to make fun of him. "When I told you I'd never undressed in front of a woman, I meant it. You were the first."

All the lines went out of her face. She simply looked at him. After a minute, she lifted her hands to frame his hard cheeks and tug his head down. She went on tiptoe then, touching her mouth tenderly to his, breathlessly tender. There were tears on her mouth, and he tasted them.

"You're crying," he whispered softly.

"I always thought you were experienced," she said simply, smiling even through the mist of tears that blurred him in her sight. "I thought sex was something you just... sort of took for granted."

"I never took it for granted." His face went hard again. He let go of her and sat down on the sand, resting his arms on his drawn-up knees as he watched the horizon. "Sit down a minute."

She moved close beside him and leaned her head against his shoulder.

"My father hated the whole world after Mother left," he said. "Most of all, he hated women. He told me..." He hesitated, scooping up a handful of sand and absently drifting it onto the beach. "He told me that sex was a weapon. That women used it to get what they wanted, to keep a man in line. To rob him of his manhood." He laughed softly, bitterness in his deep voice. "I didn't understand what he meant, but as I got older, he drilled it into me. He never let me look at the kind of magazine most boys had tucked under the mattress. He wouldn't let me date or go out with girls, he even got hot if I talked to a girl. After a while, he began lecturing me about how dirty sex was, and how women would cow a man by getting him stirred up and then pulling away. He said the only purpose it had in life was the begetting of children." He sighed heavily. "I was just a boy, Kate. Just fifteen when my mother walked out. I could never understand why my father didn't love me. I did my best to please him, to be what he wanted. Finally, when I realized his attitude was warping me, I stopped trying to please him. Just before he died, we got along pretty well. But the damage was done."

Kate felt his body going more and more rigid as the minutes passed. She understood him better at that moment than she ever had in their relationship. "Do you still feel that way?" she asked softly.

"Sometimes." He drew in a long breath. "I don't like losing control, Kate. Not even for those few wild, sweet seconds…"

"Oh, Jason." She put her arms around him and nuzzled her face into his shoulder. She'd done that to him just today, she'd knocked him off balance and he'd lost his head. She hadn't understood his remoteness, not then. Now she did, and she felt guilty for doing that to him.

"I'm not blaming you," he said. "I don't think you have any more resistance than I do, when we make love."

"I'm a woman," she whispered. "It isn't the same for me." She smiled shyly and dropped her forehead against his shoulder. "I like giving up control, as long as I'm giving it up to you."

She knocked the breath completely out of him with that soft little confession. His arm slid around her, hesitantly. He drew her close against his side and felt her body relax immediately, submissive and warmly responsive.

He looked down into her eyes, searching them in the windswept darkness. "You said I never let people get close," he whispered. "Is this close enough to suit you, Kathryn?"

Tears came warm and soft down her cheeks. She drew his face down to hers and kissed him, tenderly, amazed at the way he indulged her hunger and fed it.

He eased her down against the grainy sand and smiled as his mouth warmed hers in the darkness. His lean hand found her belly and pressed there, savoring the knowledge of what lay under it.

"Did I ever tell you that pregnancy suits you, Mrs. Donavan?" he whispered against her lips.

She smiled, nuzzling her nose against his. "I'm glad," she whispered back. "Because I like carrying your baby."

Wild shivers of emotion went through Jason like fire when Kate said that. His lean hand flattened, became caressing. His mouth slid back over hers and grew slowly more insistent, warming with desire.

She reached up to draw his broad chest down against her and all at once he felt the danger and drew back.

"No," he said huskily, pulling her up to sit beside him. "We can't risk that again."

She knew what he meant, and why. She sighed, leaning her head against his shoulder. "I know. But it was so sweet, Jason."

"Sweeter than wine," he agreed. "And I want you every bit as much as you want me. But we're going to be parents. We have to protect our baby."

"That sounds nice," she murmured. "Our baby."

"I think so, too." He got to his feet reluctantly and drew her up with him. "You need sleep."

"Do I get to sleep with you?" she asked, searching his eyes.

"I guess I can grit my teeth all night," he sighed, smiling. "All right, but keep your hands to yourself, Mrs. Donavan. I know about you fast country girls."

"You ought to. You taught me everything I know," she laughed softly.

Her gentle teasing delighted him. He slid his fingers into hers and led her back down the beach toward their room.

Kate curled up against him in her thin blue cotton gown, listening to his heart beat in the darkness, loud against the faint hum of the air conditioner and the even fainter roar of the surf outside the window. He wasn't asleep, but she didn't speak. It was new and exciting to sleep with him, to lie in his arms in bed and not have to worry about being caught or hiding from prying eyes.

"Are you asleep?" he asked, and she saw the glowing orange tip of his cigarette as he turned slightly toward her.

"I can't sleep," she confessed. "It's different, sleeping with someone."

He laughed softly, the sound pleasant and deep in the quiet, dark room. "I know. I'm having the same problem. I've never spent the night with a woman before."

That was exciting. Apparently his few interludes were conducted in places where he didn't want to spend the night. She smiled to herself. "I'm glad I'm the first," she said quietly.

He took a draw from the cigarette. "You really don't mind that I don't have a lot of experience, do you?" he asked suddenly.

"Of course not," she returned drowsily. "I don't like

playboys. I really don't want a man who uses women the way he uses cars."

He burst out laughing. "What a hell of a way to put it!"

"It's true," she said doggedly. "A man who can go from one woman to another without sentiment or loyalty isn't the kind of man I want to father my children."

His lean hand brushed gently against her soft dark hair. "It was like the first time, that day I made love to you," he said quietly. "I did things with you that I'd never thought of before."

She buried her face against him, shy all over again as she remembered what they'd done together. "You seemed to know exactly what to do."

"I was bluffing," he whispered. "I was scared to death I was going to do the wrong thing and hurt you."

"Jason!" Her eyes came up, shocked as she searched past the orange tip of his cigarette for his face.

"The very few times I gave in to desire, it was always with women who knew the ropes," he said simply. "I heard one of the boys talk once about his wedding night, or I wouldn't have had a clue about how to keep from frightening you."

Her face, she knew, was red. "Well…it wasn't bad at all."

"Yes, I noticed that it wasn't bad at all," he laughed softly. "My God, you made me feel ten feet tall. Those sweet little noises you made, the way you held me. You'll never know how whole I felt with you. Or how it hurt me to walk away."

"I thought you were feeling guilty."

He shifted. "Maybe I was. Guilty and a little vulnerable, too. I didn't want to get married."

"Neither did I," she lied. She drew in a slow breath. "But here we are."

"And here we'll stay," he added. "I don't believe in divorce. So you're stuck with me, Mrs. Donavan, and I may even make you like it one day."

She kissed his bare shoulder. "I like it already. I just hope I can be the kind of wife you want. I know I'm naive in some ways, and country, and I don't know much about high society. But if you'll be patient, I'll learn those things. I'll try to make sure you're never ashamed of me again, the way you were that night Cherry invited me to supper."

He pulled her against him roughly, a sound that was almost a groan passing his lips. "I was cruel because I wanted you so badly, Kate. I'd missed you like hell, forced myself to stay away. And then I looked up and there you were, and I caved in. I didn't want to give in to it, so I fought back."

"You did a good job of it," she sighed. "Until I agreed to go out with Gabe."

He sighed at the memory of that confrontation. "And I lost my head completely. I couldn't even stop."

"Neither could I, so don't agonize over it. You never seduced me. It was as much my doing as yours, and I don't have one single regret, Jason. Not one."

He felt his chest swell at that confession. He brushed his hard mouth over her forehead. "Neither do I. Least of all now, with a baby on the way." He started to tell her that the baby hadn't been an accident, not on his part. But he held back. He'd already told her more about his deepest feelings than he really wanted to. There was time for confessions. All the time in the world.

"You'd better get some sleep, cupcake," he murmured. "We've got a lot of exploring to do in the next few days."

She smiled against his shoulder. "Good night, Mr. Donavan."

"Good night, Mrs. Donavan." He kissed her forehead before he put out his cigarette and curled her into him. At that moment, he wouldn't have minded if the world ended. He was happier than he'd ever been in his life.

They spent three more days in Jamaica, exploring the elegant landscape and getting a look at the drastic difference between the luxurious tourist houses high on the hills and the less than adequate houses that many Jamaican people lived in.

"The economy here is very unstable," their cabdriver told them as he drove them around the island. "We go from prosperity to poor to worse than poor."

"What about tourism?" Jason asked curiously.

"We don't get as much of that as we'd like," came the resigned reply. "Riots, you see. And people hear how violent we are…violent, my God. Violence everywhere in the world, my friend, but people only notice it here. You can get mugged and killed in New York City and that doesn't even slow down tourists there. But here, there's one riot completely across the island, and nobody wants to come to Jamaica."

"I love it here," Kate confided, and meant it. "It's beautiful and unpolluted, and the people are marvelous."

Barton Cox grinned at her. "Thank you, ma'am."

She flushed. "Well, they are. We've been treated so nicely, in the hotel and in the restaurant…everywhere we've gone. And people haven't talked up to us or down to us. Here, color doesn't seem to matter."

"How could it? We don't have the history your country has," she was reminded. "In Jamaica, there was no Civil War."

"No, there were just bloodthirsty pirates who killed and robbed everybody," she laughed.

He lifted his hands briefly from the wheel. "Local color," he corrected, chuckling.

He took them down to the public beach, to the docks where huge cruise ships were anchored, and then up to the tip-top of one of the mountains that rose almost from the beach itself. On the top was an elegant restaurant with a Greek motif and parrots in cages.

"How beautiful they are," Kate enthused, and started to stick her finger into the cage.

"If you like having ten fingers, don't do that," Jason cautioned, catching her hand. "Those are Amazon parrots, and they can crack nuts with those beaks."

"They wouldn't really bite me, would they?" she asked Barton. "They look so tame…."

"The tamest Amazon will nip occasionally," the cab-driver responded. "Hello, Chico. Hello, Maxine."

"Hello," one of the parrots replied. As the bird climbed by his beak to the side of the huge wrought-iron cage, his pupils dilated and contracted so that they seemed to be flashing. He ruffled and made a purring noise, then spread his wings and tail feathers. Next he made a bobbing movement with his head and regurgitated.

"He likes you," Ben told Kate. "That's a compliment, from a parrot, at least."

"I'm flattered. I think," Kate murmured dryly. "They're very pretty."

"Amazona ochrocephala auropalliata," Barton said in Latin. "Yellow-naped Amazons. The noisiest, most vocal, and most acrobatic of the big parrots. I have one of my own at home. He sits on my lap, to watch the news with me, and shares my dinner."

"I never knew birds were like this," Kate said, fascinated. "I thought they just sat in cages and sang."

"These are allowed out of their cages during the morning, and late afternoon. It's cruel to keep them inside all the time, you see, and they don't stray far. They're climbers more than flyers. They're every bit as affectionate as a cat or dog, and very intelligent." Barton smiled. "Mine can sing grand opera and carry on a conversation. But they're unpredictable, and they can damage a poking finger. Mine doesn't like to be touched except when he invites it."

Kate sighed wistfully and glanced up at Jason, but he put his finger on her lips.

"No, you can't have one," he told her firmly. "We've got several thousand head of cattle scattered over two states. That's enough animals."

"You are a rancher?" Barton asked Jason.

"That's right. Kate and I come from south Texas."

"A state I have often wished to visit. But Jamaica is home." He lifted his shoulders. "I could never live anywhere else. Say, do you see movies often?"

"Once in a great while," Jason told him.

"A black woman I admire has become a big movie star in your country," Barton replied as he led them back out to the cab. "She's known there as Whoopi Goldberg."

"I think she's super," Kate sighed. "She was on one of my favorite weekly television shows, and in a variety show special…she was even nominated for an Oscar for the film *The Color Purple*."

"She has a great talent," Barton agreed. "And she is an inspiration to our young people, who see what can be done if one aspires."

Kate wondered if Jason understood her own aspirations, but she wasn't spoiling the delicate balance of their comradeship by asking. She slid her hand into his and smiled at him. After a minute, he smiled back. The lowering of barriers that first night had made him less antagonistic, but he still had a great deal of reserve left. Kate knew it was going to take time and patience before Jason trusted her fully. He might go far enough to share some secrets from his past, but that was a long way from telling her everything that was in his heart, especially where she was concerned. But she had time. Worlds of it. Her life had never been sweeter than it was here, in this beautiful place, with the man she loved most in all the world beside her and his child nestled under her heart.

They did a little more sight-seeing before they returned to the hotel, where Kate laid on the beach in her one-piece black swimsuit. She bought some shell necklaces from a big Jamaican who carried his wares on a small raft that he pulled along in the shallow water near the beach. Jason didn't go swimming. He lazed beside her in his white shorts, so devastating in his almost nudity that Kate hid behind her sunglasses and just stared at his darkly tanned, hair-roughened muscles with pure delight.

They had most of their meals near the pool, where odd-looking black birds with sideways tails called kling-klings begged for crumbs from the tables. Kate had gotten used to the kling-klings sharing her breakfast. The small blackbirds with their pale greenish yellow eyes and distinctive cry were a sight that, like the Amazon parrots, would stay in her memory for a long time. She'd also gotten used to the slower pace, the sultry Caribbean breezes, the beach, and the thrilling sight of octopi chasing hermit crabs along the surf, throwing their tentacles onto the sand in an attempt to harness their meals.

They'd met other tourists who became recognizable,

and a school marching band had performed for the hotel's guests. Kate had enjoyed that most of all, since it had given her an incredible feeling to stand as the American national anthem was played. Used to being a Texan in the States, she was now a minority in a foreign country—an American, not just a Texan. It was new and interesting, to think of herself in those terms.

Jamaica had been a learning experience in many ways. Kate felt that she had gained a better understanding not only of geography, but also of world economics. And of her new husband.

Their relationship had changed for the better during those lazy days in the sun. Kate had slept in his arms every night, although he hadn't slept a lot for the disturbing proximity to her. She knew how badly Jason wanted her, but they were both too afraid to risk any more danger to the baby. He kissed her occasionally, but only lightly, briefly, so that the chemistry between them didn't flare up too high and become unmanageable.

Jason's distance from Kate since his loss of control in their hotel room never fully disappeared. But when they got back to San Frio, that distant attitude grew even more rigid, and she wondered if he meant for intimacy to be banished from their relationship forever. They shared a room, but not a bed now. He slept on the daybed and she had the king-size bed, and if she saw him at night, it was only as she was drifting off to sleep.

It didn't help Kate that her cramps were coming back, and that she had more spotting. She had a terrible feeling that she was going to lose the baby, and it was the most unsettling worry of all.

Jason settled back into ranch business with a vengeance, leaving Kate to her job with ill-concealed irritation. His attitude toward her work only made the distance between them grow. She wished they were back in Jamaica, where they'd been close, where their budding affection could have blossomed. Now, they were growing apart at a rate that frightened Kate. And because it did, she worked harder than ever, burying her fears of losing Jason in her work.

During the day, she went to the plant as usual, but in the evenings, she found herself at the mercy of newfound society friends who called with overwhelming frequency. She was invited to a coffee for a bride-elect early the next week, and Jason told her in one of their infrequent meetings at the supper table that it would be a good idea to attend.

She couldn't really spare the time. Things were hectic at the plant as she finished the last ten garments for the collection. But she asked for the morning off, and went. She was afraid that her casual things would be too informal for a coffee. She didn't really know how to dress for a coffee. She didn't want to distress Jason, and despite her knowledge of casual fasion, she still had no real idea of the kind of thing one would wear to a spiffy morning coffee. So she wore a black cocktail dress. Unfortunately, Cherry was out and couldn't tell her that it wasn't appropriate for a morning social event. A neat suit or even a dressy dress would have been adequate, but Kate did the thing properly in spaghetti straps, sequined jacket, and black pumps with rhinestones. With her perky short haircut, she wouldn't have been out of place at a Roaring Twenties party. But she stood out at the sedate gathering in the big brick mansion.

Her hostess didn't gasp when she opened the door, but she came close. She tried to smile and invited Kate into the parlor, where about two dozen women were milling around the silver service and refreshments. None of them had on cocktail dresses, and all of them stared blankly at Kate when she walked in.

She went red in the face. Not a single one of those women had on anything comparable to Kate's ensemble. Just my luck, she thought, to overdress again, and in black, again. She should have remembered her last social evening at Jason's house, and the disastrous results, but she hadn't been thinking clearly.

"Mrs. Donavan, isn't it?" one of the women asked, and nearby, Kate saw that horrid blonde woman who'd been at Jason's dinner party.

"Mrs. Donavan indeed," Kate said with a resigned sigh. "Overdressed as usual and as out of place as a pumpkin. I'm pregnant, you see. I guess my mind stopped working at the moment of conception."

That casual remark, thrown out with panache and an impish smile, took the cool edge off the social set. They crowded around her, and she found herself caught up in conversation about the wedding and her own gown, that someone had said she sewed herself.

"This is Edna St. John, our bride-elect," her hostess introduced a shy little dark-haired girl in a rich beige suit that did nothing at all for her petite figure with its ankle-length straight skirt. "She's being married to Barnett Coleman in March."

"Congratulations," Kate said with a smile as she tried to balance her coffee cup and saucer.

"Thank you," Edna replied. "You were just married last week, weren't you?"

"That's right." She bent closer. "It was a shotgun wedding," she said in a stage whisper. "I got Jason pregnant, too."

Edna giggled and so did their hostess. The blonde

came ambling up and lifted a lazy eyebrow. "That would be one for the books, from what I've seen of Jason Donavan," Daphne drawled. "He isn't the world's most notorious playboy."

"Still waters run deep," Kate told her, hiding her nervousness as she remembered her last confrontation with the woman. "And here we are again."

"You were right in what you said to me that night," she said levelly. "So I did something about it. I'm divorcing my husband, who loves my money more than he loves me, and I'm going to Libya to become a harem girl or some such thing. I expect to be involved in a juicy international scandal in no time," she mused, tongue in cheek.

Kate burst out laughing. "How delightful." She grinned. "I'll look forward to reading all about it."

"It will be your fault," Daphne drawled. Then she smiled, and turned away to another guest, and Kate realized then how much of a disguise the woman's bored expression and sharp tongue were. Like Jason's bland poker face, this woman had her own mask, but it wasn't an obvious one.

"How could you advertise something like pregnancy when you've barely been married for a week?" a hatchet-nosed matron demanded shortly, offense in every line of her flushed face.

Kate noticed her hostess's sudden pallor, and turned back to the matron without letting her own nervousness show. "Because it's something that everyone will see soon enough," she replied. "I made a mistake, but at least I'm not trying to hide it. I want this baby. So does my husband. If that makes me a scarlet woman, then I suppose I am. Oddly enough, I have very old-fashioned ideas about babies. I think people should be married before they make them, and that a baby's life is precious, not something easily disposed of just because it interferes with a woman's pleasure."

"I'll bet the pro-abortion people love you," Daphne murmured in a stage whisper.

"Oh, they're perfectly entitled to their own opinion," Kate replied. "I can even see their point of view, under certain circumstances. I simply don't share it, that's all." She leaned forward. "I'm a prude!"

The matron flushed even more, and stormed off to whisper something to another ruffled-looking older woman. Kate just smiled and lifted her coffee to her lips. Not bad, kid, she told herself. At least, not for her first coffee, even if she didn't know quite what to wear or how to act. Society ladies were just like the ladies at the plant, except for the size of their bankrolls. There were nice ones and nasty ones, caring ones and uncaring ones. Kate didn't have another worry about fitting in. This had been a piece of cake.

However, when she turned to thank her hostess for inviting her, she tripped, and poured coffee down the back of the ruffled matron's expensive suit and knocked her into the coffeepot.

CHAPTER FIFTEEN

KATE LET HERSELF into the house, smeared with finger sandwiches and canapés and stained with coffee. While she was afraid that her face was going to be permanently red, her most immediate concern was keeping Jason from finding out about what she'd done. She barely remembered how she'd managed to get out of her hostess's home, blurting apologies and promising to make good the expense of replacing everything. The expensive silver coffeepot had an equally expensive dent in it. The china was in shards. Two crystal lazy Susans were also gone. Kate imagined it would take at least thirty or forty dollars to replace the things, and thank God she had an account of her own and a good deal of money in it from her designing.

"What in heaven's name happened to you?" Sheila explained when she saw her. "What are you wearing? Kate, you didn't go to the coffee dressed like that?!"

Kate swallowed. "Yes, I went to the coffee like this. And I was congratulating myself on how well I was doing when I bumped into a plump lady and knocked her into the canapés and fell on her." She burst into tears. "Oh, Sheila, I'm sure God never meant for me to be a society butterfly!"

Sheila drew the sobbing woman into her arms and rocked her against her huge bosom. "There, there, my pet, there, there. Sheila will teach you everything you need to know, don't you fret."

"I broke the china," she wailed. "I dented the silver coffeepot. I broke two..." She hiccuped. "...two crystal platters on pedestals. I promised to replace them."

Sheila froze. "You were at Mrs. Warden's house?"

"Yes."

"Oops."

Kate lifted her tearstained face. "Oops?"

Sheila let out a long breath. "Kate, honey, that silver coffeepot dates to the time of the Alamo. It came over from England with one of Mrs. Warden's ancestors. The china is Wedgwood. Expensive stuff, Wedgwood. And the crystal, I'm sorry to say, is Waterford." She realized that she might as well be speaking Greek. "I bought a salt and pepper set for our service two years ago—I paid almost a hundred dollars just for those small items. Or, rather, Jason did."

Kate was going pale. "You're telling me that I did more than thirty or forty dollars' worth of damage."

Sheila pursed her lips and nodded. "You might say that. I'd estimate it at about six hundred, by the time she has that coffeepot repaired by a master silversmith."

"I need to sit down." Kate dropped into a chair in the hall, pale and sick and terrified. "Jason will have to know. He'll kill me."

"He would never kill a pregnant woman," Sheila assured her. "And six hundred dollars isn't so much. Jason will hardly miss it."

"I knew I shouldn't have gone."

"Nonsense. After all, honey, mingling with society people is something you'll have to get used to. But it won't always be so agonizing, honest it won't." She helped Kate off with her stained jacket. "Now you go upstairs and change clothes, and I'll make you some nice decaffeinated coffee."

"Yuck," Kate muttered. "I hate decaf."

"Well, baby won't. Go on, now."

Kate got up, wobbling a little. She started for the staircase, but she turned back before she went up and smiled. "I love you."

Sheila smiled. "I love you, too, pumpkin. Go on."

After Kate bathed and changed into oversize blue knit pants and a worn, stained white top that she'd embroidered herself, she felt worlds better. If only she could be sure that Jason wasn't going to find out what a fool she'd made of herself at the Warden coffee. He'd be disappointed, at the very least.

She went back downstairs and had coffee, barefoot and relaxed at last. And as luck would have it, all bad, Jason chose that minute to walk in with two very distinguished businessmen.

"Hello, Jason," Kate said shyly, getting to her feet.

He looked at her with obvious irritation, from the stained old shirt to the pulled places in the knit pants, to her bare feet. "Gentlemen, my wife," he introduced her to two Stetson-decked cattlemen who took off their Stetsons and smiled politely.

"I'm Kate," she introduced herself with an equally polite smile and no trace of self-consciousness. "Are you in the cattle business, too?"

"Afraid so," the oldest man said. "I'm Ed Blaine. This is Harry Sanders. We're from Montana. Got a feedlot up there, raise purebred Beefmasters."

"My dad had a few head of those," Kate said proudly. "Mom and I still own them, although Jason keeps track of them for us. They're bred from yours, too, if you're S&B Beefmasters, that is."

"We sure are." Harry, the smaller man came forward.

"Well, those heifers threw the prettiest little calves you ever saw," Kate told them, "and we've bred them just this past spring to a champion Santa Gertrudis sire. We're expecting some fine results in the way of improved stamina and other good heritability factors."

"My God, she speaks cattle," Ed Blaine exclaimed, his huge jowls tugged up in a delighted smile. "Little lady, Jason's a lucky man if he's got himself a woman who can understand the cattle business. My wife doesn't know an Angus from a Hereford."

"All mine thinks about is diamonds," the other man agreed with a weary sigh. "She's allergic to cattle, you see."

Jason's irritation was gone by now, and he was frankly astounded at the way Kate was charming his business associates. He'd been just slightly embarrassed at her lack of decorum and her ragged clothes, but nobody seemed to be noticing how she was dressed.

"Jason taught me about cattle," Kate confessed, and she smiled at her husband with real warmth.

He found himself lost in her soft green eyes, and for one long moment he actually forgot what he was going to say. He jerked his eyes away finally.

"Her father was the Spur's foreman for a number of years," he told the other men. "And Frank Whittman knew cattle. Kat learned as much from him as she's learned from me."

"Sit," Sheila said to Kate as she joined the small group, coaxing the younger woman down into a chair. "She's in the family way," she told the older men. "And she's had kind of a rough morning."

The cattlemen grinned. "Style and personality, and a baby to boot. Damn, you lucky son of a…" He cleared his throat. "You're a lucky man, Jason."

"Thanks, Ed," he mused, but he was watching Kate. She looked pale under that forced good cheer, and there were lines of strain in her face. "Why don't you gents go into the study and I'll organize us some coffee and sandwiches. We can eat and talk business at the same time."

"Suits me. No need to show us the way, I know it," Ed said. He and Harry lingered for a minute to say good-bye to Kate with obvious reluctance, and then they wandered off down the hall, murmuring to each other.

"What happened?" Jason asked Kate.

"Do you want the whole horrible thing, or will you settle for an abbreviated version?" Kate asked miserably.

His chin lifted. "Abbreviate it."

"We owe Mrs. Warden six hundred dollars."

He cocked an eyebrow. "Any particular reason?"

"Broken china and crystal and a dented silver pot," Kate sighed. "We also owe a Mrs. Gills twenty-five dollars to have her suit cleaned. It's got some kind of paste with little tiny fish and mayonnaise and coffee stains all over it."

"Is that all?" Jason asked politely.

Kate grimaced. "Well, I stained my cocktail dress and some of the sequins got knocked off, so I'll have to have a new one. I got it for ten dollars at the San Frio thrift shop…"

"God almighty!"

Kate grimaced and Sheila shushed him, but he was going right up through the ceiling anyway.

"You wore a cocktail dress with sequins to a coffee

and got anchovy paste on Mrs. Gills and broke the Wardens' china?" He seemed lost for words. "How?"

"I backed into Mrs. Gills. Sort of. With my coffee cup. It was full. I'm sorry," she moaned.

"You backed into Mrs. Gills."

"That's right."

"What was she doing at the time?" he asked.

Kate hesitated. The woman might be a friend of his. But in the long run, the truth was the only chance she had against that cold, challenging stare. "Well, up until then she'd been telling everybody what a slut I was for getting pregnant before I got married."

He studied her wan little face. And then he bent unexpectedly and softly moved his lips against hers, smiling as he nibbled them and then lifted his dark head. "Good for you, honey," he said so tenderly that she almost cried. "I'll settle the bills, don't worry about it." He stood up. "Sheila, how about some sandwiches and coffee for some hungry cattlemen?"

Sheila was wiping away an unexpected tear. "You can have a fried horse if you want one, after being so sweet to my Kate. I'll bring it in." She turned and went to work.

Kate got up and slid her arms around Jason's hard waist under his jacket. "I think you're a nice man," she said softly, trying not to notice the way he stiffened at just her touch. He'd been physically distant since that afternoon in Jamaica. They shared a room, but not a bed, and he was careful not to come in before she was asleep. He left before she woke. It was even getting to be a rare thing to see him at breakfast, lunch, or supper. But she wouldn't give up. She couldn't. They were married, and as long as they were, there was still hope.

"I think you're a nice girl," he replied. He bent and

kissed her gently, but he drew back almost at once. He couldn't take much of that. His body reacted too suddenly to Kate, so he was careful to keep his distance most of the time. He wasn't risking the baby twice.

"Oh, come back," she whispered, and she moved closer.

But he took her by the thickened waist and lifted her gently away. "None of that, Mrs. Donavan," he said gently. "I'm a busy man. Are you taking the day off?" he added curiously.

"The whole day," she said. "I can't really spare the time, but I was too tired to go in."

"Good girl. The job will still be there when you're gone. And, Kate, get yourself some clothes, will you?" he asked gently. "Some maternity outfits and some evening things. And a suit. To wear to coffees," he added firmly. "Ask a saleslady. She'll tell you what to buy."

"All right." It was hard not to take offense, but she knew he meant well. She smiled up at him. "I'll try not to disgrace you."

He bent and kissed her forehead. "You won't disgrace me. Still doing okay?" he asked, and his lean hand touched her waist gently.

"Doing fine," she assured him. Why worry him with things that might never happen. She forced a smile to her lips. "Just fine."

"Okay. I'll get back to work then."

"You do that." She watched him go, her eyes brimming over with love. He was her whole world. If only she could tell him what he meant to her, how much she cared. But while he might like her, his feelings didn't go that deep. She had to remember that she was only here on sufferance, not for any other reason. The thought kept her depressed for the rest of the day.

So she dove into her work. Her coworkers were puzzled. They expected her to slacken up a little because of her marriage and her pregnancy, but if anything, she did more and worked later.

That finally captured not only Jason's attention, but his anger as well. And when she announced one evening two weeks later that she was flying to New York the following day for the showing of her collection, and two days later to Atlanta for another one, he hit the ceiling.

"Like bloody green hell you're going," he said coldly. They were in his study, with the door closed. He'd been doing paperwork, but now he rose from his desk like a dark-haired volcano, bristling with fury.

"I have to be there," she repeated. "Jason, I've worked for months on this collection. They've gone to a lot of trouble and they've invested a lot of money in my talent. I can't let them down. The media will be there…."

"And hot to write about a nobody from rural Texas who can sew a skirt?" he asked with ill-concealed bad temper. "Set me right, Kate, is that how it goes?"

The mocking tone hurt. So did his lack of faith in her ability. "I'm a good seamstress, if nothing else," she said, struggling not to lose her temper. "You used to think so yourself."

"Sure, when it meant sewing things for your own use," he agreed.

"Why does it bother you so much that I want to do something that you can't control, Jason?" she asked bluntly.

He turned away to light a cigarette, staring blankly at the painting of his prize Santa Gertrudis bull on the wall behind him. The bull had been a grand champion, a huge moneymaker.

"It isn't that," he said finally. He turned back. "You're pregnant. The last thing you need is to be jetting around the country."

"You took me to Jamaica on a plane, just three weeks ago," she pointed out.

"I was with you," he replied curtly. "If anything had gone wrong, I'd have been right there."

"Nothing went wrong," she said. "And nothing will. I'm not having any problems, not even any more nausea." She crossed her fingers behind her back. "There's no reason I can't go."

"I don't want you traveling alone," he shot back, his eyes intimidating.

"Then go with me," she said daringly.

He hesitated. It was a temptation. But he had roundup staring him in the face, and business was keeping him jumping. One big deal had fallen through already, what with fluctuating cattle prices and low sales figures. They were headed for financial difficulties no matter what he did, but he couldn't tell Kate that, or how important it was that he personally stay on top of things.

"I can't go," he said. "I'm selling off calves and up to my neck in ranch work."

"You and your cattle and me and my designs," she said. "Tit for tat."

He blew out a cloud of smoke in an angry breath. "Damn it, Kate, you don't need to work!"

"Of course I don't," she agreed readily. "Not from a financial standpoint. But what do you want me to do, Jason, sit at home and have babies and go to social functions?"

"That's a woman's place," he explained.

"What do you know about a woman's place?" she asked quietly. "Your father ran your mother off with just that kind of attitude, didn't he, Jason? He made her life miserable and ordered her around and abused her until she couldn't take it anymore...."

"Shut up!"

His voice was deep and icy, so quiet that it was frightening. His eyes stared at her with that cold intensity that chilled her to her toes.

She watched him, shocked at her own unexpected bravery for asking a question like that. Something in Jason's face prompted an even braver one, because he never talked about his mother. Not ever. "He beat her when he drank, too, that once, didn't he?"

He turned away blindly. He couldn't talk about it. He didn't want to remember. He didn't want to face the implications of his father's life, of his father's drinking that had turned a kind, loving father into a brutal stranger. Yes, his father had done all that. And caused his wife to leave him, although Jason had never admitted it until now. The admission hurt. It made him sick with worry about himself. What if he became like that? What if he caused Kate to leave him? Or was he going to lose her anyway, to her damned career? The baby might not be enough to hold her....

"Jason..."

"Go to New York," he said, blind with sudden fear. No. He wouldn't let her do this to him. He wouldn't let her see how easily she could cut him. "Go to hell for all I care."

He went back behind his desk, sat down, and pulled the ledger under his cold eyes. He didn't look up again.

Kate felt empty and cold. Tears ran down her cheeks, but he wasn't looking at her. She called his name, and he didn't even flinch.

Finally, with black nausea in the pit of her stomach,

she turned and went out the door. It closed behind her with sickening finality. Still, Jason didn't look up. He couldn't.

There was a letter in his middle desk drawer. Quietly, he opened it and looked. The writing was neat as a pin, very steady and confident. There was his name and address. And at the top left-hand corner of the small envelope, there was hers. Nell Caid Donavan, Apartment B22, 125 Costa Drive, Phoenix, Arizona, and the zip code.

He fingered it. Then, with a rough sigh, he picked it up. He usually threw these cards away without opening them. This one he'd kept, although he hadn't opened it. It was too early to be a birthday card, though. That puzzled him. She only sent cards once a year.

Kate's determination to pursue her career had hurt. Apparently her damned job meant more to her than his baby. But hadn't he known that all along? From the beginning, she'd said that she didn't want ties any more than he did. But he'd made her pregnant. He'd done it deliberately, because part of him was obsessed with her. And now she was straining at the bit, even with his baby in her body. She didn't really want the baby, he reasoned, because it interfered with her freedom. What if she found some way to lose it? The thought haunted him. He knew she wouldn't have an abortion. Kate was too tenderhearted for that. But she could fall or something, and even do it subconsciously.

He tore open the envelope and found a floral card inside, with no writing on the front. He opened it. There were only two lines inside, in the same neat hand that had addressed the envelope.

"Please come and talk to me," it read. "There may not be much time left."

It was signed Nell Donavan, in a different hand, an oddly unsteady and slanted hand. He frowned at it. Perhaps she had arthritis, or perhaps…his face hardened. Perhaps she drank, like his father had.

He stuffed the card back into the envelope and shot it into the drawer, closing it roughly. Not much time, the devil, he thought as he pulled the ledger close again. That was a trick. Just a trick to get him to come and see her. What did she want? Forgiveness? More than likely, she wanted money.

He leaned back in the chair. Kate hadn't, though. No, he thought bitterly, Kate wanted to earn her own with her designs. She wanted to be rich and famous, not just Mrs. Jason Donavan. He thought about her the way she'd been in Jamaica, that wild afternoon she'd deliberately led him on. He still worried about whether they might have harmed the baby. It didn't seem natural for a woman to bleed when she slept with a man, unless she was a virgin. Jason had wanted to discuss it with her again, but he felt uncomfortable talking about such things with Kate. He felt uncomfortable a lot lately. He wanted Kate to come home and be his wife. He wanted to sleep with her at night. He wanted to take her with him everywhere he went, and never spend more than an hour away from her.

Most of all, he wanted her silky soft body against his in the darkness, giving him the sweetest oblivion he'd ever known. He wanted to stroke her hair and kiss her until he went blind. But she wanted to go to New York and get famous. He glared at the ledger as if it were responsible for all his problems. After a minute he picked up his pencil and started again. All the brooding in the world wouldn't change anything. He had work to do.

Cherry heard Kate sobbing and walked into her room hesitantly. "Kate?"

She lifted her tearstained face. "Hi," she sniffed. "Sorry. I think it has something to do with being pregnant. I cry all the time lately."

"Maybe it's the water?" Cherry suggested with a warm smile. "Can I help?"

"You can help Gene look after Jason while I'm gone. I'm flying up to New York tomorrow for the showing."

"Wow," Cherry sighed. "Well, have fun. I guess I'll pose for Gene again. He's determined to do portraits now. He's even got a commission to do one for a friend, and they're paying him three hundred dollars. We haven't told Jason yet," she confessed. "We're hoping that it will lead to more commissions. He's really very good, you know."

"I do, indeed," Kate replied. "Keep him at it. He'll make it, if he sticks to his guns. Jason can be very hard to fight."

"I've noticed that," Cherry murmured. She winked. "Sleep tight. How's baby?"

"Doing fine, as near as I know. The nausea has stopped. I hardly even feel pregnant," she smiled.

"Good! 'Night."

"Good night."

Kate touched her stomach. Odd how she felt lately. But the cramping and bleeding were infrequent, so everything must be all right. And after the showings, she'd have some time to enjoy being pregnant. Maybe even to enjoy being married to Jason. She'd involve him with the baby, she decided. She'd get him to help pick out names for boys and girls, and shop for baby things. Yes. That might help heal the breach between them. But it was going to be so difficult to forget and forgive his coldness tonight. She hated to leave with a drawn sword between them. Perhaps in the morning, they could patch things up before she left.

She phoned her mother. Despite the fact that they had lunch together almost every day at the plant and talked on the phone a good deal, their relationship was different now. It was more like friend to friend than mother to daughter. Not that Kate loved her mother any less than she ever had. But now she was a woman, and she felt a new kind of maturity, of understanding.

"How are you doing?" Mary asked when she answered the phone.

"Better than the last time we spoke," Kate mused, tongue in cheek, and trying desperately to hide the hurt Jason had inflicted. "I haven't been to another single party. I'm leaving in the morning for New York, for the first showing of the collection, and then I go to Atlanta and Dallas."

"That's a lot of going, honey," Mary said.

"I know. But Dr. Harris didn't tell me I couldn't go," she told her mother truthfully. The obstetrician might have had something to say about it, but her appointment with him was still in the future, because there hadn't been an opening. "And I'll be real careful."

"See that you are, honey," her mother said gently. "You could lose that baby more easily than you realize. I lost two before I had you."

That was a comforting thing to say, Kate wanted to reply. But she forced herself not to say it. Mary never meant to hurt, she just opened her mouth and words came out.

"I'll be careful, Mama," she said, her tone a little stiffer. "I'd better get some sleep."

"Kate, I'm sorry," Mary moaned. "I didn't mean to worry you. I just don't want anything to happen…."

"If I'm not meant to have this baby, all the protective instincts in the world won't do any good," Kate said reasonably. "I can't stay in bed for nine months, not with the best will in the world. I feel fine. Well, pretty fine. I'm tired a lot. But the nausea seems to have passed and there's only a little spotting. I'll take it easy and I'll get plenty of rest. After all," she added, "sitting down at a showing is a lot easier than putting a collection together."

"Well, I won't argue with that. Call me when you get back, honey, and have a safe trip."

"I will. Love you."

"I love you, too, baby."

Kate hung up and put on her gown. She was nervous and a little scared, and she'd have given anything to go downstairs and beg Jason to go with her. But that would be admitting defeat. She couldn't let him dictate her whole life for her. If she was going to have any independence in the future, it had to start now. And she had to have money. That, she'd have to earn, so she couldn't afford to start treating herself like an invalid.

She touched her abdomen gently. She didn't feel pregnant. She felt strangely empty, and that worried her. She didn't know what to expect if anything was wrong, how she'd feel physically, and she didn't want to call the doctor at home just to ask. Probably she was just overworked and overtired. She'd get some rest on the trip.

If only the collection went well. Tomorrow, the burden would be on her. She'd see her designs on real models while buyers gave them a critical and unbiased eye. This would be the acid test. She'd make a reputation or not make it on her talent.

If the designs didn't sell, she didn't know what she was going to do. Jason was going to be hard enough to live with either way. He didn't want her to have a career that didn't involve him. It seemed to bother him to not be able to control things and people. Looking back at his childhood, she even understood his reasoning. He'd had no control at all over his father. His mother had deserted him. He'd had the responsibility for not only the ranch after his father's death, but for bringing up his young brother as well. All his life, he'd been kicked around and made to do things. Even now, he had the entire burden of the ranch to bear, because Gene didn't really want any part of it. Jason had never been allowed to enjoy himself. He didn't know how. Until Kate had entered his life, he'd hardly ever smiled at all.

She sighed, thinking about how fortunate she'd been in comparison. She'd had two parents who loved her dearly, and though she'd been disciplined, she'd never been abused. If only she could show Jason how beautiful it could be, belonging to a loving family circle. But he didn't seem to want that now. He didn't even seem to want her anymore.

With a long sigh, Kate put out the light and climbed into bed. She laid awake for an hour or more before she finally dropped off to sleep. And still Jason hadn't come upstairs.

CHAPTER SIXTEEN

CLAYBORN'S NEW YORK showing wasn't the extravaganza Kate had somehow expected it to be. She'd thought of women dripping diamonds and furs, a regal atmosphere with crystal chandeliers and plenty of space, and a band and photographers shooting off flashbulbs like crazy.

Actually, it was rather a cozy setting, in a showroom that Clayborn's parent company maintained on Seventh Avenue. There were a number of buyers around, sensibly dressed in business suits or dresses, and only a handful of photographers in attendance. The music was taped, and Kate had trouble understanding both the woman who was introducing the fashions and the models who wore them.

Roberta was on hand, looking just faintly bored with the whole business, and Kate got a glimpse of Clarisse in one of the seats reserved for Clayborn people.

Kate chewed nervously on a fingernail when the first of her embroidered skirts was shown. The model swung gracefully down the runway, and Kate wished that she was back home in Texas sitting in a patch of sunshine surrounded by wildflowers. She was scared to death that someone was going to laugh at her unsophisticated designs.

"Don't worry so," Roberta whispered, touching her bare arm gently. "They're going to love your ensembles."

But Kate wasn't convinced. She shifted, uncomfortable in the gray knit suit she was wearing for the occasion. It was store-bought, and the skirt was too tight in the waist. She'd unbuttoned it, and the zip kept trying to slide down. God forbid that it should fall off in the middle of the showing!

The woman at the microphone was describing another of Kate's creations, a khaki shirt with epaulets worn with a denim skirt with khaki appliqués. But there was no wild applause, and nobody stood up and suggested that Kate be crowned queen of the fashion designers. On the other hand, no one booed her. That alone was encouraging.

Kate was sweating when the last of the models wearing her collection left the runway and went backstage.

"Well?" Kate groaned as the announcer told the audience that the program was concluded and thanked them for attending.

"We won't know yet," Roberta said gently. "These things take time. We can tell how successful your collection is going to be by the orders we…well, hello, Carla. Nice of you to stop by."

A tall, elegant woman nodded and fixed Kate with her jet black eyes. "You are Kathryn of Texas, yes?" she asked in a voice that was just faintly accented.

Kate smiled. "I have to confess. I am."

"I like very much the comfort of your basic silhouette, and the functional direction of the fabrics you use. It is very different, this collection, but that will give it distinction. I will include at least ten of the pieces in my spring lines. I thought it might encourage you to say that before I place the order," she added with a smile. "You have flair, mademoiselle. I think you will succeed. 'voir, Roberta."

"Thank you," Kate said, smiling broadly. "You flatter me."

"It is not flattery," the woman named Carla replied

smoothly. "Flattery does not sell garments, and that must be our collective concern, *n'est-ce pas?*" She nodded to Roberta and moved away.

"It is definitely not flattery, coming from Carla Roche," Roberta said with a breathless laugh. "My God, such praise. Didn't you recognize her?"

Kate shook her head and smiled apologetically. "I guess I should, but I don't."

"She's the head buyer for Savant."

"Savant?" Kate asked. "*The* Savant? The very expensive Savant stores that are mentioned in the same breath with Saks and Neiman-Marcus?"

Roberta grinned wickedly. "Now what other Savant is there in this country?"

"I think I'm going to faint," Kate informed her.

"Not yet, you don't," Roberta laughed. "You've got to meet the press, lady, and here's where I come in. You just follow my lead."

Being interviewed was as new an experience as being a designer had been, and Kate found herself enjoying it. It wasn't anything like the ordeal she'd expected, although there were some questions that she had a hard time answering with a simple yes or no. But eventually it was over and Roberta rescued her.

"Kate, let's go and talk to Clarisse," she said, and once she had her out of earshot of the fashion reporters, she grinned from ear to ear. "I eavesdropped. You did great!"

Kate relaxed only then, and smiled as Clarisse approached them. She hugged the taller woman. "It's good to see you again. I heard about your good fortune."

"I was lucky," Clarisse laughed. "And Roberta's brother is a very nice man. Are you both coming to Curt's showing tomorrow at the Waldorf?"

"I'm flying to Atlanta," Kate said, shocking Roberta. She smiled apologetically. "I'm really sorry, but I'm pregnant and I'm not doing too well. I'm afraid to push it too hard, so I'm going to go to Atlanta tomorrow and then home to see my doctor."

"Pregnant?" Roberta asked.

"You know, as in 'with child,' or 'in a family way'— that thing that happens when you sleep with a man…?" Clarisse prompted.

Roberta glared at her. "I know what happens when you sleep with a man. You take precautions."

"Guess who didn't?" Clarisse said easily, folding her arms over the bodice of her simple, very chic black dress.

"So that's why you got married so suddenly," Roberta mused.

"Jason wants the baby, too," Kate sighed. "I'm hopeful that things will work out for all of us."

"They will," Clarisse said optimistically.

"Well, if you ever turn that gorgeous hunk of yours out to pasture," Roberta said with a sly grin, "I'm going to be first in line with a lasso."

"Shame on you, talking like that to a pregnant lady," Clarisse scolded only half jokingly.

Roberta blushed. "Yes, shame on me. Well, let's mingle, Kate. If you're only here for the day and the evening, let's milk it for all we're worth."

Kate did that, but finally, the fatigue began to tell on her. She began to feel nauseated and went off into a corner, where she stayed until Roberta rescued her.

"Are you okay?" Roberta asked. Kate was almost white in the face.

"I will be, after a good night's sleep." She sagged a little as she spoke, and she was uncomfortable. There was some cramping now, probably from all the standing. "I'm so tired, Roberta."

Roberta patted her arm. "Well, honey, from your standpoint, I guess it has been a long day. I'll go back to your hotel with you, and we can have an early dinner. Then you can get some rest. I'll put you on the plane in the morning. You'd probably get lost halfway to La Guardia."

Kate grinned. "With my track record, I'd probably find the airport but get on a plane to some foreign country. Roberta, thanks for all you've done," she added sincerely.

"You had the talent, kid," Roberta joked. "I just helped point you in the right direction. I have high hopes for your collection. It was a pity your Mr. Rogers had a sick wife and couldn't come. He'd have been proud of you. Come on. I'll get you out of here."

Kate slept from the time her head hit the pillow, and she slept most of the way to Atlanta the next day on the plane. She was spotting heavily now, and the cramps were more frequent than they had been before. She had a bad feeling, and she wanted to go home, where Jason would be there if she needed him. But once she got to Atlanta, she was going to find a doctor and have herself checked over. She should have done it before, and she cursed her own inaction. She'd put it off out of fear that she was going to miscarry. Now, it might be too late.

She wondered if Jason had missed her. He was busy with cattle, and their argument was still fresh. She wondered miserably if he'd meant what he said about not caring where she went or what she did. She'd wanted to call him the night before, but she was too hurt.

An elegant woman with blue eyes and jet black hair met her at Hartsfield International Airport in Atlanta, and Kate groaned as they walked for miles after leaving the jerky confines of the people mover, a subway train-type conveyance that was fast and efficient. But there was still a long way to walk, past rushing travelers and security guards, children playing in the long walkways, and only a handful of small shops, which seemed odd in such a staggeringly big airport.

By the time they got out the door and were headed toward the parking lot, Kate was sick.

"Is it much farther?" she asked the woman, Angela Marshal, as they started under the parking deck toward the widespread economy parking area.

"Quite a bit, I'm afraid," the older woman said in her gentle drawl. "Honey, you look bad. If you'll wait, I'll go get the car and pick you up here. Let me have that bag, too."

Kate was on the long covered walkway that led to several different sections of the parking lot. She smiled gratefully. "I'm so tired...I'm pregnant, you see."

"Don't say another word, I know just how you feel." Angela grinned. "I got two girls, three and five years old and I spent a total of eighteen months throwing up. You just hang on right there, I'll be back in a jiffy!"

Kate held on to one of the round supports, feeling gruesome. She didn't know how much farther she could go. The pain was getting worse and she felt a wetness that was sudden and frightening, and nausea that almost brought her to her knees.

As Angela pulled up, tears were rolling down Kate's cheeks.

"Honey, what is it?" Angela asked quickly.

"Oh, God...I think I'm losing the baby," Kate whispered, her face white and pinched and full of horror.

"Grady Memorial is just down the road a few miles," Angela said as she jumped out of the compact Chrysler she drove and helped Kate into the passenger seat. "Sit tight. I'll get you there as soon as I can."

She got back in under the wheel and pulled the car into the lane to pay the parking ticket, then onto the crowded expressway with its maze of new construction.

The ride was a nightmare of congested noontime traffic. Kate was barely conscious when Angela pulled up at the emergency room entrance of Grady hospital and ran in to get help.

Kate was lifted gently onto a stretcher and taken inside, groaning in pain that had become unbearable.

She was examined presently by a young physician, who confirmed her fear of miscarriage, and told her that an emergency dilation and curettage would have to be done. The nurse came and took her away to be prepped, had her sign a form, then took blood to type and cross match and shaved her for the operation. By the time she was given the necessary injection, she was in such misery that she didn't care what they did if they could just make it stop hurting.

She came to in the recovery room, trying to grab at the skirt of a passing nurse. It was so odd, the feeling that she needed to touch another human being, perhaps to reassure herself that she was still alive.

"So you're back with us," the nurse said with a gentle smile. "Good girl."

Kate tried to answer her, but she was too groggy.

They took her to a bed in a semiprivate room, but the other bed was unoccupied. She was still hooked up to an IV and she felt sore. Even worse, she felt empty. Horribly empty. And her first thought was that her baby was dead, and that Jason would blame her for losing it. She'd gone to New York against his wishes, and despite

Dr. Harris's long talk about it, she felt guilty, too, because she'd been too afraid to tell him the truth about her cramping. She'd been terrified to hear him confirm what she'd known somehow—that she wasn't going to be able to carry the baby to term.

All day long, she worried about what to do, about whether or not to have them call Jason. Angela came in to see her briefly and promised to return that evening and tell her all about the showing, but Kate was unenthusiastic.

One of the doctors came to talk to her, and found her in tears.

"None of that, now," he said gently, smiling. "You're young and healthy, and there will be other babies. Some women are never able to get pregnant in the first place."

She dabbed at her eyes with the sheet and looked up at him. He was blond and wore glasses and he didn't seem to be much older than Kate herself. She tried to smile back.

"My husband will blame me for losing it," she blurted out. "He told me to stay home...."

"Staying home wouldn't have helped, in this case," he said quietly. He pulled up a chair and sat down. "I don't like to discuss miscarriages in detail, but if you want to know, I'll tell you."

She searched his face. "Please."

He took her hand and held it gently. "The fetus had terminated some time ago."

"You mean...it was dead?"

He nodded.

She felt the hot sting of tears rolling down her cheeks. "What was wrong?"

He told her, gently but in detail. "There was nothing anyone could have done."

She burst into tears and he patted her hand. It sounded so horrible. Poor little thing. Poor, poor little thing.

He called the nurse after a minute and ordered a sedative. "Here," he said when the nurse returned, injecting it into the tube that led down to the needle in Kate's blue-veined wrist. "This will relax you, and make it easier for you to get through the night. You can go home tomorrow."

"My husband," Kate began.

"He was notified when they brought you in," the doctor said. "I assume he's already on his way. I go off duty at seven, but I'll try to wait around and talk to him."

Kate managed a watery smile. "Thank you. That would help."

He patted her hand again. "Take care of yourself. And don't dwell on this too much. I've seen a lot of women miscarry their first child and then have twins on the next try."

"You're very encouraging."

"We do our best. Good afternoon."

She watched him leave and then she was asleep again. When she woke, it was dark, and Jason still hadn't shown up. She felt a cold shiver of fear. He might not come. He might leave her to make her way home alone. She was frightened and sick and miserable, but he must be, too. She remembered Melody and the abortion that sent Jason half out of his mind. He'd be remembering that, too. He'd be remembering a woman who wanted a career too much to let an unwanted baby stand in her way. He'd remember what she said that afternoon before he'd found out she was pregnant, about careers and babies not mixing. He'd remember that she'd insisted on going to New York and Atlanta against his wishes. And he'd add all that up in his mind and come up with a deliberate act.

She closed her eyes. Well, if he insisted on a divorce,

she'd manage. She'd go on with her career. But she thought about Jason grieving over the child he'd wanted so much, and the tears came back. She wanted to hold him, to comfort him. Jason would be hurt and sick, just as she was, and nobody else could get close to him.

The drugs they'd given her brought a slow, sweet oblivion, free from tormenting thoughts and the grief of loss. Her last thought was of Jason, and how she wanted him here.

BACK AT THE Diamond Spur, the man sitting in the high-backed leather chair at his desk was as quiet as death. He'd locked the study door and he had a bottle of whiskey that he was trying not to open. This had been his father's answer to pain. One drink had led to another, and another. But when the pain was this bad, how did a man face it?

Kate had gone to New York against his wishes. She'd deliberately put the baby at risk, to further her career. If she'd stayed home where she belonged, it would never have happened. Or...would it?

He remembered with horror that afternoon in Jamaica, in their hotel room. He remembered the violence of his lovemaking, and the fear that he'd hurt her, that he'd jeopardized the child. And that was what made him open the bottle and pour some of its amber contents into a glass. No, Kate wasn't wholly to blame. He was. He'd lost control and killed the baby. He knew it, because that doctor who'd phoned him had said that the fetus had been dead for some time before Kate's body expelled it. His violent hunger for her, that he hadn't been able to control, had done that. He was responsible.

But something in him couldn't bear the thought. He pushed it to the back of his mind. Kate's career was at fault. Her determination to get ahead at any cost. Yes, that was the problem. It wasn't his fault. It wasn't!

He lifted the glass to his lips and took a long, slow swallow. One helped. Two made it better. He didn't usually turn to alcohol to help him through things. Oddly, Kate had been at the bottom of his last two real bouts, the day he learned she was pregnant and today, the day she wasn't anymore.

He wondered what she was feeling. Relief, probably, he thought bitterly. Then he remembered her tender heart, and was ashamed of himself for the thought. No, she'd grieve, a little anyway. But now she could have her precious designing. She could travel without any hindrances. She could leave him, too, and she probably would. He didn't have any illusions about that. She'd told him, hadn't she, that her career came before any man.

The alcohol slid smoothly down his throat. He remembered his father mumbling something about women being at the root of all a man's deepest wounds. He hadn't understood at the time, but he did now.

His teeth ground together as he thought of all the plans he'd made for her and the baby. He hurt to the soles of his feet, but this time there was no one to take his hand and smooth back his damp hair and make him feel whole again.

He lifted the glass back to his lips, with a new and tormented understanding of his father's drinking habit. Just this once, he promised himself. Just this one last time, he'd never resort to the bottle again. Just to kill the pain…

A half hour later, he was mercifully asleep in his chair and oblivious to the world.

CHAPTER SEVENTEEN

KATE PUSHED THE eggs and grits around on her breakfast platter. She hadn't heard from Jason yet. She didn't know if he'd gotten the message, or if Sheila or someone at the house had taken it and they hadn't been able to reach him. He could be out of town. But with the ranch so busy right now, that was unlikely.

No, she thought miserably. More probably Jason had just been too angry to come running, and he wouldn't be reasoning logically. Not now.

Angela had come back to see her the night before, telling her how the buyers had raved about Kate's collection. That would mean sales in this area of the country, and that was reassuring. But Kate was sick over the loss of her baby right now, and too worried about Jason's reaction to care overly much about her designs. After all, Jason's initial rejection of her was what had prodded Kate into trying to make a career of design. She'd wanted to show him that she could make a good life for herself. But this had gotten way out of hand.

She didn't know whether to try and go to a hotel after she was discharged, or to try to get back to San Frio. She was still worrying over the problem two hours later when Jason came in the door of her room.

The other bed was still empty, but Kate wished there was someone else around. He was wearing dark glasses so that she couldn't see his eyes. There were new lines in his face, and he looked as tired as she felt. He didn't come far into the room. He stopped at the foot of the bed, just looking at her. After a minute, she thanked God that she couldn't see his eyes.

"Your doctor said that you could be discharged about eleven," he said curtly, glancing at his watch. "I'll see to the paperwork while you change and get your things together. I assume you're finished with marketing and promotion for the time being?" he added in a tone that could have taken rust off a car.

Kate shuddered at the way he sounded. That was cold fury, not concern, and all her worst fears were being realized. "I know what you're thinking," she began. "But I'm not totally to blame...."

"I'll be back when I've checked you out," he said, ignoring her defensive remarks. "I have a car to take us to the airport, and I've chartered a flight home."

She held on to her pride by a thread. "All right," she said in a voice devoid of life.

"The doctor here advised me to keep you away from work for a few days, to give you time to heal," he continued. "After that, you can do as you damned well please."

Kate couldn't fight that tone. She knew it all too well, and it broke her heart. She leaned back against the pillows with a weary sigh. She'd have to get up in a minute and dress. Then she and Jason would go home and be polite strangers for...how long?

"Do you want a divorce, Jason?" she asked in a voice as cold as she felt inside, and because of the dark glasses, she couldn't see the effect that question had on him.

"There's never been a divorce in my family," he returned after a minute, his voice strange and deep. "It won't start with me."

"All right." She didn't look at him.

He stared at her with his heart like lead in his chest. God, she looked tired. Raw with weariness. He wanted more than anything to take her in his arms and hold her, to share the grief that was eating him alive. But he couldn't bend that far without breaking.

"Are you all right?" he asked after a tense minute.

"Yes. I just feel...empty." She had to fight not to let her pain show, but it flashed across her face despite all her efforts to control it. She bit back tears. "It was nice of you to come after me."

"You're my wife," he said curtly.

She looked up then, suddenly. "Why didn't you come yesterday?" she asked.

He laughed bitterly. "Because I was too damned drunk," he replied.

"Oh." She stared at the starched white sheet. "Oh. I see."

Did she, he wondered. He turned. "I'll take care of the bill and sign you out. Can you get dressed alone?"

"Yes."

He waited, but she didn't look up or say anything else. He went out, closing the door quietly behind him.

An hour later, they were flying back to Texas. After he got Kate comfortably settled, Jason sat in the cockpit with the pilot. She imagined that he couldn't bear being in the same seat with her, after what had happened. She couldn't even blame him for feeling that way. She had acted like an ostrich, hiding her head in the sand, trying to go on normally and pretend that she wasn't having problems. Trying to pretend that it was a normal pregnancy, when she'd known all along that it wasn't, that something was badly wrong. She'd only been hiding from the truth because she'd wanted Jason's baby so badly. But he wouldn't see it that way. He could hardly bear to look at Kate, and that told her all she needed to know. He blamed her. He hated her. And now she wondered if there would be anything of their marriage that they could salvage.

She closed her eyes and tried not to think about the baby. She'd had such sweet dreams for it. Tears burned her eyes. It would never know the warmth of the sun on its laughing face, or touch a leaf and feel the silky softness of a rose. It would never feel grass under its little hands or run after butterflies by the riverbanks. Kate would never hold it and see generations of Donavans and Whittmans in its sleeping face. She felt the tears, and let them pour out her grief.

She cried and cried. Long before they reached San Antonio, she was drained of emotion. The tears had a calming effect. The woman who got off the plane and into Jason's waiting Mercedes was quiet and very pale. And she didn't say one word all the long way to San Frio.

Mary was waiting at the house. She ran to Kate, wrapping her up in loving, grieving arms, but Kate only acknowledged her presence. There were no more tears. She fielded Sheila's equally concerned welcome and managed a smile for Cherry and Gene. Then she went to her room and changed her clothes, and not for anything elegant. She put on her worn oversized jeans with an old smock top and her sneakers. She was never going to try to be anything except herself ever again. If Jason wanted a society butterfly for a wife, he was in for a shocking disappointment. Mrs. Jason Donavan was going to be just plain Kate Whittman Donavan, as long as she lived at the Diamond Spur.

The atmosphere at the house was strained. Jason didn't

come into the room he'd reluctantly shared with Kate during her pregnancy. He left her there and moved himself into a guest room down the hall. His clothes and toiletries had already been removed before she came back, obviously before he came to fetch her from Atlanta.

She saw him at meals, but he was as distant as she was, and Cherry and Gene tried to carry the conversation alone. They didn't have much choice, since Jason and Kate barely spoke.

Kate went back to the plant after a week's rest. The design staff seemed to know about the miscarriage because they were careful not to mention anything about the baby and they kept her mind occupied.

The first news she got of her collection was when Mr. Rogers came into the office with a sheaf of paper, grinning from ear to ear.

"Orders," he said, showing them to Kate and Sandy and Dessie and the girls. "Orders! Kate, only about fifteen of your designs weren't accepted. We've got orders, overwhelming orders, for all the rest—especially for that denim and khaki ensemble. We'll make a killing on these designs! Kate, you're set for life. The higher-ups have already given me the green light to commission you for a second collection, for fall this time. Want to try it?"

"I might as well," Kate said with a quiet smile.

Mr. Rogers was thinking she meant that she had to fill her time with something, and he wasn't completely wrong. He smiled and patted her shoulder. "Good girl. When you're a little better, we'll talk about the next collection. Right now, just play around with your ideas until you have a direction for the fall line. We could even send you overseas to look at what the couture houses are coming up with, if you want to try a different style. And we'd like you to go back to New York when we show your fall styles, of course."

She didn't want to go overseas, but she wasn't going to tell him just yet. She was already thinking of something else in a regional theme. Khaki and denim, but this time in a collection built around the Alamo. Big stars and Mexican prints on fabric, and buckskin. But it wasn't quite organized, so she didn't mention it.

"That will give me some time to recuperate," she agreed. "And to organize things at home."

Home as a word sounded strange these days. But she and Jason were going to have to come to some kind of arrangement.

"Okay. And thanks for getting our leisure line off to a tremendous start."

Kate smiled at him. "Thank you for giving me a chance."

"You made your own chance." He named a figure they'd arrived at for the second collection—a dramatic improvement on the first. "You can look over the contracts with your attorney, and let us know. Eventually, you might want to go into licensing...."

"I don't have that much ambition right now," she replied. "The glitter isn't worth the pain, did you know?"

Mr. Rogers pursed his lips. "Glitter is something you read about in sexy novels, Kate," he said with a smile. "The garment industry is just hard work with a little success thrown on top. It's something you have to love to be good at, and you get back only what you put in. The rich lifestyles and jet setting exist for some of the couture designers, that's true. But everybody who gets that high pays his or her dues on the way up. Many people think the dues are exorbitant."

"Yes," Kate agreed. "I'm one of them. I have little desire to have a couture house." She shrugged and forced a smile. "I want to design leisure clothes. But I wanted my baby…." She turned away, fighting tears. "Sorry. I'm sorry. It's still fresh in my mind. I'll get over it, I just need time."

"If you want more rest, Kate, say so," Mr. Rogers said gently. "We know what you've been through in the past few months."

"I need to work," she said unsteadily. "I'll be all right, you know."

He smiled at her. "Of course you will."

Kate dragged herself home that night. She was still in working clothes, a pair of embroidered jeans and a tank top. Her casual attire was an outward expression of her feelings about everything else. She'd been too concerned about fitting in—with Jason's world, with her false ideas of what a designer should be. But as Jason had told her once, she'd always be plain Kate Whittman from San Frio, Texas, no matter what happened. She was trying to remember that now. She might as well try to be herself starting now.

Jason was already at the supper table, studying a contract he held in his hand. Nobody else was around, not even Sheila, but there were cold cuts and bread and spreads on the table, and a half-empty pot of coffee.

He looked up, his glance quick and not very flattering. "Been to a rodeo?" he asked.

"I dress for comfort at work," she replied easily. "If you want me to wear ball gowns and diamonds at your dinner table, then buy them for me and I will. Otherwise, I'll do it my way."

He put the contract down and his dark eyes glittered over her. She was thinner than she'd ever been. She was living on her nerves, and she looked it. Her green eyes were dark-circled, and her dark hair was down below her collar now, a little unruly. It needed cutting, but he hesitated to say anything to her. She didn't seem to care very much about how she looked anymore.

"You don't look well," he remarked quietly.

"I've just lost a baby," she said shortly. "How should I look?" She lifted her eyes and glared at him after she'd filled her china cup. She put cream in her coffee with a slender, graceful hand that trembled a little. "They've asked me to do a second collection, one for next fall, and I've agreed. It will mean more travel, to New York at least, and perhaps to some of the regional markets."

He leaned back in his chair, dark and quiet and arrogant. He was wearing a blue checked Western shirt, sleeves rolled up to the elbows, the buttons at his throat undone. He looked cool and calm and totally unruffled, but his eyes didn't blink as he spoke to her.

"How convenient that you aren't still pregnant," he said. "You'd have had to curtail some of your jet-setting."

She stared at him for a long moment. Like old times, she thought, seeing beneath the raging mockery to what was really underneath. Odd how well she knew him. How completely. She'd come into the house fuming and irritated, and now she could feel the impact of his pain. The anger and frustration drained out of her, leaving only the shared sadness. Kate couldn't see what was under the pain, but that alone was enough to soften her.

She got up from the table and went to him, ignoring the surprise on his dark face as she bent and brushed a soft, tender kiss across his forehead.

"I wanted the baby, too, Jason, despite what you think," she whispered softly and managed a wobbly smile.

She moved away with tears in her eyes. It still hurt, just as much as it had in the beginning.

Jason watched her go with a face he could barely keep calm, hurting from his heart down. She saw too much, damn her. He slammed his napkin down and went to his study without even his coffee, and he slammed the door behind him. Damn her!

He sat down at the desk, his head in his hands. Now he knew that she'd been grieving as much as he had. She'd just learned his gift of hiding it. He wished they could talk. But he still couldn't bend enough to tell her how he really felt. Until he could, there was no hope of a reconciliation.

The whole family was at breakfast the next morning. Kate smiled vaguely at everyone as she sat down, trying to put the night before behind her.

"You won't be on the road anytime soon, I gather, and not working impossible hours until you start on your new designs," Jason said unexpectedly.

"Not right away, certainly," she said quietly.

"Then you'll have time to do some things for me," he said, leaning back arrogantly in his chair. "I want you to organize a few dinner parties for me. I'm trying to drum up some support for a feedlot operation I have in mind. I'll give you the names of the men I want to invite, and you can get them here in different parties, so that we have a full table. Sheila can help you."

Kate shifted uncomfortably in the chair. "I don't know anything about dinner parties," she said shortly. "Or don't you remember my first one?"

He only lifted an eyebrow as he sipped black coffee. "It's time you learned. If you're going to live here, you can't walk around in rags and bare feet forever."

Kate glared at him, oblivious to the shocked faces around her. "I'll dress as I please in my own home, as long as it is my own home," she informed him. "I'm not high society, as you once told me." She poured herself a cup of coffee and buttered a slice of toast to go with her eggs, glaring at him. "As for organizing dinners, if Sheila will help me, I'll try. But don't expect miracles. As you once said, I'm just a poor little country girl."

He actually grinned, a painful reminder of the old camaraderie they'd once shared. "Don't wear black sequins, will you?" he murmured.

She lifted her coffee cup and came within a hair of throwing it across the table at him. "Damn you!" she breathed.

Jason lifted his chin, delighted at her show of fury. It meant there was still some feeling in her. Even subdued fury was better than her constant coldness. "Damn me, by all means, but buy a new dress."

"I'll be delighted to buy an original at Neiman-Marcus," she promised with icy sweetness, "and give you the bill. If you want rich, you can have rich, but you'll pay for it."

Gene chuckled. "She's got a point," he began.

Jason glared at him. "You can shut up," he said flatly. "I've had more than enough advice from you. I'm carrying the load for both of us while you strut around pretending to be the next Renoir."

"Renoir was an impressionist," Gene replied imperturbably as he buttered a biscuit. "I'm going to specialize in portraits. Right now, I'm working on one of Kate, from a sketch I did when she didn't know."

Kate was flattered and surprised. "Are you, really?" she asked.

"He really is." Cherry grinned. "And it's beautiful. He's putting you in a green satin gown...."

"Don't tell her yet!" Gene burst out. "It's a surprise."

"If you want to paint Kate, put her in blue jeans in a patch of sunflowers," Jason said lazily, studying her with eyes that were dark and quiet and oddly attentive. "Not in an evening gown."

It was the first thing he'd said to her since she'd lost the baby that didn't have an edge to it. Her green eyes searched his dark ones in a long, tense silence. He didn't look away, and the tension burst into sparks as it lengthened and pulsed with excitement.

"By all means," she said, tearing her eyes away. "Show the world what a country hick looks like." She put down her napkin and stood up. "I'm late."

Jason hadn't meant it that way, and he almost said so. But she was gone, and Gene and Cherry just sat staring daggers at him. He finished his coffee and got up leisurely, his mind on that helpless softness in Kate's eyes. It seemed like a long time since he'd made love to her. He thought about it a lot these days. Altogether too much, when he should be thinking of ways to keep from losing the Spur. None of them, not even Gene, knew how critical his situation was getting. He'd bought additional land when interest rates were sky high. It had seemed a good idea at the time because a recreational facility had been planned for that land, and Jason was worried about having four-wheel drive vehicles worrying his cattle, or drunken party-goers shooting them for sport. Now, when he was struggling just to pay the interest on the loan he'd taken out to pay for the land, it didn't seem overly wise. But spilled milk was spilled milk. He'd just have to do the best he could.

"Why is he so cruel to her?" Cherry asked when Jason was out the front door.

Gene shook his head. "I don't know. It isn't like him to hurt Kate. But they've had an odd relationship. Our father had warped ideas about sex and women. I think Jay's having a hard time reconciling what he's been taught with what he feels for Kate." He sighed and touched Cherry's hand gently. "I hope he can work it out. Losing the baby has done something terrible to both of them."

"Yes, I know," Cherry replied. She linked her fingers into his. "That's why I haven't said anything about our baby." She searched Gene's eyes and smiled softly. "But we'll have to tell them someday. I'll start showing before much longer."

"And I have to start showing a profit," he mused, lifting her fingers to his mouth. "Now that I'll have three mouths to feed instead of two. Jason's never taken my art seriously, but when he sees what I can do with this portrait of Kate, he'll be convinced. I'm certain of that, Cherry."

"So am I," she said firmly. "And if we have to starve in a garret and beg milk for the baby, I'm with you all the way. Every step."

He took a slow, proud breath. "I love you," he whispered.

She leaned toward him, smiling as she touched her lips to his. "I love you, too."

THE WEATHER WAS slowly getting cooler as October turned to November, and Thanksgiving came into sight. Kate, well into organizing the first of three of Jason's dinner parties, was very nervous. She wasn't sure about the guest list, and Jason had been vague. He usually was, expecting people to read his mind if they wanted answers he was too impatient to give.

She did the best she could, worrying over the caterer and the seating arrangements, whether or not she'd chosen the right kind of wine to serve with the poultry dish and the sweet. She didn't know beans about wine. She didn't know beans about place settings, either, not formal ones. Sheila had to teach her. If designing was hard, creating a formal table wasn't much easier. She'd never known how many utensils it took just for one big meal. A knife, fork, and spoon had been adequate when she was growing up.

The past two social events she'd gone to had led to disaster because of the way she'd been dressed. But this time, Jason's mocking attitude had sent her to a boutique, where she found a sedate gray crepe dress with a high neckline and bishop sleeves that suited Kate very well. She had her hair trimmed and a body wave put in it, so that it curled softly around her oval face. She wore a minimum of makeup and very sophisticated perfume, and not too much of that, either. From her dark hair to her sedate gray kid high heels, she looked perfect as a young society wife. And she was certain that even Jason couldn't find fault with the way she looked this time.

She'd done some reading in her spare time—bestsellers, and some historical novels. She'd boned up on elegant cuisine and art. She knew a lot about costume already, from her design training. Kate wasn't polished, but she felt she could hold her own. Hopefully.

She went downstairs just before the first guests arrived. Jason was in a neat gray vested suit, holding a glass of whiskey. That alone was odd, because he never drank. The last time had been when Kate lost the baby, and she scowled a little as she went into the living room.

"I'm not going to stagger, don't look so worried," he taunted.

"You never stagger," she replied quietly. "But it's odd to see you drinking."

Yes, he thought bitterly, but she couldn't see inside him, to the dark places filled with guilt and frustrated desire. His dark eyes ran down her slender body. Still too thin, he thought bitterly. Too thin, too distant. He tried occasionally to approach her, but more often than not his pride held him back at the last minute. And as for Kate, she never came near him voluntarily anymore. She never touched him. She was a stranger who lived in his house and avoided him most of the time.

"You look very elegant, Mrs. Donavan," he said, and without his usual sarcasm.

"I found it at a boutique," she replied. "Even though I design clothes, they're all casual things. I never knew much about evening gowns and such." She lowered her eyes to his chest. "It was Cherry who told me about the boutique. She does know style, probably because she and Gene hang around with an artistic crowd."

He watched the way her hands folded and unfolded, as if just being around him made her nerves stand on end. "They want to move out."

She stared at him. "Do they? Cherry didn't mention anything…."

"Oh, she wouldn't," he said with a cold, bitter laugh. "She's trying to protect you."

Kate frowned. "I don't understand."

He smiled mockingly and lifted his glass to his lips. "She's pregnant."

It shouldn't have hit her that way. It was only a state-ment, after all. Just that. But the way he said it, the bitterness in his deep voice, the faint accusation in his eyes brought back the agony of her own loss. Kate felt the floor go out from under her. Her blood beat in her head as great waves of shock hit her from all sides. She just stood and stared at Jason, like a calf waiting for the bullet....

He caught her as she swayed, spilling whiskey as he dropped the glass and swung her up in his hard arms with a muffled curse. He laid her down on the long couch, noticing how frail her body was and her face, pinched and white. Memories flooded him of Kate running to him across a meadow, laughing, her green eyes sparkling. That child no longer lived in this old, tired woman who lay so still on his living room sofa.

He fumbled with the brandy bottle just as Gene came in and suddenly stopped at the sight in front of him.

"What's wrong?" he asked.

"Get Sheila," Jason said shortly. "Tell her to bring a cold wet cloth."

"What happened?" Gene persisted.

"I told her about Cherry," Jason muttered. "Will you get out of here?"

Gene went, hastened on his way by those cold black unblinking eyes.

Jason looked and felt dangerous. He knelt beside Kate, furious that his hand was unsteady as he lifted her head and put the brandy snifter against her lips. She made a face and groaned, but he held her until some of the brandy got past her tight lips.

"Don't," she moaned, pushing at it.

He set the glass aside and held her shoulders down when she tried to sit up. "Are you all right?" he asked tersely.

"No thanks to you," she whispered shakily, her eyes accusing. "Was it necessary to fling it at me like that?"

He got slowly to his feet. "You had to know eventually," he returned, standing over her with a face like stone. "Why hide it?"

"Why, indeed?" She did sit up then, fighting the urge to burst into tears. "If Cherry had told me, at least she would have led up to it first. She wouldn't have tried to hurt me with it."

He glared at her. "Why should hearing about another woman's pregnancy hurt you?" he asked coldly. "You told me in the beginning that you didn't even want my child! Your career came first, you said!"

She didn't think she could breathe again. The ice had finally cracked. His remoteness had caught fire, and for the first time, he was letting out his feelings, without making her have to guess at them.

Now if she could only draw him out, keep him going. Kate got to her feet slowly. "Is that what you think, Jason?" she asked, fighting for composure. "That I never wanted the baby, that I deliberately put his life in jeopardy because of my work?"

He straightened, staring at her. She was oddly still, as if she were waiting for something. And it was such a relief, suddenly, to have it out in the open. "You told me that no man would ever matter more than your damned job, didn't you?" he asked with a cool smile, the alcohol mercifully numbing his own guilt about Jamaica. "And that you didn't want a string of preschoolers hanging on your legs."

"I lied," she said.

He turned abruptly. "You what?"

"I lied, Jason." She took a slow breath, her pale green eyes holding his. "I knew you didn't want to marry me.

You felt guilt that you'd seduced me and got me pregnant, but I was never sophisticated enough or cultured enough to suit a man like you and I knew it. So I lied and told you that I didn't want you or a child because I thought it would make you go away." She smiled bitterly. "And it did. Except that you found out the truth and forced me to marry you anyway."

She turned away, missing the rigid shock on his dark face. "As for having problems, I had them from the beginning. I refused to have the tests they wanted because I was afraid they'd find something and ask me to have a therapeutic abortion." She sighed wearily. "I couldn't have let them. So I hid my head in the sand and pretended that everything was all right. But it wasn't. Everything went wrong, and maybe it was because of the way it happened." She toyed with a fold of her dress, fighting tears as she remembered it all. "Babies should be made by people who love each other, Jason, not because of… of an uncontrollable desire. And love on one side isn't enough. Even when it's as strong as mine was for you."

CHAPTER EIGHTEEN

JASON DIDN'T MOVE. It all came rushing on him like a tidal
wave. Why in God's name hadn't she told him that long
ago? Or at least, when he'd gone to Atlanta to get her?
And then he realized how little chance he'd given her to
tell him anything. He'd been unreachable. Then, and since.

She'd lied to save him from a marriage she didn't think
he wanted. She'd wanted his baby. That had to mean that
she'd wanted him. But he'd been so cold to her that she
couldn't have any feeling left for him now. He'd shifted
his own guilt about the baby on to her thin shoulders,
and now his own inability to accept blame had cost him
the woman he wanted most in the world, and his child.

"I wish you'd trusted me, just a little," she whispered,
turning to take a tissue from the ceramic decorator box
on the cream-colored end table. The room was done in
chocolate and cream, with modern furniture and innovative designs in the carpet and drapes. Kate had always
loved it, but right now she could have dropped a match in
the middle of it. She sat up, dabbing at her eyes.

"I've never learned to trust, Kate," he began quietly.

She got up. "I know that," she agreed, averting her
gaze. "I even know why. But I'd never have hurt you
deliberately." She smiled wistfully. "I loved you, Jason.
Didn't you know?"

He felt sick to the soles of his boots. "No," he said

tautly. "I swear to God, I didn't even suspect it. Not even when you gave in to me…"

"You needn't worry," she said quickly, shooting a wary glance in his direction. "I'm over it, now. I won't fall at your feet or anything. I'm cured." She stared at the tissue in her cold hands. "I'm really cured. You've made it very clear that you don't want anyone to love you. You look on love as a weakness, Jason. I can't blame you, you've never had much experience of it. But I feel sorry for you. Even when it hurts, it's better than being dead inside."

His dark eyes flashed wildly over Kate's wan little face, and he had the sensation of tearing the wings from a butterfly. She looked almost damaged, and he wanted to tell her the truth. That he did know how to love, that he wasn't dead inside. That he wanted her love, needed it, hungered for it. If only he could make her understand the darkness inside him, the fear that drove him sometimes to strike out, the fear of ending up like his father….

He moved toward her, his hard face oddly still. "Kate," he began softly.

But before he could speak, Gene and Sheila were back, and Cherry was with them. They'd ganged up in the kitchen, to protect little Kate from that cold man who seemed bound and determined to drag the heart right out of her.

He glanced toward the door and the impulsive words died inside him. He laughed ironically. "Don't worry, Kate, here comes the cavalry. They'll save you from me."

"I don't need saving," she returned quietly, her hands folded at her waist. "I'm not afraid of you, Jason. I never have been."

"Are you all right?" Sheila demanded, dressed up for once in a perky mauve dress that almost concealed her abundant weight, her salt-and-pepper hair neatly curled. She glared at Jason. "Done it again, have you? Why don't you go cut up a calf, that ought to improve your disposition!"

He didn't flinch. He went back to the bar and poured himself another whiskey, a larger one, and threw it down.

"Go ahead, get drunk," Sheila persisted. "Be like your daddy…!"

He whirled, his whole expression threatening. "Damn you!" he breathed, almost shuddering with rage.

"Sheila, no!" Kate cried, horrified at what Sheila had said, at what it did to Jason's eyes. She couldn't bear to see him hurt. She got between them, so that she was right in front of the belligerent housekeeper. "We have guests coming. This won't do." She swallowed, sniffling as she tried to compose herself. "Gene, take Cherry out of here, this isn't good for her." She smiled gently at Cherry. "I'm so happy for you, honey."

Cherry ran to her, hugging her warmly. Tears ran from her eyes, spoiling her mascara. "I didn't know how to tell you. I didn't want to upset you."

"Babies shouldn't upset people," Kate said with a forced smile. "And it will be wonderful to have one in the family. Go with Gene."

Gene looked worried, but Kate nodded, smiling.

They went out and Kate turned back to Jason, who was staring out the window without moving, the whiskey glass clenched in one lean hand.

She stopped beside him, searching for the right words. She alone knew how vulnerable he really was.

"She didn't mean that," she said softly. "She thought she was protecting me."

He looked out the darkened window blankly. "My

father was never a cruel man, except when he drank. When he drank, he raged. And while he raged, he hit." He looked down at the whiskey. "I can remember a time or two when I've raised my hand to another man, when I had too much to drink. But maybe I'll break one day," he said absently, not looking at her. "Maybe I'll try to find my answers in a bottle, like my father did. Maybe I'll end up just like him…"

"You won't," she said quietly. "Jason, you aren't your father. You're a totally different man. You aren't cruel."

"That's damned funny, coming from you," he replied shortly, glaring down at her.

She drew in a gentle breath. "You aren't a cruel man," she repeated, searching the dark, tormented eyes above her. "Oh, Jason, I'm sorry," she whispered achingly. "I'm so sorry, about our baby…."

She touched his arm, and he flinched. He actually flinched away from her, his entire body going stiff, his face rigid with self-control. No, he thought in anguish. No, she didn't love him anymore. He couldn't let her see how desperate he was for her touch. If he couldn't have her love, he didn't want her pity.

But when Kate saw and felt his reaction, she interpreted it a different way. He wasn't going to stop blaming her for the baby's death. She'd failed him, as she'd said, and he didn't want any part of her. Even her touch repulsed her.

Blindly, she withdrew her hand, staring at it as if it weren't even part of her body. "Excuse me," she said in a tone that barely carried to his ears. She turned and went quietly from the room in a kind of stunned daze. She didn't know how she kept from screaming. It was the last straw. There had been too much pain already, but this was insupportable.

Jason watched her go, his eyes quietly haunted. He stared at the glass in his hand for a long moment, studying it. Slowly he made himself put it down and leave it. Not me, he thought. No. Not ever again. He turned away and left it sitting there.

He didn't know why he'd poured the first glass, except that the dinner tonight had worried him. He was entertaining potential business partners, and it was a critical time for him. He had some land he wasn't using for any other purpose. If he could involve some potential backers, he might still pull the Spur out before he had to file for bankruptcy. He was living on his nerves already because of the tension between himself and Kate, and now he realized that he'd created it.

Kate thought he was ashamed of her, that she'd let him down. That was almost laughable. She was the only bright spot in his world, and she had a heart so tender that she could even try to comfort a man who'd hurt her. He closed his eyes and his lips compressed as he fought down a wave of remorse that cut off his breath. Softhearted when she'd needed someone, when she'd lost a baby that he realized now she'd wanted desperately, he'd turned his back on her.

He turned, staring blankly at the door. He loved her with a passion so primitive it struck him like lightning, almost bringing him to his knees. He'd have given anything to take back the past few months, to make it all right again. But the road ahead looked dark. He wondered if Kate would ever let herself care about him again.

He reached the doorway as the bell rang, and guests started pouring in. Minutes later, when they were sitting around the table and he got a look at Kate's too-composed features, he knew that it was going to be too late. When she turned and looked into his eyes, he was sure of it. There was such indifference in them that he knew without a word that she'd given up on him at last.

The dinner party might have been a huge success, if Kate hadn't been so upset. But she was nervous and unsure of herself, and having Jason sit at the head of the table like a man ready to order an execution didn't help. She felt out of place, and she looked it.

One of the society matrons mentioned a book she'd read. It happened to be one of the ones Kate had thumbed through, and she quickly said so and praised the author's talent.

The matron was immediately affronted, because the book had been a satire on the oil business, which her husband made his living from. Then while Kate was trying to talk her way out of that faux pas, another of the wives mentioned the rates her CDs were getting. Kate didn't know what a certificate of deposit was, so she assumed that the woman meant the mileage her car was getting, and Kate began talking about hers.

The woman laughed, thinking Kate had made a funny joke. How cute, she told Kate, to pretend to think that a certificate of deposit was a sports car. But to Kate, it was just one more example of how silly she looked trying to be a society woman. She excused herself from the table without saying where she was going. She went upstairs, changed into her jeans and boots and a pullover sweater, and went out to the barn to see about Kip.

Jason had given her a stall for her quarter horse when she'd married him, and she'd moved the horse over after they returned from Jamaica. Having Kip was comforting. He was someone to talk to, who understood her.

She groomed him, talking to him gently. She began to feel like herself again. One thing she knew. She might design clothes well, but she wasn't cut out to be a hostess. Jason would just have to divorce her and try again. That would probably suit him, too, since he couldn't stand to let her touch him anymore!

She pulled the curry comb harder through Kip's dark mane.

"Don't pull it all out," Gabe teased.

She smiled out the stall at him. Gabe, at least, liked her the way she was. He was a nice man, even if he did fall in and out of love every second week.

"I won't," she assured him. "I'm hiding out. Don't tell anyone where I am."

"What's going on?" he asked.

"The social set is having dinner with Jason. I've just started a fight between two ladies who have opposing views on the latest bestseller, and still another lady thinks I'm hilarious because I don't understand finance." She sighed. "Oh, Gabe, I'm just hopeless. I'm not cut out to be anything but a designer."

"The boss didn't marry you because you were a designer," Gabe mused.

"That's true." She sighed. "God knows why he did marry me," she added under her breath as she drew the comb along the sleek withers. "What are you hanging around the barn for?"

He shrugged. "I've had a fight with my girl," he confessed. "She thinks I've been two-timing her with one of her friends."

"Have you?" she murmured, tongue-in-cheek, because she knew Gabe.

He shrugged and stuck his hands in his pockets. "Just a couple of dates, that's all. Nothing for her to go and get upset about."

"You'll never keep a girl with that attitude," she said easily. "No woman likes being two-timed."

"I know, Kate, but I like girls," he groaned.

"So I've noticed," a cold, unpleasant voice said from behind him.

He turned on his heel and the boss was standing there, looking mad as hell and dangerous to boot.

"Uh-oh," Gabe said under his breath.

"Better find someplace to go to ground, old son," Jason told him with a smile that was spoiling for a fight.

"No sooner said than done, boss man." Gabe grinned sheepishly. He nodded to Kate and took off, while there was still time, with only a twinge of regret for leaving Kate to face Jason.

"What in hell are you doing?" Jason asked Kate. He was in his shirtsleeves, bareheaded, with his black hair faintly disheveled in the stark light from the hanging bulb overhead. His white silk shirt was unbuttoned halfway down his broad, hair-roughened chest and rolled up to his elbows. He looked frankly sexy, if it hadn't been for the set of his head that alerted her to his state of mind.

"I'm grooming Kip," she said pleasantly. "I hope your dinner is going well. I had a terrible case of polite indigestion, from an overdose of social leprosy."

He actually laughed, his stance less threatening. "Well, it's not fatal."

"Have they gone?" she asked tersely.

"They're still arguing about that damned book. At

least, two of them are. The other one is in tears because she suddenly realized that she'd upset you. She honestly thought you were making a joke."

"Sorry," she murmured regretfully, and pulled the comb slowly along Kip's flank, watching the way it rippled with pleasure at the touch.

"The men are deliberating about whether to drink all my whiskey or just go home. They don't think they want to invest in a feedlot." He tilted his head back. "If you want to walk out, honey, this is a good time to leave. I may go bust any day."

She stopped the comb altogether. "I didn't marry you for your money."

He sighed heavily. "No, I guess you didn't at that, did you? You married me because you were pregnant with my baby. You told me a few white lies to keep me from sacrificing myself, and I've given you hell ever since." His dark eyes caught her shocked ones. "I know I'm the devil to live with. Well, maybe I didn't want to get married, but I wanted the baby. I had so much riding on that little one, Kate. I went crazy when we lost him. But I never really blamed you, despite what I said."

She frowned. "I don't understand."

"It doesn't matter anymore." He gestured toward Kip's mane. "You missed a spot."

She had. She pulled the curry comb over it. "What will you do, if you lose the Spur?"

"Blow my brains out, probably," he said easily. "It's the only thing I ever cared about."

Yes, she thought bitterly, it probably was. God knew, he'd never cared about her. "I'm sorry if I ruined your chances in there," she said after a minute.

"You didn't. I'd already ruined them, just by showing weakness," he said. "People attack it instinctively, Kate, haven't you noticed? They smell blood. Especially businessmen. They knew I was in trouble when I invited them here."

"I thought ranchers helped each other," she said. "You always helped Dad."

"We're not talking family ranches here, honey." He pulled out a cigarette and lit it, and then leaned lazily against the stall to smoke it. "We're talking millions, not nickle and dime. The bank is two steps away from foreclosure. I've defaulted, Kate. I can't even meet the interest payment. The feedlot was a long shot, but I took it." He shrugged. "And I lost."

She put away the comb, patted Kip's neck and gave him a sugar cube, and went out, latching the gate behind her. "What will you do?" she repeated gently.

He blew out a thin cloud of smoke. "I don't know."

She searched his hard face. "A lot of it was my fault, I guess..."

"None of it was your fault," he said curtly.

"I'm not cultured enough to be the kind of wife you need," she said from between her teeth. "I grew up poor and even if I know how to design, I don't even know how to dress...."

"Just hold it right there," he said shortly. His black eyes bit into hers. "You weren't the only one who told a few white lies. I never thought you wouldn't fit into my world." He moved restlessly, avoiding her shocked gaze. "I just didn't want you fitting into anybody else's. You'd already said you didn't want to get stuck on a ranch in Texas."

"You didn't want me," she reminded him. She flushed at the look on his face. "Well, only in bed." She lowered her gaze back to Kip's mane. "I tried to be the kind of wife you wanted, but I wasn't meant for fancy parties and high society. I do like going barefooted and wearing jeans, just like you told Gene to paint me."

"I told Gene to paint you in jeans because you're a country girl and I like you just that way," he replied gently, taking a draw from the cigarette. "I meant it as a compliment, not an insult. I guess with things so strained between us, though, you didn't expect compliments from me."

She forced a smile to her lips. "Thank you for telling me," she murmured.

He had to force himself not to make a grab for her, throw her against a wall and make violent love to her where she stood. It was what he wanted to do, and it might have given her a hint about his feelings. But she already seemed to think that desire was all he had to give. It was going to take a long, slow courtship this time to win her back. His eyes kindled and a faint smile touched his hard mouth. Well, he'd managed to do that once. Why not twice? Maybe it wasn't hopeless.

"How do you feel about your career now?" he asked, and without mockery or anger.

She looked at him and shrugged. "I don't know, Jason. I like doing it. But it isn't my whole life. It's just a job that I enjoy. That's all."

He pursed his lips and had to fight not to grin. He stared at the glowing tip of his cigarette.

"I do make a lot of money at it," she added hesitantly. "If you need help, I don't mind contributing what I've got…"

"I'm the head of the household," he returned. "That may sound old-fashioned, but then, so am I. In my family, I make the living. I'd starve before I'd take a penny from you."

"You're such a chauvinist, Jason," she sighed.

His broad shoulders lifted and fell. "Is that new?"

She managed a sad smile. "No. You always were."

He smoked his cigarette silently. The barn was cozy against the chill of cooler weather. "Have you started your new collection?"

The question surprised her. He sounded genuinely interested. "Why, yes. I'm building it around the Alamo," she said. "I drove up with Cherry a couple of days ago to look at it again, to get the feel of it. Mr. Rogers thinks I may be able to get a fabric designer at one of the Clayborn mills to design a fabric just for my things. Isn't that something?"

"Oh, yes," he agreed absently. "That's something."

"Well, it is to me," she said quietly, turning away. "I put in a lot of hard work to get where I am, even if you do hate my work."

"I don't hate it," he said. His broad shoulders rose and fell. "I resent it sometimes, and don't bother asking me why, I won't tell you," he added curtly.

"Why not?" she asked, her green eyes twinkling for a change. "Are you dying of love for me and madly jealous of my work?"

He actually laughed. It was the truth, and she didn't even believe it. "Wouldn't you fall in the floor if I was?"

"I'd do that, all right," she agreed, finishing up Kip's withers.

"About what happened in the house; what I said to you earlier about the baby..." he began gruffly.

She put up the curry comb. "If you apologize, I will fall on the floor, of shock," she said without looking at him. "You never apologize, because you never make mistakes."

His eyebrows went up and he grinned. It was the first time he'd ever been able to face that imperfection. "I'm perfect," he reminded her. "Didn't you know?"

She let her eyes wander over him with shocked delight, and he felt light-headed at the soft appreciation in them before they averted to the business of putting Kip into his stall. "Physically, I wouldn't have an argument," she murmured daringly.

He smiled wickedly. She came back out of the stall, and found herself suddenly caught and held against his broad chest, with his dark face just inches from hers.

"You're pretty devastating yourself, Mrs. Donavan," he breathed, and bent to her mouth.

He hadn't kissed her since before she lost the baby. It was new and exciting, as it had been in the early days of their courtship. She caught her breath as his lips nibbled and teased hers, while that whipcord lean arm held her closer in the soft silence of the barn.

"Kiss me back, Katy," he teased, nuzzling her mouth. "I dare you. Open your mouth, the way I like it, and kiss me blind…!"

She didn't want to. She didn't mean to. But when she turned her head, his mouth was there, hard and warm and smoky and expertly demanding. She caught her breath and it went into his mouth, sighing out helplessly. He turned her and backed her up against the wall, his lips hard against her, his broad chest shaking with the force of his heartbeat, his body causing an instant answering desire in hers.

She put her hands on his chest to push him away, and he chuckled deeply, nibbling her lips while he jerked open the shirt buttons and pulled one of her hands inside, to tangle it in the thick hair over the warm, hard muscles.

"Go ahead," he invited in a husky whisper. "Touch me."

"I don't want…" she began.

"Don't fight me," he whispered. "I'm not going to seduce you or force you into a relationship you aren't ready for. Touch me. I won't lose my head again, I promise."

Tears stung her eyes. "I didn't blame you for that, Jason," she whispered softly. "I shouldn't have said what I did…."

He lifted his head, just enough to see her eyes. "I didn't like having you see me that way. I felt helpless."

"I know," she said gently. "And you don't like losing control."

He lifted an eyebrow ruefully. "You know too much about me."

"That's right." She moved her hand experimentally on his chest, liking the way he moved sinuously under her light touch. "Watch your step, cowboy, or I'll tell on you."

He chuckled softly. He hadn't laughed in a long time. She hadn't, either. He liked the way she lit up when she laughed. "Who will you tell? I can't think of anybody else who'd care." He drew his nose softly against hers. "Your legs are trembling," he whispered.

"Don't get conceited. Yours are, too," she whispered back.

He knew they were. His dark eyes searched hers gently. His hips moved once, slowly, and his gaze went to her mouth, watching it part. She still wanted him. If he took his time, and didn't rush her, there might be a small chance that he could make her love him again.

"I want you," he whispered. "But I'm not going to do a thing about it. See how that ties in with your theory that I only made love to you out of desire."

And with that he levered away from her, his whole look

frankly amused and a little predatory as she stared blankly at him, her body shocked by his sudden withdrawal.

"I don't understand," she said unsteadily. The whole tone of their relationship had changed pitch since she'd told him the truth about the baby. She couldn't understand the sudden change. She didn't quite trust it, either.

"I know that. But you'll figure it out one day." He finished his cigarette and ground it out under his heel. "Let's go inside. And one more thing, honey, no more midnight conversations with Gabe in the barn," he added, and this time there was venom in the stiff wording.

She looked at him, shocked. "Well, I didn't plan it," she said hesitantly. "He'd had a fight with his girl."

"He doesn't have to cry on your shoulder."

"I'll tell him that, if it happens again." She glanced at his hard face. "I wouldn't have let him do anything, you know."

He nodded. "I know that." He searched her eyes quietly. "Gabe will never know that we got married because he was going to take you to a square dance," he remarked, watching her go beet red. "Remember, Kate? I dared you to go with him and you tried to slap me again, and I pushed you against the door and went crazy the second I kissed you. My God, I don't even remember how we got on the sofa, I was so far gone."

Remembering that day always embarrassed her, and it was too fresh a memory to talk about. She moved away from him, clearing her throat.

"I'd better go back in and face the music, I guess," she sighed, leading the way out of the barn while she tried not to hear his amused soft laughter behind her. She glanced at him. "I'll never make a socialite, you know. But I guess I can try again."

"We'll lay off inviting businessmen over, for the time being," he said as they reached the porch. "You'll have enough to do, with those new designs."

She was touched by this odd and unexpected concern for her feelings. She turned at the bottom step and looked up into his dark, impassive face. "Jason, it's important, isn't it? These business dinners, I mean."

He studied her face. "I don't know, Kate," he replied honestly. "If I can get some backing, with what I learned in Australia about breeding new strains of Indian cattle with my own, I might pull us out of the fire. It will take time, and I need a feedlot to start out, but it's an investment that may pay off big. I just need a little leeway. A backer might make the difference."

"And if you had a decent hostess," she said miserable, "you'd have a better chance. I've let you down badly. You never should have married me. I know you never would have, if I hadn't gotten pregnant."

"Don't bet on it," he said, and looked down at her with darkening eyes just as the front door opened and Gene came out.

"Oh, there you are," he said, smiling when he noticed that Jason had apparently been reaching for Kate when he opened the door. "Our guests are getting ready to leave." He grinned from ear to ear as Kate and Jason came through the doorway. "I just sold a portrait to the crying lady."

Jason blinked. "What?"

"She's still crying, by the way, Kate," he told her. "She's really sorry that she hurt your feelings."

"My sensitive feelings will be the death of us all if I don't get them under control," Kate remarked ruefully.

"You've been through a lot," Gene said gently. "Nobody's mad at you, least of all family, isn't that right,

Jay?" when he noticed that Kate's mouth was swollen and so was Jason's, and they both looked flustered.

"The only person I'm mad at is you," Jason shot back. "Get in there and sell cattle, not portraits."

"Spoilsport," Gene muttered. "What in hell do I know about the cattle business?"

"And that's the whole problem." Jason was on his favorite subject now, just warming up. "You never have taken an interest in it."

"Why should I?" Gene demanded. "You're the one with the ranch know-how, not me. I never wanted any part of running it, but you're determined to try and force me into a mold I don't fit!"

"You could fit if you wanted to."

"Then why don't you paint?" Gene replied. "Why don't you become an artist, just because I want you to?"

Jason glared at him and he glared back. "Excuse me," Kate murmured, escaping while she could. She darted down the hall, past the open living room door, and had almost made it to the staircase when the weeping woman came after her.

"I'm so sorry," the matron apologized. She was at least fifty pounds overweight, white haired and blue eyed, and her whole face was red. "Honest to God, Mrs. Donavan, I didn't mean to embarrass you."

Kate turned around, her eyes as kind as her smile. "I've just lost my baby," she said softly. "I'm hurting, a lot. I wouldn't have taken offense ordinarily," she added, tossing off the white lie with panache.

"I lost my first one, too, honey," the older lady replied, "but then I had three in a row." She smiled. "You'll have other children."

Kate liked her. From a bad beginning, this lady was

turning out to be a jewel. "Mrs…. Drake, isn't it?…" she asked. "You're very kind. I hope you'll come back to dinner again, and maybe I can be a better hostess." She flushed. "You see, I'm not used to this kind of thing. I worked in a sewing plant before I started designing. In fact, I still work there." She threw up her hands. "Oh, what the devil. I don't know anything about cocktail parties and CDs and sports cars. My gosh, until just recently, the best car I'd ever owned was a twenty-year-old Ford with ninety thousand miles on it!"

Mrs. Drake brightened. "Would you like to learn all about cocktail parties and CDs and sports cars?"

Kate stared at her. "What?"

"My children are grown. I sit around all day long with nothing to do except in the spring, when I get outside and plant flowers until even the bees complain." She grinned. "I'd just love to instruct you in the fine art of being rich. It's fun."

Kate burst out laughing. "You snob, you."

Mrs. Drake did laugh then, her broad face almost young. "You bet, honey. Well?"

"I'd love it," Kate said. "If you won't expect too much. I guess you probably heard what I did to poor Mrs. Halls…"

"…who should have had coffee dumped on her years ago, it might have improved her," Mrs. Drake said pertly. She smiled. "What are you doing Saturday afternoon?"

"Not a thing in this world," Kate replied. "If you're sure."

"I'm sure."

She told Kate how to get to her house before she left, and paused on the way out to remind Gene about her portrait.

"What about my portrait?" Kate asked when the guests had gone.

"Next Monday, for sure," Gene assured her. "I'm just finishing the face now."

"I can hardly wait to see it," Kate sighed. "Did you paint me in blue jeans?"

Gene grinned. "Wait and see."

Jason had already gone into his study, and where the door was open, Kate noticed him hard at work on the books as she went past it. He didn't look up, and she didn't speak. But she noticed that he only had a cup of steaming coffee on the desk beside him—and some homemade cookies. She had a good idea where they came from, too.

"If I dry the dishes for you, can I have a cookie, too?" Kate asked Sheila, peeping her head in while the housekeeper put everything away.

Sheila turned from the cabinet, looking sheepish. "I felt sorry for him," she muttered. "I shouldn't ever have said that about his daddy."

"He'll get over it," Kate assured her. She smiled impishly. "Especially if you keep pumping cookies into him."

Sheila grinned back and offered her the platter of freshly baked goodies.

Later, Kate went back by the study on her way to bed, but the door was closed and she heard Jason's deep, curt voice. He was obviously on the phone and it was a business call, she could tell. She almost knocked, but she was still a little shy of him. Well, tomorrow she'd know if it had only been the alcohol that had made him forgiving and approachable and ardent. But she prayed that it wasn't. For the first time in weeks, she felt a glimmer of hope for their marriage.

CHAPTER NINETEEN

JASON WAS SITTING all alone at the breakfast table when Kate went downstairs.

She stopped in the doorway, her eyes quietly hungry on his dark, abstracted face. He was wearing jeans and a chambray shirt, an echo of her own clothes except for the softer cut and decoration of her own. He was hatless, pushing a knife around on the spotless white tablecloth. It was odd to find him there this late, since he was usually up and out at daybreak. There was a production sale underway soon, and he had been pushing things and people trying to prepare for it. He was selling off more stock than he wanted to, Kate knew, in an effort to try and meet at least part of the note hanging over the Spur.

"Good morning," she said softly, more responsive than she'd felt in weeks.

He looked up from his brooding into her freshly scrubbed face. She looked young and pretty and his heart ached for her. He smiled gently.

"Good morning yourself," he replied. His eyes slid down her body to her tight-fitting jeans before he averted them. "Have some breakfast."

Kate sat down next to him, glancing pointedly at the single biscuit, tablespoon of scrambled eggs, and one link sausage remaining on the platter. "Can you really spare me this much?" she asked teasingly, and lifted the platter to look under it. "Or is there more that you've put in your pocket for later?"

The change in him at that teasing remark was amazing. All the darkness left his eyes, replaced by a faint but steady twinkle.

"I work hard," he pointed out. "I have to have a big breakfast."

"That's right," she agreed as she put what was left onto her own plate. "Yours and mine."

He chuckled softly as he poured himself a second cup of coffee and creamed it. "You're bright this morning. I'll have to hide you under a bushel so the sun won't be ashamed to shine."

"You're brooding. Why?"

He leaned back with his coffee mug in his lean hand and stared at her. In that position, with his shirt pulled tight over his broad chest and his jeans making his flat stomach even flatter Kate was pleasantly reminded of what was under his clothing, at how fit he was, how powerfully muscled. She ate eggs and didn't even taste them.

"I'm worried," he said, telling her the truth. He was going to do a lot of that from now on. It might even improve things. "We're in the hole and going deeper, and I don't like the number of calves I'm having to sell off."

"Wintering them would be expensive," she reminded him.

He smiled ruefully. "I keep forgetting how well you know the cattle business. You charmed those Montana cattlemen, did I ever tell you? I made a sale because my pretty wife complimented their bull's calf-producing ability."

Her eyebrows went up. "My, my. So the little woman does have her uses."

He pursed his firm lips. "If you want to pick a fight,

go ahead," he said softly. "But things might get physical. You look cute in those tight jeans."

She almost dropped the fork. He'd flinched away from her only the day before, and here he was making suggestive remarks. She stared at him. "Physical, how?" she asked. "Did you plan to hit me with a switch?"

"If you're remembering yesterday, Kate, you might consider that a hungry man can't hide it." He watched her flush with renewed delight. Despite marriage and the intimacy they'd once shared, she was still shy with him. "I see you understand me. I didn't think it was the proper time or place to advertise the effect you had on me, when you'd just accused me of seducing you purely out of desire."

She sat with her fork poised in midair. Her mind just wouldn't work out the implications of what he was saying, or his sudden change from cold tolerance to amused honesty.

He had her confused. Good. Throwing her off balance worked nicely into his plans for the future. He finished his coffee and got up, reaching for his hat on the table behind him.

"You don't want me here," she began, fishing.

He picked up his gloves, worn and stained with grease and grass, and flicked them against his muscular thigh. "That's why I've divorced you and thrown you out the door so fast," he agreed pleasantly.

This man was some stranger who'd sneaked in the front door. It wasn't Jason Everett Donavan. She leaned her head back to look up at him, her eyes wide and curious.

"You're confusing me," she faltered.

He smiled slowly. "Progress at last," he murmured, and bent.

She watched his face come closer with shocked delight. He nudged her mouth with his until her head was at the back of the chair, and then he lazily eased her lips apart and took possession.

But before she had the time or presence of mind to kiss him back, he lifted his head, smiling a little when her mouth tried to follow his.

"If you meant it, about trying that dinner again, how about next week, just after my production sale? A buffet dinner, for a few visiting cattlemen and their guests." His mouth quirked. "Just a small thing. About a hundred and fifty people."

"That's small?" she whispered huskily. It was hard to think after what had just happened. He'd kissed her, voluntarily. He even seemed to like her again.

"This is Texas, baby doll," he reminded her. "I'm going out to check fences down on the Smith Bottoms. You can come with me, if you want to."

She must have a fever. That would explain these delusions.

"Yes or no, honey, but make up your mind quick. I'm in a hurry," he added with the same faint smile as he towered over her.

She cleared her throat because part of her mind seemed to be stuck in it. "I guess I can let things slide today," she excused her work. "It's Saturday, after all."

Sitting in the big Bronco beside Jason, Kate felt as if they'd started all over again from scratch. It was like the day she'd made him go to the doctor with his arm. He talked easily about the ranch and the new strain of cattle he wanted to breed with those Indian bulls. He talked about the cash flow and the bad decisions, as casually as if he and Kate had discussed it time and time again. It was husband-wife talk, except that he'd never spoken of it to her in this way. He was treating her as an equal for the first time.

In fact, his whole manner toward her was new and different. It was as if he were trying to make up in some way for his recent treatment of her. Not an apology, exactly, but as close as he'd ever come to one.

"You look thoughtful," he remarked, smoking a cigarette as they bounced over the fields where tall, bare live oaks stood like dark sculptures against the horizon.

She sighed, leaning her head back against the comfortable seat. Her leather jacket and his sheepskin one were tucked away, not needed just yet because the cab was comfortably warm. "I'm not, really. I'm…" She glanced at him shyly and away again, her heart going double time in her chest because she was so close to him. "I'm happy."

He felt those words to his toes. He smiled under his fingers as he put the cigarette to his mouth. "So am I," he said surprisingly. "We always did get along well, Kate."

She folded her hands on her jeans, lifting one to touch a ribbon of embroidery she'd put down the outside seam of the legs. "Until we got married."

He hesitated. It was still hard to talk about it. "And stopped talking," he said. He glanced at her, his eyes lingering on her soft mouth and the pretty embroidered chambray shirt that she'd left open and tantalizing at her throat. "You'll never know how hard I fought to keep away from you," he said surprisingly. "You were right when you said I never saw you as a threat. I hadn't. And then I touched you and my life fell apart."

"Yours wasn't the only one," she replied, her tone cool.

He laughed softly. "Don't get your back up, honey, I didn't mean it the way you're taking it. My life fell apart because that's when I realized just how empty it had been.

I'd been kidding myself that I could live alone all my life and never mind it." He shrugged. "Then it got to the point where I couldn't sleep without dreaming about you."

She wasn't going to give in, she told herself firmly. She wasn't going to let him rush her. She glanced out the window at the dead grass and the long stretches of pasture where great rolls of fall hay had been put in cattle feeders for the various lots of cows and bulls and steers.

"Neither one of us was very experienced," she explained it, "and you said yourself that you'd been celibate for a long time."

He lifted an eyebrow under the shadowy brim of that battered black Stetson he always wore. "And desire was all it was on my part, is that how you see it?"

She shifted restlessly. The conversation was getting all too personal, too soon. She lifted her eyes to his dark face and studied his profile curiously. "I didn't think it could be anything else," she said honestly. "I was just a country girl with a few big dreams, after all. I didn't have poise or culture. I still don't," she added. "We both know if you'd had a choice about who you married, it wouldn't have been me."

He stopped the Bronco in the middle of the pasture and cut off the engine. When he turned toward her, his black eyes were narrow and intent. "Listen here, honey, if I'd had a choice, I'd never have married anybody," he said shortly. "I wanted an heir, but not enough to suffer a woman in my house. Or so I thought."

She felt as if she'd stopped breathing. "You…you wanted our child more than you wanted me."

"I wanted our child," he said slowly, "because he was our child. Not because I wanted someone to inherit the Spur."

"But, you said…!"

He leaned toward her and brushed her soft mouth with his hard one, nuzzling her nose gently. "You stopped looking under the words when we got married, didn't you?" he whispered. "You started taking me at face value. I couldn't bend enough to tell you what I really felt, and you didn't try to find out." He nibbled at her lower lip, liking the way she caught her breath and relaxed to let him do it.

"I thought you hated me," she whispered.

"Your mistake," he breathed as his mouth worked on hers. "Open your mouth a little more."

"Only if you'll put out that cigarette and kiss me properly," she whispered back, shocked at her own boldness.

He chuckled delightedly. "Okay," he murmured. He put it in the ashtray without even looking at it and drew her face up to his with the hand that wasn't cupping the back of her head. "It's been a long, long time since we did this together," he whispered, and his lips eased under hers, pushing them gently apart.

It began tenderly, but their hungers had gone unfulfilled too long. In no time, her arms were clinging around his neck and his mouth was grinding hers against her teeth, its feverish pressure arching her neck. His hard chest was crushing her back against the seat.

"Jason," she whispered brokenly, trying to get closer.

He murmured something rough, fighting her out of her seat and across him, her head against his window, his mouth still possessing her lips. His lean hand glided under her shirt, fighting a front catch that must have been invented by a ninety-year-old virgin.

"Help me," he groaned, his big hand all too big for such a dainty fastening.

She could barely find enough breath to laugh because he sounded as desperate as she felt. She helped him, and watched his face as he peeled the lacy covering away. He was watching her eyes, not her body. Her shirt wasn't even unfastened. His fingers traced only the outside edge of the soft satin mound, just lightly touching, and she gasped.

"You were always mine the minute I touched you," he said roughly, searching her wide, darkening green eyes. "You never held back from me, or played games, or pretended to be shocked at my hands on your body."

"I was innocent," she reminded him. "It was all new and exciting."

He bent, brushing his mouth tenderly over her eyes to close them while his hand drove her slowly mad with its lazy teasing. "It still is," he whispered. "Oh, no you don't, Mrs. Donavan," he added unexpectedly when her fingers went instantly to his shirt buttons. "This is my party, I'll call the shots."

Her eyes opened, questioning. His hand moved and she gasped involuntarily as it teased closer and closer toward a hardening tip. "Jason…!"

"I like being in control, didn't I ever tell you?" He smiled as he bent toward her, his lips smoothing lazily over her mouth. Her body was beginning to tremble. Second by second, she was twisting, just barely moving, trying to trap that hand where she wanted it most. He knew that, and it delighted him, but he wasn't going to give her what she wanted. Not yet. His mouth pressed her lips open and he kissed her with a deep, slow pressure that made her moan.

Finally, his teasing touch reached the hard aching center of her, and he touched it, lifting his head to watch her face at the instant he did it. She actually shuddered, and a tiny cry pulsed out of her throat. She looked incredibly sexy that way. He covered her with his warm, callused hand and she buried her face, embarrassed, against his shirt.

"My God, there can't be another woman like you in all the world," he whispered at her ear. He caressed her tenderly, his lips on her eyelids, her nose, her flushed cheeks, her trembling mouth. "I want you, baby doll. I want you badly, can you tell?" he whispered against her lips, and gathered her hips into his.

She flushed red, astonished that even marriage and a pregnancy hadn't acclimated her to this kind of masculine teasing. "Yes," she managed, "I can tell."

"And do you know what I'm going to do about it, Kate?"

She let her cheek slide against the warm, hard shudder of his chest, hearing his wild heartbeat. Then she lifted her head to meet his black, glittering eyes. "No, what?" she whispered, excitement bearing down on her.

He bent and brushed his lips against hers. "Absolutely nothing." He moved his hand and put her back in her seat, gently but firmly. Then he picked up his cigarette pack from the dash, shook one out, lit it with faintly unsteady hands, and started the Bronco.

Kate felt as if she'd been dropped from a great height and had just hit the ground. Her wide eyes stared at him with slowly dawning comprehension while her body trembled and her breath came like a runner's.

"See how that ties in with your theory that I only seduced you out of desire," he invited with twinkling eyes, and turned the Bronco back onto the rutted path with a touch of the accelerator.

For the rest of the morning, he was friendly and attentive, and she sat on the chrome-plated running board of the Bronco and watched him use the complicated wire stretcher to put two strands of barbed wire back in place. Muscles rippled under the sheepskin jacket he'd left open, and her eyes watched his lean, sure hands with memories lying soft and vulnerable in them.

"That does it," he sighed when he was done, tossing the wire stretcher into the back, where the seats had been let down to make more storage room. "God, that's work."

She watched him flex his shoulders, admiring the very set of them. "I know it is," she replied. "I tried it once, and almost ripped my arm off." She laughed. "Dad yelled at me and then he hit me, and then he hugged me."

"Which is probably what I'd do, except for the hitting part," he added, tilting his hat back to stare down into her eyes. "I'd never hurt you deliberately. Not even if I was stoned to the back teeth."

She smiled softly. "I know that." She lowered her eyes to his open jacket. "There was still a full glass of whiskey sitting on the table in the living room last night," she remarked. "Untouched."

He stripped off his gloves slowly. It was hard to talk about, but after what he'd done to her, she deserved the truth. "I'm not going down the road my father did," he said then. "No matter what comes, from now on, I'm going to face it without crutches."

She looked up, shocked. "Jason, you've got it all out of perspective," she said softly. "An occasional drink isn't a crutch."

He shifted uncomfortably. "Maybe it was only an occasional one with him, at the beginning."

She went close to him, and she had to lean her head

back a long way to see his face. He towered over her. "You won't ever become an alcoholic," she put it bluntly. "Because as long as I'm alive, as long as we live together, I'll make sure of it. I'll take care of you."

"I've given you hell," he breathed.

"Yes," she admitted. She searched his hard face, seeing now the avalanche of emotion under that taut look. Someday, perhaps he'd trust her enough to show her all those violent feelings he was still afraid to reveal. "All your friends get that special treatment," she added with her tongue in her cheek.

He relaxed into laughter, tapping her on the cheek with a hard finger. "Shut up. Let's go home. I've got to talk to Sheila about getting everything ready for the production sale next Saturday."

"Can't I help?" she asked. He hesitated and she grinned. "I know I don't have a very good track record, but that was at formal dinners. A production sale means a barbecue and country people. And those," she added wickedly, "I know very well."

"I hate formal dinners," he said unexpectedly. "You needn't look so shocked," he added. "I do. I hate dressing up and trying to act like a gentleman and say and do all the right things. I can, and I've learned to bluff my way through, but I've never learned to like it. Hell, I was dirt poor before I built up the Spur."

She had forgotten. He seemed so suave and comfortable at those affairs that she'd actually forgotten his beginnings. "You never told me you hated it."

"I never told you a lot of things I felt," he said shortly, his eyes narrowing. "I'm trying. Can you see that? I'm trying not to hold things in."

She'd sensed it, but it was nice to know it. She reached

out hesitantly and touched his hand, loving the way his fingers curved towards hers, gathering them in.

His fingers contracted. "I feel guilty about Jamaica," he said tautly, bringing her shocked eyes up. "I lost control and I hurt you. I thought I'd killed…" He averted his gaze.

She gasped. She'd been too wrapped up in her grief to see through his cold, angry mask. Tears stung her eyes. She went against him without hesitation, just as she always had when he needed comforting, without a single sane thought of her own survival.

She clung to him. "You didn't kill our baby." She held him closer, feeling the shudder that ran through him. "Stop blaming yourself."

"I blamed you instead." He gathered her against him convulsively. "I'm…" He hesitated. He had to swallow to get it out. "I'm…sorry."

Kate cried. It was that much a milestone in their rocky relationship.

"Oh, don't cry, for God's sake," he muttered, hiding his embarrassment in bad temper. "Stop it, Kate."

She laughed through her tears. He didn't realize it yet, but they were on the way to a brand new relationship, to a future that was going to be so bright it might blind them both.

She threw her head back and looked up at him with her radiant face. "Okay," she laughed. "God forbid that I should embarrass you."

"Yes. God forbid." He searched her wet eyes slowly. Then he bent and kissed away the tears, smoothing them away from the warmth of her eyelids. "We'd better go home," he whispered. "If you're going to help me with that sale, I'll have to tell you what I want."

She nuzzled her nose against his. "I'll give you three guesses what I want right now," she whispered at his lips.

But he put her away from him firmly, his eyes faintly amused. "No."

She blinked. Her eyes searched his face, looking for cracks in the armor.

"Sex," he said slowly, "is an exquisite way to express what two people feel for each other. But it shouldn't be the foundation of a marriage." He scowled, searching for words. "We put the cart before the horse, just like you said last night. You don't really know me, except in a surface way, because I've never shared what I feel with you. What I'm trying to say is that I think we should turn the cart around, Kate."

Her face at that moment was beautiful. She smiled at him, her eyes alive with feeling. "Does that mean we'll see each other besides at the supper table once a week?"

"That's what it means." He slid his hands warmly up her arms. "And I'll try to stop living in the past."

"Then, isn't there something else you need to do?" she asked quietly.

He knew without asking what she meant. His face went hard. "No."

"Jason…"

"No!"

She sighed, lowering her eyes to his chest. "All right, I won't push." But it was depressing that, even with this new attitude, he still couldn't find a way to forgive his mother. Nell Donavan would die sooner or later, and it would be tragic if Jason never tried to see her and hear her side of the story.

CHAPTER TWENTY

KATE'S PORTRAIT TOOK longer than Gene expected it to. It was just past Thanksgiving Day when he finally produced the painting.

They had just finished supper and Kate and Cherry had gone to visit Mary. Gene ushered Jason into the living room, where he had the portrait on an easel, to watch his older brother's reaction.

Jason didn't move an inch. His smoking cigarette hung limply at his side while he stared and stared at the canvas with eyes so hungry that Gene actually looked away in embarrassment.

Kate was running through a meadow of wildflowers. Daisies and black-eyed Susans, Indian paintbrush and bluebonnets dotted the lush grass, and behind her a big mesquite tree's feathery fronds danced in the same wind that blew the skirt of her white lacy dress against her legs. Her long black hair hung over her shoulders, and she was wearing a big brimmed, floppy lace hat on her head. She was laughing, as Kate always had in earlier times. The green eyes that shone out of her lightly tanned, oval face gave her a sweet mystery, an elusive beauty that held Jason spellbound.

"Did you do that from memory?" Jason asked him after a long pause.

"Most of it," Gene said quietly. "All of it, except for

the dress and hat—I had a photo of her in those when she came to our wedding, it was a dress that Cherry had loaned her. I remember she didn't want to risk ruining it, and Cherry insisted. It suited her."

"Yes," Jason said idly. He couldn't look away from her pretty, impish expression. "Gene…that look in her eyes…you did that from memory?"

"She looked like that the day you were married," Gene replied, knowing that it was a delicate memory for his brother, and his voice was soft and hesitant. "When she looked up at you, just before you kissed her…."

Jason had thought about that a lot, lately, now that he and Kate were speaking to each other, laughing together, getting acquainted all over again. They were growing closer in every way, except physically. He held back because he didn't want her to get the idea that all he wanted was her body. But his hunger for her was getting more unmanageable by the day, and that painting succeeded in arousing him as much as Kate did.

He wanted it. He'd made a new payment on the interest, although the next one would get close pretty soon and he wasn't sure he could meet it. He'd pay Gene on the installment plan if he had to, but he wanted that portrait. "You can name your own price for that," he said, staring at the open doorway that led into the hall. "Anything you want."

"You name the price," Gene said. "I'll even give it to you, if you like it that much."

"Like it." Jason laughed, but there was an odd huskiness in his voice. He took a long draw from the cigarette, and his posture was rigid. He blew out a cloud of smoke on a heavy breath, and finally he turned, composed again. "It's the best work I've ever seen," he told his brother with genuine praise. "If that's the kind of thing you want to do for a living, I expect you'll make more than I ever do raising cattle."

Gene flushed with embarrassment. He hadn't expected anything more than a grunt, or maybe an argument. He hadn't expected this. "Thanks, Jay," he said.

Jason smiled at him. "Okay, son, you've made your point. You're a damned good artist. I'll help you, any way I can. But that," he added, nodding toward it, his eyes narrowing with possession, "that doesn't leave this house, even if it is your best work. It's mine."

"So is Kate. Isn't she?" Gene asked gently.

"God, I hope so," Jason said with unexpected fervor. "At least we're making a start again."

"You'd make it quicker if you stopped having separate bedrooms," Gene murmured dryly.

"Tell me about the portrait you're doing for Mrs. Drake," Jason asked.

"You're avoiding the issue."

"Which means I'm through discussing it." He turned. "Come on. What are you painting for Mrs. Drake?"

"Her youngest grandsons," he sighed. "She's already approved the preliminary sketch. Nice lady. Did you know she'd been teaching Kate how to give parties?"

Jason's eyebrows arched. "What?"

"Well, Kate thought you were ashamed of her, so she's trying to bone up on manners and deportment. Mrs. Drake is teaching her. She says she'll shock you with the Christmas dinner party she's throwing for the rest of those businessmen on the list you gave her."

"I told her I wasn't ashamed of her. I thought she'd given up on all that." He frowned.

"Surprise, surprise." Gene grinned. "Kate's full of them."

"Yes, I know." The older man's dark eyes went back to the portrait on the easel, caressing it. "God, she's beautiful," he said half under his breath.

"Indeed she is," Gene murmured. He smiled softly at his own handiwork. "She was pregnant when I painted her, just like Cherry is now. There's something about a woman when she's carrying a child. Something gentle and mysterious. Elusive."

"I guess Cherry's already picked out a name," Jason replied, trying not to sound bitter because their baby was only a memory now.

"Several," Gene admitted. "Along with a hundred dollars' worth of baby clothes, a bed, and so forth." He glanced at Jason. "And it cuts you to the bone to hear about it, I know. That's another reason Cherry and I want to get into our own house by Christmas, Jay. It will be better for you and Kate to have some time alone. Oh, Sheila's around, sure, but she never intrudes."

Jason felt hunted. "I'm over it," he said shortly. "There's no reason for you to have to buy a house...."

"But we want to," Gene replied. He stuck his hands in his pocket and stared at his older brother, smiling. "Look, Jay, if I have normal bills, I'll have to produce. I have Cherry and a baby to think about now, and I'm responsible for them. It will be for the best, in the long run."

"If you need help, any time," Jason said. "I'm here."

"You always have been." Gene's face hardened. "My God, even when I was a kid, you were always there, taking licks I deserved, doing anything to protect me from Dad when he was drinking; do you think I could ever forget the sacrifices you've made for me?"

Jason couldn't handle that. He moved away. "Stop it," he said curtly. "You'll have me in tears."

Gene didn't realize that it was the truth. He thought it was just more of Jason's standoffish dry humor. "Okay," he murmured, and forced a laugh. "As long as you know that I'd die for you."

"I'd do the same for you, Gene," came the quiet reply. "Now can we talk about something else? Like how much I'm going to have to come up with for that painting?"

Gene gave up. Jason couldn't let people get close. He wondered if Kate would ever really get through that wall around him, or if that was the real problem in their marriage.

They talked about the painting, and then Gene got something off his chest that had bothered him for days.

"Jay," he began, "do you remember the day you sent me to get a stock quotation out of your desk drawer in the study."

Jason turned. "Sure. Why?"

The younger man hesitated. This was even more sensitive ground than Kate. "I saw a letter."

"She deserted us," Jason reminded him. His eyes grew cold, hard. "She walked out on us and let that drunken tyrant beat and bruise and humiliate us. Can you forgive that? Well, I can't. I want no part of her."

"Then why keep the letter?"

Jason hated questions he couldn't answer. That one disturbed him. Without a word, without a gesture, he turned on his heel and left the room. Gene watched, wondering. He had an odd feeling that if Jason ever bent enough to admit how he felt about Kate that it might thaw him just a little. Maybe it might make him more human, more responsive to the human frailties he seemed to hate in himself and everyone else. He wanted Kate, Gene knew that. But if he loved her, some of Kate's natural empathy might get through to him. Everybody in the family, except Jason, knew how Kate felt. It was only getting Jason to accept the cost of love that was the problem. But perhaps one day he would. And if Jason didn't, Gene would go to see that woman in Arizona. But he wasn't giving up on big brother yet. He knew there was a soft spot in that hard armor. And it was getting softer by the day, thanks to Kate.

Kate got to see her portrait later that night, when she walked into the living room. It was hanging over the fireplace. She gasped at the sight of herself in such detail.

"My goodness," she burst out. "Is that me?"

"It looks like you," Cherry replied. "You dish! Doesn't my husband paint pretty portraits?"

"I love it. It's too pretty to be me," Kate sighed, smiling up at it. "My, my, you're going to be so famous, Gene, and I'll be able to say that I knew you in your starving garret days."

"Speaking of which, we move Saturday," Gene mused, winking at Cherry. "Into our own little house, with our own little mortgage."

"I'll miss you both," Kate said honestly.

"You can visit," Cherry said. "And we're not moving that far away!"

"Well, in that case, I'll visit a lot," Kate returned. "Especially when the baby comes." In that instant, even as they began talking about baby furniture, she grew morose. She thought about the baby she'd lost, for the first time in weeks, and she could have cried with the emptiness she felt. She and Jason were growing closer, but he never touched her these days. He was gentle and affectionate. But affection wasn't love. And she began now to worry about the future. What if he never loved her?

At least she'd shown her abilities as a hostess at that production sale, mingling with guests, talking cattle to the men and fashion to the women. It had been a lovely day all round, sunny and bright. Afterward, Jason had been lavish with praise and so obviously proud of his wife that she'd gone to bed with delicious memories. But she'd gone to bed alone. As she always did now. Jason never even opened the door of the guest room where he slept. And the nights were lonely and too long. She wished she could ask him why he didn't want her anymore, if he didn't. Perhaps he was afraid to risk another child.

The day that Gene and Cherry moved out, Kate grew quiet and brooding. They'd been so happy about having their own place. Jason and Kate had gone along with the last stick of furniture to see them settled. It was the baby furniture that had done it. Kate had burst into tears the minute she'd gone into her room for the night. She'd cried the whole time she was putting on her thin green gown with its delicate lace, and was crying still as she cleaned the makeup from her face and combed her dark hair that was slowly growing long again.

It was nearing Christmas and she wondered what it might have been like if she'd still been pregnant. It was really ridiculous to grieve anymore, she told herself, but she couldn't help it. She'd wanted the child so much.

Just as the tears were burning her cheeks and she was sniffling back more, the door opened quietly and the light went on.

"I shouldn't be able to hear you crying, should I?" Jason asked from the doorway. "But I did."

He looked tired. He was still dressed in his suit because he'd gone straight from Gene and Cherry's new house to some business meeting. He hadn't even loosened the tie, and Kate thought that, even blurred by tears, he was still the handsomest man she'd ever seen.

He came into the room, pausing beside the bed.

"What's the matter, honey?" he asked gently.

"I was thinking about the baby," she whispered, and the tears ran again as she held out her arms, like a lost and frightened child.

He didn't even hesitate. He reached down, throwing back the bedcovers to scoop her up in his hard arms and hold her, rocking her with the strength and warmth of his body.

"Shhh," he whispered at her ear. "Damn it, I should have been with you in Atlanta," he murmured huskily. "I never should have left you there alone."

"You were hurting, too," she whispered brokenly. "I understood."

Hadn't she always, he thought bitterly. He held her closer, drinking in the soft, woman scent of her body, the exquisite yielding of it in his arms. God, it felt good to hold her. To have her close and clinging to him, to smell the sweet fragrance of her clean, warm body. He could feel her through the gown, even through his suit, and he wanted so much to lie her down on that bed and make the sweetest love to her. But he had to go slow.

"You need a good night's sleep," he murmured. "It was just reaction, from seeing the baby furniture at Gene and Cherry's."

She stared at his chest. "I guess so." She sighed. "I guess I'll never have another one. It would be hard to go through that again, anyway," she added, trying not to let him see how badly she wanted it.

"Are you afraid of the risk?" he asked point blank.

She avoided his gaze. Did that mean that he was? "I

don't know," she began hesitantly, trying to think of a way to approach the subject that wouldn't alienate him.

He saw her frown and abruptly changed the subject. "Well, we've got other things to worry about right now," he said. "And Christmas is coming up."

He shifted her, so that she was closer, wrapped up in his warm arms, rough fabric against soft skin. She let him do it, too drugged by the feel of his arms around her to argue. She nuzzled under the jacket and against his white silk shirt. Under it, she could feel the hard muscle and the gentle cushion of thick hair. She remembered how it felt against her bare breasts and trembled a little with traces of pleasure. Her fingers unconsciously curled into his chest, her nails delicately scoring him with a slow, sensual rhythm that she wasn't even aware of. All the while her tears began to dry.

"Do you want to go away for Christmas or stay home this year?"

"If things are still hard financially, hadn't we better pinch pennies or something?" She didn't add that she could use those few weeks to get her designs well underway and get paid for them, so that she might be able to help him out.

His hard mouth tugged up in a smile. "Will you leave me if I lose it all and wind up living in a line cabin, posing for Gene's western landscapes?"

"Silly man," she whispered, her smile warm, her eyes full of soft affection. "Where would I go, without you?"

His dark eyes slid down to the bodice of the gown. "Isn't it a little cold for a see-through gown?" he asked huskily.

She nuzzled her face against his suit coat. "I didn't

notice the cold. I was lonely, and I'm tired of sleeping by myself."

That made his heart race. His jaw went taut. "Then why didn't you come to me and say so?" He looked at her quietly. "You say I'm always holding back, but what are you doing?"

She looked up at him. "You're the one who said we needed to get to know each other before we slept together again."

"I thought that was what you wanted," he said, puzzled. "Babies ought to be made out of love, not uncontrollable desire, isn't that what you said to me the night we argued?"

"I wish you could read my mind sometimes," she sighed as she got off his lap and moved away. "But you keep giving me what you think I want." She kept her back to him. "No, babies oughtn't to be made out of desire. But then, ours wasn't."

He stood up, studying that straight, tanned little back that was all too visible in the low cut of the gown. He wasn't sure he'd heard her right. "You wanted me," he said.

She turned, her pale eyes holding his, her body straight, her chin lifted proudly. "I loved you," she corrected, her eyes bright and steady as they met his.

He was suddenly, acutely still. "You what?"

She searched his shocked, glittery black eyes. "I loved you. I still love you. I'll always love you. Deathlessly," she whispered, ripping away the mask. "Endlessly. Hopelessly. I loved you from the very beginning, Jason." She smiled bitterly. "I tagged after you like a lovesick child, you even said so. I goaded you into making love to me, and I deliberately didn't take precautions because I thought if I got pregnant, you might love the baby even if you couldn't love me." She laughed, but through sudden tears as she leaned back against the wall for support.

He stood there like a statue, not moving. She'd said once before that she'd loved him in the past, but that she didn't anymore. He hadn't realized, until now, that she was still in love with him. It changed him. It knocked him completely off balance.

"But it all backfired, didn't it, Jason?" she was asking miserably. "Because you're never going to feel like that about me…!"

His mouth cut her off. He was close against her, his body hungry like the mouth that devoured her trembling lips. His weight crushed her gently against the wall behind her. She tasted tears on her mouth, like salt, mingling with coffee and smoke on his breath. He was hard and warm over her, and she was trembling. Then his mouth opened and his hips shifted. She stopped thinking at all.

CHAPTER TWENTY-ONE

LIGHTNING SHOT THROUGH Kate's body. It was the most primitive kind of thing that she felt in Jason as he bent over her, devouring her in a hush that was only broken by the rasp of his breathing and the rough bump of his heartbeat. There should have been thunderstorms around them, or crashing waves, or an earthquake. They should have been in the middle of an open field with the rain coming down in pitchforks around their oblivious heads. But there was only the bright room, with its pink decor and canopied bed, the soft sound of the wind outside the closed window and the hum of the furnace coming through the register behind Kate's feet.

She didn't have enough room to respond to him. His powerfully muscled body was against her from thigh to breast, one leg bent between both of hers, his hands rhythmically pulling her hips upward into his while his tongue probed past the soft trembling of her lips.

"I'm trying…to talk to you," she whispered against his hard mouth when he finally lifted it just enough to catch a breath of air.

His lean hands moved up to her breasts, slowly taking their weight over the silky fabric of her bodice. "You told me you loved me," he whispered unsteadily. "What did you expect me to do?"

"I didn't think you wanted to be loved," she breathed as his mouth lowered again.

"More fool, you," he murmured against her welcoming lips. "If you don't want to get pregnant again, you'd better tell me while I can fumble something to use out of my wallet."

"Is that where you keep it?" she whispered.

"God knows. I think the only one I have is three years old, and it's probably long since rotted," he managed with the last traces of humor in him. He was trembling, and she could feel that, and he didn't give a damn. She loved him. And he loved her. He wanted to show her how much, and it was going to take one hell of a long time.

"What happens if I say I don't want a child yet?" she asked unsteadily as he bent to lift her. "Hold the thought while you rush into town to the drugstore…?"

"Dream on, honey." He eased her onto the mattress and followed her down, his mouth nudging her gown out of the way so that he could get it over her taut nipple. She moaned when he did that, clutching at him with satisfying hunger. He knew what she liked best, and he did it, overwhelmed with the newness of knowing she loved him, wanting nothing in life more than to please her.

"Jason, the door…" she managed. It was standing open, and her eyes were like green and black saucers.

"Who's going to see us, or hear us?" he asked softly.

"What if they come back to pick up something, or Sheila did?" she asked.

"Damn," he sighed. But he got up and closed it, then locked it. He stared down at her as he returned to the bed, warm, possessive desire making him arrogant. His dark, hungry eyes ran the length of her body in the gown that concealed nothing from him, lingering on the taut tips of her breasts.

She felt all woman, letting him look at her like that. She liked it. And because she did, and because she had no more secrets from him, she pulled the bodice down and slid it over her hips. Then she lay back, her body curled and soft on the coverlet, and let him look at her.

"I love you," she whispered huskily. "I don't even care if you know it. I love you to distraction."

"If you don't stop saying that, I'll never get my clothes off," he said with black humor as he tried to work buttons with hands that wanted nothing more than Kate's body under them.

"Why?" she murmured dryly. "Does it disturb you?"

"Disturb me, the devil," he laughed. "It excites me so much I can't even feel my damned hands!"

That was new, too, to see Jason ruffled. She liked it. She watched the clothing come off that powerful, darkly tanned body with a feeling of utter possession. He might not love her, but he wanted to be loved. And as long as he was open to her, she might move in under his heart if she was very careful.

He turned finally, his body like bronze in the light except for one wide swathe because he didn't sunbathe in the nude. He was beautifully made, she thought, watching him with blatant interest. She loved the evidence of his hunger for her, the powerful masculinity that was hers alone now.

"You've never looked at me like that before," he said quietly as he eased down alongside her.

"I was too shy of you," she said gently. "I still am, a little. But you give me so much when we make love. I tingle all over, just thinking about how it is."

"You give me a lot, too." He slid his hand along her breasts, watching her stomach curve in suddenly with pleasure, and he smiled. But it was no mocking, superior smile. It was amused, indulgent, even conspiratorial.

She made his head spin. She made him invincible. He found new things to do, that made her cry out, that made her shudder. He touched her in ways he'd been too reticent to touch her before. He smoothed his mouth over silky skin that trembled. He lifted her and held her, he pushed down against her and buffeted her, and all the while she looked at him with those eyes. Those soft, green, misty eyes that held enough love to bind him forever.

It was sweet madness. She looked down where he lifted up her hips in firm, sure hands. And she watched. And so did he. Her eyes slid back up to his with new knowledge and fascinated pleasure. It was like no other time with him. Even the sounds were different. There was passion, but it was so slow, so tender. Every movement was careful and loving, and their rhythm like summer wind, slow and sultry and sweet.

She caught her breath and he smiled. "There?" he whispered, and did it again.

She gasped, laughing. "It...never felt...like this."

His hands cupped her face and he smiled down into her eyes. "We never loved like this," he whispered, and bent to her mouth. His breath caught as his hips moved again. "Don't be afraid of another baby, Kate," he breathed into her open mouth, and then his hips moved sharply.

The world exploded into a dazed kaleidoscope of color and urgent, quick movement, of jerky gasping cries and then buffeting, rough, shuddering rhythm. She felt him and heard him, and held him. And all around her, the world became red and blazing hot, and throbbed.

She couldn't get any closer. She remembered trying to. Jason was still trembling in the aftermath, his heart shaking him, his breath gasping. She was trembling, too. She thought she'd cried out his name, but she was dazed in the aftermath of unbearable fulfillment.

Kate breathed, trying to calm down. And just when she almost did, he lifted and pushed, and began to move. She started to speak, but his mouth covered hers with exquisite tenderness, and when he slid against her she realized that he was still part of her. Then the rhythm changed and he moved again.

The morning light streaming into the room woke her. Kate opened her eyes and looked for Jason, but he was nowhere in sight. As she sat up, she felt a lingering soreness and smiled.

Her eyes went lovingly to the dent in the pillow beside hers, and she leaned over and pressed her lips tenderly to it.

"What a waste," Jason murmured from the bathroom as he stood in the doorway, laughing at her.

She flushed. He was wearing his dress slacks and boots, and she could see that his naked chest bore the marks of her fingers and her mouth from the long night. "Good morning," she said shyly.

"It was a good night, too," he mused as he sat down on the bed and stripped the covers off, lifting her across his lap. Her bare breasts were now lying soft and warm on his hairy chest. "Now tell me good morning," he breathed, and kissed her.

She reached up to hold him, kissing him back, warm all over with the sweetness of belonging to him. There was nothing to compare it with. Always before, there had been some conflict, something to spoil it when they came together. If nothing else, there was his own inability to open up with her. But that seemed to be miraculously gone.

Her eyes opened lazily as he lifted his head, and she searched his face, finding no traces of conscience or guilt or moodiness.

"I thought it would only be another dream," she whispered. "I was afraid to open my eyes."

"So was I, if you want the truth," he whispered back. His dark eyes searched her, and then went over her like hands, caressing, possessing. "My God, if last night had been a dream, I'd have jumped off the roof."

"I thought we'd never be close again," she said softly, dazed by the feeling in his deep, tender voice. "Not this close, anyway."

He lifted his eyes back to hers. "You're the only person who ever was," he said gently. "I don't want anyone that close, except you."

She smiled up at him, her hand touching his hard shoulder, his chest, his neck. "Now that I'm here, do I get to stay?" she asked, only half joking.

"Suppose we start acting like married people," he suggested. He spread her fingers flat on his hard chest. "Suppose we sleep together from now on."

"And make babies?" she asked slowly, looking up, because that was the one thing she did remember from that long, sweet loving; what he'd said at the last.

"Did you hear me?" he whispered as his eyes searched hers. "I wasn't sure I'd said it aloud."

"You did." Her face flamed, like the body so close against his. "And I want to."

He hadn't been sure of that at all. She did lip service to wanting a child, but he hadn't been sure that it wasn't either grief at the loss of the other one, or just desire. He was afraid a baby so soon would tie her down again and she wouldn't like it. But if she loved him, it didn't seem to matter. To him, at least.

"Kate...your career...this traveling..." He hesitated. "Hell, I'll go with you," he said. "I'll take care of you."

"I'm not risking that again, if I get pregnant," she said quietly. "Not if it means spending nine months in bed. There isn't going to be any traveling."

"No. I won't try to chain you here," he said firmly. "You have a talent. I want you to use it."

Her eyes searched his. "You don't mind my career anymore, do you? You really don't."

"I told you once that it disturbed me, I just couldn't tell you why. Not then. You see, Kate, I wanted to come first," he said shortly, admitting it at last. "I wanted to know I was loved. All right. Now I do. I won't feel jealous of your work anymore."

She wondered if a woman could faint sitting up. She cocked her head. "You wanted to know that I loved you?"

"Is that so surprising? I made you pregnant on purpose, or haven't you even realized it?" he asked matter-of-factly. "I could have taken precautions. I didn't even try. And you never questioned it. My God, does a man who doesn't really want ties deliberately risk getting a woman pregnant when he's as old-fashioned about that sort of thing as I am?"

Her lips parted. "Oh, my goodness," she managed. "I never thought about that."

"Thank God. A man likes to have a few secrets." He kissed her softly and pursed his lips as he looked down her body with lingering desire. Then he sighed. "I guess you're going to be out of commission for a couple of days, after last night." He looked up and grinned, looking unspeakably happy and at least five years younger. "But we can always feel each other up under the covers, can't we?" he asked.

She laughed. And then she cried. She held him convulsively. "I love you," she breathed.

"Yes. I noticed that a few hours ago." He sighed, drawing her closer. "How about some breakfast? Then I can go to town and try to talk the bank out of foreclosing."

She stiffened. "But the production sale—didn't you say it made enough to pay off the interest note?"

"Sure," he agreed. "But I still have to pay off the other mortgage, honey, the one on the house and land. I paid off the interest note on the last cattle shipment, that's all." He searched her troubled eyes gently. "Kate, I don't care. Nothing comes before you, not even the Spur. If I lose it, and I still have you, then I haven't lost a thing."

He might not love her, but he certainly felt something for her, if he could make a statement like that. The Spur had always been his life.

She smiled tenderly, touched beyond reason. "It's pretty momentous, to be told that you're more important than somebody's enormous big ranch."

"I meant it, too." He brushed his mouth over hers. "Let's go down and have something to eat. Then I've got to get to town. And you've got to get to work." He grinned. "If I lose my shirt, you may have to support us."

"Oh, I would, gladly," she began.

He put his finger over her lips. "No. I was kidding. I'd sell the place before I'd let you pay for it," he said, and the look in his eyes was level and genuine. "I mean it. My pride wouldn't stand that."

"I just offered," she faltered.

"Yes. Thanks. Now get dressed, you brazen hussy,"

he said, tossing her lightly into the middle of the bed, his dark eyes appreciating every line and curve. "God, what a body! Get out of there before I go crazy looking at you."

She laughed delightedly. It was like a totally new marriage, bright with love and promise. He picked up his shirt and suit coat and tie.

"I'd better find something less rumpled to wear," he remarked. "See you downstairs, Mrs. Donavan," he added, and there was real tenderness in his voice now.

She showered and put on her working clothes—jeans and an embroidered top. Her freshly shampooed and dried hair fell like black satin around her shoulders. She felt young. Honeymoonish, in fact. Not only that, she felt determined. Jason might not want help, but he was going to get some. Now the Spur had become not only her future, but the future of her prospective children. She wasn't going to see it go down the tube because of Jason's pride. She had more than enough to bail the place out, in her own account. She was going to save the Spur and swear the bank to secrecy. Then, when things were a little more stable than they were right now, she could tell Jason the truth and wait for the explosion.

She pursed her lips. The bank president was a good friend of the family. If Kate approached him in the right way, she just might get him to discover unexpected dividends from some of Jason's stock to report to Jason. That might disguise the true nature of the deposit, which Kate had to make sure Jason didn't find out about. It just might work, she decided.

Jason was downstairs when she finally got there, always one jump ahead of her when it came to dressing. He seemed to appear in his clothing, as if he never had to put it on at all.

He was in a charcoal gray suit this morning, and he looked debonair and unusually flashy with a red pouf in his chest pocket that matched his bloodred, patterned tie.

"Well, aren't we spiffy looking," Kate mused, grinning at him as she sat down next to him at the long table.

"We sure are," Sheila remarked, grinning herself as she put a platter of biscuits next to the eggs, hash browns, sausage and bacon platters already on the table. "My, my, there's that Kate all flushed and looking like a bride, and Jason's bed not even slept in all night long. A body could get suspicious."

Kate went beet red and so did Jason, of all people. He glared at Sheila with eyes that promised murder.

"I ought to bludgeon you with the coffeepot," he said shortly.

"You'd attack your own cook?!" Sheila exclaimed, holding both hands to her breast. "You'd assault a helpless old woman who spent all morning stalking a wild hog, and hauled it up on chains and skinned it out and dressed it and ran it through a sausage grinder, just so you could have fresh sausage on your breakfast table?!"

Jason stared at her coldly. "You didn't have time to skin out a hog."

Sheila shrugged. "I had to take it out of the refrigerator and get the wrapping off, with my poor old hands eaten up with arthritis," she amended. She grinned. "But it sounded better my way, didn't it?"

He turned over his coffee cup with a smile doing its best to get past his teeth. "Oh, hell, sit down and eat your breakfast."

"Can't," Sheila said, removing her apron. "I'm on my way to Laredo with Mrs. Carstairs from down the road. We're going shopping for serapes."

"I guess that means cold cuts for lunch," Jason sighed.

"We don't have any cold cuts," Sheila replied. She smiled. "You might take Kate out to lunch."

"Kate only gets a half hour, Cupid," Kate murmured dryly.

"He could have a sandwich with you in the canteen, couldn't he?" Sheila persisted.

"Of course he could," Jason said resignedly. "I had planned to do that, without any prompting from you."

Sheila chuckled. "Now isn't that nice," she sighed.

"So you can put up your bow and arrows," he added curtly.

"I'll just stick them in the cupboard, so's I can shoot you some nice steak for your supper, my lord," Sheila murmured, dropping him a convincing curtsy.

He picked up a fork and Kate had never seen the older woman move so fast, giggling all the way.

"You animal," Kate accused.

"I wouldn't stab her," he replied. "God knows, I'm a patient man, I've put up with it all my life without killing her."

"I had noticed that you're a man of great patience," she agreed with an impish smile.

He pursed his lips and searched her green eyes. "After last night, I should hope so," he said, his voice dropping an octave.

She went red again, and he laughed, bending over to kiss her.

"What time do you have lunch?" he whispered.

She was having trouble thinking. "I...usually go at eleven-thirty, so the girls can go at twelve," she whispered back.

"Do you? Open your mouth a little...."

She did, and it was like the night before, a stormy interlude that quickened her pulse and made her breathless with undisguised hunger for him.

He lifted his head after a minute, breathing roughly himself. His dark eyes were almost black. "You can't imagine what it does to me, to kiss you like that," he whispered gruffly. "It's like making love completely when I do it with you."

"Oh, don't," she moaned, "I'll die of longing."

He took a slow breath and nuzzled her nose with his. "So will I, honey. Isn't it a sweet way to go?"

"So sweet…." She kissed him gently, loving the way his mouth responded so easily to hers. She smiled against it. "I love this," she whispered. "I could never let go completely before, but now I can, and when I give in to you, I don't feel ashamed afterward of what I've said and done and thought…."

He lifted his head, his eyes stunned. "Did you?" he asked. "Did you feel that way, after we made love?"

"Yes," she confessed. She curled her fingers into his, and tugged at them idly. "It didn't embarrass me at the time, but later, it all seemed so intimate and…and kind of…"

"…dirty?"

She looked up. "Yes," she said.

His fingers contracted. "I told you how my father felt," he reminded her. "Sex was an animal instinct, he said, and no real man needed it." He brushed his lips against her fingers. "I guess, deep down, I had learned to feel that way about it, too. But after I made love to you, that started to change. It was something more than a mating urge. It was too tender most of the time, too profound. And last night, honey, all the walls went down. Every one. Last night was creation. I learned things about you and about myself that I never knew. That wasn't lust. That was loving. That was the kind of loving," he emphasized softly, "that plants seed and grows fruit. The kind of loving that brings a new life into the world, not a seamy kind of quick satisfaction that reduces a beautiful act to a sordid coupling."

"You make it sound profound," she said gently.

"Isn't it profound?" he asked, smiling. "When two people express what they feel for each other in that way, so that the very force of the feeling creates life? My God, Kate, is anything more profound than that?"

She laid her cheek against his hand. "I thought you had hang-ups," she murmured. "It sounds as if you've gotten rid of them."

"I've gotten things in perspective, that's all." He tangled her fingers back into his. "And I'm still learning. My father had problems. But they aren't mine, unless I let them be." He searched her eyes. "What we shared in that bed last night wasn't dirty. And whatever we do together, however we do it, it isn't anything to be ashamed of afterwards. We're both vulnerable, Kate," he added softly. "That used to bother me, but it doesn't anymore. I don't mind letting the barriers down with someone who loves me."

She nuzzled her cheek against his. "That sounds nice."

"No one else ever did, Kate," he said, half under his breath, in a tone that was dark and soft. "I told you that in Jamaica, and I meant it. You're the only person in the world who ever loved me."

"Oh, that's not so," she said, getting up. She pulled his head against her breasts, cradling it there. "Jason, your father loved you. He had to. There was good in him, or how could your mother have cared about him? And your mother loved you...."

"Did she?" He pulled back, his eyes fierce. "Damn her, she put herself first. She left us here with that madman! She ran. I watched him try to go after her...." He stopped, fighting down the memory of that night. He'd been almost fifteen, he'd never forgotten what he saw, but he'd never let himself think about it. He clammed up.

Kate searched his eyes. 'You still blame your father for his drinking and your mother for her desertion, after all this time. I don't think you've ever tried seeing it from their point of view, have you?" she asked gently. "No, don't blow up at me," she whispered, and she put her hands very tenderly against his hard mouth, quietening him as if by magic. "Listen. People aren't perfect. You've tried to be. You've been afraid to make mistakes, because that would mean you might end up like they did, you might be flawed. But we all make mistakes, Jason. We're all human. Your father was weak, and in a way, so was your mother. But that's just human."

"It's weakness," he ground out. "If you're weak, you get hurt."

She smiled, nuzzling her face against his. "I'd never hurt you," she whispered, and her mouth softly rubbed over his lips. "I love you too much."

His eyes met hers, tormented. "Kate...she loved him, at first."

Kate kissed him tenderly, loving the way he was with her, loving the way he let her get close, let her touch him.

She nibbled his lower lip and smiled. "I love you," she whispered. "And you can't do anything horrible enough to make me leave you. Does that make you feel less threatened?"

He sighed heavily. "I don't know."

That was a setback, but only a temporary one. He cared for her. She could make him love her, it would just take time.

"Jason, wouldn't it be as well to go and see your mother," she suggested hesitantly. "While she's still alive? And ask her all the questions you never asked your father?"

He didn't move for a long time. His dark eyes thoughtful, he finally pulled away and got up, lighting a cigarette with steady fingers. "I don't want to see her."

"Why? Are you afraid of what you might find out?"

"I'm afraid I might break her neck," he said curtly. And in that instant, he looked almost capable of it.

CHAPTER TWENTY-TWO

"I GUESS IT'S never occurred to you that she might have had a reason for what she did," Kate murmured gently.

"She had a reason, all right," he shot back. "Her own safety."

"Have it your own way," she sighed. "You've got it imbedded in concrete, and nobody's going to change your mind. But she can't be a young woman any more," she added without emphasizing it. "Once she's gone, there won't be anyone alive who knows the truth. Not even you."

He didn't say anything. That was a good sign, she thought, silently pleased with herself. When he didn't say anything, he was considering it.

"I've got to run," she said as she swallowed the rest of her coffee. "I'll be late."

He put out his cigarette. "I'll drop you off on my way to the bank."

She smiled as he got up and slid his hand gently into hers. She couldn't remember a time in her life when she'd been happier, or when she'd felt closer to him. If only it would last, this lovely newness. Her fingers curled trustingly around his as she fell into step beside him.

Kate found herself watching the clock at work, despite the fact that she was doing some of the best work she'd ever produced. Her Alamo collection was taking shape beautifully. Mr. Rogers was delighted with her ideas for fabrics, and immediately got on the phone to one of the company's fabric designers. This was the first time she'd had access to actual fabric design, and it was exciting.

Jason came into the canteen at eleven-thirty on the dot, but he wasn't the same smiling man Kate had left that morning. He was tired and there were deeper lines in his face than usual. But he still dredged up a smile for her when she got her coffee and sandwich and sat down beside him.

"It didn't go well, I gather?" she asked gently, smoothing her fingers over the back of his big, lean hand with fascinated delight.

He turned his hand and caught her fingers gently. "You read me too well," he mused. He meant it, but oddly enough it didn't bother him anymore. He didn't mind having Kate know his secrets, because she loved him. But there was still one last hurdle. He hadn't admitted how he felt, how obsessively he loved her. He couldn't let her know just how vulnerable he was. His father had loved Nell Donavan, and she'd used that weakness against him. What if Kate someday did that to him?

She looked up and caught that strange expression. "Is my makeup smeared or something?" she teased softly.

"You look lovely. You always do, to me," he replied, putting away his disturbing thoughts. "They turned me down, Kate."

She tightened her grip on his hand. "I'm sorry. Is there an alternative?"

He laughed curtly. "Sure. There's a public auction."

Her heart seemed to stop beating. Despite what he'd said about not minding it, if it came down to choosing between losing the ranch or losing her, she knew what the Spur meant to him.

"Is that for certain, or just a possibility?"

"I can't even pay the interest, unless I start selling off my breeding herd, Kate," he replied. "And if I do that, then that's the end of the Spur anyway. I'm going to fly out to Houston and talk to some people I know. Then I want to go to Oklahoma and up to Montana. It's going to be a lot of traveling in the weeks before Christmas, but it's necessary."

She sighed. "Can't I go with you?" she asked hopefully.

"I have to keep my mind on business for just a little while," he said, smiling. "Okay?"

She laid her head against his shoulder briefly, mindful of amused, indulgent smiles around them. "Okay. When will you go?"

"As soon as I can get a flight," he told her. "I'll call you every night, but it may be three weeks before I get home. I'm sorry. It's just that it might mean the difference if I can get some backers."

She searched his dark eyes. "I told you that I'd give you what I have. I've got almost thirty thousand dollars saved…."

"No." He put his fingers against her lips. That much would have been more than enough to give him the time he needed, but he couldn't bend his pride enough to take help from a woman. Not even when she was his wife. "Can you walk out with me, or will we have an audience?"

"I can walk out with you and of course we'll have an audience."

He smiled, shaking his head. "Come on, then, we'll sneak off in the car long enough to kiss each other stupid, and then I'll leave."

She found herself in the Mercedes with him, in the

back row of the parking lot, too far away for anyone to get a decent look. He kissed her until her lips were swollen.

"God, that's sweet," he breathed against her lips. "I'm going to miss you like hell, baby doll."

"I'll miss you, too. You'll really call me every night?"

"You'd better believe I will. You can have Mary come over and stay with you while I'm gone, if you want to."

"Mama has a new group of friends and they have something to do every night of the week," Kate sighed. "Sometimes I think she's forgotten that she has a daughter, although I do see her here most days."

"She's letting you get settled down," he murmured dryly. "I'll bet she remembers her first months of marriage to your father."

"Maybe she does at that." She touched his hard cheek. "Don't flirt with other girls."

"As if they'd even notice, if I did," he chuckled. He traced her nose with his lips. "You're the one I worry about, you sexy little woman. Keep those sultry eyes to yourself until I come home."

She smiled lazily. "My sultry eyes and I will be right here, waiting. As if I'd waste myself on a lesser man," she teased delightedly and was kissed roughly for her pains.

"You're good for my ego," he whispered.

"That works both ways. But I promise I'll be good."

And the promise lasted until two weeks later, when she got the first of her contract money for the new designs. She took an hour off from work and went to see Mr. Baker, the bank president of the San Frio People's Bank, and gave him her entire savings to pay off the pending note on the Spur.

She swore him to secrecy, but she knew that Jason wouldn't let it rest until he found out where the money had come from. She just hoped that he cared about her enough to unruffle eventually. She couldn't let him lose the Spur.

Later, she went to the small house that Cherry and Gene were buying, a two-bedroom brick one just down the road a few miles from the Donavan place. Since Gene had a stake in the ranch, too, she felt obliged to tell him what she'd done.

"Jason will kill you," Gene mused, adding to her own misgivings.

"Oh, I know," Kate groaned. "But what else can I do? I can't let him lose it!"

"Neither could I," Gene agreed. "And if I had any savings, I'd already have thrown them into the kitty. I have prospects and a small trust, but I can't touch it for another four years. Hell of a mess, isn't it?"

"I'm glad Kate stepped in," Cherry said as she brought in a tray with coffee and cookies on it. She didn't look very pregnant yet, but she had the glow and the soft flush that told their own story. "Jason is your husband. He shouldn't mind letting you help."

"You don't know Jason," Gene told his petite wife. "He's got the pride of a martyr. He'll never let her do it."

"He can't stop me," Kate reminded him. "It's already done. But he can be so unbending sometimes. I wish he'd go and see your mother," she added gently, meeting Gene's quiet eyes.

He sighed. "If he doesn't, within a month or two, I'm going to," he said. "We've neither of us ever heard her side of it. We never really heard Dad's, because he wouldn't talk about her. But I think she's entitled to a hearing, even if Jason doesn't."

"He may surprise you both someday by producing her," Cherry said. "Maybe he's curious, too."

"If he is, he's keeping it very quiet," Gene said.

Kate studied the face that was like the shadow of her rugged husband's. "Gene, do you hate her?"

He shrugged. "I don't feel anything. I was too small when she left. I'm curious. I don't think I hate her, although I could for what happened to Jason because she left. He protected me. But there was never anybody to protect Jason."

Kate could have cried, thinking about that lonely boy that Jason had been. It was so painful that when Cherry began to talk about their plans for the baby, even that was a welcome change of subject. Kate still grieved for the baby she'd lost, but now there was at least the hope of another child. In fact, it might be more than hope, because her period was late and by the third week Jason was gone she was feeling some vague nausea.

The time Jason was away was cheered only by the nightly calls, which he was careful to make after Sheila had gone to bed. Probably, Kate thought, to spare her blushes, because he talked to her like a lover, now. Conversation was laced with shared memories, and endearments, and lazy teasing. He was like a different man, so open and loving and warm that Kate was lulled into a sense of fantasy.

She had Red Barton drive her to the airport the day Jason got home. He looked tired, his powerful body a little sluggish as he moved through the milling tourists with his travel bag over one shoulder, his Stetson hiding his dark eyes, and his navy vest suit straining against hard muscle as he moved with lean grace.

He looked up as she approached him, and like magic,

all the weariness left him. She ran to him, laughing, her green eyes full of love.

He dropped the bag and caught her up by the waist, swinging her up against him with pure delight in his smile.

"Well, what a sweet surprise," he murmured as he bent to her mouth. "Dessert already, and I haven't even had lunch…."

She smiled under his hard, hungry mouth, clinging to him with loving abandon.

"I missed you," he whispered. "The nights went on forever."

"So did the days," she whispered back. She sighed happily, her eyes lost in his. "Don't go away again."

"Not for fifty years, at least." He kissed her again and then let her down, his dark gaze approving her neat black and white fitted suit. "Nice," he murmured. "Did you make it?"

"I sure did. On my very own sewing machine at home. Maybe someday we'll have a little girl, and I can make things for her," she added, her voice soft with dreams. And he knew then that her fear of losing another baby was fading. She was looking ahead, not behind.

"I'd like that, too." He touched her neat coiffure. "I'd like a son as well."

"I'll keep that in mind," she teased.

He picked up his bag and took her arm. "Well, we're not out of the woods by any long shot, but I've got enough backing to keep us running for six more months," he said. "By that time, I think I'll have my feedlot in operation and those new crossbreeds I've been breeding from Indian strains should be throwing calves."

Kate's heart froze. She hoped that she hadn't jumped

the gun by doing what he'd forbidden her to and bailing him out. A man's pride was a delicate thing. Especially a man like Jason. She'd only been thinking of helping him, but he liked to stand on his own feet and do things his way. He might not see it as helping. He might actually see it as an attempt to take him over, to buy him.

She looked up at his dark face, and she almost told him. But he smiled, and bent, and brushed his mouth with exquisite tenderness over hers. Later, she thought. She'd tell him later.

"Welcome home, boss man," Red Barton drawled as Jason and Kate got out to the ranch pickup truck.

Jason glared at him. "What the hell are you doing here?"

"I drove Miss Kate," Red replied. He raised his eyebrows at the unfamiliar sight of his taciturn boss with an arm around Miss Kate and a look on his face that even a blind man would have recognized as a frustrated desire to be alone with her. "Gosh, I'm sorry I didn't bring the car. Then you two could have sat in the backseat and... talked," he added with a meaningful smile. But the smile vanished when the look in Jason's eyes made him immediately into a dignified cowboy. "Just get right in, Miss Kate, and I'll have you two home in no time!" he said with exaggerated politeness.

Jason muttered as he tossed his bag in the boot and got in beside Kate. "I wish to God I understood the perverted sense of justice that makes me keep you around, Barton."

"Well, boss, what it came right down to was that you either had to keep me or that rattlesnake I saved you from," Red told him reasonably as he started the truck with a wry glance. "And we both know how you hate snakes."

Jason actually grinned. But he didn't let Barton see him do it.

That night was like the first time. He made love to her with such aching tenderness that she clung to him afterwards, trembling in the aftermath of a loving like none she'd experienced before.

He kissed her mouth, his dark eyes watching her in the swath of moonlight that filtered across the bed. "Happy?" he whispered.

"So happy," she whispered back. She nuzzled her face against his damp, hairy chest, loving the abrasiveness of it against her body. "It gets better every time."

"You make me whole," he said quietly. "The world begins and ends with you, now."

She kissed his throat. "And for me, it begins and ends with you. I never knew I could be so happy."

"Tomorrow, suppose we go Christmas shopping?"

"Just the two of us?" she asked drowsily.

"Just the two of us. I'll drive you into San Antonio and give you a credit card."

"I already have one, thanks. Not with your credit line, I'll bet," she teased, "but I have a respectable one of my own."

"You're my wife," he reminded her. "You have the right to my card."

She started to argue, but it was too sweet, this intimacy, to be shattered. "All right," she whispered, remembering that compromise had to be the hallmark of any successful marriage. "You win."

"I usually do," he murmured wickedly, and rolled over against her. She started to push at his broad chest, but he caught her mouth, laughing, and in seconds, she was moaning. The sudden shift from humor to passion always startled her. She wanted him obsessively since the first time. She had no way of knowing if it was normal or not, but he seemed to share it. She closed her eyes and held him closer, and gave up trying to sort it out.

The next morning, she got up and dressed, puzzled by Jason's absence. She didn't know why he hadn't waited for her. But when she got downstairs, and saw him, she had a premonition of disaster.

He whirled at her step, his face unmoving. He'd been to the post office, she knew by the stack of mail on the table. By the look on his face, the mail wasn't all he'd found there.

"Mr. Baker was in the post office," he began quietly. He studied her face as if he'd never seen it before. That tall, arrogant stance spelled trouble. He looked the way he had years ago, formidable and unbending.

"And what did the bank president have to say?" she prompted. She folded her arms closely over her breast.

"He said I didn't have a thing to worry about, that the payment had been made. I asked him how, and he wouldn't tell me. At least, he wouldn't tell me immediately," he added, with a narrowing of one eye that spoke volumes. "But I got it out of him, Kate."

She let out the breath she'd been holding, pausing on the bottom step, nervous. "Now, Jason," she began, "it's my home, too...."

"To hell with that!" he said, his voice cutting like a whip, as knife-edged as the fury in his eyes. "I pay the bills around here! This is my ranch. You had no right to go behind my back and make me look like a damned kept man!"

She pursed her lips. It was hurt pride, that was all.

He'd calm down. All she had to do was hold on until he got over it, until she could reason with him.

"I never meant to do that," she said. She looked him right in the eye, spoke softly, and made no sudden moves. She'd read that advice in a book about how to ward off attack by man-eating guard dogs. Maybe it would work on unreasonable husbands, too.

"Whatever you meant to do, you've made me look like a damned fool in the eyes of the community," he shot back. "My God, Kate, I've spent half my life trying to live down my father's reputation and my mother's desertion. And now, on top of all that, I've got to live down the fact that there's a woman paying my bills!"

It was even worse than she thought. Well, maybe reason would work. So she moved down one more step and went close to him. "Jason, we're married. My money is yours, too...."

His pride hit him between the eyes, and he didn't stop to choose his words. It all boiled over, all of the shame that had festered in him all the way home. "I won't take money you earned by putting your career before your husband and child!"

She gaped at him. This wasn't a reasonable man talking. This wild-eyed man wasn't her Jason. That feverish accusation didn't have a grain of truth in it, and he knew it. She was even pretty sure that he didn't mean it. He was just taking out his wounded vanity on her in the best way he knew.

"My, we are in a snit, aren't we?" she asked, refusing to let him push her into an argument over an issue that had already been settled. Once, she might have resorted to tears. But she'd learned a lot in the months they'd been married. She knew exactly what he was feeling, and she was sorry she'd caused it. He was going to hate himself later for the accusations he was spouting with such conviction right now.

"In a snit!" He took off his hat and slammed it onto the floor. His black eyes were blazing with fury. "My God, how could you do that to me? How could you go behind my back like that?!"

"It was safer than doing it in front of you," she returned reasonably. "I couldn't stand by and do nothing, and let you lose your birthright."

"You could have let me handle it," he said coldly. "You could have trusted me to do the right thing, instead of taking things into your own hands."

"And challenging your control," she replied, because that was what was giving him fits. He couldn't stand losing control. She lifted her soft eyes to his. "I hurt your pride, and I'm sorry. I didn't think about how it might look. I had the money and you needed it. I just wanted to help."

"How? By killing my pride? I trusted you, and you betrayed me," he shot back, almost shaking with fury. "You're no better than my mother!"

She glared at him. "All right, then! I'll take the money back…."

"It's too late for that. You think you can wear the pants around here, do you? Okay, honey. You made the payment, you make the rest of the decisions. You run the damned place."

Her green eyes widened. "Do what?" she asked blankly.

"You run it, Kate," he said, his chin jutting in anger, his eyes glittering blackly. "Let's see you do your Ms. Macho act down here in Texas. Go ahead. You give the orders. You get the men working. You herd cattle and sell cattle and keep the records and handle the money. After all," he added with a cold smile, "women can do anything, can't they? I guess next you'll want me to get pregnant so you can have me under your thumb completely!"

It was terrible that she should laugh. She didn't even want to. But the way he said it, and the way he looked, brought her to her knees. She started and she couldn't stop. The thought of a pregnant Jason made her hysterical.

"Oh, for God's sake!" he burst out. He threw up his hands and swiped up his hat and stalked toward the front door.

She came to her senses as he opened it, and ran after him. He kept going, right toward the Mercedes, the very quickness of his strides an indication of how furious he really was. It was just plain bad luck that Red Barton and Gabe and a couple of the cowboys chose that moment to come riding by on their horses. Their denim jackets were buttoned against the cold wind that Kate didn't even notice in her shirtsleeves as she followed her angry husband to the car. It was where he'd left it, just in front of the house.

"Where are you going!" she cried.

"I don't know!" he shouted. That alone was unusual. He never raised his voice, even when he was the most angry.

"Jason, come back and talk to me!" she pleaded, aware that the cowboys had halted a few yards away and were leaning forward, helplessly intent on the unfolding drama in front of the house.

"I don't want to talk to you," he said, whirling. "The way you're taking over everything lately, you'd have me modeling those damned embroidered skirts you design and wearing high-heeled shoes and petticoats!" He became aware suddenly of the hysterical laughter coming from the direction of the driveway, and turned to find his four men doubled over.

"If I had my rifle, you wouldn't be laughing half that hard, Barton!" Jason raged at him.

Kate was trying to keep a straight face. "Don't shout at my men," she instructed. When he gaped at her, she reminded him, "You said it was my ranch, now. That means I get all the men, too, doesn't it?"

"You bet, Miss Kate!" Red Barton called. "I'm yours!" And he put both hands over his heart and assumed a pose that doubled the men over with laughter again.

"By God, I'll break your neck…!" Jason shouted, taking a step forward.

"Save him, Gabe!" Kate yelled, and Gabe grabbed the grinning cowboy's reins to lead his mount and the other cowboys quickly down the road.

"Now see what you've done!" Jason growled at her. "Damn it, Kate!"

"I thought you were leaving home," she reminded him, lifting an eyebrow. She'd decided that she wanted him to get away for a few days and get his perspective and his temper back. It might do him some good. "And while you're away, you might think about the fact that most people are human and make the occasional mistake. Then you could join the rest of the human race."

He clenched his hat in his hand, staring down at her with his lips set in a thin line. "I've already made a mistake," he said icily. "I married you!"

She lifted her chin and smiled sweetly at him. "Thank you. How comforting to know that our marriage has served a useful purpose."

He was ready to throw something. "It's your fault that

we ever got married!" he accused blackly. "You never had to start saving me from myself and driving me nuts…I'm not through! Where are you going?"

She was going inside, that was where she was going, and she was through even if he wasn't. She heard him still raging behind her when she went up the steps. By the time she got inside, his language was blue. She heard the furious roar of the Mercedes down the driveway just as she was closing the door. She wondered if he wasn't already regretting his impulsive offer to leave because now his pride was forcing him to do it. Without even a toothbrush, too.

She prayed that she'd done the right thing. Under the circumstances, she'd done the only thing possible.

CHAPTER TWENTY-THREE

JASON DIDN'T KNOW where he wanted to go. He felt betrayed. His pride and his honor were hurt. He couldn't understand why Kate would do such a thing to him, especially if she loved him.

Considering Kate's point of view hadn't even occurred to him. He was in a black mood. All the worries and anguish of past and present seemed all at once to congeal inside him. And all of it, he decided, was because of his mother.

As he drove, he thought about her. He thought about her desertion and how it had almost killed his father. How her leaving had brought about the horrible corruption of the father he'd adored, and turned him into a drunken tyrant. His adolescence had been the purest kind of hell. That, too, was his mother's fault.

The more he thought about it, the madder he got. He'd ignored her pleas to come and see her, all these years. Now he was going to take her up on her invitation. With cold fury he turned the car onto the highway that led, eventually, to Arizona. She was going to pay, by God. For every anguished year of his life, he was going to make her pay.

Back at the Spur, Kate was reconciling herself to the fact that Jason wouldn't be home that night. She had a lonely supper, ignoring Sheila's pointed questions, and then she went to bed alone.

How different it was from the night before, when she'd slept in Jason's arms with the sound of his heartbeat at her ear. Everything had seemed unbearably sweet, and the future had held such promise. She couldn't be sure, because it was too soon, but her period was almost three weeks late now. And she was regular as a rule. They'd taken no precautions at all, and Jason was potent. But she was glad now that she hadn't mentioned her suspicions to him. After that nasty crack he'd made about her career, he could just wait and find out along with everybody else.

Kate wished he'd go see his mother. She had a feeling that his anger at the older woman was responsible for a lot of his problems. If he could hear her side of it, he might be able to get his own life into focus. Jason was so afraid of failure, of becoming like old J.B. He didn't realize that Kate loved him too much to care if he failed, and that she'd never leave him. Which brought to mind the fact that Nell Donavan had run instead of trying to help her husband. Why?

She turned over in the big, lonely bed with a sigh. She wished she had as many answers as she had questions. Most of all, she wished that Jason would call. But he didn't.

The second day after he left the Spur, Jason arrived in Tucson, Arizona. The huge, jagged Santa Catalina mountains ringed around the far-flung city on its desert plain.

He had the address on Nell Donavan's letter memorized, after having seen it so many times. Two days of lazy travel had made him angrier about the whole thing. He felt murderous. That cold, hard woman had made his life and his father's and his brother's hell. He wanted nothing more than to pay her out for it.

He turned onto the street and looked for the number. Odd, the only building with that particular number was a facility of some kind. A retirement village of a sort, but it had a strangely medical appearance.

He parked the Mercedes, now covered with dust from his journey, and got out. There was only one door, and it led into a lobby with a reception desk, and nurses.

He frowned. This was like a hospital. Perhaps he'd gotten the address down wrong.

"I'm looking for Nell Donavan," he told the white-capped woman at the desk.

"Oh, yes," she said pleasantly. "One of our nicest patients. Are you a relative? She doesn't have visitors."

He ignored the question, because it irritated him. He was girded for battle. He didn't want to hear any kind words about his icicle of a mother.

"Has she been here long?" he asked instead.

The woman looked puzzled. "Why…yes. This is an intermediate care facility. Much like a retirement home, you see, except that we have round-the-clock nursing staff and a resident physician. Mrs. Donavan has been with us for quite some time. Here we are." She stopped in front of a door, the number that had been on the return address of her cards. It wasn't an apartment number. It was a room number.

Jason hesitated. He frowned. Well, this was why he'd come, wasn't it? To tell her what he thought of her. He thought about all the long, wasted, cruel years. His eyes began to glitter. Damn her!

He pushed open the door, oblivious to the slow retreat of the white-capped woman, who was curious about his odd behavior.

Inside the room there were two beds, but only one of them was occupied. There was a small, frail-looking woman in it. A woman with silver hair and odd-looking dark eyes. She was propped up, wearing some kind of plain cotton gown and robe. She had a look on her heavily lined face that combined resignation with faint good humor. Not the woman he remembered at all. Of course, she would have changed in the fifteen years since he'd seen her.

"Yes?" she asked, her voice as soft as Kate's. She smiled quietly. "I know you aren't the nurse. I know her step. You have a heavier one, and hard-soled, as if you wear boots. I think that you must be a man."

That was when he realized why her eyes looked odd. She was blind.

He moved closer to the wall, for support. She was blind. Blind. Blind! The word echoed in his mind until he felt as if he were going mad.

"Are you still there?" she asked. She sat up slowly. "Please. Can I help you?" She stretched out a hand. "Shall I call the nurse?"

"When..." He cleared his throat and tried again. He had something stuck there, he could hardly get words out. "When did that happen?"

"I'm sorry?"

"Your eyes," he bit off.

She took a slow breath, because the sound of that voice was oddly familiar. Her eyes searched helplessly, but she was long past the ability to see anything. "About fifteen years ago," she began, and she tried to smile because she had a faint suspicion about her unexpected caller's identity. Please, God, she thought. Please God, let it be him this time!

"What made you...like that?" he asked hesitantly.

"There was an automobile accident. I was going to my brother's house, to get help. My husband..." She paused for a minute. It was hard to talk about it. "We'd had a terrible fight, and he'd hit me, for the first time ever. I was frightened. I ran and got into the car and started for Tucson, where my brother lived." She smiled sadly. "It was a crazy idea, but I had a concussion and didn't know it. I wasn't thinking straight. On the way there, I blacked out at the wheel."

Jason was barely breathing. Nightmare images were fogging his mind. He remembered the night she left. He'd blocked it out for years, forbidden himself to think about it. But he remembered a scream just before she came running down the staircase with blood streaming from her face. His father had been just a few steps behind, white-faced and raging…crying. His eyes closed. It hurt to remember. His father had been crying. That was something Jason had never done in his life. He'd never been weak, as his father had…

"You wrecked the car?" he prodded, when she didn't continue.

"Yes." Her sightless eyes closed. "When I came to, I was blind." She laughed softly, bitterly. "You can't imagine how I felt. I had two sons." Her voice broke on that last word. "I couldn't persuade my husband to get counseling, so I was going to bring my boys out to Tucson with me and force J.B. to choose between his family or the past." She drew in a slow breath, and her age sat heavily on her then. "But I was blind. To make matters worse, my brother had just had a heart attack and was in the hospital himself, so I had nowhere to turn. I couldn't go back home. Blind, I would have been helpless, I couldn't have done any of us any good. So I went to my sister-in-law, just until I could be placed here."

Jason was staring at her, trying to reconcile what she

was saying with all the horrible things he'd thought. He'd hated her. He stared at her frail, helpless figure with eyes black with pain. "You didn't contact…your husband?" He almost said "Dad," but he changed his mind. He didn't want her to know who he was, not just yet.

"He'd thrown me out," she replied. "He'd hit me and told me he didn't want me anymore. I was afraid of him, then." She smiled softly. "But I would have gone back, even then, if I'd been sighted so that I wasn't at his mercy. I never really blamed him, you see. I understood him. He was part of me. When he died…" She swallowed, because her voice had broken, "when he died, a woman I knew called and told me, because she'd read it in the San Antonio paper. I don't think I've stopped grieving since. For him. And for my poor boys."

This wasn't what he'd expected. She wasn't what he expected. He didn't know what to do.

Because of the odd silence, her dark eyes began to search aimlessly for him again, with such loving anguish in them, such pain. Her voice trembled a little as she added, "I know that it's you, Jason," she said suddenly. "I don't even know how, but I know it. And I prayed that some day you'd come. Even if it was only to tell me how much you hate me." She clenched the sheet over her body, gnawing her lower lip, wrinkled with age and pain.

He didn't move. His boots were fixed to the floor. He just stared at her, helpless. She wasn't the medusa of his dreams. She was a tired old woman who'd lost everything, and had to suffer the mercy of strangers because she'd had none from her children.

It suddenly occurred to him that she'd called him by name. His head lifted, his eyes faintly clouded. "What did you call me?" he asked huskily.

"Jason," she whispered brokenly. She pulled herself up against the pillows, her face open and vulnerable. "You are, aren't you? You're my son…!"

Her voice broke and he couldn't bear it. He went to her without hesitation and dropped down onto the side of the bed to scoop her roughly into his hard arms.

She clung to him weakly as he held her, rocked her, feeling her frailty, her helplessness, hearing the sobs and feeling the hot tears against his skin.

"My boy," she whimpered, her thin body shaking. "My son."

He couldn't have answered her to save his life. His throat felt parched with emotion, his eyes were swimming in moisture. What a waste, he thought. What a horrible, ironic waste. He'd never asked about her side of it. Just as Kate had accused him, he'd never seen her side of it, he'd never thought of forgiveness. He'd never allowed for complications. He'd wanted perfection, and there wasn't any. Not even in himself. He'd made one horrible mistake after another, and this poor, tortured creature in his arms was the biggest of his life.

The nurse, who'd been concerned by the subdued anger in the tall man's face, had come to the door to peek. But what she saw touched her. That man wasn't going to hurt anyone. She turned quietly and left the room.

"I know how much you must hate me," she was whispering, her voice thick with tears. "I can't blame you, I left you, I deserted you."

"My God, shut up," he breathed, holding her closer. "I didn't know. I didn't know!"

"I was too proud to tell you," she whispered. She sniffed, rubbing a sleeve across one red eye. "I didn't want you here out of a sense of responsibility. You owed me nothing, and I knew that you and Gene most likely hated me, blamed me. It must have been a nightmare. I tried to get in touch with you, but as long as he was alive, he made it impossible. He never understood how far gone he was, Jason. He hurt me, so badly, when he drank, and I couldn't make him get help. I was coming back for you and Gene, oh, Jason, I was. But I had nothing. I was blind. I didn't even have a place to live. I couldn't work…." She sighed. "What good are words?" she asked with a sad smile. "They won't erase the years, or the misery I caused."

He patted her back awkwardly. "Gene paints," he said after a minute. "He's damned good. He's doing portraits now. I wanted him to be a cattleman, but he's as stubborn as I am. He's married. She's nice. Young, but sweet, and they're expecting a child."

She sat back up, dabbing at her eyes with the handkerchief he'd given her. "And you, Jason?" she asked gently. "Are you married?"

"Just recently," he said on a heavy breath. "Although I may not be by the time I get home. I've given her a lot of trouble. It amazes me that she hasn't murdered me in my sleep."

She laughed a little, hiccuping. "You should be at home. Christmas is only a few days away. I could have waited."

He felt a heavy weight of guilt for the years when he'd ignored her existence. "You mentioned in your last letter that there might not be much time," he said, recalling those words now with faint terror.

"Oh, yes," she recalled. "They'd just done some tests, and I hadn't had the results. But the tumor was benign. I'm a tough old bird."

"That's the O'Hara side, I guess," he remarked to

lighten the atmosphere. "Sheila always said you had spirit."

"Sheila! Is she still at the Spur?" she asked. "Lord, she was good to me. And to the two of you. She helped me to keep you out of his way. That was the only consolation I had, knowing that Sheila was with you. He didn't fire her?"

"Oh, no. She ran interference. She's still doing it, but for Kate now, not for me."

"Kate is your wife?"

He smiled faintly. "She was, until I shot my mouth off. I don't know if she'll want to live with me anymore now." He sighed. "She's young and tenderhearted, and she loves me. I didn't really want her to, but I've kind of gotten used to it."

"She sounds very nice."

"She designs clothes. I didn't like that, either. I didn't want her to have a life apart from me." He touched the silver hair gently, amazed at how easy it was to talk to her, as if all the years between had fallen away with his need for revenge. "She accused me of wanting to own her, and maybe I did. I was so afraid I'd lose her."

"Did you tell her that?"

He laughed. "Of course not."

"You might consider that some people won't hurt you deliberately, even if you provoke them," she said. She touched his hand, where it rested on her hair. "Do you have children of your own yet?"

He hesitated. "There was an almost child. Kate lost him on a business trip."

"And of course you blamed her," his mother said indulgently. "And you couldn't forgive her, or yourself for not stopping her."

"Stop that," he muttered. "You're as bad as she is."

"Mothers have intuition," she said. "And I remember your father, so well. When he died, Jason, was it easy?"

"In his sleep," he replied. "It was quick."

"I'm glad." She wiped away more tears. "I loved him so. I never stopped. He was my whole world."

He frowned a little, watching her. "I don't understand."

"There was a third baby, Jason," she said after a minute, and she felt for his hand, holding it hard as she spoke. "A little girl, barely three days old. Your father had gone to get the car, for us all to go to church. He didn't see me when he started to back up, and he backed into me." She stopped. "The baby died and I almost died. I could never have any more children. He started drinking then. That was just before Sheila came to work for us. I tried to make him get help. But he wouldn't admit that he needed it. He grieved himself almost to death, God love him. At least, he's at peace now."

"My God. Nobody ever talked about that," he said. "And he mentioned a girl from time to time, but I didn't realize it was a child."

"We kept to ourselves back then," she replied. "Not many people even knew I was pregnant, and after it happened, I guess they all assumed that I'd miscarried. By the time I left, it was ancient history." She smiled wistfully. "But you see, Jason, people aren't ogres without reason. I understood him, but at the last, he became so violent. I would have kept trying even so, but when I was blinded there was no hope. So all these years I've lived with the terror of how it would be for you and Gene. I even tried to intervene once, through a teacher, but they told me it was no use. Your father could be so kind, so gentle, when he wasn't drinking," she recalled. "I loved him so much. And I'm so sorry that you and Gene had to live that way. That I deserted you…"

"Gene and I are survivors," he interrupted. "We have good marriages, and we have the Spur." He muttered. "We have it because of Kate, but we have it."

"What?"

"She put every penny she had in the bank into the Spur and stopped them from selling it at public auction." He grimaced. "And I gave her hell."

"It hurt your pride," his mother agreed. "Yes, I can understand that. But your pride won't make up for losing a woman like that. Why don't you consider going home?"

"I just got here."

She smiled. "Then you'll know the way back." She settled into her pillows. "You can bring Gene and the wives to see me. I'd like that."

He studied the timeworn features quietly. "I'll do better than that. I'll take you back with me."

Her face tautened. "No."

"What's the matter?" he asked.

"I don't want to go back to the Spur."

"It's not the way it used to be," he said gently. "And memories aren't so horrible, once you get control over them. Think about the happy times."

"Can you?"

He shrugged. "I've gotten to that point, yes. He didn't drink all the time. He had the occasional good day. There were times when he sat and talked about you until he got hoarse. He never stopped loving you."

She bit her lower lip. "If only," she whispered.

He nodded, although she couldn't see him. "If only."

"It's a long drive back to Texas," she remarked after a minute, and looked worried.

"I don't speed," he told her. "And you can lie in the backseat if you'd rather."

"Lie in the backseat?" She stared toward him. "I'll have you know that when I'm in between bouts of bronchitis like the one I've just beaten, I play golf."

He gaped at her. "Alone?"

"It's safer for the spectators that way," she murmured, tongue in cheek. "Blindness isn't so horrible. I have memories, you know, of sunsets and lazy spring landscapes and Texas bluebonnets. And I get around pretty well. They're letting me get up this afternoon, and I'll show you what I mean. If you're still around, that is."

There was soft hope in that careless comment, and he smiled. "Oh, I'll be around for a while," he mused. "I want Kate to miss me bad before I go home. And I'll take you with me for a peace offering."

She chuckled. "Well, I guess I'll go with you, then." She smiled to herself. "I'll be your navigator. We can go home by way of Alaska."

He laughed delightedly. "That's a deal. We'll make it home in time for Christmas," he told her. "Sit tight. I'm going to talk to the administrator and your doctor, and we'll see what we can arrange." He bent down and kissed her wrinkled cheek. "Don't you worry, honey, I'll break you out of this place, if I have to use a nail file on the bars."

She laughed. The sound was odd because it had been a long time since she had. And when she heard him leave, the tears fell again. So much happiness, after so much pain. Her son. Here, and not hating her. That was all the Christmas present she needed. Thank God for miracles, she prayed silently. Oh, thank God!

CHRISTMAS EVE CAME and Kate had eaten supper by herself. Then, feeling a need for it, she'd gone to the Christmas Eve service at the local Presbyterian church, where they had a candlelight service and sang Christmas hymns. She found a measure of peace in the small, very old confines of the small seventy-year-old church. She still hadn't heard from Jason, and she was worried about him. She didn't even know where to look.

Gene had been equally upset, but he was no more capable than Kate was of tracking down a man who didn't want to be found.

"Maybe he's holed up in a motel somewhere," Gene sighed.

"I hope so," Kate had replied quietly. "Oh, Gene, I wish I'd listened to you. I've done it again."

"Your heart was in the right place," he comforted her. "He'll get over it. It may take a while, but he'll get himself straightened out and when he does, he'll come home."

"He'll probably divorce me," she laughed miserably.

"A man who could look at a painting of you the way he did won't divorce you."

Kate had thought about that. But it was only desire on his part. He'd never professed any undying love for her. He'd never pretended that he wanted any more than her body and her loyalty. He had those. But she loved him as well. And while he was willing to take the love she offered, he had none to give.

She went back home alone, tossing her purse onto the hall table as she entered the well-lit house. She took off her burgundy wool cape and smoothed down the emerald green silk of her high-necked dress with its bishop sleeves and faintly full skirt. Her hair was loose around her shoulders, soft and silky. And when she looked in the hall mirror, her face had a new light, a glow almost. She smiled at her reflection, because she felt pregnant. If only she were.

A sound in the living room caught her off guard. She turned, and there was Jason, looking taller than ever in a gray suit, watching her curiously.

"So you came home," she said icily, when she wanted to throw herself at him and kiss him until he was in danger of suffocating. But she kept herself aloof with an effort. She wasn't taking one step toward him ever again. He was going to have to do the work this time.

"I own it," he replied, his smile resigned. She wasn't disposed to forgive and forget, that was obvious. He'd outraged her feelings. Again. But there was still time, he felt sure of it. He knew she was glad to see him, even if she was hiding it fairly well.

"Part of it," she agreed, her green eyes steady. "Would you like to split it up into his and hers, or would you rather I just asked for my money back and let the bank have it?"

"Suit yourself, honey, but I don't think we'd enjoy living in the bank," he replied dryly.

She cocked her head and stared at him curiously. He was oddly easygoing, as if he'd never stormed out of the house and vanished.

"Where have you been?" he asked.

"I could ask you that if I cared," she said with sweet venom in her tone. "I've been to church."

He smiled at her temper. "It's Christmas Eve."

"Nice of you to remember," she said unsteadily, because he was moving closer. She didn't want him to touch her. She backed away. "I didn't think you were coming home at all."

He stopped when he noticed her withdrawal. Slow, he told himself. Don't rush it. "Sheila left about the time we got here. She made us some coffee."

Us. He'd said us. For one wild, horrible moment she thought he'd brought some woman home, until her common sense got control of the panic. She straightened. He could mean a businessman, of course.

"Us?" she asked.

"Yes." He turned, gesturing for her to lead the way.

There was a small, old woman sitting in an armchair by the crackling fire. Her silver hair framed a worn face containing quiet, unseeing brown eyes under dark eyebrows. She was wearing a simple brown cotton dress with stockings and old-fashioned lace-up black shoes with wide heels. And beside her was a coat that Kate might have found at a rummage sale several years back.

"Mrs. Donavan," Kate said, because she felt it. Knew it.

Nell's face lit up. "Yes," she said, laughing. "Kate!" she guessed with uncanny accuracy, and held out her arms.

Kate went into them without a word, holding the older woman, rocking her gently. So this was why Jason looked so different, so relaxed and quiet and tender. He'd gone to see his mother. He'd made his peace, at last. She wouldn't ask how, or why. It was enough that he had.

"How lovely to meet you at last," Nell sighed. "I've heard a lot about you over the past few days." She touched Kate's face, tracing the perfect features, the long hair. "Yes. I pictured you this way. You're very young, Kate."

"Almost twenty-one," Kate said.

"I was a year younger than you when I had my first child," Nell said. "When I had Jason. He was the sweetest baby. So easy to care for, so undemanding."

Kate glanced at him. "My, my, how he changed," she said with a poisonous smile.

His eyebrows arched. "Naughty, naughty," he scolded. "It's Christmas."

"Not quite," she replied. "Have you called Gene?" she added.

"That should be him, now," he said, nodding toward the headlights that briefly sprayed the window, followed by the sound of an engine dying and two doors opening.

"I'll let him in," Kate volunteered, and went briskly to the front door.

Gene looked ruffled. Really ruffled. Cherry was with him, and her eyes were bright with excitement.

"She's in there?" Gene asked. "What's she like, is she nice?"

"Go and see for yourself," Kate prompted, smiling.

Gene walked into the doorway, smiling hesitantly at Jason. "Mama?" he said as he looked at the small, frail woman. Unlike Jason, he didn't recognize her. He'd only been around six when she'd left them.

Her head turned, but her eyes didn't focus. She smiled. "Is that Gene?"

Gene's face froze. When he realized that she was blind, he understood, as Jason had, without a word being spoken, without a single explanation. He moved closer, going down on one knee beside the frail figure with eyes that were misty and searching.

"Yes, it's me," he got out. He touched her wrinkled hand, held it gently. "It's me."

She reached out to his face and smiled as she touched it, felt the sudden wetness under his eyes. "There, there," she whispered. "It's all right."

He held her, as Jason had, his head on her thin shoulder, his heart breaking.

Cherry and Kate went into the hall, and Jason followed them, giving Gene the time he needed to speak to her alone.

"She's not as old as I thought she'd be," Cherry said. "And she seems lovely."

"She's had a hard time of it," Jason replied. "Gene can tell you, later. How about something to drink? Milk for you," he told Cherry with a rakish grin and a glance at her midriff. "But Kate can have something stronger if she likes."

"I'll have coffee, if there is any," Kate said coldly.

"I'll get my own milk," Cherry sighed. "The sacrifices I don't make for baby."

Kate's face closed up at that innocent remark, and Jason saw it and felt even worse than he had.

She poured herself coffee, and got down another cup and saucer when he announced that he thought he'd join her. She filled it and pushed it toward him without looking. Then she led the way into his study, where she sat down on a leather chair, looking unapproachable.

Cherry, sensing undercurrents, excused herself on the pretext of making more coffee for Gene and Mrs. Donavan.

Jason sat down in the armchair facing Kate's. Balancing his coffee cup and saucer on his lap, he proceeded to light a cigarette.

"Are we still speaking?" he asked after a minute.

"You had more than enough to say before you left," she reminded him. She sipped her coffee, grimacing when she scalded her lip.

"I guess I did." He leaned back, smoking his cigarette quietly. "When we go upstairs, I'd like to talk to you, Kate."

"No you wouldn't," she said with a mirthless laugh. "You'd like to take me to bed. That's all you've ever wanted from me. It's all I've come to expect. And when you've finally had your fill, and you're satisfied, you'll turn your back and walk away." She wasn't sure she believed that, but her emotions were all over the place lately and she was still angry at him for going off and not letting her know where he was.

He didn't believe what he was hearing. Didn't she know how he felt? Didn't she have any idea?

"Kate, it's not that way," he began.

But before he could say any more, Gene was standing in the doorway, smiling. "Isn't she a doll?" he asked Jason. "My God, I hardly believe it."

"I know," Jason said gently. "I've got a lot of guilt to live with over the way I've treated her these last years."

"She doesn't blame you," Gene reminded him. "Nobody does. Except you, Jason. You're the one with the hang-up about perfection. The rest of us just live with being human." He said it lightly, and in a way that didn't offend, but it cut Jason to the heart.

"I always thought I had to be more than that." He looked at Kate. "I thought everyone did. Now I'm sorry I didn't realize it before," he added.

Kate looked up, studying him quietly. That felt as if he were trying to tell her something.

"We don't have a present for Mama," Gene said suddenly. "And tomorrow is Christmas."

"You two are the best present of all," Kate replied. "But I have a bolt of satin and I'm quick. I'll bet I could make her a robe by midnight, if I start now. She's an eight petite," she murmured, rising.

"Not on Christmas Eve," Jason protested.

He was thinking of her comfort, but that wasn't how she interpreted it. She gave him a look that could have curdled milk.

"Sewing isn't work to me. It's pleasure. Right now, it's about the only one I have."

She turned and left the room and Jason cursed roughly under his breath.

"Now what have I said?" Jason muttered. "My God, I can't open my mouth...."

"Pregnant women get fussy," Gene sighed. "I can't say good morning to Cherry without getting my head snapped off."

Jason glanced at his brother. "Kate isn't pregnant," he said slowly.

"Well, well," Gene mused, pursing his lips as he studied his brother's hard face. "Talk about the husband being the last to know. Sheila says Kate thinks she is."

Jason started toward the staircase, his eyes horrified. Again. It was all happening again. The disbelief, the distrust, the doubt. But on her side this time. Something inside him snapped. Not again!

He left Gene standing there and started up the staircase, his eyes blazing. No, by God, not again! Not this time. She was going to listen to him if he had to tie her to her sewing machine.

CHAPTER TWENTY-FOUR

KATE WAS IN the guest bedroom where she kept the sewing machine Jason had given her that long ago Christmas before they were married. The bed had long since been taken down to make room. She had a drafting board in there, along with a table for cutting cloth and a dressmaker's fitting form to use when she draped designs. She had threads and needles, scissors, tailor's chalk, vellum paper, tracing paper, and all the other accessories of her trade. There was an iron and ironing board, too, and a rack to hang garments on.

Jason paused at the doorway, watching her pin a pattern into place on a length of blue satin.

She glanced at him, but that was all. "Did you want something?" she asked defiantly, remembering the day he'd left and his parting shot about their marriage being his biggest mistake.

He sighed. He hadn't expected her to make it easy. He hadn't left her like a loving husband, and he had some regrets about the things he'd said to her. He could imagine that she remembered every single one, verbatim, judging by the look on her face.

He studied her quietly, a kind of aching pride at her softly glowing beauty. She looked pregnant, if that was anything to go by. And he felt warm and delightfully hungry all over, just looking at her.

He put his hands in his pockets and leaned against the door facing, looking elegantly sexy. He'd taken off his tie and suit coat and loosened the top buttons of his white silk shirt.

"Go ahead, Kate," he invited wryly. "Give me hell. God knows, I deserve it."

She really glared at him. Did he have to go and steal her thunder? She had to force down a smile. He was doing to her what she'd always done to him when he was in a temper.

"You said our marriage was a mistake. You said…"

"I know." He looked at her quietly, with eyes that saw her differently now. "I've had some hard lessons since I left here. I've learned a lot of things about myself that I don't like."

She looked up, stunned. That was new. "Did you?" she asked, her hands hesitating on the pattern.

"Guess what, Kate. I'm human."

She had to fight down a smile. "Are you, really?"

He pursed his lips amusedly. "I suppose you knew it all along, but I had to learn it the hard way."

He took a cigarette out of his pocket and lit it, careful to leave the door open so that he wouldn't irritate her lungs. If she was pregnant, the smoke might harm her.

"Were you in Arizona all that time?"

He nodded. "Getting to know my mother, all over again."

"I'm glad about that. But I guess you couldn't spare the time to let the rest of your family know you hadn't died in a wreck or something," she added coolly.

His eyebrows levered up. "I wasn't sure you wanted to hear from me." His dark eyes wandered over her. "You were pretty hot when I left. You hurt my pride, but I gues[s] I didn't do yours much good, either."

"And that's a fact, you cold-blooded snake," she tosse[d] right back. "You accused me of letting my career com[e] before anything, even our baby."

He didn't even lose his temper at the name-calling[.] That alone was unlike Kate, and if she was pregnant[,] her emotions would probably reflect it just that way. H[e] smiled at her. "And you knew all along I didn't mean it,["] he replied. "You always had an uncanny knack for read[-] ing my mind." He took a long draw from the cigarette[.] "Anyway, I didn't mean that about the baby. We'll hav[e] another one someday, Kate. And a new baby would hea[l] almost all of the old wounds."

He was fishing, but she wouldn't take the bait. "Well[,] if I ever get that way, you'll never know until I look lik[e] Moby Dick and you can see it. I won't tell you," she sai[d] curtly. "You'd tie me up and lock me in my room fo[r] nine months. Then if anything went wrong, you'd say i[t] was my fault. That I'd put the baby at risk for the sak[e] of my career."

She sounded calm, but her hands were trembling. "No[,] I wouldn't," he said.

She picked up her scissors and started cutting out fab[-] ric, her movements quick and deft. "I like your mother,["] she said to ease the tension.

"So do I." He studied the cigarette. "I told her that w[e] wanted her to stay, for a little while," he said gently. "An[d] despite what I said about our marriage being a mistake[,] I don't want it to end."

She looked up with eyes that were dark green, soften[-] ing. "I don't, either," she said gently. "I've never wanted[ ] that."

That was encouraging. He searched her eyes quietly. "We can always start over again. One more time," he added dryly. She was still hesitating, and he wondered if she was afraid he might want her to sleep with him. She might be afraid of risking the baby, and so was he, suddenly. He frowned. "You don't have to sleep with me," he added.

She bit her lower lip. "Oh, Jason," she murmured huskily.

"I'm not the world's most lovable man. I never pretended to be." He let his eyes run down her body with pure possession. He looked at the polished wooden floor instead of at her. "Kate, I've had to be strong all my life. I've never bent, because I was afraid of breaking. So I kept it all inside. I hid my feelings, and my fears, and I never let them show." He looked at her warmly. "But when I saw my mother, and heard her talk about those reasons you said she'd have had for leaving, I got my mind together again. I'm still going to find it hard going for a while, to let the last barrier down. But I think I can, now."

She was still wary of him, but he was telling her things he never had before. She touched the cloth gently, tracing the brocade with a slender, pink-nailed finger.

She dropped her eyes to the cloth. "This will only take about an hour," she said. "But I think your mother will like it. She has an elevated sense of touch, because of her blindness. She'll like the feel of the satin."

How like Kate to think of that. God, how he loved her! He moved toward her, his heart full and aching.

"She'll like it," he said quietly. "But don't wear yourself out, honey."

His concern touched her. She stared at his shirt front. "I won't."

He touched her cheek gently. "Got a kiss for a bad-tempered, tired husband?" he asked only half jokingly.

She hesitated, but after a minute, she moved, surprising him by reaching up to touch her lips softly, shyly to his.

He stopped breathing. She hung there, so close yet so far away, and something in him snapped.

"Kate," he whispered huskily.

She saw the hunger burn in his eyes, and for one long moment she managed to deny herself the pleasure of his body. But she wanted him so. She reached up, feeling the shock of his arms coming around her, waiting for his mouth, her lips parted and pleading.

"It's been so long," he said, and his mouth covered hers.

She felt him lift her. He held her so close that his hard chest bruised her swollen breasts, but she was touching heaven and she couldn't complain. Her mouth answered his, echoing its long, sweet pressure, drinking in the magic and mystery that they shared.

He let her slide down his body after a minute, and he actually laughed at his own body's helpless, immediate reaction to the smooth brush of her belly.

"Damn," he chuckled.

She flushed. "Stop that," she mumbled.

He grinned. "I'm sorry, honey, but I can't do much about it," he said softly. "It's as natural as breathing, under the circumstances."

"Oh, for heaven's sake, I don't mean *that*...!" She colored even more and hid her face against him. "Jason Everett Donavan," she murmured wearily.

He smoothed her long hair, loving its silkiness. "Don't stay up here too long," he said, his breath stirring it. "We've got a big day tomorrow."

"I got you something," she said shyly. She had, too. A new watch that did everything, like the one she'd noticed that he'd worn for the past several years without getting a new one.

"I got you something, too," he replied. "Something that sparkles."

She lifted her head. "Not a diamond," she said. "Not that, not when you're already tied in knots financially, I couldn't bear it."

He traced her lower lip with a finger that wasn't quite steady. "Thanks to you, Mrs. Donavan, I'm not tied in knots financially. With the time you've bought me, I'll fight my way out."

"That isn't what you said when you left."

"Of course not," he sighed. His voice was husky. He drew in a slow, unsteady breath. "My God, I've learned whole volumes about forgiveness in the past few days. I've learned things about my mother and my father that make me sick with shame."

"You've learned that people are human, that's all," she said gently. "And that there are always reasons for the way they behave. Sometimes you have to dig very deep to find them. But they're always there."

"How did you learn so much, so young?" he asked after a minute.

She nuzzled her face against his hard chest. "I had you to practice on," she whispered. "You were a hard case, but eventually I wormed my way into your arms."

His arms contracted. "Did you really want that so badly?"

"With all my heart." She sighed contentedly. "I'm sorry I complicated things for you, Jason. Maybe it would have been better if I'd never let you touch me in the first place."

"And give up all those sweet memories?" he whispered softly. "God forbid."

"They aren't all sweet."

"Is life?" He tilted her face up to his. "Don't leave me," he said tautly. "Don't give up on me, Kate."

"Oh, how could I?" she whispered tearfully. "I love you so much!"

He felt humble. She still loved him. He hadn't killed it after all, even with his bad temper and abrupt departure, thank God. He drew her tenderly against him and rocked her. His body trembled with need, but he banked down the fires. Kate needed tenderness now, and she was going to get it. He was going to prove to her that she was his life.

"You'd better go back downstairs, hadn't you?" she asked after a minute, although she hated to let him go. "I want to get this robe sewn. It won't take long, and I won't get tired."

He let her go, reluctantly. His dark eyes searched hers. "Okay." He turned toward the door and stopped at the facing. "Sleep tight, honey," he said, glancing back.

She started to speak, but she bit her lower lip. She wanted to sleep with him, but she couldn't quite get the words out. "You, too," she said instead.

He nodded, and after a minute, he went back downstairs and settled into a chair to listen to his mother talk about the long years they'd all been parted.

When it was bedtime, Kate rejoined them, looking a little worn, but smiling.

"Can I help you upstairs, Mama Donavan?" she asked.

'We've got a lovely guest room. All pink and carpeted, with a canopied bed."

"Such finery," Mrs. Donavan laughed. "You'll spoil me."

"That isn't likely," Kate said gently, taking the thin hand to help the older woman up. "You aren't the kind of person who ever demands anything."

"Neither are you," Mrs. Donavan shot back, smiling. "All right, then, point me toward the staircase and watch me shoot up it."

Gene and Cherry said their good nights, and Jason kissed his mother's cheek before Kate followed her up the staircase.

She settled Mrs. Donavan in the guest room, which was where Kate herself usually slept.

"Thank you, sweetheart," Nell Donavan said gently when she was in her long flannel gown and tucked up under the covers. Kate had shown her where the bathroom was and made a row of chairs to it, so that the older woman could feel her way there in the night if she needed to. "I'll be fine."

"It's good to have you here," Kate said, and meant it. "It's even better to see you and Jason speaking. He's different since he went to find you."

"I can sense that," Nell said quietly. "I've heard only a little of what his life was like, Kate, but I think I'd go mad if I knew it all. The sad thing is that J.B. was the kindest man I ever knew—when he wasn't drinking. But alcohol got a hold on him when grief came, and he couldn't shake it. I tried, but I wasn't strong enough to help him."

"That's nobody's fault, you know," Kate replied. "None of us are perfect. We do as we're able. That's the best we can hope for."

"You're very old for your age," Nell said. She smiled secretly. "Have you told Jason about the baby?"

Kate blinked. "I'm not sure that I'm pregnant," she faltered, fascinated by the older woman's uncanny perception.

"Oh, I have a feeling that you are. I've developed a rather startling kind of sensitivity since I've been sightless. I don't understand it, but it helps to make up for not being able to see," she added. "You love him very much, don't you?"

"With all my heart. I can't remember when I didn't love him."

"Do you know how he feels?" Nell asked with a faint smile.

"He wants me," Kate said bluntly.

"I think you'll find it's a good deal more than that," she said, sighing as she closed her eyes. "Sleep well, my dear. I'm glad we have a chance to get to know each other. I seem to have been alone for a very long time. Perhaps I deserved to be. But it's nice to have a family again."

"I hope you'll stay," Kate said softly.

Mrs. Donavan smiled. "For a little while. But you see, I have friends in Tucson, Kate. People my age, whom I've known for a long time. They're all the family I've had, and Tucson is home. Eventually, I'll want to go back. But by then, I hope we'll be good friends, and that you'll visit me with Jason."

"That will be delightful. We'll bring your grandchildren with us."

"I thought I'd never have that kind of pleasure," Nell confessed. She stared up at the canopy with sad eyes. "We expect so much from life. And sometimes, we get so little. It's important to appreciate what we have." She turned her head. "I think Jason has it wrong. I think you want him far more than you want fame. If you do, tell him so now. Don't let him go, Kate. He needs you more than he realizes."

"I'm not about to let him go, Mama Donavan," she replied gently. "Now you go to sleep. I'll see you in the morning."

"Yes. Good night."

"Good night."

Kate closed the door with a sigh, turning out the light on the way. The hall was quiet and deserted, only the wall sconces providing enough gleam for safe walking.

She turned down the hall. She'd only gone about five steps when Jason appeared in his doorway, watching her, with a smoking cigarette in one hand.

"Where did you plan to sleep?" he asked softly. "The guest room has the only made-up bed, except for mine."

She moved closer, until she was close enough to feel the heat from his body, smell the thin smoke from his cigarette. "I guess I can sleep on the sofa...."

"Won't you be uncomfortable?"

She smiled. "Yes."

"Want to sleep with me?" he asked hesitantly. "Just sleep," he added, so that she wouldn't get the wrong idea. "It's a big bed."

"Okay." She stopped. "My gown is in the guest room," she said, hesitating. She'd been sleeping there since he left, but Mama Donavan was in it now.

"You can have one of my pajama jackets," he offered. "I never use them."

"Thank you."

He closed the door behind them and searched through

his chest of drawers, tossing her a pale blue silk jacket. "How's that?"

"Fine," she said. She hesitated, framed in the soft glow of the bedside lamp. This was ridiculous. They were married, weren't they?

With a resigned sigh, she took off her clothes and as she shed the bra, she noticed his dark eyes blatantly on her swollen breasts, the tips darker than usual, bigger.

And because of the way he was looking at her, with something like reverence, she turned slowly toward him, to let him see. Her lips parted on a rough breath at the intent, hungry expression on his face as he let his eyes caress her boldly.

"You're beautiful, Kate," he said quietly. "Every inch of you."

"I'm very swollen," she whispered.

"Isn't that natural, for your condition?" he whispered back.

"You knew...when I was talking about not telling you if I ever got pregnant again," she said, shocked.

He nodded, smiling gently. "Sheila mentioned it to Gene. But I knew you'd tell me in your own good time. I guess that's what you're doing right now. I remember what your body looked like when you were pregnant before. I recognize those subtle changes."

"I'll get fat," she breathed. "I'll look like a pumpkin with arms."

"Yes." He moved closer, his hands slow and exquisitely gentle as they touched her, cupping the tender weight of her breasts. "I'll take good care of you."

"Haven't you always, in spite of everything?" she mused. She held his hands to her body, loving their rough strength. "I haven't been to the doctor. But I'm almost sure," she whispered, pulling his hands closer. "Are you glad?" she asked, looking up with her heart in her soft green eyes.

"Yes, I'm glad," he whispered. He bent, lifting her clear off the floor. He carried her the few steps to the bed and laid her down, stretching out beside her. "Don't worry," he said, his voice like velvet. "I won't risk this baby. I just want to hold you."

She smiled up at him, loving him with her eyes as he touched her body with tender, patient hands. "Oh, Jason, if I die tomorrow, I won't care now."

"You said that once before," he reminded her. His mouth touched warm, bare skin, making her jerk suddenly with warm pleasure. "Hmmmm," he mused, "I like this, too. I like the very taste of your skin, and you like my mouth on you, don't you?"

"Blackguard," she breathed huskily, gasping when he did it again.

"That's no way to talk to your husband," he mused. He arched over her, his dark eyes smiling down into hers. "I want a son."

"You may get a daughter."

"I'll divorce you if I don't get a son," he threatened at her parted lips.

"No, you won't," she laughed. "You'll spoil her rotten and then blame me when she gets out of hand."

"I probably will." He lifted his head and searched her eyes quietly. "I'll love any child you give me," he said softly. "But not half as much as I'll love his mother. Not a fraction as much as I love you, tidbit," he breathed, bending.

The words went into her mouth as his covered it with aching tenderness and soft hunger. He moved down, his chest rubbing gently against her breasts, and he reached between them suddenly to pull his shirt out of the way so that he could feel her softness against his bare chest.

Kate wondered if she'd heard him, or if she was dreaming. It sounded so unreal to hear him say that he loved her. But it felt as though he meant it.

"Did you hear me?" he whispered against her eager lips. "I said I love you."

"I didn't think…I heard you properly." She looked up at him. "Do you, Jason? Really?"

"With all my heart. My mind. My body. Every part of me." He kissed her roughly, feeling her lips part and beg for his. "God, I want you. I need you…!"

She softened under him, her hips liquid, soft moving and arousing. He groaned at the blatant seduction of them, and she smiled under his mouth.

"I want you, too," she whispered. "No, don't pull away. There's nothing to be afraid of. You won't hurt me or the baby. I want you."

"Kate," he groaned. "The risk…!"

"Darling," she breathed, moving softly, "the only risk is in your mind. This baby is going to happen. Now you just lie still, Mr. Donavan, and let me show you how desperate I am…."

He felt her hands at his belt, and he actually gasped. She'd never touched him like that. She'd never ventured past his belt, but her hands were bold. They trespassed under the fabric that covered him, and he arched up and groaned with a shuddering kind of pleasure at her tentative touch.

"Oh, yes, I like that," she whispered. "I like pleasing you. Up until now, you've had to do it all. But I want to learn. I want to know…how to please you. Show me, Jason. Teach me."

He didn't know if he could get enough breath to teach her anything. His body was already shuddering. He pushed her hand hard against him and he found her mouth. And seconds later, explosions of pleasure rippled down his back.

That was only the beginning. She kissed him and caressed him, undressed him and learned his body with her hands and her mouth. And all the while he watched her with delicious disbelief at the things he was letting her do. This, too, was new; this ability to let himself be touched, to give in to her. To deliberately lose control.

She seemed to sense it, because she was smiling. Until he found her mouth and eased her under him. His hands began to smooth down her trembling body, arousing her lazily, bringing her softness gently against his hardness. And then she gave in to him, smiling against his mouth, laughing through the fierce passion, until tremors shot through her and she arched up toward him.

"I love you," she whimpered at the last. "I love you."

"I love you," he whispered into her soft mouth. He moved down against her hungrily, feeling his mind explode into the achingly sweet fulfillment that he only knew with her. He groaned. And finally, there was peace.

"Jason, it's Christmas," she whispered later, lying against his broad, sweaty chest in the darkness. She smiled and kissed his shoulder. "Our first Christmas together."

He tangled her fingers with his, feeling his wedding ring on her finger. "Yes." He nuzzled his mouth against her soft hair. "Warm enough?"

She was nude, as he was. They'd both been too tired

to worry about clothing. "I'm warm enough," she murmured drowsily. She curled closer. "See?"

"You'll see something, if you do much of that," he whispered in her ear. "I'm still hungry."

"So am I." She slid her arm around him. "Again," she murmured, moving sensuously. "Please."

"Are you sure?" he asked, and when he leaned over her, she could see the concern in his eyes from the faint light coming through the window.

"This time, I'm sure," she said, smiling. She reached up, her arms soft and loving. "Merry Christmas, my darling."

"Tomorrow," he murmured, "I'll have the moon gift-wrapped for you...."

"Why would I want the moon, when I've got you?" She smiled lovingly, and put her mouth softly to his.

Christmas morning dawned, and excitement lay like a soft blanket over the reunited family.

Kate and Cherry helped Sheila in the kitchen, while Mama Donavan and her boys got to know each other all over again.

"Isn't it terrific?" Cherry sighed. "Oh, gosh, I never dreamed that Jason would actually go looking for his and Gene's mother."

"Neither did I," Sheila confessed. "But I hoped he would, someday. I didn't know about the baby that J.B. cost her, but I did know that they never stopped loving each other."

Kate glanced at Sheila. "The gossips always said that you had a crush on J.B."

She smiled. "Gossips always find something to talk about. Honey, I was deeply in love with a man who went to Korea in 1952. He never came back, and I never wanted anybody else. J.B. wasn't my kind of man from the beginning. We'd have fought like cats and dogs, and believe me, that's no way to make a marriage. You have to have things in common."

"But J.B. and Nell did," Cherry said. "Didn't they?"

"They had a lot in common," Sheila agreed. She finished the dressing and put it in the oven to bake in a huge pan. "But once he started drinking, there was no stopping him. Eventually, he let it take him over and destroy his life. It almost destroyed the boys, too. They never talk about him. He left scars on them that they'll never really get over. Jason, especially."

"Oh, he seems to be managing all right," Kate said demurely.

"Don't get smart," Sheila said. "Anybody can get pregnant. Look at Cherry."

Cherry's face lit up. "Kate! Are you pregnant, too?!"

"I don't know yet," Kate replied. "But there's a very good possibility. Although," she added with a dark glance at Sheila, "it's amazing how everybody seemed to know it before I suspected. I seem to remember that Sheila asked me point blank."

"Some of us are perceptive," Sheila returned. She lifted an eyebrow and extended a pan of boiling potatoes in Kate's general direction, watching Kate fight down nausea. "You did that same thing when you were pregnant before. Couldn't stand the smell of boiling potatoes. It doesn't take a mathematician to add two and two."

"It's more like one and one making three," Cherry murmured dryly.

Kate chuckled and Sheila grinned.

They ate Christmas dinner before they opened the presents. Mrs. Donavan seemed to manage very well without help. She asked Kate to fill a plate for her and

tell her where everything was, like the face on a clock.
Kate described beans at three o'clock, turkey at six, and
so on until she'd gone around. Mrs. Donavan grinned
and dug in, and she ate heartily.

Kate produced the blue robe first thing. She hadn't
wrapped it. She placed it on Mrs. Donavan's lap and
watched the sightless woman touch it, caress it, feel the
length and width and shape of it.

"Oh, my," Mrs. Donavan gasped. "Satin brocade. A
robe." She touched it again, lightly. "Kate, it's blue, isn't it?"

Kate laughed delightedly. "Yes!"

"Amazing," Jason murmured.

"Color perception," Gene agreed. "I've read about un-
sighted people being sensitive to colors, but I didn't believe it until now."

"The body compensates," Mrs. Donavan told them. "I
hear better than I ever could before. I sense things. It's a
nice recompense. Thank you for my robe, Kate."

"I whipped it up last night, while you were talking to
Jason and Gene," she admitted.

"You sewed this yourself?" Mrs. Donavan gasped.

"I'm a designer," Kate said proudly, and she smiled at
Jason, who didn't fuss or protest. He only smiled back.

"You certainly are, if this is a sample of your work.
I'll treasure it," the older woman said softly.

"I'll play Santa Claus for the rest of us," Gene volunteered. He passed out packages and for the next few
minutes, everyone in the house, Sheila included, tore off
ribbons and paper, ooohing and aahing over their gifts.

Kate sat in Jason's arms that night, under the Christmas tree lights shimmering in colors around the lighted
fireplace. The two of them listened to Christmas hymns
while Gene and Mama Donavan and Cherry talked about

the Christmas season and Gene told her about their forthcoming baby.

Kate wore around her neck a delicate silver filigree necklace with a crystal charm enclosing a tiny mustard seed. It was the sparkly thing Jason had bought for her—an expensive little bit of nothing, but with a profound message. It came from a passage in the Bible, which referred to all things being possible if the believer had only faith as a grain of mustard seed. Jason smiled at her, the wonder of shared love in his dark eyes. And when Kate felt his warm, strong hands linking it around her neck, and he whispered that he loved her, she cried.

His watch had less of a message, but he was proud of it just the same. But his finest, most precious gift, he told her, was his Kate.

Jason looked down at Kate with delight, his fingers lightly brushing her waistline, smiling tenderly.

She pressed his hand against her. "It's still too soon to be sure," she whispered.

"I know. Let me dream," he whispered back.

"You look so different," she murmured lazily, nudging him with her head. "Relaxed. Less tense."

"I should, after last night," he whispered. "My God, what a Christmas present you gave me!"

"I got one back," she said, smiling. "Jason, I've never been so happy."

"Neither have I." He glanced past her at his mother and Gene, heads together, looking so much alike that it touched his heart.

"She's happy, too. I've talked her into staying a week. Gene and I want time to get to know her. We've got a lot of time to make up."

"She's a character," Kate mused. "I love her to bits already. I want Mama to meet her."

"We'll have her over to dinner tomorrow night."

"That would be nice." She yawned. "Goodness, I get tired easily these days."

"No wonder," he teased.

She linked her hand into his. "Will you be terribly disappointed if I'm not pregnant?"

"No. Because the way things are between us, before much longer you will be." He kissed her forehead. "I love you, sweetheart."

She smiled, tingled at the words. "I love you, too."

The days passed lazily after Christmas, and Kate grew close to Mama Donavan, as her boys did. But all too soon, the older woman grew restless for her own familiar room in the nursing home, and Jason reluctantly agreed to drive her home.

"I'll come back," she promised. "But I miss my friends. You don't mind, really, do you?"

"I mind," he told his mother gently. "But we'll keep in touch now. You're part of us. We're part of you. We won't ever be strangers again. Or enemies."

She hugged him close, her eyes full of tears and love. "Thank you," she managed huskily. "Thank you for coming to see me. Thank you for forgiving me."

"There was nothing to forgive," he said quietly. He kissed her wrinkled cheek. "Tell Kate good-bye. Then I'll drive you over to Gene's and you can say good-bye to him."

"I'll see you when the baby comes, Kate," Mrs. Donavan murmured as she kissed Kate warmly. "Take good care of my boy."

"The best I can," Kate promised, and hugged her back. "Godspeed, Mama Donavan."

"You're a good girl. I'm glad you're my daughter-in-law. Okay, son, let's go," she told Jason. "And don't think you can drive me around in circles and bring me back here and tell me we're in Tucson. I may be blind, but I hear really well."

Jason chuckled. "Okay. No tricks."

"And when we get to El Paso, you can let me drive," the older woman said with a twinkle in her eyes. "I'll get you through that city traffic in no time!"

"She might do better than you do, at that," Kate began.

Jason glared at her. "At least I can get the car through the gate without losing a fender," he shot back, and grinned when she blushed. She'd done just that not a day before.

"I didn't see the gate," she defended herself. "It jumped out in front of me."

"Sure it did, honey." He bent and kissed her softly. "Take care of yourself until I get back."

"You, too," she murmured, and kissed him back. "I'll put a candle in the window."

She watched him drive away and this time she smiled. It was so different from the last time he'd left. But now he'd be back. And she knew almost certainly that she was carrying his child. Life was going to be sweet from now on. She touched the tiny mustard seed charm around her neck, marveling at the small miracle that was even then growing in her body.

CHAPTER TWENTY-FIVE

"Is HE AWAKE, do you reckon?" a drawling voice murmured.

"I don't think so. He looks pretty flat to me."

"Maybe he's hiding."

"Could be. I heard the baby crying most of the night. My God, that kid's got a set of lungs!"

"So has his daddy," came the laconic reply. "And if you wake him up, you'll hear 'em."

"Well, we can't get anything done until he tells us what to do about that new lot of cattle he bought."

"Let's try calling him," another voice suggested.

"How about if we do that from outside?" a younger one replied.

"There's a bucket of water by the front porch."

Jason opened one eye under the concealing brim of his hat. The cowboys were gathered around the bunk he was lying on in the bunkhouse. Red Barton was grinning, Gabe looked worried, and the others were just plain amused.

"What do you want?" he asked curtly.

"New breeding stock's coming in, boss," Gabe announced. "Where you want us to put the heifers?"

"And do you want the bulls in with them, or in a separate pasture?"

"And what about that crazy looking bull?" Barton asked. "My God, boss, he's so ugly, one of the boys threatened to quit if he had to look at him more than once."

"He's just like the Indian bull I got last year that pulled us out of the hole and saved your jobs," Jason reminded him. "You thought he was beautiful when I sold that lot of calves he sired and you got a bonus."

"All that money made my eyes go bad, I guess," Barton sighed. "Anyway, right now, he's a sitting bull," he added, grinning. "He won't get up. And he looks lonely."

"Then why don't you go sing him a lullaby?" Jason muttered darkly.

"Looks like somebody else could use one of those," Gabe remarked, cocking an ear toward the house. "Your son and heir is at it again."

"Miss Kate will leave you for sure," Barton assured him. "Poor woman."

"It's tough being a baby," one of the older hands observed. "Can't do anything except lay there and have people talk funny to you. I don't blame the little guy for crying. I'd cry too if I couldn't drive the truck or eat chili."

"Fire that man," Gabe told the boss.

"Just before roundup?" Jason asked, sitting up wearily. "Bite your tongue."

"Then fire him after roundup. He snores."

"I do not," the old hand grumbled. "It's my deviated septum."

"I'll deviate your septum if you don't stop snoring!"

"What time is it?" Jason groaned. His back was half broken. The bunk was harder than his mattress.

"Nine o'clock," Gabe offered. "You must have really been tired."

"First Kate rocked him. Then I rocked him. Then his

grandmother rocked him. Then Sheila rocked him. And he never stopped, not for a minute. The doctor says it's colic. He gave us some medicine for it, but Kate won't use it."

"The baby just stopped crying," Barton remarked. He grinned. "I guess Miss Kate just gave in."

"Oh, thank God," Jason moaned.

"Poor Daddy," Gabe patted him. "There, there, you'll make it until baby graduates college."

Jason glared at him. "Of course I will," he muttered. "He's just a baby, he'll grow."

"His lungs already did," Barton said, tongue in cheek.

Jason got to his feet, unshaven and still wearing his jeans and checked Western shirt with its blue plaid wrinkled from being slept in. He hadn't even taken off his boots. He reached down and picked up his hat, stretching painfully.

"My God, how do you sleep on those things?" he asked, glaring at the bunk. "If I had the money, I'd buy you all decent mattresses."

"We're too tired to care where we sleep," Barton reminded him. "Like you must have been last night, boss man."

"I thought babies slept," Jason said dazedly. "I swear to God I did. Everybody said so. He doesn't sleep. He's been here for weeks, and he hasn't slept yet."

"He will," Gabe assured him. "Eventually."

Jason went out, followed by the men. He told them what to do with the new cattle and went into the house to check on Kate.

"You traitor," she accused the minute he walked in the door. "Hiding in the bunkhouse. Your men told on you!"

"Well, I ought to fire them," he sighed. "But I guess I

deserve everything I get," he agreed with a grin. "Wait here while I load you a gun to shoot me with."

"Don't be silly." She went into his arms, kissing him lazily. "Our son is asleep. I finally broke down and gave him the medicine. I guess Dr. Harris figured I would when I couldn't stand any more of the colic. But so many people said I shouldn't give him medicine for it…"

"Dr. Harris wasn't one of them," he reminded her. "How's baby's mama?"

She smiled up at him. "Baby's mama is still overwhelmed with being baby's mama. Oh, Jason, isn't he a little miracle, huge lungs and all? Every day he does something different, or he makes a sound he hasn't made before. He watches me and he makes the cutest expressions…. I adore him."

"So do I." He kissed her forehead tenderly. "Being with you, when he was born, was something I'll never forget. That was a miracle, too."

She nuzzled her face against him. "You poor man. These long nights are hard on you, I know, when you have to work so hard."

"Not all that hard." He smiled. "I've gotten us out of the hole and operating in the black. And your new collection made a bundle, Mrs. Donavan. And with this new licensing thing, I guess you'll have it made.

"Fame and fortune are fleeting," he whispered at her lips. "But loving lasts a long time. And you and I may set new records for it the next hundred years."

She laughed delightedly. "That suits me. As for my designing, most of that will be done at home, now. I don't want little Cade left with a babysitter. Besides, that wouldn't be easy since I'm nursing him."

"Watching it gives me the sweetest pleasure," he whispered, his eyes locked with hers. "There's something profound about a tiny mouth suckling at a woman's breast."

She blushed, but she smiled, too, because it was profound. She sighed. "I'm tired."

"I know you are. I wouldn't have run out on you, but I knew I had these cattle coming in, and I had to get enough sleep to cope with the arrangements."

"I forgive you." She reached up and kissed him. "Mama Donavan's rocking him right now. She was so delighted that we asked her to come and stay after he was born."

"She loves Tucson, but she likes being around us," he agreed. "I'm sorry Gene and Cherry and little Lisa couldn't come back to see him. But he's determined to stay in France until he gets through that international exhibit. He's doing good work. I'm proud of him."

"You can tell him that when he gets back. It will make him feel good," she said gently.

"You make me feel good," he said. "Just looking at you gives me goose bumps."

"I hope it always will." She moved away reluctantly. "Want me to fix you some breakfast?"

"Where's Sheila?"

She led him to the living room door, and nodded toward the sofa. Sheila was sound asleep on it. Mary Whittman was sprawled in an armchair next to it, her mouth open, faintly snoring.

"My God," Jason murmured. "How many people have we pressed into labor here?"

"Well, there's Mama Donavan upstairs, and Sandy's in the guest bedroom, Dessie's next to her..."

"...anyone else?" he interrupted, amused.

"Mrs. Rogers phoned and offered to come if we needed her. And Jo at the café, and…"

"Never mind." He shook his head, his dark eyes adoring her. "I hope Cade inherits your gift for attracting help. By the time he's old enough to help me work the ranch, we'll need extra hands."

"Oh, that reminds me," she continued, "Red Barton took a turn rocking, and so did Gabe." She grinned. "I wish you could have seen them."

He chuckled. "So do I. They never mentioned it when they came in to wake me up." He touched her nose. "What are you going to cook for me?"

"How about cereal with milk?" she asked hopefully.

"Okay."

"In that case, you can have scrambled eggs, bacon, and biscuits," she offered, and hugged him.

After he'd eaten, Kate led him up the staircase to the nursery. She had decorated it in soft blues with teddy bears and lambs on the wallpaper and a white baby bed with a tiny blue quilt that Mary had made for little Cade.

The son and heir was curled up in his grandmother's arms, being sung a lullaby. Kate and Jason paused in the doorway, staring at the tiny head with its cap of jet black hair, sleeping in his tiny jumper.

"He'll sleep for a while," Mrs. Donavan sighed, touching the tiny face with delicate fingers. "I can't see him, you know, but I know what he looks like. Jason, he's the image of you."

Jason grinned like a man receiving an award, and Kate reached up and kissed his cheek. "What did I tell you, Daddy?" she teased softly.

He nuzzled her face. "I guess that means I can't claim

you had a mad affair with the milkman," he murmured dryly.

"We don't have a milkman, sweetheart," she reminded him. "Anyway, he's going to have brown eyes. I can tell."

"Sassy, isn't she?" Mama Donavan grinned.

"She always has been," Jason sighed. "And I wouldn't change a hair on her pretty head." He kissed Kate and then leaned over to touch his lips to Mama Donavan's wrinkled cheek. He looked down at his son. He brushed his lean fingers over the tiny head, his eyes blazing with pride and love. Kate caught her breath when she saw his expression.

She smiled at him, her own love reflected in her eyes. I'd do it all again, she thought suddenly. I'd go through it all again, every painful minute, for this.

And Jason, watching her, read her thoughts. He smiled back at her because he felt the same way. Every day his love for her grew, but now there were no barriers, no doubts. He wasn't even jealous of her career because every night she slept in his arms, and he knew to his bones that he came first in her heart. He always would. He winked at her, and laughed at her soft, helpless blush.

Three months later, Cade Christopher Donavan was baptised at the Presbyterian church, with two grandmothers, four godmothers and three godfathers, and Kate had designed and made the baby a long, lacy baptismal gown and cap for the occasion.

Afterward, Mary and Mama Donavan sat with Cade while Kate and Jason drove out to the pasture where the new Indian bull lived.

"Red Barton was right," Kate remarked. "He sure is ugly."

"He saved us from bankruptcy," he reminded her with a grin.

"Well, maybe he does have a glimmer of beauty. Right there under his left ear…."

He turned off the engine. "Come here."

His arms reached for her, and he pulled her across him. "Alone at last," he mused. "Remember the first time I kissed you?"

"On your porch," she recalled. "You came on pretty strong, and I was scared. I almost cut and ran."

"I did cut and run," he said gently. "But I came to my senses finally, thank God." He kissed her again. "Kate, are you happy?" he added, his dark eyes searching hers, softly.

"Yes." It was only the one word, but in that word she put all her love and the memory of perfect nights of loving, long days of being together and learning about each other. In it she put her heart and soul, and all the love she felt for him. One word. But in it, she gave him the world. And he smiled.

* * * * *

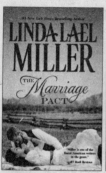
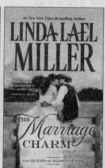
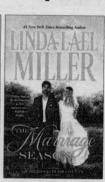

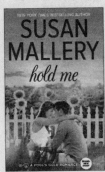

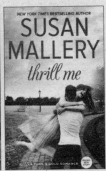

REQUEST YOUR FREE BOOKS!

2 FREE NOVELS
FROM THE ROMANCE COLLECTION
PLUS 2 FREE GIFTS!

YES! Please send me 2 FREE novels from the Romance Collection and my 2 FREE gifts (gifts are worth about $10). After receiving them, if I don't wish to receive any more books, I can return the shipping statement marked "cancel." If I don't cancel, I will receive 4 brand-new novels every month and be billed just $6.49 per book in the U.S. or $6.99 per book in Canada. That's a savings of at least 19% off the cover price. It's quite a bargain! Shipping and handling is just 50¢ per book in the U.S. and 75¢ per book in Canada.* I understand that accepting the 2 free books and gifts places me under no obligation to buy anything. I can always return a shipment and cancel at any time. Even if I never buy another book, the two free books and gifts are mine to keep forever.

194/394 MDN GH4D

Name	(PLEASE PRINT)	
Address		Apt. #
City	State/Prov.	Zip/Postal Code

Signature (if under 18, a parent or guardian must sign)

Mail to the **Reader Service**:
IN U.S.A.: P.O. Box 1867, Buffalo, NY 14240-1867
IN CANADA: P.O. Box 609, Fort Erie, Ontario L2A 5X3

Want to try two free books from another line?
Call 1-800-873-8635 or visit www.ReaderService.com.

* Terms and prices subject to change without notice. Prices do not include applicable taxes. Sales tax applicable in N.Y. Canadian residents will be charged applicable taxes. Offer not valid in Quebec. This offer is limited to one order per household. Not valid for current subscribers to the Romance Collection or the Romance/Suspense Collection. All orders subject to credit approval. Credit or debit balances in a customer's account(s) may be offset by any other outstanding balance owed by or to the customer. Please allow 4 to 6 weeks for delivery. Offer available while quantities last.

Your Privacy—The Reader Service is committed to protecting your privacy. Our Privacy Policy is available online at www.ReaderService.com or upon request from the Reader Service.

We make a portion of our mailing list available to reputable third parties that offer products we believe may interest you. If you prefer that we not exchange your name with third parties, or if you wish to clarify or modify your communication preferences, please visit us at www.ReaderService.com/consumerschoice or write to us at Reader Service Preference Service, P.O. Box 9062, Buffalo, NY 14240-9062. Include your complete name and address.

DIANA PALMER

77977	LONG, TALL TEXANS VOLUME III: ___ $7.99 U.S. ___ $8.99 CAN.		
	ETHAN & CONNAL		
77976	LONG, TALL TEXANS VOLUME II: ___ $7.99 U.S. ___ $8.99 CAN.		
	TYLER & SUTTON		
77975	LONG, TALL TEXANS VOLUME I:		
	CALHOUN & JUSTIN	___ $7.99 U.S.	___ $8.99 CAN.
77941	WYOMING TOUGH	___ $7.99 U.S.	___ $8.99 CAN.
77910	WYOMING STRONG	___ $7.99 U.S.	___ $8.99 CAN.
77854	PROTECTOR	___ $7.99 U.S.	___ $8.99 CAN.
77762	COURAGEOUS	___ $7.99 U.S.	___ $9.99 CAN.
77727	NOELLE	___ $7.99 U.S.	___ $9.99 CAN.
77724	WYOMING BOLD	___ $7.99 U.S.	___ $8.99 CAN.
77696	WYOMING FIERCE	___ $7.99 U.S.	___ $9.99 CAN.
77666	MERCILESS	___ $7.99 U.S.	___ $8.99 CAN.
77631	NORA	___ $7.99 U.S.	___ $9.99 CAN.
77570	DANGEROUS	___ $7.99 U.S.	___ $9.99 CAN.
77283	LAWMAN	___ $7.99 U.S.	___ $7.99 CAN.

(limited quantities available)

TOTAL AMOUNT $ _____
POSTAGE & HANDLING $ _____
($1.00 FOR 1 BOOK, 50¢ for each additional)
APPLICABLE TAXES* $ _____
TOTAL PAYABLE $ _____

(check or money order—please do not send cash)

To order, complete this form and send it, along with a check or money order for the total above, payable to Harlequin HQN, to: **In the U.S.:** 3010 Walden Avenue, P.O. Box 9077, Buffalo, NY 14269-9077; **In Canada:** P.O. Box 636, Fort Erie, Ontario, L2A 5X3.

Name: _____
Address: _____ City: _____
State/Prov.: _____ Zip/Postal Code: _____
Account Number (if applicable): _____

075 CSAS

*New York residents remit applicable sales taxes.
*Canadian residents remit applicable GST and provincial taxes.

HQN™

www.HQNBooks.com

PHDP0215BL